AFTER

MIDNIGHT

Book design by Stacey Aaronson

Published 2014
Printed in the United States of America
ISBN: 978-1-63152-913-9
Library of Congress Control Number: 2014933539

For information, address:
She Writes Press
1563 Solano Ave #546
Berkeley, CA 94707

After Midnight

Diane Shute

SwP

SHE WRITES PRESS

This is written for my mother, Irene Ruth Lasserot, whose name is in the book.

Contents

CHAPTER I

TROUBLE IN LONDON

Alix knew she was in trouble. She dared another peek through the curtain, but the crowded street and towering buildings remained. Defeated, she stared into the shadowed corners of the carriage, searching for a key to the chaos surrounding her.

Her sister's ermine muff rolled to the floor. Alix retrieved it, mourning the beautiful animal. She pushed it to the far corner of the red, diamond-tucked leather seat so she would not have to hold it. Did her dear sister Lily customarily forget things in the carriage? How could Alix guess, when she knew nothing about Lily? It was another hallmark of how this shocking scheme was doomed to fail, since it was impossible to impersonate someone completely unknown.

The continued clatter of carriage over cobblestone frayed her unsteady nerves. Though her uncle Quenton was driving, he showed no sign of stopping. Certainly he had recognized that it had been she getting in to take Lily's place when they had left the farm. Even though they were twins, Quenton would have noticed the difference at once. No matter how much he needed his job as Lily's driver, he was sufficiently immune to any threats to have contacted Alix first. He must have a counter plan in place if he brought Lily to the farm. Along the road to London, Alix had expected him to pull over and share it, but her heart sank when they turned onto smooth pavement. Another chance peek through the curtain made her cringe. Greensward and tall houses rolled past the coach, signaling arrival in Westminster.

If Quenton planned to shed a little light on his intentions, he was fast running short of time. Alix lost all hope of any last-minute chat when her uncle called to his horses.

"Look lively now, lads!" The carriage lurched in response and suddenly clattered to a halt at the curb.

Resolutely, she straightened her position, for there would be no last-minute reprieve. Alix smoothed her sister's skirt and adjusted her sister's bonnet strings, waiting for the door to open. As her uncle jumped down from the box, she drew a deep breath and assumed Lily's vacant expression.

Quenton opened the door without regard for her. He did not know she had been riding inside Lily's coach, dressed in Lily's clothes, and knew nothing about Lily's plan to exchange places. It was too late to tell him, because now the cost of his outrage at the detestable scheme would be his employment. Determinedly, Alix mustered the will to step down from the carriage.

NICHOLAS MEASURED SILENT PACES against the pendulum of the Bavarian floor clock. Only the snap of the fire, the pelting rain, and the redundant tick marked his trek down the length of the library. Upon reaching his desk, he turned to start his journey again.

"I beg your pardon, milord."

It was the butler, Percival Winston. Nicholas avoided the man's sympathetic gaze, but he hovered in the doorway, awaiting permission to enter. Finally discarding the need, the butler came in regardless. His presence made no difference to Nicholas, as long as his visit was brief.

"I thought you might like a lamp or two."

"If you must," Nicholas responded, unwilling to concede a reminder of the waning day.

"Thank you, milord; I'll just be a minute."

The strike of the tinderbox invaded his seclusion and sparked thought. The clock chimed, igniting the parody of his most recent afternoon. When he had rolled out of bed that morning, he had scarcely imagined this finish to his day. His schedule had started as routinely as usual, save he had been fortunate enough to have missed Lily going up to bed as he went down to breakfast. He made no pretense of avoiding his wife; he could scarcely stand the sight of her, let alone stomach the caliber of people she entertained.

Once Lily Radcliffe had set her sights on the Griffon fortune, there had been no chance for a reprieve from his reckless marriage. He loathed acknowledging he was a fool for the fortnight that had ended his delusion on their wedding night. Now, while Lily lived the high life as his entitled wife, Nicholas was left with the price of folly. It did not matter what she did, so long as she did it outside his knowledge. Until recently, she had seemed so clever, coming off scot-free from every escapade, that he had mistakenly come to rely on it. He should have anticipated the proverbial hens coming home to roost. Her error might have granted him a hearty laugh, except he was the unwitting cuckold.

Not that it mattered what others thought, beyond the mockery she made of his name. He had no desire to see the

Griffon reputation sullied or to gain notoriety as a laughing-stock. To date, the worst he had managed was his marriage to Lily Radcliffe. Little had he thought it would lead to scandal, but it had not taken her long; barely had the ring been on her finger when he had discovered his blunder. It had taken the better part of a year to emerge from a bout of self-loathing, and now this.

He would have been wiser petitioning for immediate annulment, but he was too busy drowning in one hell of a bender. To be precise, it was not a bender inasmuch as it was a drunken row night after bloody night in the saloons along the river. When he could not drink anymore and his legs gave out, some passerby would take sufficient pity to pour him into a bunk on one of his frigates lining the docks. If not, he would remain where he fell until morning patrol, when a bobby woke him sufficiently to stagger to a berth on his own.

It was a shameful pastime for a man of his position, but he would do anything to keep from returning home to the disgrace of his marriage. By the time he scraped himself together sufficiently to look in the mirror, his wife constructed a new pratfall.

"Would you care for a scotch, milord?" Winston suggested, smoothly pouring without regard for a reply. "In my opinion, a drink goes down nicely on a day like this."

Nicholas did not like living with the intimation that he was fast becoming a wastrel. "Are you suggesting there's a reason I should be drinking?"

"Not at all, milord."

"In that case, I might like one."

"Will you dine in tonight?"

"God, no." He grimaced at the unwarranted suggestion and tasted his whiskey. "I'll be at the club, as usual."

"Very well, milord. May I be of further assistance?"

"No, man. Go along."

"Thank you, milord." Winston capped his performance with a bow and disappeared through the door.

Nicholas waited until the butler was gone to take a decent drink of scotch. Winston was right: It cut the bitterness of learning about the D'Arcys' European tour, right after he had received the message that Lily had spent the night at their country estate.

It was the reason he had stormed home to meet her when she surfaced. If Lily's cohort, Beth D'Arcy, was out of the country, then how in the devil could Lily have been visiting her? The short answer was the obvious lie, but it did not furnish anything about where she had actually been.

After watching her having a go with his brother, Phillip, all winter, he was sick to death of her flagrancy. He was not so much worried about her as he was concerned her rendezvous would become public fodder. He wished not to see her but to hear the lie straight from her lips. Then he would take his complaint to a judge and end the sham of their marriage in divorce, without exposing her disgraceful affair with his brother.

Divorce was ugly and would cast aspersion on his reputation, but with unassailable proof and without involving Phillip, it would not be as painful as it could be otherwise. Someday his worthless brother might even thank him, but for now, Phillip would learn of the dissolution in a letter. By the time Phillip's ship returned from Calcutta, the public disgrace would be forgotten. Nicholas would prefer for his brother's indiscretion never to emerge in court; the disgrace of marital incest would be sufficient to oust his seat in Parliament. To save the tattered remnants of a once-reputable name, they might need to sell their London properties and move Lion Shipping Company up the coast to continue the family business in relative obscurity.

Lily. She could not be content with the ruin of one Griffon male; she had to have both. Nicholas's gaffe in marrying her jeopardized both brothers' reputations. She was worse than a siren, simply devouring any man foolish enough to look at her. How many others had she enticed to their downfall? There was no need to count any of them, when by marrying her he was the king of them all.

Now it would end. He was finished living in a self-destructive prison. He might be guilty of falling for her angelic image of soft blue eyes and lustrous hair. Her sweet facade hid one of hell's most heartless demons, and he had paid full price for his blunder. Tonight, he would watch her squirm; tomorrow, he would enlist a petition for absolution.

He sipped his scotch, reveling in the anticipation of victory, while a carriage clamored to a stop on the street below. He did not need to part the curtains to recognize his black landau pulled to the curb. Nicholas turned to the liquor cabinet to refresh his drink. His wife was home, and now the final act could begin.

LORD NICHOLAS GRIFFON did not rise when she entered. Alix knew he was waiting for his wife, when his sharp gaze pinned her with a challenge to falter as momentum brought her through the door.

"Milady is home, milord," the butler announced. With a solemn bow, he turned to her next. "Might I be of further service, milady?"

While she struggled to summon her poorly practiced approximation of her sister's voice, Nicholas dismissed him curtly. "That will be all, Winston."

"Yes, milord."

At least the butler was well trained. Did he sound pleased to be released? Alix could not blame him. She pasted on a Lily smile and, tugging on the tips of Lily's white gloves, carried her performance to the fire. The library hearth was polished black granite veined with white. Under ordinary circumstances, she would have remarked on its beauty, but now her back prickled while the earl's gaze burned through her.

"Lily, where have you been?"

Lily's husband asked the question quietly, but dread pooled in her stomach. Why had she not suspected her sister of deceit when Lily had described her husband? Dear Lily had maintained him to be as foolish as any coxcomb, a complete wastrel, and both as distant and as conceited as a fop.

The man sitting at his desk did not appear to be any of those things, but she dared to sweep him with the mocking gaze dear Lily prescribed for challenging situations. What she glimpsed chased her eyes away, because he deliberately planted his hands on his desktop and pushed to his feet.

Nicholas Griffon was taller than she expected when he moved from his chair. The square of his shoulders and imperious lift of his chin made for an imposing figure. Bright coals flickered in the darkness of eyes burning beneath the formidable frown of intelligent-looking brows. Dark hair framed his angular face with unruly curls, despite the ribbon holding it, and his chin bore witness to neglect of a razor.

It might have been a trick of uneven light, but his tan moleskin breeches evidenced the same weather staining as his black riding boots. His unbuttoned forest-green coat and burgundy brocade waistcoat were a rich, pleasing combination but wrinkled from wear. His starched collar was open, leaving a well-matched ascot trailing ribbons down his shirt. He was far from any popinjay she had ever seen, and leonine smoothness as he moved around the desk lent him a dangerous impression.

Her heart quivered, but she willed her fright into submission by studying the deceptive flames of the fire. "Don't tell me you didn't get my message about being round to D'Arcy's," she managed in Lily's snide snicker.

"If you insist."

Loud silence followed his determination, filled by the clock's ponderous metronome. Scrambling to rally a defense against this inexplicable change of character from the man her dear sister Lily had claimed she would meet, Alix found she was woefully short. Lily had offered no advice for direct confrontation; she had maintained she acted without constraint and that a simple claim about spending the night with a friend would suffice as explanation.

"It's a lie, isn't it?" It was not an accusation, and the gentleness of his tone belied his conviction. It fanned her spark of fear into a flame of desperation, for her unintentional crime was indefensible.

"This is unlike you," she replied cautiously, although she realized she had not a clue as to whether it was like him or not, since dear Lily was clearly unreliable. Was he gentleman or beast? How could she possibly guess? She knew nothing about the man towering over her. Even her uncle had never mentioned anything about him, beyond that this man was his employer.

"Did you think no one would learn about the D'Arcys' European tour?"

Mayhap if Alix had had time to recover her wits from the stunning revelation of Lily's having set her up as a ninny for the fall, her sister's winsome bonnet strings might not have encircled her throat when his heavy hand fell on her shoulder.

He may have intended only to stop her instantaneous flight, but instead of a run for freedom, the ribbons created an instantaneous chokehold.

His curt exasperation terrified her. "What the devil are you doing?" he snapped, interfering with her desperate fight with the strangling ribbons tangling on his sleeve.

"I'm not who you think," she tried to claim, but lack of air throttled her assertion. "Please, release me." She gagged on the stinging gash of unyielding ribbon.

"Hold still," he demanded in disgust, grappling with ribbons while she twisted frantically. "You're going to bleeding well garrote yourself!"

"Stop pulling," she begged, staving off his hold as darkness began to crowd her vision with a weird delusion she had died this way before.

"Damn it, stop this!"

"I can't breathe!" She collapsed helplessly at his feet.

"Bloody hell, you're killing yourself! By God, Lily, if this is a joke . . ."

Lily. The name meant nothing to her. Darkness rushed to her release.

A WATERY WORM slipping tenderly across her temple woke her. Muttering mingled with a noisy trickle, and a sponge mopping her forehead dripped afresh. Thought followed sensation with suspicion she had fallen, haplessly thrown from an unruly horse. Opening her eyes brought odd distortion instead of clarity, and a frightening woman peered into her face.

"Glory!" The word gagged her. She struggled to rise, pushing the unwanted sponge away.

"Fie, what is the meaning of this? Have a care, you ungrateful child!"

Alix tore at the dreadful tangle of strings wrapping her throat, yanking the absurd bonnet askew until it smothered her face.

"Do you mind? That bonnet is new!"

"Not any longer," she wheezed, tearing the hateful thing off to fling it away.

"That'll cost you! You'd do well to remember your place!"

She struggled to sit up while the maid scrambled after the bonnet. A painful attempt to swallow tore her throat as she looked around, feeling caught in a nightmare. "Where am I?"

"In London—where do you think?" the maid retorted tartly, with a flatly disapproving look, preening the unlucky goldfinch on Lily's bonnet. "These," she added, sweeping it in a grand gesture at the sitting room, "are Lady Griffon's chambers."

"Lily." She choked on the hated name. It was not a dream that memory returned to her, but the deplorable act of the outrageous scheme that ensnared her.

"Yes, nothing but the finest for milady," the maid sniffed. "She promised someone suitable would return in her place. My guess is that it's supposed to be you."

"Milady." The entitlement curdled on her tongue. What kind of lady contrived hateful intrigue? Where was the decency of thrilling in manipulation, or the victory in deceit? The shock of being involved in such an egregious deception set her reeling. "Have you any brandy?" Her pitiful entreaty came painfully, as a croak.

"Brandy." The maid met her request with a distasteful sneer. "Milady drinks nothing but sherry."

"If it was sherry I wanted, I would have requested it," Alix coughed, rubbing her bruised neck and disliking the tart maid at once. She added it to her displeasure at Lily's tasteless furnishings. She rose from the white damask couch, displacing a crimson pillow. It plopped onto a Venetian red carpet; the shades were garish together. Alix's love for color cringed and cried for justice from the mismatched hues. She turned from the horror of the room to find the maid gaping at her, and her patience with Lily's charade reached its end. "Why are you standing there?"

"You look just like her."

It would be her misfortune to have an identical twin like Lily. The fortunate event was that they had not been raised together. Save Lily's exploitation of their differences, Alix heretofore had managed to eke a life for herself. It may not have always been fortuitous, but, mercifully, she had forgotten most of it. What was important was here and now, and Alix did not like the way it looked.

If the past was history and one managed the present, the future might still take care of itself, but not with Lily flying widdershins over it like the proverbial fairy-tale witch. Perhaps she was more of the wicked stepsister; Alix would have to think on it later, because the maid mercifully appeared with the entire brandy decanter.

"Here, be careful," the maid complained when Alix grabbed the glass.

"Thank you," she managed to rasp after the liquid's welcome burn soothed the torture from her throat.

"Go easy," the maid counseled with flat disapproval. "Percival Winston keeps track of his liquor cabinet."

"Why? Do you have trouble with thieves?" Alix asked prosaically, snatching the bottle by its neck to take it to the fire. She drank down another glass and managed to land safely in a chair, when the pedestal heel broke on Lily's shoe.

"You're a souse!"

"Not yet, but give me a few more minutes in this place, and I will be."

"Aye, and I knew it; who else would take on this lark?"

"Lark?" Alix's laughter issued as a cackle. She would have to be careful, lest Lily's spell transform her permanently into her sister's evil part. "You must be Jenny."

"And who else would I be?"

Alix shrugged with indifference and poured another drink. The brandy splashed carelessly, but at least the alcohol was quick to work. With luck, she might still make it home and be in the barn on time for morning feeding.

"Hand that over before you drink yourself sick."

She evaded the maid's grab by springing adroitly and dancing away, kicking off the cumbersome burden of dear Lily's ridiculous shoes.

Darkness waited at the window. Swirling mist haloed the streetlamp in gold on the curb. Across the street, a brougham hitched to a handsome four-in-hand of white horses waited by the sidewalk. The door of the house opened, spilling light on a couple sheltered by enormous umbrellas toted by accommodating servants. A footman hopped from his perch to open the carriage door, while the driver waited bareheaded in the rain.

"You're already drunk," the maid accused.

"Do you blame me?" Alix returned with numb lips and a thick tongue. Would that she were free of this obligation and could join the pair leaving as the coach rolled away from the curb.

A fleeting memory of her mission returned. There was a plethora of hiding places in the knickknacks and whatnots on the shelves. With a wink from one of the Fates' wily sisters, she could find what she needed within the hour, but then the deceptive room shifted, tilting her into a nearby lamp.

"Fie, I knew it! You're going to set the place afire!"

Maid Jenny did a fine job of catching the wobbling lamp. Considering her nimble retrieval of Lily's bonnet earlier, Alix deduced the maid had grown up with boys. In Alix's case, it was her uncle Quenton, but she could not reveal such to good Jenny.

She sat on the couch a little more heavily than she intended and spilled fresh brandy into her glass.

"Fie, you're not getting sick, are you?"

"Not yet."

"Good—give me this before you do," Jenny insisted, pulling the decanter from her unwilling grasp. "Let's go to bed while you can still walk."

"I don't have time to go to bed; I won't be here very long."

"Now you're rambling. Up you go," she grunted, doing her best to heft Alix from the couch.

"Thank you for your assistance." Alix regarded the uncertain approach of the bedchamber door warily. "I don't suppose you know where Lily keeps everything, do you?"

The maid hesitated when a distant door closed, and then pulled her on with a look of warning. "Of course I know where you keep your things, milady."

Alix grabbed the door frame to stop their progress. "I told you, I'll be here only a few minutes."

"Before going to bed . . . yes, I remember."

"No, I've got to find something."

The maid tugged relentlessly. "It'll be there in the morning."

"No, you don't understand . . ."

"Pishposh. There's time enough for everything . . . now come on," Jenny grunted, pulling her loose.

Unbalanced, Alix stumbled and careened to the strategically placed bed. She groaned upon landing, thankful it saved her from the floor.

"Come on, climb up. I've done this plenty of times. Will you just lie here quietly while I find a nightdress?"

"I'm not making any promises."

"Fie, now I'm a nursemaid for a tippler," the maid muttered in retreat.

CHAPTER 2

HORSE SALE AT OXLEY COMMONS

idnight Star snorted and picked up his pace to outstrip the stride of the hired horse beside him. Nicholas tightened the reins reflexively, as John Wesley resorted to his riding crop to keep the rented horse abreast.

"It would be simpler to say yes," he complained.

Nicholas laughed. "For you, perhaps . . . but take my word for it, because my horse isn't for sale."

"Blast it—leave it to you to come away with such an engaging animal."

"I wish I could take credit, but I'd never have found him without my stable master's acquaintance with Sterling."

"All you have to do is name your price."

Nicholas shook his head. "Midnight Star is worth his weight in gold; your bank account wouldn't cover it."

"Then I hope Sterling Wood Stable has another like him on the lists today. Fair warning that he's mine if it does."

"Quincy Hill was noncommittal about today's sale, but Midnight Star's a fine example of what the stable is producing. I'm just fortunate he's a close associate of Alex Sterling's."

John eyed his horse covetously. "My life would be easier if you'd agree to sell him."

Nicholas laughed. "I'm not interested." Nor would he ever be. Midnight Star was not merely a horse; he had a sentience above that of other animals. The idea of the stallion having an elevated awareness might mark Nicholas as an eccentric, but it did not stop his conviction. His initial admiration of the previous summer had deepened to such fondness over the winter that he would never part with the horse, even to his best friend.

It did not matter if he and John Wesley had a history dating to school at Eton or if they sailed on the same ship in the King's Navy; whenever they were back-to-back, fighting pirates, Nicholas was fortunate for John's presence, and as their lives had settled afterward, he had never hesitated to share anything. It ended with this horse, and his friend did not quite know what to feel about his change in fortune. Nicholas understood, but their bond recently had suffered a few bumps, including the giant hurdle of his wife. If Nicholas could rise above their brief affair, his friend could get over his desire for the stallion.

John laughed, shaking his head. "It's not fair you get all the looks and the horse, too."

Nicholas was accustomed to John's good-natured bedeviling, but his friend was the one with women chasing after him. Before marriage, Nicholas had been content to linger in John's excess. When John had insisted Nicholas take the lead with Lily Radcliffe, it had prompted the worst mistake of his life. Although it had not stopped John from having an affair with her soon after, it had been too late to keep Nicholas from ruining his life by marrying her.

That was old news from the previous summer, though.

Over the winter, Lily had moved on from his best friend to Phillip, and now Nicholas smelled fresh blood. He did not know why he should dwell on it, especially since John was newly married to Sarah Newton. The day was fine and held too much promise to revisit old offenses. Besides, with luck, the next time Lily tried to kill herself, Nicholas would have witnesses sufficient to vouch for him at the inquest.

"Only you could be so damned fortunate; I suppose the stars are making up for their shameful performance with Lily. Did you see her this morning?"

"No, thank God." The admission soured his mood, but Midnight Star struck up a parade-ground prance to cheer him. Nicolas checked his horse, shifting his weight comfortably in the saddle. "I presume she's alive, because no one's informed me of her death."

John threw back his head to laugh. "That's quite an admission for the detectives!"

"I'd nothing to do with it. Don't bleeding ask me how those damned ribbons tangled on my sleeve. I carried her upstairs; I don't know what more could've been done under the circumstances. She may've throttled herself silly, but the maid's my witness she was breathing when I left."

"I've never heard a more bizarre story, old chum; you'd better keep it to yourself in the future."

A distant cry of "Hi there" interrupted their ride. "Ho, Little John! Wait!"

"Sam," John noted needlessly of his new brother-in-law, looking around to see who hailed them. A black cabriolet rattled around the corner with Samuel Newton, the Fourth Earl of Stragglethorpe, waving his top hat from its window, revealing his carrot-red hair.

John shook his head regretfully. "Whatever you do, don't

tell him Sterling Wood will be at the sale today."

"Lists will be posted everywhere . . ."

"Just keep him busy," John suggested quietly. "Sam!" he called back as the taxi neared. "I didn't know you were joining us!"

"You never asked, but Sarah said I'd catch you on the road! How can I resist a sale at Oxley Commons when I hear Sir Gordon from Sterling Wood is going to be there? Good morning, Griffon, old boy . . . I don't suppose we'll find your stallion on any of those lists."

"Not a chance, Sam," Nicholas replied, shaking hands through the open window. "In case you haven't heard, Midnight Star isn't owned by Sterling Wood any longer."

"His horse isn't for sale, but if he was, I'd have first chance to buy him."

Sam was quick to rise to John's challenge. "I'm afraid you'd have to fight me for him, chap."

"Just because I married your sister doesn't mean I have to hand over all my rights, blast you."

"Give it up, lads," Nicholas interceded cheerfully. "Midnight Star will never be for sale."

"That's not fair, when Quincy Hill works for you; he's thick with Alex Sterling and has his choice of horses."

"Except when he's racing for the Royal Stud on Sundays," Sam corrected. "Then it's a jolly 'tallyho' and every man for himself."

"He'd ride in races for Sterling if the man paid him enough. Frankly, I'm surprised he hasn't quit you, Nicholas. He makes good money as a jockey."

"He likes working for me," Nicholas assumed. He had never considered the possibility of Quincy Hill's quitting. The man managed every aspect of Nicholas's stable and was beginning to make his country estate notable for fine hunters.

"I'll pay you a hundred quid more than Little John's best offer if you change your mind."

"You might be my brother-in-law, but keep out of my business."

The watchman waved them through the gates with the river of others winding through the maze of fields. Their banter carried them past the hotel, with its single coach waiting by the doors.

"You can drop me anywhere on the Commons, Cabbie," Sam directed his driver. "I say, isn't that Sir Robert Gordon?"

John stood in his stirrups. "Where?"

"Don't you see that swashbuckling chap by the causeway? He wasn't just granted his golden spurs; he earned them the hard way at Waterloo."

"Let's hurry; we might be able to catch up with him," John proposed, directing his horse toward the assortment of stablemen loitering near the entrance.

"Hey-ho, milord," one of the residents called to Nicholas in a lilting Irish brogue. "Sterling Wood is down in Barn Two. You've just missed Sir Gordon, don't you know?"

"Did we, now?" John mimicked him easily, handing off the reins of his hired horse without a second look. "Gads, Nicholas, your horse is famous. Barn Two, did you say?"

"Aye, milord," he answered, busily looking over Midnight Star. "Isn't this fellow entered in Sunday's steeplechase?"

Nicholas jumped to the ground lightly. "No, I'm afraid you have the wrong horse."

"Then this big lad is a dead ringer for Dark Star. He won the three-mile at Somerset, don't you know."

"My horse is from Sterling Wood originally."

"Begorra, milord, you've the luck of the saints."

"Let's hurry, or we're going to miss Gordon."

Nicholas trailed along, eager only for a distraction. Barn Two was not hard to find, and neither was Sir Robert Gordon; his commanding voice carried across the gathered crowd. He was tall enough to be imposing, and broad of chest, with gray sprinkling his hair. His august beard left only a square chin exposed. He cut a fine figure standing next to a first-rate chestnut Thoroughbred he passed off to a waiting groom. Parting the crowd, Gordon came forward congenially. "Gentlemen," he smiled, offering his hand to each of them, with a grip suggesting he crushed rocks as a hobby. When his ice-blue eyes settled on Nicholas, they turned pensive with his inspection. "Midnight holding up well for you, is he?"

"I wouldn't trade him for another horse."

"Frankly, Sir Gordon," John said, taking advantage of the opening, "we hope to find something of the same quality for ourselves."

Gordon laughed. "Well then, let's have a look around. "

Resigned to waiting, Nicholas propped himself against the nearest stall. A glance at his watch counseled another hour until lunch, but a roast beef sandwich with horseradish already sounded tempting. Apathetically, he noted where dust had smudged his sleeve. *What next?* he wondered wearily.

THE ANGELIC SINGING that awoke Alix did not ease the weary thumping in her head and ended abruptly when a vague realization prompted a frantic escape. "By Jove," she wheezed, fighting unwieldy sheets. The velvet bed curtains gave way and fell atop her when she crashed to the floor amid the clanging of a bell.

Silence might have settled in the aftermath, if not for someone moaning. The calamity brought a pair of sensible black shoes to the carpet before her. "What is it that you're doing?"

Alix rolled over to look at the maid. "I'm getting up."

Jenny clasped her hands beneath her apron doubtfully. She might have been prettier if her auburn hair were not pinned severely under her cap. Alix was uncertain, since the maid's lips were pressed into a thin and disapproving line, but she had round green eyes and honest brows that might be delightful if not flattened by a frown.

With a determined look at the mattress, Jenny reached for her. "Let's get you back into bed," she grunted. "I didn't expect you awake so early."

Alix fumbled for purchase against a slippery slope of pink satin, encumbered by a metal rubbish can stuck on one foot, until Jenny pried it off.

"Try to sleep. It's too early to start your day."

With dizzying sickness spinning her head, Alix dully accepted her advice. "Has anyone ever suggested you're a joy?"

Jenny paused to consider her with cautious reservation. "Not before now."

Later, when she opened her eyes again, Alix found her sickness abated. The room seemed to have righted itself, but her fearful nightmare remained. In it, Lily was a wicked queen who bade a kingdom to sleep while Alix filled the role of her reflection. Unlike in most fairy tales, she would not reap a rich award of treasure; her happily ever after would be to continue as before . . .

A horse! A horse! My kingdom for a horse! Shakespeare's infamous line in *Richard III* pushed her from the bed. What she would not give for one of her horses to escape—but the kingdom of Sterling Wood Stable was what she had to save.

She toured her sister's place with naked feet. The garish, mismatched colors were no better in the inoffensive daylight. Trying to define her strange situation, she forced her mind to think. Frustration nipped her; at home, the stable's schedule packed her agenda. Besides managing the overall farm operation, Robbie was busy with horse sales. As the jockey, Ozzie had no time for anything but the horse-racing trials on the track, and Molly's cousin from Galway, Finghin, had his hands full with schooling novices in the field. Who had time to pick up Alix's share of the work? A dizzying fear of failure swam over her. She sank into the nearest chair and clutched her head dismally.

Her angst brought the maid's return. "I was expecting you in the dressing room."

"Coming," Alix whispered hoarsely.

"I have your bath drawn," Jenny continued, satisfied that Alix would follow. "Everything's in order, including your cup of tea."

Lily would drink tea, but Alix wished for coffee with a good shot of Irish cream, and a fast horse away from this place.

"While your hair dries, we'll have plenty of time for a manicure . . ."

Jenny did not mention breakfast, although Alix suspected it was closer to lunchtime. At home, meals arrived punctually. Her stomach suddenly realized it was empty.

"And a pedicure." Jenny lifted her eyebrows, staring meaningfully at Alix's feet.

Alix peered down at her toes defensively. She had a crushed nail from a horse stepping on it, but she had planned to trim them on Sunday.

"Now," Jenny directed, leading her to the tiled bathroom, where an overflowing tub swelled with bubbles. "Go ahead and get in. Just relax while I undo your hair."

Obediently, Alix stepped out of her nightdress and into a

bath of warm and heavenly lavender-scented shivers. At the farm, bathing was a necessity; the last wonderful bath she had had was . . . she could not remember. Still, once she found what she was here for, she would not hesitate to quit this mad game.

Only Lily would consider putting such a wild caprice in motion. Although her plan had been conceived in desperation, how many people would gamble on something so outrageous? "You don't understand" and "It's the only thing that will work," had punctuated her sister's bizarre proposal, which had changed into a treacherous ultimatum when Alix had refused to budge.

"I'm pregnant," Lily had finally confessed. "My husband will know it can't be his child; he detests me."

Alix's solution was simple by comparison. "Take a long holiday."

The suggestion set her sister mewling pitiably. "The father is someone in his family," she said, adding, "Nicholas caught us together."

"You've been dallying with one of his relatives?" While Alix struggled with the revelation, Lily hurried to make it worse. "It's a sticky complication with his brother. Don't you see this is the only solution?"

"Lily, if your husband knows you're involved with his brother, you're better off confessing—"

"Alix, if you don't help me in my darkest hour, I'll have to disown you."

"Disown away, dear Lily," Alix challenged in brazen ignorance of her own susceptibility.

"Since you force me to it, either you assume my place or I'll make use of the King's grant for your guardian's estate, given into Mother's care before her death. Save me now, and you'll secure his property. Turn me out, and I'll be forced to sell it—you might imagine how I'll need the money."

"Lily, don't be ridiculous."

"Ridiculous is how you'll feel when you see your family standing outside these gates."

Nothing could compare to the helplessness Alix experienced by facing such dire consequences. Even with time to reflect on the road, she was mired in the unseemly idea of pitting their lives against each other in a wager. Should she fail, pleading for mercy from Lily's husband would be useless; had she any doubts about his reaction, her bruised throat was a fine indication.

Her effort hinged on finding the land grant and escaping. While getting dressed, as the maid arranged her hair in Lily's style, Alix pondered how to find it without anyone's noticing her search.

"You must have said something. Lord Griffon has a fine reputation," Jenny concluded, lifting a pearl necklace from the jewelry box. "This should cover the bruising. Take my advice and keep mum when you're down at tea."

Alix kept her eyes averted from the mirror, lest she see Lily's reflection. "I thought tea would be brought up on a tray, as lunch was earlier."

"Pishposh, milady takes meals in her room only when she's not presentable, and enjoys practicing her piano in the afternoons. Besides, the chambermaids are due any minute, so go on and play the piano." Jenny hesitated when Alix blinked at her blankly. "You do play, don't you?"

"Yes." She battled her frustration futilely. Now that she finally had time to look for the deed, the maid was banishing her from the room. "How long will the maids need?"

"Until after tea. You do know how to play more than one song, I hope."

"Usually."

"Good, then away with you."

"B-but . . ." Alix stammered as Jenny steered her to the hall. "I don't know where I'm going."

"All the way down, and the second door to your left."

"Oh." She was terrified to leave. "Where's His Lordship?"

"Milord's never home before six o'clock. He returns only to change clothes for the evening."

"But yesterday—"

"Oh, fie, now here they are!" Jenny pushed Alix into the hall. "Don't dillydally."

"But—" The door closing in her face effectively silenced her protest.

The butler appeared, watching her with impassive reserve, as Alix reached the bottom of the stairs. It was too late to worry about her appearance as Lily. Unable to do anything else, Alix kept marching, wearing her sister's petulant smirk, until he bowed hesitantly.

"Good afternoon, milady."

His dry greeting did not evoke goodwill between them. "Good afternoon," she managed, testing her voice beyond her whispered exchange with the maid. It quavered painfully, but she dared not evidence weakness as he led her to the parlor.

"May I bring anything before tea?"

"No, thank you," she managed firmly, drifting to the black piano in the far corner. Piano was not her favorite instrument, but she did not mind playing. She used the excuse of folding the cover from the clavier to survey the room, but the butler had fled and closed the doors.

It was impossible to know if eyes were pressed to keyholes, examining her performance, yet she took heart if the butler did not immediately suspect her. Alix hesitated. Perhaps he had, and had hurried out to summon police, though the view through the windows did not evidence anyone running for the constable.

Determinedly, she smoothed Lily's skirt and assumed the seat. The beautiful fishtail grand had its lid propped, exposing an ornate soundboard, but the music desk was empty. Alix froze with her fingers touching the keys, perplexed by a new dilemma. What did Lily play? Her sister had not mentioned music before shoving Alix into the carriage.

Now, while Robbie was at Oxley Commons, selling horses culled from the racers or trained as hunters, Lily was alone in his house on the farm. Robbie's wife, Molly, was, mercifully, in Ireland, visiting family. There was the couple who took care of the place, but Mabel and Jerry were in no position to gainsay anyone. Alix had not thought what mischief Lily might create in her absence. She had been too stunned by her own unexpected predicament to ask Lily about her plans.

Alix could scarcely believe that when Robbie returned, he would accept the brief explanation Lily had insisted Alix write in a note, about the necessity of meeting a solicitor to settle their mother's affairs. Lily had promised to handle the details, but Lily was supposedly on holiday until Alix's return. In a fortnight, Alix was to post an additional letter describing an interminable delay, but as soon as Alix found the title Lily held over her, she would be quick to wave it under her sister's nose.

Alix preferred not to consider why Lily had done what she had. She moved her mind beyond the frustrating spiral to her problem of the empty music desk. Alix could not recall a single piece from Lily's lessons during their brief history in the same house. Seconds marched by while she waited for inspiration. Perhaps she could simply rise, as if suddenly remembering music was kept in the bench. The invisible eyes hidden behind keyholes weighed in with judgment. Once questions began, they would swell with gossip's contagion. Lily's husband would denounce her as a stranger, and the constable would lock her in prison.

Alix was not Lily, nor did she wish to be. She wished only to find the land grant and end this insanity. If she imitated Lily for a few hours, she might find the document to release her. Mozart always soothed her angst, so she began with his Minuet in G. The piano's resonance proved its value beyond that of a lovely piece of furniture. Soon, the smile curling her lips was her own. Carefully rearranging her expression into Lily's petulant pout of concentration, she switched to J. S. Bach and tinkered through the dignified baroque.

Percival Winston waited silently, hands clasped at his back, at the tea cart, complete with a decanter of sherry. "Would you care for me to pour, milady?" he asked when she faltered to an uncertain finish.

"No." Her lips formed the word without a voice. Glumly, she swallowed her fear. "Thank you. You may go."

Did he pause? Alix nearly sprang from the bench when he closed the door on his exit. She avoided sherry in most cases but now gulped it as water. It left her gasping as she sank to the couch and poured tea for a chaser. The blend was a surprising Darjeeling with orange and clove. Pleased, she added a dot of cream and settled back cautiously.

If Lily frequented this parlor, Alix gauged she exerted little influence over its aesthetics. Its airy feel was a charming difference from the gaudy apartment upstairs. Everywhere was color: greens mixed with gold, yellows with persimmon. It drew her into a tour along the graceful fireplace mantel. She was smiling again. A quick sip of tea hid her pleasure as the louvered cupboard beckoned. Instruments hung on the back panel, and drawers revealed a variety of equipment, including a silver flute.

Her half-realized recognition brought a pause when she found her fingers on the sound holes and her lips pursed over the embouchure. She did not know how to play flute, did she?

FRISK POSED WITH THE RAZOR under Nicholas's nose. "I don't know, milord, but Percival found it significant." Skillfully, he returned to business with his straightedge.

"I've never heard so much poppycock."

"I can't substantiate his claim, but there's common agreement belowstairs."

"Winston is simply mistaken about Lily's being alone."

Albert rinsed the razor. "According to my understanding—"

"Everyone likes to talk," Nicholas interrupted flatly. "The blasted lot have gone tone-deaf if they think her playing's improved, but frankly, it doesn't matter. What's important is that Lily's not strangling herself in some corner, because then I'd be obligated to respond to an inquiry about her death."

"I'd say that's a little harsh, yet I understand completely."

"I've never experienced anything so absurd. Damn me, Frisk, I don't know how her bonnet strings tangled on my cuff buttons. If she hadn't fainted first, she might've managed to choke to death. It was almost as if she wished to send me to the gallows."

"Perhaps she panicked, milord."

"Kindly remember whose side you're on, if you don't mind, if called on to testify as a witness in my divorce. It's as though something has driven her near the edge."

"Yes, milord."

The steaming towel Albert put on Nicholas's face muffled his words. "Damn you for sounding so complacent."

"I beg your pardon, milord."

"At least tell me what you're thinking."

"Obviously, if she had succeeded in sending you to the gallows, she wouldn't have been alive to enjoy it."

"Very funny, Albert, but it is not you who is in this predicament."

"I think you should know that what they're saying might be true."

"We've known one another our entire lives. Since when have I ever heeded household gossip?"

"You can't deny the fling with Phillip spawned a great deal of speculation."

"When isn't gossip rife with conjecture?"

"A few months have elapsed since his ship sailed for Calcutta. While it's not my business to elicit information, remember it was Martha who brought the incident with Phillip to the forefront, and you can't deny she's been a credible source. Now everyone's talking about milady's mysterious maladies. You know how that maid of hers, Jenny Smith, isn't anyone's favorite."

"I was unaware that there were popularity contests for maids."

"There doesn't need to be a contest for that one," Albert opined sourly, rattling the shave kit when putting it away. "She's been acting oddly, even for her. The secrecy surrounding milady since Phillip's departure made Martha curious, and she showed me a calendar she's kept of certain dates. I must say it's compelling, even if it's hearsay."

Nicholas pulled off his shaving towel and climbed out of his chair to his waiting scotch. "I don't know if I like the direction this is heading, Frisk."

Albert glanced at him cautiously. "She marked the days milady's been ill."

Nicholas stripped off his undershirt in exchange for another. "It's no secret Lily enjoys her liquor. She's only feeling the aftereffects."

"She doesn't touch her favorite foods and rings for something different, but then today she ate everything, including the crusts of her bread."

"I couldn't give a fig what Lily eats."

"The bottle of brandy Percival found missing turned up empty in her room. On top of these odd events, there's the occasional stir over unusual thefts from the meat locker."

"What the devil does that have to do with anything?"

"I'm not certain if there's a way to put this delicately, milord. At first Martha did not pay much attention, but Jenny Smith suddenly refused to allow anyone near the laundry on certain days. When it happened again the next month, Martha put everything down on her calendar. To be completely straightforward, the thefts concur with milady's customary time of indisposition."

"I knew I didn't like where this was going. Now gossip is rampant that the meat was taken for its blood to soil the linens, and it all dates back to the affair with Phillip."

"Aye, milord, and, unfortunately, it makes a sensational story."

"Well, don't stop now, man—go ahead and say it: Rumors are flying that Lily's carrying Phillip's child."

Albert coughed into his handkerchief. "I beg your pardon, milord."

"Blasted Phillip—I knew nothing good would come of this! Now the rotter is off scot-free to Calcutta, leaving me to clean up after him!" The unexpected development was shocking. Not only did it pose a giant hurdle to Nicholas's intention to catch Lily in flagrante and give her plenty of reasons to wish herself dead, but it also put a new wrinkle in his plans for a divorce. He felt his chances shrinking immensely, for there was not a judge in the land who would allow for dissolution with a child involved.

QUENTON'S EYES SNAPPED OPEN. He had not meant to fall asleep. Recognition of the shadowed room spurred his languor from satin sheets. Pinching the sputtering candlewick as he moved from the bed, he felt in the dark for his cast-off clothes. After tucking in his unbuttoned shirt, he grabbed his coat. His tie still hung on the bedpost, and he was pushing his bare feet into shoes when Gwynne's arm came around him.

"Marquis," she purred sleepily.

Determinedly, he kissed her objection into silence, until her body rose with a throaty laugh. "The hour's late." How he would miss her wanton willingness. His cloak was where he had left it, by the balcony door, and he reached for his hat while he kissed her. "Bonsoir, *ma chérie.*"

"Don't tease—you know I love to hear you speak French."

"Au revoir," he replied, as he opened the balcony door and stepped out into the swirling mist of night. His hastily donned cloak billowed when he hopped the iron railing and landed beneath her room for the final time. He fixed his tie and buttoned his shirt as he slipped between houses. Had Gwynne disclosed their affair to anyone but Lily Griffon, he might have disavowed his part entirely. He had not planned to bed her again; that had been mere surrender to temptation.

Quenton checked his watch in the light from the neighbor's porch. The hour was late, and the long day weighed on him heavily. He hoped when Lily next called for the coach she would not have another twisted desire to see Alix. As he reached the sidewalk, his anger returned. Lily was relentless when given the opportunity. Had Gwynne not confessed when Lily had spotted him slipping away from her at Brighton Hall, he might have been anyone. Even though she had not realized him as her coachman dressed in a gentleman's guise, he was in no position to survive a scandal or an ensuing investigation.

He stepped from the curb, relegating Gwynne's perfumed memory to the past. He would be fortunate if nothing worse than taking Lily to visit Alix transpired in the aftermath of Gwynne's betrayal. While Lily's anomalous demand to meet with Alix might have been prompted by the untimely death of their mother, Mary-Margaret, it defied explanation. Lily had been raised an only child by her mother, who posed as a widow whose husband was lost at war. When Quenton had brought Alix to her door, the woman had promptly whisked his niece from sight, lest anyone question the fabrication. Quenton was in no position to judge the course of their mother's lies, but by the time he had secured employment, Alix had already been living with the Gordons. He had not seen Lily until she had Nicholas Griffon on a string, and by then he had been glad she had never learned of his existence.

He had not planned to work for Nicholas Griffon forever, nor had he bargained to become Lily's personal driver after the hasty marriage. If he won the Newmarket Hunt Cup in a fortnight, he would be in a position to work at Windsor exclusively for the Royal Stud. The unexpected stumbling block was his vow to care for Midnight Star. Now he wished he had never coerced Alix into selling the colt to Griffon last summer, but before Lily came along, Quenton's intent had been to improve the bloodline of the Thoroughbreds on Griffon's country estate.

What twisted deception had invaded their lives! When Quenton had brought Alix to England, he had not been able to guess whether anyone would try to follow from France. Intent on a complete break with the past, he had made up a new name. He had not considered it then, or he might have imagined something more original than the colorless name of Quincy Hill when applying for a job as a servant.

Pausing near a haloed streetlamp, he retrieved his half-smoked cigar from his lapel pocket. At one time, he would have cast away the butt for someone else's enjoyment. Now he was in the ranks of the less fortunate and smoked them through until he needed a pin to hold the stub. He carried a pipe when wearing livery, but in honor of the man he used to be, tonight he lit a cigar.

He blew a puff of smoke to watch it dissolve in the English mist, and sauntered on. If he were in Paris, the night sky would be filled with stars, but he was accustomed to English weather and had never cared for Paris anyway. Tomorrow he would dutifully shoulder the yoke of work, but tonight he clung to a rare moment of liberty.

"Good eve, milord; might you spare a light?" A strolling bobby hailed Quenton from the mist.

"Certainly, Officer." He found it preferable to be congenial to the police, and assumed a British inflection.

"Bit wet tonight," the stout fellow remarked, digging his pipe from his coat.

"When's it not, this time of year?" Quenton replied, cupping his cigar for the bobby's pipe.

"On your way home, milord?"

"Indeed, Officer," he agreed, although he knew the man's name was Mark. He was the regular neighborhood bobby working the nightshift and might have recognized Quenton in Quincy's black uniform.

"Right-o. I beg your pardon, milord; it doesn't hurt to ask."

"Nay, your curiosity is reassuring, Constable."

"Thank you, milord. Good night."

"Cheerio."

Quenton touched the brim of his topper as he continued across the street to the gloomy protection of the trees there. The Burton dog barked at his passing footsteps. When he reached the curb where he usually parked the coach, he stopped to enjoy a last puff on his cigar. Silence returned as the dog quieted, signaling that the constable had moved on. Knocking the ember from his smoke, Quenton pocketed the stub on his way to the carriage house where he lived on the second floor.

The pungency of new-mown hay and a hollow echo as he climbed the wooden steps welcomed him home. At the top, a square space sufficient for a table with two stout chairs, and an antechamber for his bed, comprised his quarters. After lighting his single tallow candle, he undressed to put his suit away in the cupboard hidden behind his narrow wardrobe.

He had drawn the cold water for his evening bath from the well earlier. His nightclothes were a thin nightshirt and the plaid flannel robe Alix had given him two birthdays ago. He poured his nightcap of single-malt scotch into a battered cup, snuffed the sputtering candle, and took his drink to bed. He sipped it sitting on the edge of the thin straw mattress, carefully devoid of thought.

"*Santé*," he finally bade the night.

Quaffing the last of his scotch, he pitched the cup across the barren floor. Its clamor woke the horses and caused a few wary snorts, before silence returned. Quenton caught his piece of blanket as he folded himself onto the narrow space afforded for his rest, resigned to a darkness without dreams.

CHAPTER 3

FITTING IN

"This'd be faster if you'd hold still," Jenny complained around the pins pressed between her lips.

"It'd be faster if you knew what you were doing," Alix corrected, half-turning to watch the maid in the dressing-room mirrors.

"Fie, I can't take in this waistband with you twisted around."

Alix bit back her exasperation. "You've got a pucker there," she noted instead.

"Fie!"

At least the painful bruising on her throat had abated, although she still dared no more than a whisper, considering the maid's constant admonition about eavesdroppers.

Jenny hesitated at a soft knock on the serving door. "Hush, who's that?"

"Maybe it's lunch."

"Is food all you think about?" Jenny peered around the edge of the wardrobe. "It's too early for the chambermaids."

"Why don't you answer it?"

Jenny pushed her pins into the pincushion as the caller rapped again. "Wait here."

"Don't worry." Alix retreated to dressing couch. The mirror on the open wardrobe door reflected the mirror near the dressing screen. She retrieved her lukewarm tea to watch the combined reflections of the maid as Jenny smoothed her apron, adjusted her cap, and then opened the door. An impressive gentleman waited on the opposite side, with his hand poised to knock again. Either he was in a hurry or his insistence proved he was unaccustomed to waiting—an air that lent his rank importance. From his impeccable appearance, Alix guessed his position was significant indeed. Although he was strikingly well presented, Lily's maid was unimpressed by his interruption.

He smiled belatedly. "Good morning."

Alix immediately liked his smooth baritone voice, but Jenny's brevity quickly established he was not a gentleman caller. "Yes?"

"I have a few errands to run down in Mayfair. I thought you might need to go that way as well."

"No."

Although Alix winced at her curtness, Jenny's flat reply left the man unscathed. "More's the pity," he replied pleasantly. "Percival didn't have the Tuesday shopping list from you, so I thought you might've planned to go out."

"No, but thank you," Jenny concluded, moving to close the door.

"I say," he interjected smoothly.

Had he put his foot in the door? From what Alix could glean by the slice of reflection showing Jenny's expression, she appeared perturbed.

"Yes?"

"Since I am going in that direction, I don't suppose you have your shopping list ready."

"No," Jenny stated flatly, and pushed the door closed.

Alix lowered her eyes to her teacup and assumed an innocent tone. "It wasn't lunch?"

Jenny frowned disparagingly at the door. "It was Albert Frisk."

"Oh, I see."

"No, you don't see," Jenny countered precipitously. "The man is a bounder. He must be growing tired of his little Martha if he's decided to pick on me."

"Albert Frisk has an eye for ladies?"

"That's putting it lightly." Jenny snatched the pincushion. "Up with you now; let's finish this skirt."

Alix obeyed meekly. "Who's Martha?"

"Martha's one of the upstairs maids."

"Is Albert Frisk a chamberlain?"

"No, he is Lord Griffon's man."

"Oh." Alix recalculated her assessment. If Lily's husband employed a ladies' man, what did that say for Nicholas? Lily maintained her husband was a preening peacock, but so far, Alix had a different impression.

"He's as slippery as an eel. He probably wouldn't even work here, except he was born to his position."

"You're creating another tuck there," Alix noted gently.

"His parents were milord's personal servants, God rest their souls. They say Albert Frisk grew to manhood with milord. He thinks he's above the others, just because he's been to school with His Lordship."

"I see."

"Of course, his father is retired on the family estate up north. I don't know what milady told you," Jenny sniffed, appraising Alix carefully. "The old lord died a short time after his wife was lost at sea."

"How tragic."

"Yes. Apparently the gaffer did not feel the same way about his wife, because after their drowning, he's survived to a ripe age, hasn't he?"

"You are speaking of Albert Frisk's father?"

"Yes. They call him the old gaffer up north. He's well respected, mind you, but that son flies high on his father's coattails. Up all hours, gambling and chasing skirts—he's taken full advantage of his position. Men all think alike, and don't try to tell me otherwise. I have raised four brothers, haven't I? I know how they sniff around, looking for a likely partner in crime."

"Is that so?" Alix sighed.

"Hold still. I'm almost finished," Jenny sniffed, tugging on the waistband. "He even has Percival Winston putting wagers on horses. Fie, a man in his position—I don't know how Mary puts up with it."

Alix stifled a sigh. "Who's Mary?"

"Mary Winston, the cook."

"Oh."

"I'd not stand for such nonsense for more than five minutes."

"Cooking?"

"No, gambling! Do you ever think about anything but eating? We're wasting time if I'm only going to let everything out again. There, I think we've finished, but I don't know . . . it needs a little something."

Alix twisted to look at the uneven alteration. "Perhaps tossing it out would be reasonable."

"This skirt is going to take some doing. Here's your

dressing gown—hurry up and change."

"You didn't mark any buttonholes. How am I supposed to get out?"

"Oh, bother! You're pinned in? Fie, you need an entire new wardrobe! Wherever you're from, it's a pity they didn't feed you better! No wonder all you can talk about is food. Hold still and let me undo this; you can't wear a single skirt for every occasion."

Alix did not dissent, but her problem had nothing to do with eating; it was searching for Robbie's land grant without anyone wondering why she was rummaging through cupboards.

"There's your lunch," Jenny noted, detecting activity in the sitting room. "Minnie's cousin just opened a dressmaking shop down on Kindly Street. When we took tea together last week, she said her cousin's taking new clients. You'll need something to wear for the evenings, and don't forget appearances at tea."

"Thank you for reminding me to ask the butler to cancel upcoming engagements."

"We can't forget the ball at Clarence House! Fie, what day is today?"

"Don't worry, I'll ask him to decline that, too."

Jenny hurried past Alix to look cautiously into the hall. "Have you forgotten you're to go with milord?"

Alix paused while inspecting her plate. "Lord Griffon?"

Jenny closed the door swiftly. "Your husband," she hissed, rushing to take control of the tray. "It looks like I'll have to go out after all. Sit down so I can arrange this properly. It shouldn't take very long for Minnie's cousin to fit you in."

Alix's spirits lifted; while Jenny was away, she would finally be able to search for Robbie's grant. She tarried through a lunch better forgotten and nearly bolted from her chair the moment she heard the maid leave through the dressing room. Halfway up, she remembered the swarm of servants working in the enormous house, any one of whom might be watching her through an odd keyhole or slender slice of door.

She finished her wine and made a deliberate show of folding her napkin before going to the desk. There, she pulled aside the lace curtain to watch a brown spaniel lead someone's butler down the street. Feeling she had pretended long enough, Alix let the curtain drop and sank into the desk chair. The little drawer in the hutch contained a misplaced thimble among the nibs of pens. A variety of fine stationery and card stock was stacked in the organizer, but her interest was in the daunting disarray of correspondence in the drawer.

She was on her knees on the floor with a half-sorted lapful of cards when a door snapped shut. Alix hastily scrambled to her feet, grasping haphazardly at the cascade of letters.

The chambermaid's broom clattered to the floor as she curtsied hastily. "I beg your pardon, milady!"

"It's quite . . . all right," Alix responded hesitantly, pushing the letters into her pockets as she glanced defensively at the clock.

"Please, allow me," the maid insisted, diving to retrieve the letters without waiting for a reply. She made short work of raking them into a pile while Alix urgently closed the drawers and restored the desk.

"I don't know quite what happened . . ."

The maid insisted, "I didn't mean to make you drop everything!" as she delivered the rest with a regretful curtsy.

"I was just going to take these downstairs," Alix lied, adding them to her pockets. "I'll be off," she added hastily, edging for the door.

"All right, milady, if you're sure you don't want me to come back later."

"Nonsense, don't be silly," she protested, and fled into the hall.

ROBERT KICKED THE FRONT LOG on the fire, added another piece, and arranged it with the poker. When satisfied the blaze would keep all night, he poured a second whiskey before returning to his chair.

This was Alix's room. It was the drawing room, but he always thought of it as Alix's, just as the parlor belonged to his wife, Molly. In truth, the rooms belonged to everyone, but each one had its own presence. His was his office, which was more of a study, since Alix usually handled the bookwork. He was not fond of keeping records. He never worried about having an adjunct to do it; in his line of service, records made dead men.

He packed his pipe with Egyptian tobacco while looking at the portrait of the golden stallion North Star that Alix had painted after her horse won the Newmarket Cup at Oxley. It had marked the beginning of the fruition of her dream, achieved through long hours of work, but the girl never wasted a moment on laurels. She was her father's daughter, and on most days, Robert suspected Henri would have been proud of her. On the others, he wondered how different would have been his circumstances if his friend had still been alive.

Robert never dwelled on the past. It had too many skeletons. Alix helped keep his mind on the future. What he would do in her absence, he was uncertain. He did not survive by rushing to conclusions. What to do about her sister sleeping upstairs was easy, but what it eventually meant was indeterminate.

He always thought life was like an onion. The surface layers had thicker ones shielding the heart where it grew. On the surface, it did not look the same. The weird analogy did not faze him as he blew a puff of smoke and propped his boots on the footstool, aware he was a perfect illustration. Anyone would see him as a country squire smoking a pipe in front of a fire. No one would see what he kept inside, but most would not want to know what was hidden.

It did not bother Robert. He minded his own business. For the most part, it was for the best. His days of worrying about what was going on inside another man's mind were better left unrepeated. He knew he was lucky; there were more just like him, but dead. He never wanted to exchange places with any of them. He had always found it more fulfilling to live in the moment—until Lily had created an unknown. As with the proverbial stone displacing still water, where the ripples would lead eventually was still uncertain.

He might have laughed had circumstances been different. In many ways, Lily was as much her mother's daughter as Alix was her father's. It would make sense, since they had grown up so differently, but Mary-Margaret had forgotten to teach the one she had raised how to use a little finesse. Robert might have come home to find the years unchanged and Alix sitting in Lily's place for lessons so Lily could sneak out to play. The girl was in a tight spot, to be sure, but one of her own making. She thought of herself as a puppeteer pulling strings to make Alix do her bidding. In a larger sense, Robert owed it to Mary-Margaret to take care of her daughter, just as he did Henri for Alix.

No one had ever promised his life would be uncomplicated. He was fortunate his wife was in Ireland, because Molly's reaction would not have been generous. If Lily were going to stay, Robert would have to write to Molly not to return for a while. His wife did not like Mary-Margaret on a good day; he could imagine what she would say about Lily's staying in her house.

By the time his pipe was finished, the idiotic situation weighed him with fatigue. He doused the lamps and wended to bed.

PACING THE FLOOR was a tiresome habit. Alix stopped by the marble mantel to stare into the fire. No answers were there, so she lifted her eyes to Lily's shadowed room in search of its secrets. Somewhere in here, Robbie's land grant had to be hidden. Nowhere else in Lord Griffon's enormous house would Lily have been able to conceal it suitably. As her exasperation with the ridiculous pretense deepened into desperation, Alix feared she needed help from her uncle.

She did not want to involve Quenton. While it was better to confess than to let him realize she was parading in Lily's place, she loathed the idea of his learning of her gaffe. Lily's ruse had returned Alix's helpless uncertainty from the turbulent time when she had lived with her mother—a time that Alix had imagined to be forgotten. As if her years of hard work and determination had vanished, she felt the same bewildered girl her uncle had brought from France.

Alix did not like to dwell on her confusing impressions of life at Mary-Margaret's house and had relegated them to the past, until in a handful of minutes Lily had resurrected them. In those long-ago days when Alix had been coerced into taking Lily's lessons, the worst she had expected was a beating with Mary-Margaret's riding whip, but now the stakes were imprisonment for criminal impersonation.

Nicholas Griffon would not hesitate to prosecute, and Alix felt the Damoclean sword poised over her. The land grant she had been certain to find easily was not only critical to save Robbie's farm but a stay of prosecution as well. Once the magistrate began to bang his gavel on her future, it would seal the dissolution of Sterling Wood Stable and expose the scandalous truth about Alex Sterling. Alix was caught in a snare of lies at the first mention of her name. Under oath, how could she answer? She had not expected the racing commission to misinterpret her licensing application. When it had granted Alex Sterling, Esq., a permit to race, it had made Alix guilty of misrepresentation.

With a frustrated sigh, she sank to the couch and retrieved the book on Michelangelo Caravaggio. The kindly butler had promoted it condescendingly, assuming she would prefer looking at the colorful lithographs of Caravaggio's paintings to reading the book of poems she had had when he had discovered her. Her boon had been the pocketful of invitations scooped from Lily's desk when a chambermaid surprised her. She had used the excuse to cancel Lily's engagements and had come away from that encounter with no more than the butler's thoughtful hesitation.

It was only a matter of time. Although she and Lily were identical in appearance, inevitably someone would realize a difference. Thus far, Alix had escaped notice by remaining in seclusion. She had neither books nor paints to grant relief from tedious inactivity. Playing the piano in the afternoon was her singular break in monotony.

She remembered turning the page, and then Jenny woke her from a dream of a fruit bowl. Its likeness was reflected on Caravaggio's page, but the wall Alix dreamed was white, with an unsettling dissimilarity.

"Breakfast, milady," Jenny announced as she approached with the tray, and then hesitated. "Fie, did I wake you?"

"No, I was only resting," she responded, feeling vaguely disoriented by surreal incongruity.

"I beg your pardon, milady," the maid continued loudly for

the benefit of anyone eavesdropping. "I've brought your kippers and eggs for breakfast. Remember, your appointment at the dressmaker is this morning."

"Oh," Alix replied dully. Her mind was mired in the room in her dream with the white wall. The room's ceiling was high, and the day was bright. Sun had spilled through open windows, along with a breeze that carried the heady scent of roses.

"Here we are," Jenny proceeded, removing the cover on the plate to reveal blackened fish so shriveled its stench banished any thought of roses. "Kippers and eggs, as promised. Crumpets, your favorite strawberries, and cream." She shook out the napkin triumphantly. "I'll pour your tea. Now, is there anything else I might bring?"

Alix responded with an imploring look at the domed cover, but Jenny leaned closer to whisper, "They're supposed to be crisp."

"Bacon," she corrected a little too loudly, and then lowered her voice, "is supposed to be crisp. This is not bacon."

"Fie, haven't you ever eaten a kipper before?"

"Thank you," Alix deemed firmly.

"I'll be in the dressing room if you need me. Don't forget, the coach will be ready at nine thirty."

Alix retrieved the silver dome defensively, but the stench of scorched fish clung in the room. She sipped her tea while staring at the open page with the painting of the fruit bowl. Why had she dreamed of replicating it with edelweiss added at its base?

Stifling a sigh, she poured another cup of tea. As she released a few drops from the creamer, the blue fishing boat on it caught her attention. Its scene was different from that of the row of skiffs on the sugar bowl. Intrigued by the changing view of the harbor, she placed them side by side. Stacked buildings behind a seawall blended, but the spire marking a cathedral gave an impression of its immensity. She turned over her saucer to find the familiar factory seal of an oak tree, and the name Fontenot Porcelain, in Limoges.

Curiously, she examined her spoon. The silversmith's name, William Vincent, stamped on the reverse did not conjure recognition. Jenny watched her with narrowed eyes from the doorway. Dutifully, Alix dotted her lips with the napkin and placed it atop the untouched plate.

"Your bath awaits, milady," she fussed, coming to count the silver. "We'd better hurry before your water's cold; you know Quincy's prompt with the coach."

"Quincy?"

"Yes, the coachman."

"I know who he is . . ." Stunned, Alix trailed Jenny into the bathroom and shrugged out of her dressing gown. "I didn't know he'd be driving."

"Who else would drive but the driver?"

How was she going to walk out of the house without Quenton's recognizing her? Alix puzzled over the hopeless question throughout her bath and dressing in Lily's clothes. Her sister's pink bonnet was no sooner tied beneath her chin than Jenny prompted her toward the door.

"Just go downstairs and get your cloak. I'll be waiting in the carriage."

Alix was getting tired of the maid pushing her into the hall with cursory instructions. "You should have made an evening appointment, preferably well after dark."

"Fie, just get on with it, will you? If anyone noticed anything different, I would have heard about it by now."

"That's easy for you to say, but remember, you're an accomplice," Alix muttered as the maid hurriedly closed the door. She dared not explain that her uncle was certain to recognize her when she made the long walk to the waiting carriage. With no other idea than to keep her face averted, Alix assumed her sister's finishing-school walk and tried not to think of the ramifications. Perhaps if she had been watching where she was going, she might have avoided Nicholas Griffon at the bottom of the stairs.

"Lily. Good morning."

His tone was civil, but his stiff expression hinted at his disapproval. Too frightened to reply, Alix wished for the proverbial hole in the floor. He perched a silk topper on his head as the butler brought out Lily's vermillion cloak. "You'll forgive my wonder if you realize it is morning. If you're sneaking up to bed, you're going in the wrong direction."

Alix dutifully slipped into her sister's cloak, infinitely grateful for the layer of makeup concealing the heat that flamed in her face.

"Your coach awaits, milady," the butler announced, offering a convenient escape, but the sight of the black landau at the curb had assumed the appeal of a gallows.

Alix edged through the door, watching Quenton warily. Her liveried uncle stood stiffly by the lead team of polished coach horses. His attention was riveted on the appearance of Midnight Star as a stableman brought the black stallion to join the coach at the curb.

"Do me the decency, will you?" Lily's husband snapped, and he took Alix's elbow in a viselike grip to march her into the morning mist. "It's my foul luck you didn't hesitate at the sight of the altar." He lifted his hat as a flashy red-wheeled gig rolled by on the street. "Let's pretend your reason for marrying me has something to do with your new neighbors, shall we?"

Given a choice, she would have transformed her faltering step into a mad sprint to Midnight; with a leap onto his saddle, she could have galloped away. As quickly as her desire fleeted, the black stallion swiveled his ears and lifted his head to look at her.

Alix swallowed her heart as she realized her pet recognized her. As beautiful and intelligent as he was, Midnight Star was no longer her horse; he belonged to the churlish man pushing her toward the gleaming black carriage. Quenton bowed studiously as he held the door but took note of Midnight's inquisitive whicker without shifting his careful obeisance. What might have become her uncle's quick awareness that she was not Lily unraveled completely when the stallion boisterously neighed a happy greeting.

"Keep a firm hold on him, lad," Nicholas ordered crisply. As the stallion's whinny echoed along the street, Lily's husband glanced at Alix narrowly. "Hurry it up a little, will you?"

Midnight Star's confusion rang loudly when the horse squealed in protest. He reared on his hind legs to pull free from the unsuspecting groom who was suddenly in a fight to stop him from breaking away.

"Hold him, Georgie!" Quenton abandoned the door and ran to block Midnight as the horse surged toward Alix, dragging the unfortunate man clinging to the reins.

"Damn it, get in!"

Nicholas pushed her toward the coach and ran to help Quenton. Her uncle boldly tried to block Midnight and barely jumped to safety as the unruly horse charged past him. Alix clambered into the coach in a scramble for the door, to use it as a shield while the men converged around the stallion.

"Watch it!" Quenton shouted when Nicholas snagged his horse by the flailing reins. Georgie jumped at Midnight's bridle as Alix's uncle hooked his arm over the stallion's head behind the ears.

"What do you think you're doing?" Jenny hissed, grabbing Alix around her waist to pull her back from the door.

"He's going to get hurt!" When she looked again, Midnight was on his hind legs and Quenton dangled in the air. "Be careful!"

Jenny reached to slam the door closed. "Fie, are you out of your mind?"

Alix bit down on her reply and dismally assumed a seat as the clamor died. Midnight's disobedience was her fault. He was only happy to see her, but she dared not reveal herself as the reason behind his sudden revolt. Defeated, she slid to the corner. As peace returned, she listened to the reluctant tattoo of her beloved pet's hooves on the pavement when Nicholas rode Midnight away. The coach rocked on its springs when Quenton climbed into the driver's box. As the horses started from the curb, they took the carriage in the opposite direction.

CHAPTER 4

The Piano

Jenny rattled through the cupboard contemptuously.
"Fie, I've never seen a man so bold."

"Perhaps he had business," Alix suggested, sliding to her chin in the warm luxury of the bathwater.

"The shops along that row are for ladies."

"He might've been running errands for his wife."

Jenny came down from the stool with a laugh. "Albert Frisk isn't married! There's nary a woman with any decency that would take him. I've raised four brothers, haven't I? I'm nobody's fool—least of all that one's!"

"Then what do you think he was doing?" Alix probed conversationally, as she reached for the sponge. It had been the same since lunch. At home, she did not fritter away time with gossip, for she would be at work schooling horses on the track. Even during her monthly bouts of indisposition, she was busy in her painting studio. She thought longingly of her painting kit and her unfinished portrait of the white colt Mercury.

The maid shook out a Turkish towel to hang within easy

reach. "You sound like one of those detectives from Scotland Yard."

"I scrub floors for the Metropolitan Police," Alix joked, but Jenny's odd look suggested the maid might have believed her.

"He didn't even have the decency to appear he'd been at the haberdasher's; he simply walked up and tipped his hat, as if he expected to find me at the dressmaker's."

Alix sank beneath the bubbles and held her breath. When she surfaced, the maid had arranged scented rainwater rinse with the egg shampoo. "He was right by the door when I came out with the new underpinnings!"

"If he's the rascal you maintain him to be, he's seen plenty of those things before."

Jenny dumped shampoo onto Alix's head and began scrubbing her hair. "That bounder! You're defending him?"

"I'd never dream of it."

"He said something like, 'I didn't imagine I'd bump into you down here,' as if I'd be bowled for six at the sight of him! I gave him tit for tat, didn't I? I asked if he was following me, but then he denied everything and offered to carry my parcels. That rake knew they were underpinnings, brown paper wrapping or not! As if I'd allow such liberties! I should've had a go at him with my umbrella, right then and there!"

"Perhaps it's fortunate you didn't, or you may've had a constable escorting you home."

The maid deftly rinsed away the shampoo as she laughed. "Fie, that'll be the day, when I let the likes of him get the better of me. Then he asked if I'd like to take tea with him; I've never heard of such cheek!"

"I can't imagine."

Reaching for a towel to blot the water from Alix's curls,

Jenny smirked knowingly. "Now you see what I mean. Let's just hope your hair dries before bedtime. I didn't plan to be gone all afternoon."

"By the way," Alix mentioned as she wrapped herself in a thick bathrobe, "would it be an imposition to ask Winston for a painting kit?"

"Like an artist uses?"

"Yes, you know. It doesn't have to be elaborate—just a few paints and crayons."

Jenny leaned closer to whisper a warning: "Milady would never ask for such things."

"It would help if you could nick a few books from the library. When I ask, Winston gives me something with illustrations."

"That's because milady isn't a bookworm; she's too busy to read."

"I must do something besides stare at walls."

"Next week there'll be plenty to do."

By next week, Alix planned to have the deed to the farm that was her key to freedom. She could only imagine the stack of paperwork piled on her desk: bills of sale and contracts, unpaid invoices and solicitations. Add in her work with the horses, and she would forget about boredom.

"Don't forget the Midsummer Night Ball at Clarence House," Jenny added.

"Certainly," Alix agreed heedlessly.

"You'll be the envy of the evening in your new gown, mark my words."

She was relieved not to worry, because she would certainly be at home before then. "Winston canceled everything," she reminded Jenny.

"Yes, but you've obligations with milord. There's still the

ball and whatever else comes up before the weekend at the races. We'll stay the night at the Commons Hotel, so you'll need plenty of things to wear, since everyone will be there."

The idea of going anywhere to dance with Nicholas Griffon made Alix queasy. Even if he did have plenty of money, either Lily must have been desperate to marry or he had been her only choice.

The maid leaned closer to whisper. "In case you've never heard of Oxley Commons, it's a racing establishment on the road to Berkshire. The place is enormous. Besides two tracks, there's the grand hotel where everyone stays whenever the Duke of Wellington is in attendance."

"Oh." The weekend races Jenny described culminated in the Newmarket Hunt. She had originally planned to be there, too, but not in the spectator grandstands. She had reservations in the owners' area on the green beyond the paddocks, where she would watch the races with Robbie. Midnight's brother, Dark Star, was entered in the Newmarket Hunt.

Obediently, Alix moved at Jenny's direction to the fireside. While the maid combed out her hair, she mentally eliminated the places she had already searched.

"Of course, I might've never thought of it on my own. It was milady's idea," Jenny revealed. "It took a bit of imagination, but I'm glad I don't have to pilfer any more meat from the cellar. Making that bloody mess to stain the linens was a shame, but it kept anyone from being suspicious about milady's monthly indisposition."

Alix swallowed her disgust. The planning for every contingency had put Lily in the lead before Alix ever heard the sound of the starter's pistol.

‿ ⁀

MIDNIGHT STAR PRANCED across the cobblestones outside the park gates. "Easy does it, old son." Nicholas rubbed the black stallion's neck companionably. The diversion of riding through the park on his way home was the singular high point of his day. The lake was larger than his pond at home, and a gathering place for couples with their children. Fathers taught their sons to sail toy boats, and mothers fussed like hens over a spot of dirt. The sound of laughter filling the air was a sad echo of what his life was missing, and better than the silence waiting for him.

The lonely clatter of Midnight's hooves bounced through the quiet neighborhood, until he stopped his horse at the curb as a faint melody someone played on a piano spilled into the street. Even Midnight Star seemed to appreciate the gentle tune. His horse bobbed his head with a throaty whicker and heaved a rattling sigh.

"It sounds as if someone has company for tea." Nicholas left Midnight at the tie stand, intrigued by the music, which grew louder as he walked up the steps. He double-checked his house number as Winston pulled the door open.

"Good afternoon, milord."

"Hello, Winston. I was unaware we're entertaining."

"Not at all, milord. Milady's practicing her lessons."

"Lessons," Nicholas echoed doubtfully as he stepped inside. He handed off his top hat and gloves, happy his mother was not here to see his damaged reflection in the hallway mirror. "It doesn't sound like lessons to me."

"I daresay it's the only explanation."

In his estimation, it would take a fortune to teach someone who stumbled through even "The Dilly Song" to play the rendition of "Greensleeves" he heard coming from his parlor. "Do you mean that's Lily on the piano?"

"Yes, milord."

Nicholas headed determinedly for the closed doors, but Winston rushed to block his entrance. "Please allow me, milord. May I suggest a bit of caution? Milady is shy and easily startled."

"Damn it, I have a right to go into my own parlor!"

"Quietly, I beg of you."

Nicholas's caustic reply died with the music. He suffered a reproachful look from Winston as the butler opened the doors silently. Unable to deny the challenge, Nicholas entered as Lily scrambled up and stood with hands clasped guiltily behind her. He took a defensive position at the hearth, as Winston brought in the tea service.

"Hello, Lily."

"Good afternoon."

If her goal was to impress the butler with her sudden uncertainty, Nicholas had to admit that she played an exceedingly fine part. If her intention was to discredit Nicholas for an unwarranted intrusion into her leisurely afternoon, it came across admirably. If she wished to lay further ground-work for a charge of brutality, she did so suitably. The stage was set, but Nicholas waited for Winston to leave and close the door before continuing.

"Did I startle you?"

Even without witnesses, she gauged him indirectly. "I . . . did not expect anyone."

"I wished only to see how you're feeling." His attempt to be magnanimous sounded pompous, considering her affected pose. He needed to regain the equanimity he wished the staff to describe if they were later called to testify in his divorce proceedings. "Naturally, I'm concerned about learning you've canceled your upcoming engagements."

"Oh."

Her soft response resembled the coo of a dove. His immediate annoyance put a brittle edge to his tone of voice, so that he sounded officious, even to himself. "Was it in error?"

Her eyes flitted to him fearfully. "No."

He could not help but pursue his suspicion that she might be pregnant. "You don't mind if I wonder whether to be worried about your health?" He should have known she would never confess about Phillip's child.

"I'm fine, thank you."

She had a new way of interjecting a delicate space of indecision, as if she were deliberating how best to deal with him. No wonder she had cleared her calendar; she needed time to practice in the mirror. If Nicholas was not careful, any judge in his right mind would find for her defense. She would paint him as an ogre who lacked understanding, and perhaps even as a defiler of innocent character. If she cast her timorous look at any man, his factual evidence would melt into insignificant gibberish.

He dared not look at her further and turned to smash a glimmering coal in the fire with the toe of his boot. "I can't express my relief to hear you say so," he lied.

"Is that everything?"

Surprised, he looked around to find her by the door. Clasping her hands behind her back lent her an absurdly schoolgirl-like appearance. Deepening his impression, she dropped her eyes to the floor. "With your permission, I'll retire upstairs; I've decided against tea."

"As you wish."

"Thank you." She maintained her ridiculously engaging civility despite his curt response. The doors behind her opened to allow her exodus, then closed silently.

Nicolas stared at the white panels blankly, not quite certain what the encounter had accomplished besides making him feel awkwardly alone.

CHAPTER 5

THE MIDSUMMER BALL

*L*ong before Jenny hooked the back of her dress, Alix had resolved to hide behind the first curtain she found at Clarence House, and not to emerge until it was time to return home.

"I'm worried about this neckline. Milady won't have an evening gown with anything but bare shoulders. It's a pity about this scar, but I still say enough paint could cover it."

Alix tugged at the plunging bodice to conceal a bit more cleavage and adjusted the shoulders before her bodice was too snug. The scar on her shoulder was the singular physical dissimilarity between her and Lily. "If your paint smudges, I'll not be in a position to repair it."

"It's a pity; you've such a fine and delicate complexion. There're some who'll have their maids paint blue under their powder for this milky appearance."

"You know a lot of beauty tricks."

"Well, I've been around, haven't I? Some people don't even look the same when their maids are finished. How did you get such a terrible scar?"

"I don't remember," Alix replied truthfully, but noted the maid's skeptical glance in the mirror. Even if she could reveal her identity to Jenny, she would hesitate to share her uncle's story of the day that was the secret behind her mad gap in memory. She had always considered their past a fable to compensate for his inability to provide for her by working in Lord Griffon's stable. Alix had never really questioned why she was living with the Gordons; she was constantly busy with the horses. Now that she was in London, she understood her uncle was trying to save her from taking a position in a household like this. She may have ended up working as a scullery maid while her sister lived as her mistress.

"'Tis for the better, I guess, but still, it's a shame." Jenny paused at a gentle knock on the dressing-room door. "Now, who's that?" the maid murmured as she hurried to answer it.

Alix remained behind the dressing screen but peered over its edge. Jenny straightened her cap before opening the door. The gentle baritone of Albert Frisk's response explained the reason for Jenny's crisp response. "Thank you, but it's unnecessary. Good-bye."

Alix winced at the definitive snap of the door latch. "Does he still have a nose?"

"If he doesn't, it'll serve him right for putting it where it doesn't belong."

"Albert Frisk seems steadfast in his interest."

Jenny briskly returned to the work of finishing the back of Alix's dress. "It'll last only as long as he thinks he wants something. Don't forget, I know a thing or two about men."

"Not everyone is the same," Alix ventured carefully, but far be it from her to offer advice about men. Her experience was limited to her uncle and the men working around the farm. Ozzie Gladstone was the youngest of the butcher's family, and

Finghin Dunnigan was typically as good-natured as he was hardworking. The stableman and smithy was the resourceful Big Tim Riley, who was married and lived down the lane. Jeremy Parker and his wife, Mabel, worked in the house. Everyone was respectful and congenial; it left Alix poorly equipped to suggest anything about Jenny's opinion of the elegant Albert Frisk, beyond noticing that he found Jenny interesting.

She thought at the very least he must realize that Jenny could turn herself out stylishly if she wished. The maid's auburn hair had luxurious copper highlights, and she had her own share of milky skin. To complement such pleasant coloring, her heart-shaped face would be lovely with a less austere hairstyle, and anyone would notice her green eyes were luminous, if she did not squint with disapproval. But Alix reminded herself that it was none of her business, and that soon she would be gone from here.

"Now then, let's take a look at you," Jenny proposed, with a startling smile eclipsing her habitual frown. "My oh my . . . I have a feeling that Minnie and I will go mad tomorrow giving out her cousin's name!"

"MILORD, MILADY IS ON HER WAY DOWN," Winston advised through the parlor door.

Nicholas drained his scotch with relief. The oddity of leaving on time might be a promising sign, but Lily was undoubtedly anxious to display her delicate new image after a fortnight of confinement. "After you," he said, waving her ahead, so as not to have to look at her. Using his watch for distraction on his way to the curb, he scarcely had time to reach for her elbow before she flashed her slender ankle in a show of black lace and climbed adroitly into the coach without assistance.

"Make haste, if you will," he responded to Quincy's dutiful greeting, and settled onto the white leather seat beside his wife, determined to make a connubial show.

Her hand trembled when smoothing her cloak away from him. Did she think he wished to touch her? Nicholas smothered a laugh at her absurdity and propped his topper so its brim blocked her from his vision. While they rolled through the neighborhood and past the park, he posed with a congenial smile and studiously looked anywhere but in her direction. Occasionally, he caught a whiff of a pleasantly different rose-scented perfume. It mingled with her newfound silence and made for an enjoyable drive, for a change. When Clarence House came into view, doormen swarmed around the incoming coaches, and in a manner of minutes they were making their way through the crowd.

Just as soon as they were announced, Nicholas made a break for the bar. He heard his wife's name behind him, but John Wesley came to his rescue with a fistful of scotch.

"Ah, there you are, old chum! We're in for a jolly show tonight," his friend laughed. "Two more here," John called to the nearest waiter, moving Nicholas from the walkway with a friendly nudge. "How now," he wondered as he stared at the crush of people. "What've you done to Lily?"

"Why, nothing, old man—you should know better than anyone."

"Don't look now, but she's stealing the show."

Nicholas sipped his scotch with annoyance. "When doesn't she?"

John elbowed him meaningfully. "There's Newton; I'd say he's forgotten all about his cousin Mary. Maybe you'd better have a chat with him."

"About what?"

"About *that*," John counseled, with a wave of his glass toward the gaggle concentrated on Lily's appearance.

Sam Newton hurried over and pumped hands with them jovially. "Good show, Griffon, old boy. What're you and John doing, just standing around? I came over hoping for permission to take your wife out on the dance floor."

Before Nicholas could respond either way, Millicent Fabersham's shrill voice trumped the noisy room.

"Lily, don't you look fabulous!"

As her declaration parted the crowd, necks craned to see the cause of excitement centered on a woman wearing a gown of flowing color. Whenever she moved, it transformed from wine red to black with a rippling effect so transfixing that Nicholas found himself staring, too, until he realized he was looking at Lily. Her elusive gaze faltered when slipping past his. She turned into her minions and left him gazing after her in puzzled silence. He could barely stand to look at her, and yet he was as dazzled as if he had glimpsed the sun eclipsing the clouds in her eyes.

"LILY, WHAT A LOVELY GOWN," said a willowy woman, as she forged a brave alliance through the snide sighs of impatient greeting rising from Lily's followers. The woman wore a gown of celadon satin, a striking complement to her fiery hair and milky complexion. A veneer of powder did little to challenge her rash of freckles, but she had merry green eyes that twinkled and a voice musical with laughter.

Sniggling whispers swirled behind Alix. "Sarah Wesley . . . That's Sarah Newton. . . . She's Johnny's new wife. . . . They were married a few weeks ago. . . ." John Wesley's name emerged with an overtone of inclusion in Lily's crowd, marking him as one of their own. With the woman's resume provided, Alix smiled Lily's trite grimace and played with her glass of champagne in tired affection.

"Sarah," Alix droned in mimicry of Lily, "you look stunning tonight."

"How kind of you," the other replied artlessly, and drank too deeply from the glass of champagne she carried. "I see you've lost your husband. I was looking for mine, too, and since Johnny said he was going to find Nicholas . . ." Chancing a speculative glance at the absorbent crush surrounding Alix, she continued, "I don't suppose I could pry you away."

Her suggestion aroused debate amid Lily's tittering entourage, and yet if Sarah Wesley had been going anywhere but in the direction of Lily's husband, Alix would have agreed. So far, she had found the anonymity of Lily's group preferable to Nicholas Griffon's steely eye. "Actually, we're just on our way to the card room."

"All right, then don't worry. I'll let Nicholas know where I saw you."

Fortune smiled on Alix as Lily's crowd watched Sarah's departure with smug speculation. Unobserved, Alix slipped behind a passing assembly and maintained their pace. When they came to the drawing room where chamber music played, she sidestepped into a tearoom, where she found a pair of closed draperies with a window seat.

"Finally," Alix breathed, sinking gratefully in the quiet, wishing she had thought to bring along an auxiliary glass of champagne.

A clock chimed the half hour, marking the evening progression. She did not know how long she could continue without discovery, when she filled awkward gaps in her grasp of Lily's behavior instinctively, although blending in had been ridiculously easy with Lily's friends. They were so enamored of themselves, they would never think differently, but Lily's sharp-eyed husband was not that affected. If she were not careful, when she least expected, he would summon the police to end her cheap impersonation of his wife.

She could ill afford a formal investigation. Her precarious position as a poseur teetered between Lily and the fictional Alex Sterling, Esq., of Sterling Wood Stable, who must remain a vague figure, simply because the business of racing was not acceptable for a woman. The license for Sterling Wood Stable was nothing short of a hoax, however unintentional. Every paradoxical hour Alix remained in Lily's shoes thinned the fabled ice beneath her feet.

Her champagne glass was empty when a nearby giggle warned of her imminent discovery. "Come on, let's have a go," a man urged quietly.

A woman protested incredulously. "Not here!"

Her reverie forgotten, Alix moved to avoid their approach. She made her precipitous leap to freedom scarcely in time, fleeing to the outside of the curtains just before the couple ducked in. She did not realize until she was midway to the door that she had forgotten her glass. The trickle of people with whom she had entered earlier had increased to a swarm flooding the room. She was nearly to the threshold when the man cried out, "Ouch! What the blasted hell?"

While surprise pulled curious onlookers to the window, Alix ducked through the door as a murmur of wonder rose in the room. "I beg your pardon!" she blurted when she accidentally barged into someone.

A pair of hands caught her deferentially. "Hello . . . Lily." Nicholas Griffon scrutinized her briefly and then looked behind her at the gathering crowd. "Where've you been hiding?"

"I was . . . looking for Sarah!" Alix grasped at anything for a reply but regretted uttering an inane lie when Nicholas's distrust sharpened accordingly.

"Lady Wesley?"

"Yes." She braved through her mistake amid eager exclamations when someone opened the curtains to reveal the hapless couple. "She was looking for her husband," she babbled nervously as she edged away from the scene that she had unwittingly created, while laughter erupted in the room. Arranging her expression in Lily's smug smirk, she stood on tiptoe and craned her neck to make good on her ploy to survey the passersby as they hurried to share the spectacle.

Nicholas ushered her away from the increasing surge of people. "She found him, but why are you concerned?"

Recalling her sister's conceited crowd, she sniggered Lily's laugh through her nose. "Well, one must do what one can when one finds someone so misfortunate."

His regard hardened in response, and he tightened his grip. "We're late to be seated for dinner," he advised as he marshaled her against the current.

Why did she experience a fleeting feeling of sympathy when he terrified her so? How deeply he must detest Lily, and it was her own bad luck that he mistook her for her sister. Her heart was dredging up this portion of pity because he was as firmly fixed in Lily's ruse as Alix was trapped herself.

CᴜSTOM DICTATED THAT NICHOLAS sit opposite Lily. Even with Helen Childs on his right and Sam Newton's cousin Mary to his left, Nicholas had little to distract him from Sam's surreptitious observation of Lily. For her part, his wife feigned indifference, apparently reluctant to lose her new reticence acquired through hours of practice. Just when Nicholas was optimistic that Lily might maintain her composure, he caught her watching him. The idea in itself was unnerving, rather like being the proverbial bird caught beneath a cat's paw without a clue of its intent. He resolved to avoid noticing her unless conversation warranted an exchange. There was no reason why his meal should suffer simply because she had decided to switch tactics. He would accept it as a warning that she planned a new display to be the culmination of tonight's event.

Midway through the soup, Sam was sufficiently enamored to forget about his pledge to his cousin Mary and opened a conversation with Lily. Until then, Lily had seemed unusually subdued, but however she finally managed to manipulate him into asking a question, she hesitantly responded so quietly that she gave the impression she shared a secret.

As if Newton's acting the fool were insufficient, the Frenchman to her left made it into a game of one-upmanship. Meanwhile, Lily remained aloof, with a smirk of quaint new diffidence. Nicholas turned to Helen Childs and struck up a conversation about the weather. It went well, until the Frenchman became concerned that Lily did not like the stuffed mussels. His excited insistence effectively killed the ebb of conversation, and with the stage set, Lily glanced at Nicholas hesitantly.

Helen peered through her lorgnette at Lily's empty plate as the waiter hovered expectantly. "Perhaps you should try them, Lily."

"Yes, yes, see?" the other man urged with typical French over-exuberance. "They're good, no, Helen?"

"I think so."

"Lily, try them," Newton chimed in, with a defiant look at Nicholas, before turning to his cousin. "You like them, don't you, Mary?"

"Why, yes, of course!" she agreed, and then blushed prettily when the Frenchman looked at her with approval.

"Really, I . . . ," Lily protested as they all exchanged furtive looks. Casting another reluctant glance at Nicholas while reaching for her wineglass, she paled as if her position as the center of attention was suddenly overwhelming.

The Frenchman swiftly waved off the offending course of mussels but, undeterred, looked to his hostess for support. "I find them pleasant."

Nicholas had been about to enjoy his own but doubted why he should take them. It had nothing to do with liking mussels, inasmuch as Lily's performance damned him either way. Should he not touch them, he would be in accord with Lily. If he ate them, he would be siding with the blasted Frenchman. How in blazes had a simple course of mussels become complicated? Did he want them or not, and devil take the lot of them. Although Lily managed to be center stage, for once she seemed discomfited by her own results. Defiantly, he cut one in half and tasted it. It was not bad, but neither was it good. It left his opinion flat, as if it were a waste of his time to consider it.

Quickly, he washed down a gulp of wine to rinse the flavor from his mouth. It was regretful, because ordinarily he liked mussels. The fact that he chose a few crab puffs when they came around had nothing to do with Lily's having allowing one to be served onto her plate. So what if she had? They were better than the mussels.

Talk around the table stuttered and died as men took note when Lily plucked a morsel from the center of her bread to place between her ruby lips. Bleeding Newton was as agape as if he had never seen such a magical performance. Her glance encompassed the assembly with a semblance of surprise.

Nicholas would have shouted with laughter, save for his own physical reaction to the suggestive disappearance of bread. What the devil was the matter with him? He knew better than anyone else about the games Lily played.

Nicholas returned his attention to his plate with fresh resolve while Newton and the Frenchman continued to vie for Lily's elusive attention. By the time dessert began to circulate, Nicholas imagined the meal as one of the longest of which he had ever partaken, especially when the Frenchman insisted the waiter put chocolates on Lily's plate.

Helen finally lost patience and glared at her guest through her lorgnette. "Charles, what are you doing?"

Ridiculously, the fellow rolled his eyes. "Yes, my pet?"

Poor Helen's face flushed so deeply that Nicholas felt it fortunate she was not combustible, or she might have gone up in a spontaneous burst of flame. "She does not care for any."

He waved away her protest presumptively. "But everyone likes chocolate."

"Charles, you are incredible! Lily, I'm sorry for my guest!"

"But why are you sorry?" the Frenchman interjected indignantly. "I don't need you to apologize for me."

Nicholas harrumphed expressively, hoping to avoid an escalating scene, but Sam overrode his caution.

"Helen is right," Newton decided, leaning forward to address the Frenchman across Lily's plate. "She doesn't want your chocolate. Take it away," he waved, summoning the hapless waiter to remedy the error.

"*Vous êtes impossible!*" the Frenchman erupted angrily.

Helen was quick to defend Sam. "*Je suis impossible?* Vous *êtes impossible!* Who do you think you are, telling people what they like?"

"I say," Nicholas risked interrupting. "After all, it was only a chocolate—"

The Frenchman jumped to his feet and threw down his napkin as a declaration of independence, toppling his dessert wine. "This is absurd!"

Helen yelped with indignation as the crimson flood splashed over her gown. "My dress!" Every waiter in the room rushed forward with towels to defray the damage, and the mishap drew the attention of the entire dining room. "Charles, how could you?" Helen wailed incredulously.

The blustering fool hurried to blot at her gown ineffectually with his napkin. "I'm sorry, Helen; it was an accident! *Naturellement, vous savez que je ne voulais pas—*"

Sam interceded coolly as Mary appropriated a towel to do more than just dab at the stain splattering Helen's lace. "I say, old man, you've made quite a mess of things. If I were you, I'd say it's time to call it a night."

The Frenchman turned his anger on Sam. *"Qui es-tu pour me dire quoi faire?"*

"S'il vous plaît," Lily interjected, reaching to stop the Frenchman when he started around her chair. *"Pardon—je ne voulais pas offenser quelqu'un."*

He looked down at her in surprise. "Madame, this has nothing to do with you."

She released his sleeve but implored engagingly, "I'm afraid it does. Please accept my apology."

Helen was not about to forgive the Frenchman. "Lily, don't encourage him; if he wants to be an ignorant ass, then let him."

Lily gazed wistfully after Helen as the woman pulled her rescuers away to find the nearest lounge.

CHAPTER 6

SEEKING ADVICE

uenton rode away with her dream. Alix lay motionless, willing the return of the afternoon he had scolded her for standing on her saddle to pick apples for Chevalier, the white pony that her papa had brought home for her from Toulouse. Quenton had taught him all manner of tricks on command, including how to bow on one knee. The afternoon sky was filled with the kind of clouds that piled into castles and flying dragons or scattered herds of elephants, and the air hummed with the shimmering of cicadas and the rhapsody of birds. Quenton had been riding near the orchard on a warhorse he was schooling when he had caught her in an apple tree.

The dreams occurring nightly made her long to sleepwalk through the day. Quenton had shared stories, but they were akin to fairy tales, compared with now, and his vague allusions were deep with meaning but elusive, since he was always careful of being overheard. What Alix dreamed was not extraordinary, but it dazed her so that she carelessly spoke French or was helplessly tempted by the flute in the parlor to rediscover her forgotten music.

She had idolized her uncle as a child and thought him capable of anything. Now he worked as a servant and lived in the stables. What had happened to their lives?

With a yawn, Alix shrugged into a dressing gown and went to build up the fire. It had become her habit to draw the images from her dreams so she would not forget them. If nothing else, the dream of Chevalier suggested she should not wait any longer to solicit Quenton's counsel. He might not be as lenient as he had been in her dream when he caught her standing on her pony's saddle, but he would help her find a solution. The end to Lily's mad game was long overdue. For Alix to try to deceive someone as assiduous as Nicholas Griffon indefinitely was impossible.

THE MELODY OF A FLUTE stopped Nicholas in the hall. Winston closed the parlor doors silently at his approach.

"Does Lily have company?"

Winston put a cautioning finger to his lips and spoke quietly without yielding his post. "No, milady's practicing."

Abruptly, Nicholas pulled Winston aside. "What the devil do you know about this?"

"I don't know what you mean, milord," he replied, straightening his suit coat with an indignant tug.

"You know exactly what I'm asking. When did Lily start playing flute?"

"Just a few days ago. I'd say she doesn't wish anyone to know about it yet."

"If no one's teaching her, how is she learning?"

"Perhaps she came upon a book of lessons in the library."

"Lily frequents the library?"

"I never thought you'd deny her a book, milord."

Nicholas was astounded that Winston would suggest

anything so lowbrow. "Why would I prevent Lily from the opportunity of reading?"

"That's my point exactly. Milady has been working diligently to improve her mind."

"I'll eat my hat," Nicholas concluded, with an incredulous cough into his fist.

"Is there something wrong with bettering oneself?"

"No," he replied, realizing the implication should the question be posed in court, and pulled himself together. He could ill afford to make an incriminating statement when his divorce proceedings were imminent. "Of course not; I daresay I'm pleased Lily's taking something serious for a change. I was caught by surprise, that's all. Since I returned only to change for the evening, I'd better get on with it."

Nicholas came away with the awkward opinion that Winston had protected her. To prove his disinterest over Lily's performance, he jogged upstairs. He was still puffing from the exertion when he found Albert in the dressing room.

"Good afternoon, milord. I wasn't expecting you home early."

"Wesley wants to have a few drinks before the theater," Nicholas explained, and used the excuse of tugging off his boots to drop onto the couch. "Do you happen to know what the devil is happening around here? I returned home to Lily playing flute and Winston questioning my intentions."

Albert came off with a boot and straddled the next. "I wish I could help, but I've gotten nowhere with Jenny Smith, and now Martha's not speaking to me because of it. I've heard rumors, but apparently everything that appeared to be evidence was coincidental after all."

Nicholas used a little more English than necessary on Frisk's backside and sent the man sprawling with his boot.

"Frankly, I have doubts about that rumor after dinner at Clarence House last week. Lily's many things, but pregnant can't be one of them." He rose to peel out of his coat. "Winston thinks she's turning over a new leaf, but she's different enough to be another person."

Albert picked himself up and gathered the boots to put out in the hall. "Isn't that a bit extreme?"

Nicholas shook his head with frustration. "It sounds irrational, but, for instance, Lily began speaking French at dinner the other night. I've never known of her to speak anything but English."

"Forgive me if I play devil's advocate, but did anyone else speak French?"

"The Frenchman she was speaking with, of course."

"Well, then I beg your pardon if I dare to point out the obvious."

"Damn you if you think you're funny, Albert," Nicholas retorted without vehemence.

"I did beg your pardon."

"Blast you anyway," he concluded, but the idea, once conceived, was difficult to dismiss. "I smell something rotten."

"A simple conversation could turn up something."

"Bite your tongue, lad; I can barely stand the sight of her, and you're suggesting I invite her for a cup of tea? I'd rather cut my own throat."

"As you say, milord, but the races will soon be upon us, necessitating her company either way."

"That's a bridge I'll cross when I come to it."

AS WITH EVERYTHING ELSE in her bizarre performance as Lily, Alix could not simply go to the stables or summon her uncle to the house. Her plan for a private meeting involved pilfering a maid's uniform from the laundry and waiting for Jenny to run errands in Piccadilly. Then she dressed in her makeshift disguise and crept out through the serving hall. The plan unfolded flawlessly until Quenton spotted her, and it unraveled from there.

Her uncle's shocked reaction cut into her heart deeply. "You there—get away from those horses," he ordered curtly when he came through the door.

"Darling, it's me," Alix replied eagerly, turning from the coach horses. She might have dropped a bucket of water on his entrance, for his outraged expression.

"Allie," he spat in complete disbelief, dropping the grain sack from his shoulder as if it contained fire. She missed that bare opportunity to run for the door by hurrying straight into his iron-fisted grip. Instead of offering a kiss and his happy embrace, he held her at arm's length by her shoulders and raked her with eyes as hot as coals. "What in the blazes are you doing here?"

"I have to talk to you," she explained, still deluded his initial reaction was only fleeting astonishment.

"Talk to me!" he parroted, so angry that his words were choked. "Talk to me?" he repeated, so incensed that his grip on her tightened until it inflamed her scarred shoulder, but he was oblivious. "Talk to me about what? Are you going to explain why you're wearing that uniform?"

"I . . . It's a—"

He cut off her words when he clamped a hard hand on her mouth. Suddenly, he looked around. "Silence," he ordered cursorily, and, snatching her elbow in his viselike hand, marched her through the stable and up the steps to a bare room above the carriage house. "When did you come to London?" he growled along the way. "You'd better not be here to tell me you've run away to become a maid, or I'll have someone's hide, and I don't care whose it is."

"Uncle—"

"Don't call me that. How did you find me? Did Lily put you up to this? Damn it, Allie! You're not working here!"

"No!" Alix gasped defensively. "I'm only dressed like this so no one will look twice at me . . . because I've been here in Lily's place." She shrank away from his well-deserved rant and waited abjectly while he paced.

Absent the work cap Quenton balled in his fist, the tips of his ash-brown hair showed blond from the sun. His trimmed beard was a striking contrast with the clean chin of the boyish uncle in Alix's dreams, but she was certain that, despite his outrage, he would find a rational conclusion to Lily's insane ruse. Finally, she drew a steadying breath and started over. "Darling, I apologize for my unlooked-for appearance."

"Hush," he warned, and went to peer warily through the thin panel of his door.

Alix mourned the sight of his mean and paltry sitting room, especially in light of her recent dreams of their former existence. "Quenton . . ."

"Speak quietly—Georgie isn't here, but he could return any moment. Allie, have you any idea what you've risked by coming here?"

Alix nodded and mutely obeyed when he waved her into one of his two chairs.

"I apologize for the accommodations, but I assure you they're such only because I'm rarely here to use them."

"Don't apologize," she protested, unable to keep from noting the bare planks of his floor, without even a rag to warm them. The walls were the same mortared stone as the rest of the building and fitted with rough-hewn timber for shelves.

The only living comfort was the old cupboard granted him for sundry. Her poor uncle had not even a cushion upon which to rest after a weary day of work. It was hard not to compare his spartan quarters with the comforts of the farm. He never once complained about the way he made his living, but now she understood why he did not speak of it.

He turned his chair backward and straddled it. She recognized the habit of old and remembered he oftentimes rocked on two legs when playing chess. The newfound connection made her smile, but she saw worry pitting his forehead beneath unkempt curls concealing his distinctive widow's peak, and his expressive brows convex with concern. Alix had always loved his golden-flecked eyes of hazel for their ever-changing hues, but now they clouded with trouble that she had no clue how to assuage.

"I must know before anything: Has Griffon touched you?"

"No." Alix dared a half-truth because she was uncertain whether the encounter in which she had choked on Lily's bonnet strings had been intentional. "He still thinks I'm Lily," she said, explaining Nicholas's propensity for avoiding her ever since.

Her uncle was so angry that his voice trembled. "Allie, you stay away from Griffon, do you hear me? I can't believe Robbie has allowed you to come here like this!"

"Robbie doesn't know everything—only what Lily made me write in the note." She hoped it was a good sign he was staring at her with shocked indignation instead of running for a sword. "I need your help, darling. I never meant to remain here once I arrived."

"Don't call me darling."

"Of course, Quenton. I—"

"And my name is Quincy!"

"I'm sorry," Alix moaned, dropping her face into her hands in despair. "I don't know how to tell you what's been happening—"

"It's Griffon, isn't it?" Quenton surmised, grabbing her up from her chair to hold her close. "If he harms you, I'll kill him!"

"It's not Nicholas! I d-don't . . . ," she stammered, confused by his vehemence. The strength of his reaction, the possibility that he would seek immediately to settle the score, terrified her. She pulled away and turned to the wall in an effort to find her thoughts. "I've been having the oddest dreams . . . of the simplest things. I don't understand them; they're just so real! I dreamt about playing a flute in a meadow, but I didn't even recognize the melody I was playing. When I tried it, I found out not only that I could play but that I knew the song. I still don't remember its name, but . . ."

His frown deepened with perplexity. "But flute was one of your earliest lessons."

"Then it's true?"

"Are you saying that all of this time, you've remembered so little of the past?"

"It doesn't mean I've never believed any of your stories," she assured him as he turned away in disbelief. "We've never really had the opportunity to discuss it. It's so rare when we're completely alone, and you've always warned it's too dangerous—"

"Allie, stop there," he warned, turning back to embrace her fearfully.

Alix crowded against him as he engulfed her in his arms. For a brief eternity, she was filled with the sweetness of her hero. His worn shirt, smelling of stable and tobacco, returned her to her carefree childhood. The protection of his embrace, his gentle and loving spirit, lifted her, reminding her how completely she loved him.

"Allie," he murmured finally, "you've got to tell me what's happening. Why did you come here like this?"

"Do you know why Mary-Margaret would have Robbie's title?"

He pushed her away abruptly. "What are you talking about?"

"The land grant Robbie won with his Golden Spurs. Lily said it was found with Mary-Margaret's papers after her death. She claimed that she intended to sell the farm if I didn't take her place because she'll need the money if Nicholas discovers she's having a baby."

If Alix had slapped her uncle, he could not have looked more shocked, but then his expression hardened with disgust. "Don't tell me," he said as he turned away. "Phillip."

"Yes."

Incredibly, he laughed. "Well, you can play with fire for only so long . . . but why does it involve you?"

"When I stayed at their house at Foreness, Lily made a game of switching places to skip her lessons and thought nothing of repeating it by holding the deed hostage."

"The farm's not all that's at stake with her husband involved. Griffon might be lost in a bottle for now, but . . ." He gripped her arms uneasily. "Promise me you'll be careful around him."

"Don't worry." When he looked at her askance, she swiftly returned to her problem. "I've searched for the title at every opportunity. It wouldn't surprise me to discover Lily's lying, but the stakes are incredibly high if I'm wrong."

"You're here to save your stable and the farm." It sounded rather grandiose, but he was serious. "The grant might not be here. If it's part of the estate, the solicitor in Margate probably has it."

The logical conclusion was dumfounding. "The solicitor?"

"If Lily intends to sell the place, who better to put it on the market?"

Alix turned away in disbelief. "Oh, glory! No wonder I haven't found it!"

"The fastest way to find out is to go and ask him."

"What a capital idea! I'd better run up and change."

Quenton tugged on his lower lip pensively. "No." He stopped her. "You'll change out of that uniform, all right, and I don't want to find you in one again. You'll be prepared to leave, but not for Margate. I'll catch the ferry alone; it'll be easier."

"But even if the solicitor acknowledges having the deed, how will you—"

He put his arm around her shoulders and guided her toward the door. "Just return to the house; I've arrangements to make for my absence here. Don't worry about Lily's solicitor. I'll do whatever's necessary. Keep your distance from Griffon," he added somberly. "I'd hate to kill a fine employer."

Alix waited uncertainly while he checked the stairs. "Darling, don't joke about such things."

"Who says I am speaking in jest, mademoiselle? Think you so little of me? Return as you came," he directed, hurrying her down the steps. "Use care when you go. Don't look back, and walk straight to the house. Should someone hail you, don't hesitate. Mostly, don't ever come down here again. Do you understand?"

"Yes, of course."

"And remember what I said about Griffon."

"Don't worry—he avoids me completely," she whispered, kissing his whiskery cheek before he opened the outer door. "Give Midnight an apple for me, won't you?"

"I give him one every night."

He held up a silencing finger before he stepped through the door and into the open. Nonchalantly, he lifted his cap to scratch his head in thought. After replacing it at an angle, he dug for his pipe and tobacco as he scanned the quiet alley. With the pipe stem clamped in his teeth, he patted his pockets for a light. Feigning forgetfulness, he turned and looked at the stable quizzically.

"Adieu," he murmured upon his quick return.

"Godspeed," Alix replied as she hurried back toward the house.

ALBERT PUT ASIDE HIS BOOK when Nicholas entered. "Good eve, milord."

Nicholas stripped off his damp evening jacket. "It's a devilish night out there, Frisk; a man can't see more than two paces ahead."

"I trust you had a pleasant evening." Albert scrutinized his condition briefly as he poured a customary nightcap.

Nicholas acknowledged that he had managed to arrive home in better shape than usual and could even remain upright without assistance. That, coupled with the return of his wicked eye, which had once earned him a spot in the top echelon of the club's dart throwers, made him deem his night an overall success. Humbly, he lifted his scotch in an acknowledgment of the momentary return of his former glory. "It wasn't anything exceptional."

He unknotted his tie on his way to the fire. "All quiet here, then? No one else disappeared on short notice?" he added in reference to Quincy's abrupt absence, while popping his collar button open and claiming his chair.

After John Wesley's speculation at the horse sales about

the man seeking employment with the Royal Stud, Nicholas could not help but wonder if Hill had been called out to Windsor to nail down the details of a new position. He was at a loss for how to replace Quincy, should the stable master quit. Although Georgie was his apprentice, the young man was hardly ready for anything more than journeyman driver, and handling Midnight Star required a certain expertise.

"Not that I've heard," Albert responded as he came to pull off Nicholas's boots. "But I'm afraid I have a confession."

Nicholas was not in the mood for soul-searching. If he wished to ponder the truth, he had plenty of his own problems to consider. He fortified himself with a sip of scotch and planted one foot against Frisk's backside while the man gripped his boot.

"Earlier, I tried to catch Martha when she was still across the hall, but she had finished in milady's chambers. There were a few papers caught in the desk drawer, so I thought to correct them before milady came upstairs." He looked around as he came away with the boot. "Perhaps it's better to just show you."

"If you've discovered love letters, I don't give a jot for them. Just bundle them for delivery to the solicitor tomorrow."

"Nay, milord," Frisk responded, retrieving a few drawings from the drawer of the end table. "Rather, these."

Nicholas put aside his drink to take the artwork Frisk handed over. "They're colorful, at least—and surprisingly well done. I never suspected Lily owned any talent."

Albert returned to the immediate task of finishing with Nicholas's boots.

"She hasn't painted before, has she? Or is this, too, a mysterious result?"

He held a scene of a high-walled courtyard to the

lamplight. White roses filled the page behind an enormous fountain where birds bathed in water spilling from a fountainhead shaped as a white-knight chess piece.

Frisk paused to peer over Nicholas's shoulder. "These were only a few from the bottom of the drawer. I was reluctant to misplace anything."

"Even under the circumstances, I can't condone your taking these, Albert. Where is this place?" Nicholas asked, considering the background of an image of an impressive yellow dun stallion pawing at a brilliant sky.

"If I were to guess, I'd think it nearby."

"It does look familiar, but it's impossible to tell," he said, dismissing it to go on to the next image, of a nobleman astride a warhorse draped with decorated armor. His high birth was evident in his fair brow, and both his engraved saber and long sword were set with multicolored jewels. Something about the man was provocative. Was it from the distinctive smile dimpling his cheek or the quality of his clothing, suggesting wealth? His horse alone was worth a princely sum. The animal posed with delicate hooves dancing on the edge of a cliff.

"Why in the blazes does this devil look familiar?" Nicholas sipped his drink, and when he thought about who could command such obedience from a horse, the impossible answer occurred to him. "Quincy?"

"It might only be someone with a remarkable resemblance."

"Damn me if it is!"

Albert quickly retrieved the drawings from Nicholas's tightening grip. "Artists paint whatever grasps their imagination; perhaps milady felt Quincy's vast experience lent well to the subject—meaning the horse, milord."

Nicholas jumped from his chair. Was this evidence of a

fantasy to raise a lover from a lowly rank to the pedestal of an equal? It gave a fresh meaning to Lily's whereabouts the night she had allegedly spent at the D'Arcys'. If she carried another man's child, was it Quincy's, and the affair with Phillip merely an ill-conceived ploy to cover the truth of her tryst with a servant?

"Milord! Where are you going?" Albert asked as Nicholas reached for the door.

"I'm going to do what I should have done a year ago!"

It did not matter if a light shone under the door across the hall—not a court in the land would bar his right to enter that hated place—but he lost all impetus on the threshold. He stalled at the sight of her sleeping in the single light pooling on her makeshift bed on the couch. She used her arm for a pillow, and the book that had fallen from her hand splayed open on the floor.

He ventured nearer only to rescue the book, but as he secured its binding, the title took him by surprise. *The Song of Roland* was an ancient epic about a conspiracy to murder a crusading knight, and the last thing in the world that should interest his wife. Coupled with the sight before him, it formed a question in his mind.

Was this Lily, with tender curls cupping her face? Free of paint and powder, were her cheeks a healthy rose? Without the smear of rouge, did her lips customarily curl with inherent laughter? Could this be Lily? A Lily who read *The Song of Roland* or *Macbeth*, which was within easy reach on the table? Had she reacted aberrantly to his rejection until she had tired of a shallow existence?

The questions formed unbidden and did not stop overflowing. Had he been wrong? Had he misconstrued her overtures by misreading her expertise? Had she taken up his challenge and rebelled to become the epitome of his hateful accusations? Had he changed a malleable ingenue through his own callous disregard for her innocence?

How could he have been mistaken by such a bizarre perception? If this were Lily, he would not have stormed out on their wedding night. He was not a prude. It was not as if he had never bedded a woman, but her vast experience bore testament against her.

That she had succeeded still reeked bitterly. His disquieting rage had chilled to dispassionate fury when he had caught Lily's duplicitous maid with a telltale vial of blood to mark a false loss of maidenhood. The initial lie had been bad enough, but to conceive a ploy to continue the unthinkable deception was the final mark against his wife, even absent the consideration that the foul consummation sentenced him to living death as her husband.

How could that same woman be this fresh-faced amateur? The inconvertibility of the two opposing images created a bizarre comparison, as if he were looking through a multitude of mirrors with distorted reflections. But if this was not Lily, then who would commit to such an unthinkable masquerade?

Silently placing the book on the table, he willed himself away from the enticement of innocence. If she were a part-time inducement designed to ensnare him, Lily would have to wait for her opportunity. He would not put it past his wife to manipulate for her own gain, and if she destroyed someone in the process, she would be the last one to be concerned.

ALBERT AWAITED HIS RETURN, pacing with perplexed uncertainty. "What happened, milord?"

"Nothing." Nicholas came up for air briefly from the bottom of his drink and then drained his glass. "She was asleep."

He was not certain what his foray across the hall had achieved. Was it a discovery, or the same damned hallucination he had idiotically married? Moreover, if the woman across, sleeping in his wife's place, was not just a charming figment of his imagination, what would he do about such a beguiling impostor?

CHAPTER 7

At the Oxley Hotel

"Ie, what are you doing standing there?" Jenny complained. "I've been expecting you at any moment for nearly the entire day."

Alix turned from the upper-story window in the Oxley Hotel, where an afternoon breeze blew back the curtains. She had been to Oxley Commons any number of times, but whenever she spent the night, it had always been in the cottages reserved for stable owners nearer the barns.

"I'm sorry, Jenny." She began her contrived apology as she followed the maid to the dressing room. "I had something of a problem after you'd left, and no one to help me solve it."

"But when I left, you were ready to leave."

"But then I noticed my bonnet in the mirror." Alix dared not try to explain the sticky situation with Lily's husband. The maid had no sooner left the house on the cart with the overnight luggage than Alix had looked out to find Midnight Star waiting by the coach.

"What was wrong with your bonnet?" Jenny asked in perplexity.

Alix removed it gingerly. She could not relate how she had waited behind Lily's door, listening to Nicholas pace in the hall. He had gone up and down the stairs a number of times, waiting for her to appear so they could leave for the races. "Nothing, I suppose, but I thought I should wear the pink serge."

Jenny took it doubtfully. "But you dislike the pink serge."

"I thought so, too, but when I looked at this ecru bonnet in the mirror, I thought, *Why not?*" After all, she had nothing else to do while biding time in the hope that Lily's husband would tire of waiting and ride Midnight Star away. She could never explain her pet's reaction at the sight of her. Not only could she not withstand a battery of questions about Midnight Star's infatuation when she was purportedly Lily Griffon, but, given her uncle's absence, she doubted the young man taking his place could manage to control Midnight on his own. To avoid a potentially disastrous scene, she made excuses whenever the butler came to inquire if she needed assistance.

Jenny considered her skeptically. "*Why not?*"

Alix tugged on her gloves to remove them and shrugged innocently. "Yes, but the amaretto was better suited to match the olive green in the paisley."

"But you didn't wish to wear paisley," the maid replied pointedly, "and you're still wearing the flowered print."

"Oh, yes, I am now." She had never changed, even though she was touting the excuse to describe her delay. In actuality, she had been pacing back and forth, too, from Lily's window to the door, waiting for her chance. Finally, one of the neighbors riding by on a white horse had stopped for a word, distracting the stallion's attention. She had fled downstairs, catching the butler at lunch. She'd had no time to wait while his assistant fumbled for her things, and she'd simply snatched them from his hands in a mad dash through the door. She had almost made it into the coach without anyone's noticing her, but Lily's sharp-eyed husband paused with his mouth agape as she yanked the coach door open, and broke off his conversation with the neighbor to glare at her belated appearance with unconcealed disgust.

Now Jenny remained unconvinced as well. "You changed dresses?" she asked, pursuing Alix's story doubtfully.

"Well, not exactly, but the idea did occur to me." Alix smiled sweetly, spreading her skirt as she settled on the dressing-room seat. "It all started with the white shoes." She hoped Jenny would explain her indecision to Albert Frisk, and that perhaps the tale would help to defray Lily's poor husband's tension, because he was nearly livid with frustration. She had not wished to anger him.

"Here now, don't tell me you were rummaging amok in milady's closets," Jenny warned sternly.

"Me? How could I ever?" Alix claimed innocently, although she would have loved to shred every piece of clothing dear Lily owned. During the morning's unfortunate delay, she had realized that she might not necessarily return to Lily's place if Quenton secured Robbie's missing deed, and so had piled sacks of lingerie in the hall for the maids. She hoped to leave Lily a strong message upon her return. The maids would have a gay time sorting through what they liked, and dear Lily could deal with a lack of underpinnings later. "You *do* see how these shoes match this gown better than the brown ones you had chosen."

Jenny dropped on her knees to unlace them. "Pishposh, who wears white outdoors? You like these because they're made for you. Haven't you ever had a new pair of shoes before?"

"I pity the penny they cost His Lordship; it's not his place to pay for my cobbler."

"Fie, as if he ever settles a bill, when that's Percival Winston's job. I've explained it to you before. It's obvious you've never lived in a fine house, either."

Alix laughed. "Begorra! In England, even the servants are snooty!"

"I'm not snooty," Jenny declared in a huff, pushing up from her stool to put the shoes away. "I never would've guessed you're Irish. You've nary an accent."

"Och, so it's an accent yer a-wantin'?" she replied in a thick Scottish burr she had borrowed from the farm's closest neighbor, Andrew MacGregor.

Jenny's eyes narrowed in suspicious surprise. "You must be one of those backstreet actresses."

Alix answered with lines from *Macbeth* as she rose to step out of her skirt. "Life's but a walking shadow, a poor player that struts and frets his hour upon the stage, and then is heard no more.'"

"Fie, I knew you were an actress," Jenny decided as she went to add hot water from the steaming kettle to the washbasin. "We'd better hurry, or you'll be late."

"Have you made arrangements for tea?" Alix changed the subject as she shrugged out of her blouse.

"Me? Why do you ask?"

"I thought you might be meeting your handsome Albert Frisk . . . Why are you laughing?"

Jenny added a towel to the rack and turned to pull out fresh undergarments. "For one thing, I'm not his type."

"I don't know," Alix demurred as she went to wash. "What would be his type?"

"Well, for starters, he likes women with a bit more up

here," Jenny asserted as she cupped her breasts. "And more here," she added, with a jocular slap on her hip.

Alix plunged into the water and spoke between splashes. "That only calls for different underpinnings. You've said as much yourself."

"As if I have time for foolish notions."

"Why not?" Alix asked as she dried herself with the towel and used it to wave at the open valise, overflowing with underclothes, on the lowboy. "Just use something from there."

"Now I *know* you're full of nonsense. Besides, don't forget I'm a little tart for that one's flavoring."

Alix climbed into a fresh chemise and settled on the bench to put on clean stockings. "What's wrong with tart? Not everything delectable is sweet."

"Do you ever hear yourself? What makes you think I'd be interested in such a man?"

"Well, he's tall, and terribly good looking."

"If you feel that way, then you take him."

"Me!" Alix laughed in a merry protest. "He's not come around to flirt with me! Besides, there are some things to admire. He has definitive taste, the same as you. His attention proves he finds you attractive."

"If that's true, then why did he just notice me? It's not as if I haven't worked here for almost a year."

"I think he caught a glimpse of your smile, or saw the sunlight in your hair that day outside the dressmaker's. You'd do well to leave it alone," she added hastily when Jenny fussed at the hairpins holding her cap. "It's far prettier with a few curls."

"It is a plain nuisance and nothing less, the way my hair slides loose from pins."

"It only proves it's soft. I could cut it, as you've done mine."

"Do you think I'd let the likes of you have a go at my hair with shears?"

"I've cut plenty of hair in my time," Alix maintained, refraining from mentioning that it all belonged to horses.

"Ha, there is a laugh," Jenny decided, hooking up the back of Alix's tea dress.

"So, are you meeting Albert Frisk for tea? I still maintain, why not? He seems to be a respectful gentleman."

"He's naught but a rake and a bounder."

"A cup of tea is hardly a commitment."

"A cuppa is only the beginning. He's a bit too smug, if you ask me. It makes me think he's up to something."

"You might find him remarkable if you sit down for a chat."

"Pishposh, Albert Frisk's too fast. He's no idea of a real man's worth."

"He must have something to keep his job. Nicholas Griffon doesn't strike me as someone who keeps frivolous servants."

"No, he's still the sea captain who runs a tight ship."

"Nicholas is a sailor?"

"Nay, not one of those scurrilous types. Don't tell me milady never said a word about how wealthy he is. He owns Lion Shipping Company, doesn't he?"

"It must be a lucrative business."

"His fleet of ships sails around the world," Jenny boasted briefly, draping a collar of Ceylon sapphires and pearls around Alix's throat. "They say he's traveled widely, too, and stopped only to get married."

"Since Albert Frisk is well traveled, it'll prove a marvelous topic of discussion at tea."

"Tea? Who said I was going to have tea with him?"

Alix hurried to the valise to rummage for a corset. "You did—don't you remember? And you agreed to wear one of these, because you can't wear your uniform to take tea with a gentleman. You'd better hurry and change," she urged, as she pushed a beribboned corset into Jenny's astonished hands.

"You're joking!"

Alix pushed the maid to the exit. "You'd best dash; we're here for a weekend of fun, remember?" She cut off the maid's protest abruptly by closing the door.

"PSST! OVER HERE," a woman hissed, suddenly crowding against the curtain concealing Alix. She shrank against the window when the co-conspirators almost trampled her toes. This, after she had purposely chosen a window without a seat as a place to hide. When she tried to escape from Lily's friends in the future, she might look for a cupboard.

"There she is!" the woman continued.

"Who?" the other whispered.

"Sarah Wesley!"

"Oh, do you see Johnny?"

"No."

"I can't believe he decided to marry her!"

"Lily says he was on the rebound after Gwynne snubbed him for that French marquis."

"Do you mean the one from Saint-Étienne who's staying over at Helen Childs's?"

"No, that's Charles du Périer. Gwynne never told anyone the name of her Frenchman, only that he is supposedly a marquis."

"Anyone could say that. Unless one's from France, who else would know? But Lily said he's so handsome that she doesn't know why Gwynne doesn't run away with him!"

"Everyone's saying he must be an impostor."

The continued mention of Lily's name inflamed a dreary throb in Alix's left temple and made her long for fresh air.

"Gwynne asked me if I've seen him—can you believe it? I wouldn't even know whom to look for! If he's not here this weekend, he's probably gone back to Paris."

Alix shrank cautiously into the narrow space the windowpane afforded her, uncomfortably aware that someone outside might notice her pressed against the glass.

"That's a sign of an impostor: They simply vanish, don't you think? Oh, look, there's Johnny!"

"Wait, where're you going? Isn't that Lily's husband with him?"

"Who cares? Nicholas was one of last season's most eligible bachelors!"

"Mother says not to let his fine looks fool you; haven't you heard the rumors that he's done something to Lily?"

"Oh, Lily's just being Lily. Nicholas used to be just as much fun as Johnny, but now he acts as if he's afraid someone will see him enjoying himself."

"Oh, don't go over!"

"Why not? He and Johnny might be married, but they're still the best-looking men here, and maybe they'll ask us to dance!"

"Oh, glory, will you just run along?" Alix breathed in their wake, and parted the curtain slightly to peer apprehensively after the pair making their way through the crowded tables. Nicholas Griffon and John Wesley had found a place to sit with Sarah. Despite her limited consensus, Alix thought if the beautiful redhead was a consolation prize, John Wesley had done well to marry her.

The sight of waiters and their laden trays reminded Alix

about the hours since lunch. Teapots and cocktails circulated freely but nowhere near her hiding place. Cautiously, she slipped from behind the draperies and drifted to a potted palm. When the next waiter passed with a tray on his shoulder, she used him as a portable screen.

"I'm sorry." He paused in embarrassment when he noticed her walking beside him. "Would you care for something?"

"Thank you," Alix agreed pleasantly, and accepted an expeditious cup of tea. After he bowed cordially on his way, she was left in the open. A survey of the table where Nicholas's party sat quickly determined that Lily's friends had provided a convenient diversion.

Deciding they would not miss her for a while longer, Alix seized the opportunity to migrate to the lobby in search of Robbie. She had just found a fruit and cheese plate on a sideboard, when men's voices echoed from downstairs. In the lobby below, a well-dressed company typical of Robbie's proximity emerged from the wagering room. She was hurrying to the stairs when she heard her sister's name.

"Lily," Nicholas Griffon's unwarranted appearance stopped her abruptly.

Sarah's laughter rose above the noise of the crowd. "Where are you going in such a hurry?"

"Yes, where are you going?" Nicholas added as they joined her.

Alix's heart plummeted. Looking futilely after the men marching with Robbie's square shoulders mustered in their midst, she watched as they pushed through the outer doors and disappeared.

Sarah reached for her hand companionably. "We've been looking for you everywhere."

Lily's husband straightened decisively. "You don't mind

visiting with Sarah while I find John, do you? He went to place wagers for a couple of your friends."

Alix bolstered her determination and propped up Lily's tired facade resolutely. "Certainly."

"What're your plans for this evening?" Sarah asked eagerly. "Have you placed any wagers?"

Alix followed her to a group of chairs to sit while they waited for the men. "In a manner of speaking, I suppose."

"Oh, good! I hope you don't mind sharing which horses have you chosen."

"You might say I've put everything on Sterling Wood Stable."

QUENTON KNEW HE WAS LATE but did not mind, for a change. He stopped to let his rented horse drink its fill at the brook and then walked beside it down the highway. When his heavy boots became uncomfortable, he tightened the saddle girth and mounted to ride. At one time, he had owned boots so fine that he had been able to walk for miles without his feet protesting. He preferred to hike adverse terrain so rugged that it was safer to climb and let his horse find its own way. He had lost an admirable stallion once when it had fallen, and then he had been lucky not to be in the saddle. That had been in the rocky Pyrenees, on the road to Zaragoza. He had been a younger man then, and the death of his experienced warhorse had been devastating. He did not know why his mind turned back to those days; he had not thought about the Spanish campaign for a long time.

It must be a symptom of the seed planted by the trip to Margate, he decided. He had not realized it until he had returned to London. So far, he had only an objective, but he was already convinced it was worth the attempt. It eased his conscience about returning to Alix empty-handed; if he were successful, it was of far more importance than the where-abouts of Robert Gordon's land grant.

It was a risky gamble, but his visit to the British solicitor had sparked his resolve. He knew Alix would not understand why he wished to return to France, but the journey came with risks he was unwilling to share. Whether it cost him his life or landed him in prison, the future was as unpredictable as it had been when he had departed. Still, if what the attorney had to say about landholdings and trusts were true for France, it was impossible to ignore.

When Quenton had taken Alix to live with her mother, the scandal of his brother's death had been fodder for speculation in midnight saloons and haute salons alike. The brutal slaughter had been a warning to anyone who opposed the imperialists in Paris. It had not mattered that Quenton had once ridden in the Spanish campaigns; the accusations against his brother, Henri, had eclipsed everything.

The trick would be managing to leave without Alix's discovering his intention. She had a way of doing things when they were least expected. He might risk his own life recklessly, but he would die for hers. He could ill afford a surprise package with soft blue eyes and golden hair if he ended at the guillotine.

NICHOLAS EXPECTED TO REGRET wearing Lily on his arm for the entire weekend but instead found himself looking for evidence that the woman in his company was not his wife. She seemed to have an odd manner of resurfacing after inexplicable disappear-ances that left even her friends guessing at her whereabouts, and by the time he had dressed for dinner that evening, he had decided to give his bizarre notion a spurious test.

He went to Lily's hotel door and rapped on it boldly.

Jenny pulled it open and gaped in surprise. "Good eve, milord. We weren't told to expect you!"

Nicholas stepped inside, immune to the maid's doubtful inspection as he retrieved his timepiece from his pocket. "Should I interpret that to mean no? I'll wait."

"Of course, milord," Jenny curtseyed and scurried away.

Nicholas paced the small sitting room, looking for opportunities to find anything out of the ordinary. His copy of Shakespeare's *Hamlet* lay on the end table, but he found no place marker when he rifled through the pages.

A rustle of lace announced her appearance before he had time to snap the book shut.

"Hello," he began, and then his mind floundered to a halt. For a bizarre instant, she looked nothing like Lily, but the illusion lasted only until she grimaced in her favorite acid smile.

"What a pleasant surprise," she deemed flatly.

He found himself choking on his stupidity. "I was passing and thought you might be ready," he managed to say on the way to hold the door.

She retrieved her painted evening fan and beaded reticule from the nearby table and adjusted her silky wrap, which shimmered in a winged reflection of her gown of outstretched cranes. The dress was another difference, if he dared to add it to his list, because he had never known his wife to wear anything so unique.

He longed to put his arm around her, just to experience what it would be like to touch her. Would he find it enjoyable, or would he recoil, as usual? He caught a whiff of her tantalizing rose-scented perfume as he reached for the door. "You look lovely tonight," he ventured as they joined the procession down the stairs.

She glanced at him sidelong, silently gauging his sentiment. "Thank you," she replied finally, instead of making one of her customary condescending remarks.

Intentionally, he pursued his premise. "I don't think I have ever seen my grandmother's black diamond quite so well showcased."

Her hand flew to the teardrop pendant clasped at her throat. "It's a beautiful piece."

How would he know if he reached a milestone? Lily did not ordinarily wear whatever family jewelry he allowed her. She preferred to spend his money to buy her own.

Heads swiveled as people stopped along the staircase to let them pass. He might have been walking with the queen of the weekend, the way a hush fell when people noticed her. Men rose to their feet, and women pushed forward to coo with admiration. Soon Nicholas was in the center of an unusual circle of conviviality, until Lily's gaggle of friends converged to take her away.

"Splendid entrance, old man." Sam pumped his hand when he succeeded in pushing through the crowd. "Don't look now, but the vision of an angel has stolen your wife."

John clapped his shoulder good-naturedly. "Why don't you give me the name of Lily's dressmaker, so when Sarah asks, I'll look better for it . . . and let me buy you a drink, because by the time my wife's finished, my bank account will be empty."

"Look sharp, lad, if you plan to keep her on your arm tonight," Sam concluded, grabbing whiskeys off a passing tray.

"Here's to us tomorrow," John toasted. He surfaced to nudge Sam in the ladies' direction. "Are we still dining together?"

Nicholas signaled the waiter before the man got away. "Bring a bottle of your best champagne, will you?"

"Oho," John chortled. "You're ordering Moisson d'Épernay? You must be planning to celebrate early, old chum!"

"Only the best is worth it, if you plan to taste the stuff," Nicholas demurred.

Sarah laughed as she turned at their approach. "You'll never guess which horse Lily thinks will win the hunt!"

"You mean you've been discussing racing?" John laughed as he slipped his arm around Sarah's waist. "That's my bride."

She giggled and playfully pushed him away. "Don't be silly; it's all Lily's doing." She joined her on the nearby settee, spreading her emerald gown so it met the black-and-white folds of dancing cranes. "You must know something about her favorites, Nicholas. What do you think of Dark Star? Is he fast?"

"Be careful, old man—my sister's serious," Sam cautioned with a wink, as he perched on the arm next to her.

"Don't ask him," John laughed, as he passed glasses of champagne. "He'd pick Dark Star solely for the resemblance to his own Midnight Star."

Uncomfortably, Nicholas realized that John knew Lily better than he did. The rumor of their affair last summer was something they never discussed, for Nicholas preferred to maintain their friendship without the taint of accusation. Still, he wondered if John noticed a difference in Lily.

Lily abruptly returned from the bridge of her thoughts as she stared into her glass and cast an oddly apologetic glance at Nicholas. Sensing his response might be of meaningful measure, he answered carefully, even though she seemed more interested in looking at the bottle's label than in what he had to say.

"Unfortunately, the Sterling Wood colt hasn't been here all week. It's rumored they've come up a bit shorthanded recently, but Dark Star doesn't seem to have suffered for it."

Sarah laughed, looking to Lily for consensus. "What does that mean?"

"It means that Nicholas isn't sharing anything," John interpreted, noticing Lily's lapse. "Now, if you ask me, the colt looks good, except blasted Gordon's been keeping him under wraps."

"I think he is too hotheaded to have a chance," Sam opined eagerly. "If it matters to you ladies, I'm putting my money on Banshee. Quincy Hill is riding for the Royal Stud. The chap wins nine out of ten of his races. Your money's as good as in the bank."

"If Quincy rode Dark Star, he'd be the odds-on favorite," John maintained, with a circumspect glance at Lily as she realized her inattention.

"Anything can happen in a horse race," she averred somberly, and finally tasted her champagne.

CHAPTER 8

The Newmarket Hunt Cup

‿❦‿

As if even the Fates were excited that it was finally the day of the races, the sun slipped from the horizon as a brilliant ball of light. It may have been Apollo, eager to show the swiftness of his horses pulling the golden chariot of the sun. It was fortuitous however the sun rose, because when it set in the evening, Dark Star could be the new reigning champion and seal the stable's reputation.

Although waiting for Sarah to get ready had taken half the morning, and they had joined Nicholas and John only for the last race of novice fillies before lunch, Alix did not feel the day had started poorly. Sarah's pick to win was a filly better suited to sprinting than running a mile, but Alix liked the brown mare that placed second and decided to make an inquiry about purchasing her. Before the afternoon sessions could begin, when Sarah wished to freshen up and the men enjoyed their pipes, Alix slipped away to see if she could find Robbie, or at least discover the spread of the odds.

The halls were quiet. Alone, she ventured down the stairs. She paused on the upper mezzanine to scan the lobby for

Robbie, but a glance at the enormous clock suggested if he was not giving Ozzie last-minute instructions at the clubhouse, he might be in the wagering room, working on the odds for Dark Star's race. She was anxious to learn the outcome of Quenton's quick trip out to Margate, and hesitated when a garrulous group of men breezed through the lobby below her vantage point. Their ranks thinned, exposing Robbie when they passed into the hall to the wagering room. Compelled to follow, she hurried to the stairs.

"Oh yoo-hoo, Lily!" Millicent Fabersham called from the upper staircase. Gathering her skirts, Millicent swooped down to join her. "Where've you been?"

"Watching the races," Alix responded. She bit her tongue impatiently and looked ruefully toward Robbie's disappearing company.

"I've heard," Millicent said, lowering her voice as she neared, "that you've been stuck with that dreary Sarah Newton."

"Don't forget she's Lady Wesley now," Alix reminded her distractedly, at a loss for a reason to escape.

"Oh well, as pitiful as that is. Where're you going?" Millicent asked, peering down into the milling throng. "Did you see someone interesting?"

"No, I'm going down to look at the odds."

"Odds," the lady repeated dubiously.

Alix was reasonably assured Lily's friend would have no passion to pursue the interest. "Sarah and I have lost the wager we placed this morning; I wish to have an advantage this afternoon."

"Oh," Millicent sniffed, lifting her lorgnette suspiciously. "I must say, it sounds boring."

"I beg your pardon, but I'd like to dash off before Sarah—"

"I'll be right there, Lily!" Sarah hailed as she hurried down the stairs toward them.

"Of course," Alix muttered in frustration.

Millicent sighed sympathetically. "I'm sorry I didn't let you get away while you still could! Oh, dear, but I'm sure you'll understand that, regretfully, I must be on my way. Ta-ta, Sarah!"

"Oh, that's too bad," Sarah replied cheerfully while Millicent rushed for the nearest card room. "What're you doing down here all alone, Lily? Where's Nicholas?"

"I'm just running down for a quick peek at the wagering boards."

Sarah's fair expression clouded doubtfully. "Oh, Lily . . . I don't know if that's such a good idea. I didn't think women were allowed there—at least, not the decent sort."

"They keep the odds posted outside the betting room; I heard some men refer to it, and I thought I'd take a look."

"If Nicholas can't go, I'll ask Johnny—"

"You wait here," Alix proposed swiftly, before she lost track of Robbie. She might sound brave, but the wagering room was the last place she wished to be caught alone. "I'll be right back."

"But aren't you worried about what people will think?"

"I'll return before anyone notices."

"Oh, Lily, please wait!" An abrupt commotion and then murmuring silence from the hallway to the betting room stopped Alix at the foot of the stairs, and Sarah ran down to pull her to safety as the gathering began to push closer. "What's happening?"

Alix could not tell beyond the sea of men, but when the tension began to draw others from the lobby, she shielded Sarah cautiously. "I don't know, but don't look; a row might be starting."

Sarah retreated up the lower steps to where she could crane her neck to see over the men's heads. "Don't tell me not to look and then endanger yourself!"

Robbie suddenly split through the crowd, emerging from the direction of the betting room with a stable boy in tow. He passed by Alix without noticing her, barking orders at the boy. "Run and show me the way, lad. Don't worry if I can keep pace. I'll be right behind you—just go!"

"Yes, sir!" The child bolted for the exit with Robbie on his heels, leaving Alix to watch, dumbfounded, as they disappeared through the doors.

"What's happening? Who was that man?"

"Look!" Alix directed Sarah to a cluster of chalkboards propped in the entry, as the crowd shifted to allow someone to write on them. Her heart plummeted when a decisive line drawn through a name gave rise to a ripple of murmuring.

Sarah peered at Alix uncertainly. "What's he doing?"

"Someone's been scratched from the race! Don't look now, by Jove, but I think it's Dark Star!"

"You can read that from this far away?"

"No, but it's why I'm going closer to look!"

Sarah caught her arm. "Lily, you daren't!"

"If my horse is scratched—I mean, if our wager needs to be changed—I have to be sure!" Anxiously peeling herself from Sarah's grasp, Alix was quickly caught in the surge of men crowding to see the changes.

Sarah suddenly squeezed through to grab her hand. "Stop! Lily, this is close enough!"

"Sarah, stay back!"

"Lily?" Nicholas Griffon's incredulous voice rose above the noisy room.

"Oh, God, now we've done it!" Sarah cringed, craning her

neck to find Lily's husband. "Nicholas, we're over here," she called with a gay wave, and tightened her grip on Alix's hand to keep from being separated. "Lily, you've got to come with me!"

Alix balked with stunned confusion in the jostling crush, unwittingly thinking aloud. "I can't believe that Star's been scratched. What's happened? Why did Rob . . ."

"Oh! Nicholas," Sarah gulped with relief, disregarding Alix as he shoved through the crowd to reach them. "You're just in time! Someone has marked out our entry in the Newmarket Cup steeplechase!"

Nicholas scowled at Alix, blocking the press of men pushing to read the boards. "Lily, what in the devil do you think you're doing?" he demanded, taking her elbow firmly to guide her and Sarah to safety.

The reminder of her sister pulled Alix from her bewilderment briefly. Resigning herself to her part, she swiftly assumed Lily's affectation. "The board's impossible to read from the lobby," she reasoned as an excuse for her unwarranted behavior.

"We were chatting with Lady Fabersham," Sarah interjected helpfully. "There was a bit of an uproar, and a man ran out just before they marked through the name of our horse."

A spectacled man in shirtsleeves appeared with notes cupped in hand. His presence quelled the noisy hall as he wiped sections of the chalkboard with his rag, and induced a fresh murmur as he began to rewrite entries.

John's initial surprise at finding his wife in the hall quickly transformed into avid interest in the changes. "I say, what's happening? Dearest, why don't you and Lily run along to the tearoom? We'll let you know what's happened just as soon as we sort through everything."

Sarah grinned at her husband with marked relief. "All right, Johnny."

"Sterling's jockey got behind the wrong horse," a man nearby shared knowledgeably. "From what they're saying, the poor fellow's been kicked into next week."

Alix's knees nearly gave way. Her reluctance to move against Nicholas's insistence abruptly changed as she clung to him for support. "Ozzie?"

Thankfully, Nicholas did not realize her reaction, as he exchanged a look of understanding with his friend. "It appears we've a few amendments to make to our wagers."

"Come on, Lily; let's go upstairs to wait where it's more comfortable."

"Right, of course," Alix conceded meekly. Her mind was too mired in unwitting disaster to counter with any sort of argument. While she was helplessly trapped inside her sister's ploy, her hard work to shape another champion for her stable had been suddenly obliterated.

"Don't worry; we'll put your money on Banshee. He's still the odds-on favorite," John promised, as Sarah tugged Alix toward the stairs.

On the lower staircase, Alix cast a final look at the chalkboard over the heads of the crowd, hoping she was only dreaming. Lily's husband had been watching their departure thoughtfully, but he turned when John urged him into the line of men forming for the betting room. Futilely, she stumbled in silent despair behind Sarah, unequipped to deal with utter defeat.

Lily had appropriated her life, and now this catastrophe. Alix was unable to reconcile the outrage that suddenly swept through her. Before she realized what she was doing, she hurried for the exit. Sarah's calls for Lily meant only that the impossible test of fulfilling Lily's role had failed. Once exposed, the lie of Alex Sterling and the stable would be public; Sterling Wood's shaky foundation quivered with disaster. The inequity of Lily's ruse ignited an overdue spark of determination that had been dampened by an impractical belief that Alix could somehow manage the charade.

Without proof that North Star could produce a championship bloodline, the breeding fees Sterling Wood Stable had commanded would be reduced to pennies. If Sterling Wood lost its budding reputation, it would not matter if Nicholas Griffon had Alix arrested for the crime of impersonation. If every newspaper in England slandered her name, she was going to meet the gates of hell in blazing glory. Even if Dark Star became notorious, he would bring sufficient money with his sale to purchase the farm from Lily, once North Star's bloodline was proven.

The freshening breeze blew Alix into the barn with her ribbons aflutter. Surprised racehorses picked up their heads to watch as she lifted her skirts to run.

ALIX HAD RIDDEN IN PLENTY of practice races but never on an official track, though only because a woman jockey was unthinkable. She was barred automatically, no matter how well she could ride. If she was discovered astride Dark Star in the race, the judges would summon the police, yet before the call to post sounded, she rode boldly onto the green with other jockeys, under the guise of Alex Sterling.

Her black horse was jubilant to see her. Although identical in appearance to Midnight Star, he was almost opposite his brother in temperament. Where Midnight was calm, Dark Star was volatile, and she could feel his passion in every bouncing stride through a high-spirited and buoyant warm-up. Star did not like the wind in his face and pinned his ears with half-closed eyes, but he was a king among followers, arching his neck and stretching long legs in a promising show while they breezed past the grandstands.

Alix rode easily, guiding him through the established routine. Her heart soared when she spotted Quenton on the striking dappled-gray Banshee from the Royal Stud, but then she ducked her head and tugged Ozzie's Sterling Wood racing cap tighter to cover her hair. Beloved uncle or not, it would not bode well for her when he noticed she was riding Dark Star. He would be so outraged to find her on the track that he would not worry about creating a public spectacle.

She turned Dark Star toward the starting post. Wind whipped against them, pressing the cobalt racing jersey of Sterling Wood Stable against the corset that she had tightened over her breasts. The crowd was too distant to notice, but judges in the weighing room and the approaching stewards were closer. Alix had scrubbed away Lily's makeup and coarsened her face with ash before joining the men in the clubhouse to report for the race. With her coiled and braided hair hidden beneath Ozzie's cap, her shocking impersonation of a man was complete, but her anxiety made Dark Star chew his bit as he sensed her nervousness as they breezed down the backstretch.

"Not now, Star," she cajoled in the lilting singsong voice her horses knew. "Patience, love, patience." She patted his neck as he puffed nervously.

A jockey picked an inopportune time to canter closely behind them. Alix would have turned in the saddle with a few short words for the inconsiderate rider as Star broke pace fretfully, but he grinned at her boyishly.

"Not a bad horse, for a newcomer."

Alix did not answer but feigned interest in Dark Star's front leg to ignore the man.

"This ain't no race for a novice."

"Never said I was a novice," Alix rasped defensively.

"Suit yerself," he laughed, riding on.

She tightened Star's reins when the departure provoked him. "None of that," she warned.

With the grandstands full and the judges arranging the finish line, Alix watched cautiously for her uncle. Banshee and Quenton's royal-purple jersey were easy to spot as the pair cut across the open green. Dark Star loved the reaction of the crowd as he cavorted past the grandstands. Alix found herself facing Nicholas Griffon as he followed his friends, but he was too busy looking for people in the crowd to notice her.

Alix knew that at any given moment, security could swarm the field. She would be notorious as the woman who impersonated a man, as well as Lady Griffon's impostor, but she was undeniably guilty. At least she was riding the best horse possible if she needed to escape, because the stamina of Dark Star's Turkoman bloodline meant that even the Royal Stud's Banshee could not keep pace with the black horse over a distance.

"Hey, watch it." Her neighbor gestured with his whip when the steward brought Dark Star up next to him in the starting line.

Alix snapped at the implied threat of the whip. "You should heed your own advice."

"Settle down, lads," the steward warned as the other horse reared anxiously.

"That damned black horse bumped me!" the other jockey lied.

She bit back her disclaimer as he sneered, but followed with mute supplication when the steward directed her to back up.

"Don't mind him, lad," the man on her opposite side said, dismissing the altercation. "He always gets nasty before he loses a race."

"Damn you, Mike—"

"See what I mean?" He spat onto the ground and settled in his saddle as the line of jockeys did the same. "All right, then, they're about ready—and here we go!"

Alix had scarcely time to take his cue when the jittery horse shied at the sound of the starting pistol and bumped Dark Star as the racers lunged away. Incensed, Star lashed out as the unfortunate horse plunged ahead, driven by his rider's whip. Alix was left suddenly alone at the starting post with Dark Star in the mood for a fight instead of a race.

They began the race in last place, behind the distancing field. "Easy does it, lovely," she consoled him. After Star cleared the first fence smoothly, he began to make up the difference. They reached the lagging runners at the next jump. He swiveled his ears toward the sound of her singsong coaxing and finally settled into an even stride as he landed easily.

Horses fell behind when he mustered a burst of speed and stretched over the water jump to come down in a hail of turf. At the next fence, one of the nearby horses fell badly. Stewards surged onto the track with a stretcher for the jockey, endangered by riders coming from behind, but Dark Star was impervious to anything but catching the leaders. Alix saw how quickly they were moving up the inside, when she spotted Quenton on Banshee ahead.

She had not considered what her uncle would do when she challenged him for the lead, but she had barely had time to consider the concept before the contentious jockey on the chestnut horse from the starting line abruptly challenged them on the outside. He grinned at her as their horses put over the wall together, with delicate syncopation. Star's ears pinned flat in immediate displeasure, but the other horse was driven by a merciless whiplash to follow when Alix urged her horse away.

They collided at the next fence. The chestnut faltered off-stride for the jump. It became a set of flailing hooves as it fell, driving a piercing pain through Alix's knee before her leg mercifully numbed. Star clipped the top of the fence and almost cost her her seat on landing, but she managed to hang on. He collected himself with the next stride, but other horses swept by to gain the advantage.

Dazed, Alix looked back at the tangle left behind as the stewards flocked to the fence. A hapless jockey flew over alone when his horse crashed against the hedge. He crumbled to the ground with horses surging over him as she closed her eyes to the disaster, unwilling to see anything more.

Resolutely, she returned to the rhythm of riding, despite the numb ache spreading from her knee. With her focus on Quenton's elusive jersey, she pressed her horse for speed. It was too late to consider the stakes of her folly, but to finish near the lead might make it worth something. Dark Star responded to the song of her voice by blurring the track with the thunder of his hooves and surging through a sea of mud.

NICHOLAS WAS UNCERTAIN if the collective groan was from the crowd or only from his box, but, unbelievably, Sterling came up in the saddle.

"Doubt you now his ability to ride?" he challenged John, who had been certain the odds were wrong when Alex Sterling had appeared from nowhere to ride in the race.

"Nay, but he's lost. You know what they say about the third time, and that makes the second after the starting line."

Nicholas focused on the big gray from the Royal Stud that was edging away from the front-runners. "Quincy's making his move."

John bumped shoulders with him, directing him back to midfield. "Look, bleeding Sterling thinks he's got enough horse to make up ground. There's no hope of catching up."

Nicholas trained his spyglass on the black horse, which looked so much like Midnight Star, as the gap narrowed with every stride. He had to admire the stallion's game effort. "I say, is he hurt?"

John immediately lifted his own lens. "It's hard to tell, but Sterling's a madman if he doesn't drop out. His horse can't keep up that pace."

In the roar rising from the crowd, Nicholas returned his glass to Banshee as the gray survived a fence that felled his nearest competitors.

"That was close." Nicholas's response was lost amid the rising noise when Sarah caught John's arm, pointing to Dark Star's systematic drive through the pack.

"Sterling can't possibly think he might still win!"

Sarah began to jump with excitement. "Look, Johnny—no wonder Lily wanted to bet on him!"

John glanced at Nicholas apologetically. "Yes, I see, dear."

Nicholas did not need their reminder of the closeness that his unfortunate marriage lacked. Determined to forget about his missing wife, he trained his spyglass on the rider on the black horse charging valiantly up the middle of the track. Dark Star made an incredible surge coming out of the last turn and romped past the flagging horses. Nicholas focused on Alex Sterling's muddied face; once again, its familiarity niggled him. He was ordinarily good with names, but he could not reconcile the feeling that he should know the jockey.

A roar lifted in the stands as the horses pounded around the turn to the finish. Who could have imagined the black horse could challenge the lead? But Dark Star landed the final jump in fourth position and bolted down the turf.

Quincy stood in his stirrups with his riding whip aloft as Banshee passed under the finish line, but Dark Star was short by only half a length, an easy second place. Another stride, and the black flashed by, leaving Quincy stiffly frozen in his saddle while he stared after Dark Star. Swiftly he collected his reins and, instead of breezing Banshee in the traditional victory lap, accepted Sterling's dare to continue the race.

People halted in the stands to watch as an impromptu chase unfolded. "What the devil?" Nicholas murmured, crowding the rail with the others. Sterling peered behind him as Quincy set the gray into a spurious gallop and then urged Dark Star faster.

"What in the blazes . . . Didn't you say they're friends?" John contended.

"Yes, of course!"

"Then they seem to have had a falling-out."

Track stewards joined the chase, riding to intercept Sterling, but the man spotted them coming. As if to prove his horse was not running away with him, he veered across the green to avoid the interference. Nicholas exchanged a mystified glance with John. "What the devil?"

Undeterred, Quincy put the gray over the rail and rode in a beeline after him. Sterling called his ruse and evaded him by escaping to the practice field while the stewards split into groups. The nearest converged on Banshee, while the others went after Dark Star. As Sterling disappeared toward the paddocks, Quincy twisted in the saddle to look after him, clearly disappointed that their spontaneous contest was canceled.

"There'll be words exchanged in the Jockey Club," John predicted with a laugh. "Damn me, old chum, but since I owe you a drink, why don't we cash in?"

Nicholas followed with mute resignation. There was plenty of time before his wife resurfaced, and when she did, he would push her winnings into her face. He decided his displeasure must have been evident while tipping his hat to Quincy when they passed the winner's circle. It was the only reason he could imagine for why Quincy would have scowled at him so furiously.

JENNY SCREAMED AND ran for the door.

Alix tripped over the chair, trying to stop her. "Jenny, wait!"

The maid grabbed madly for her umbrella. "Get away from me, you bounder!"

Alix lunged to bar the door, but Jenny employed her umbrella handily and batted her away. "Please don't, Jenny! It's me!"

"Eek!" Jenny yelped, bashing Alix until she collapsed with defeat.

"God, will you leave off with your umbrella!"

"You wouldn't get hurt if you were smart enough to get out of here!" Sudden silence fell when the sagging umbrella skewed Ozzie's racing cap. Alix huddled on the floor helplessly, as the maid gave an astonished cry and dropped to her knees by Alix's side.

Abrupt pounding shook the door, echoed by tight voices and jingling keys. Jenny called out sharply. "Here! What do you want?"

"Hotel security, miss! We're looking for one of the jockeys wanted for questioning! There's been an inquiry about an accident out on the track; he was last seen running this way."

"This is a lady's room," Jenny retorted. "There's no man in here!"

"All right, miss—keep a lookout! Sorry for disturbing you!"

Jenny inched nearer as their voices distanced in the hall. "Why aren't you downstairs acting like milady?"

"I have to change, Jenny," Alix groaned, as she used the door to pull herself up.

The maid helped her to the nearest chair. "What's happened? Don't tell me those men were really looking for you."

Alix fumbled to remove Ozzie's riding gloves. "There was a bit of a smash-up at a fence. I don't know how I managed to hang on," she continued, as the maid hurried to pour hot water into the basin and grab for towels. "I was clipped by a hoof, but I'm fortunate I didn't end up like some of the others."

Jenny shoved more wood into the potbellied stove and put on more water. "I can't believe my ears! This is a fine kettle of fish!"

Alix pushed herself up from the chair and hobbled to the dressing area to shed Ozzie's mud-stained clothes. "My leg is going to hurt like the dickens tomorrow."

Jenny came to help her pull off the riding boots. "There's dancing tonight—we'll have to say you've fallen ill and order the coach!"

Alix braced herself resolutely, relieved when the boots were off. "We can't."

"What do you mean? Fie, just look at you!"

"The track officials will check everyone leaving the Commons. Nicholas will be furious at his wife's disappearance —I've got to go on like nothing's amiss."

"Are you mad? Have you looked in a mirror!"

"You're jolly good at putting Lily together."

"You're raving! I'm a maid, not a magician!"

"You'll have to bundle these things and hide them," Alix continued, adding Ozzie's racing jersey to the pile the maid collected. "Someone'll find them in the rubbish bin. Besides, I need to return them."

Jenny's protest was cut short by a presumptive knock on the door. They exchanged a surprised look as the rapping repeated. The maid hid the filthy racing gear and wiped their stain from her hands while Alix ducked behind the dressing screen.

Jenny called, "Who is it?"

"It's Albert, Jenny. Please open the door."

"Coming," she responded evenly, and cast a cautioning look at Alix.

Obediently, Alix shrank out of sight to finish undressing while Jenny reached for the door.

"What do you want? I'm a little busy," Jenny greeted Albert crisply.

"I felt it prudent to come across and make sure everything's all right."

"Everything was quiet, until the men from security awoke milady from her nap. If any crazed man showed up in this room, I'd give him a go with my umbrella, wouldn't I?"

"Your umbrella," he repeated doubtfully.

"Aye, and why not? I have it right here!"

Albert Frisk laughed softly. "I daresay you've given more than one blighter a blow with that."

"I may not look experienced, but I have four brothers, haven't I?"

There was a pause. "Four? Why, I never imagined."

"Rascals, every one," Jenny boasted. "Now, I'm sorry, but I must hurry. Milady's going to be late for tea if I dillydally."

"I wished only to be certain you're safe."

"Thank you, Albert."

Alix drew a deep breath of relief that Jenny had planted the seeds of a story. Now she just needed to find a way to maintain it.

NICHOLAS INSTINCTIVELY DISTRUSTED everything about his wife, but her face paled when he was tapped on his shoulder for the fifth time that night. Upon each instance of someone trying to break in to their dance, she had played the same game, as if she were reluctant to part from him. Nicholas had lied to her friends so often that after another scotch, he might even come to believe the ruse himself.

He dispatched another admirer, and they began dancing to free the flow on the crowded floor. Her fragile expression blatantly contradicted the established truth. In his precarious position, Nicholas was not quite drunk enough to ignore its implication, as she watched another follower walk away.

"I'm sorry. Should I have asked first?" he alleged bluntly.

She pretended surprise with widened eyes and gasped when he pulled her toward the exit. He should have known she had been too quiet all night. He needed not guess whether what she had planned next for him was a public repudiation. Darkness lessened the effect of her delicate hesitation when she tripped down the steps. He finally stopped at the edge of the rose garden, where their confrontation would not be noticed. "What more do you want from me?"

She looked around, as if wondering whether to cry for help. Realizing her position, she struggled with her newfound diffidence. "Nothing," she claimed tremulously.

Nicholas found he was still gripping her elbow and released it, lest it lend to a charge of brutality. "You're lying."

The deceptive light shifted as elusively as faerie fire, and he was suddenly facing the guileless girl who had been sleeping on his wife's couch. She gazed wistfully beyond him at the sky, although fog moved across the grounds. "Regrettably, I owe you more than a mere apology."

Her humble admission stunned him silent, rendering worthless the scathing rejoinder he had been preparing to use. She peered at him doubtfully and then returned her eyes to the sky. "I've only a paltry plea for clemency. I've no right to ask for understanding, when I've only my remorse to offer in return for your forbearance." She did not wait for his stumbling response but abruptly turned and left him, as if he had kindly bade her good night.

Nicholas grappled with the unbelievable concept of his wife's sudden repentance as she disappeared in the mist. He lifted his eyes overhead, where the cloaking fog parted to reveal the brilliant Polaris, and realized the depth of her remorse had even altered her inflection. Dumbfounded, he looked after her, but the veil of mist concealed even the lights of the ballroom. He returned to the enigmatic North Star, suddenly convinced that she could not be Lily Griffon.

ROBERT STOOD MOTIONLESS in the darkest shadows. People passed without noticing him by the wall. He was a silent watcher, lacking desire to join the revelry and without compunction to seek the light. Being alone did not bother him. A man was born such, and died the same way, as part of the human condition.

Had he not been there, he would not have seen Alix emerge from the mist on Nicholas Griffon's arm. Customarily, he was not compelled to watch a married man bring a woman other than his wife into the night, but since it was Alix, he remained. He could not say he did not have any doubts about Nicholas Griffon. He had reservations about any man. Slippery memories clamored for recall and died stiffly when he ignored them. The darkness was no place to listen to ghosts rattling bones.

The careful stasis had shifted to split his life as easily as the night sky did the fog. Once formed, the rift would increase if disregarded, but he still might act to mend it before it transformed. It was useless to ask why things happened when there was no way for any man to know. All anyone could control was his reaction. Just like the pebble in a pond, each act would grow.

To blame Lily was a waste of his time. One day he might admit his own culpability, but it was too late for remorse. Nothing would alter the past. Once committed, deeds never changed. Intentions did not matter after a man was dead; the shape of his life was all that remained.

Quenton would seek to reclaim his fortune. Spanning the past was a dangerous endeavor for any man, so the Frenchman would wisely attempt it alone. If Robert felt the seething pit of the unknown, Quenton Saint-Descoteaux would be wise to sense it double. Robert did not wish to return to France, but the wheels were already in motion.

CHAPTER 9

THE MIDNIGHT SHIP TO CALAIS

While Quenton was at the bank, he felt the weight of his decision to return to France. Although his withdrawal was far from princely, it drained his meager savings. Was his time worth so little? If not for his winning purses from racing, there would have been precious pennies left, but the monies in Alix's Sterling Wood account kept the bank president's questions at bay. If Quenton survived the gamble in France, the amount would shrink in significance. Should he not, it would leave his niece less for her future. He pocketed the cash guiltily and used it to book passage on the midnight ship to Calais.

At the back door of the Griffon house, Percival's son regarded him blankly. Quenton could not blame the young man. After cutting his hair and shaving his beard, Quenton scarcely recognized himself either. He was hesitantly led to the butler's small chamber to pace restlessly until Percival appeared. His dramatic transformation gave even the butler thoughtful pause, but then, undaunted, Percival entered officiously. "Mr. Hill, I understand you wish to see me."

"Yes, thank you."

"Please sit down."

Their pleasantries dismissed, Percival took his chair and propped his fingers together thoughtfully. "Do you mind if I comment on the difference in your appearance?"

Quenton smiled. Until that morning, he had not shaved since the day his brother had died. At first his neglect had been unintentional, but later on his trimmed beard had become part of the persona of Quincy Hill the stableman. "No, not at all," he acknowledged.

"Young Percy forewarned me, but frankly, if we passed on the street, I don't know if I'd have recognized you. May I ask what brings this unprecedented visit?"

"I've come to resign my position."

The butler pursed his lips tentatively. "From looking at you, I presume it's due to a change in fortune."

"That remains to be seen. For now, you might say I'm answering an overdue summons."

"A summons?"

"From home," Quenton clarified guardedly. "I must leave immediately. I realize it leaves the stable shorthanded, but I'd like to recommend Georgie as coachman."

Percival tapped his fingertips together. "That's commendable."

"I'd not do so if I thought him unsuitable."

The butler reached into his lower drawer for a pair of glasses and bottle of whiskey. He glanced at Quenton while pouring and passed a drink across his desk. "I consider your opinion trustworthy."

"What do you think when you look at me, Percy?"

Percival crossed his legs when he sat back with his whiskey. "I'd say you've done well placing bets on the track."

"*Santé,*" Quenton bade, saluting with his drink.

"*Santé*," Percival echoed, as his straight brows lifted quizzically. "You're French?"

Quenton shrugged. "I'm many things."

The butler considered him somberly and then surmised, "Your name isn't Quincy Hill, is it? If you escaped Europe during the war, why'd you hide it all this time?"

"It's a complicated story—and since it comes to my leave-taking, I've a favor to ask of you."

"I understand your need for a reference."

"No—thank you. At least, I don't think I'll need one."

"You're returning to your old family, then?"

"It's a little more complicated . . . Actually, my favor is in regard to a member of that old family and requires complete secrecy, but I've always known you as a man of the highest discretion."

"I cannot say that I like the sound of your proposal, Mr. Hill." The butler rose to pace his tiny office thoughtfully. "I don't know quite how to respond."

"I hope you understand I wouldn't expect you to do anything unscrupulous, Percival. It's for the protection of another that I'm asking."

"A member from the old family you mentioned?"

"*Oui, bien sûr.*"

"I beg to know more before I make a commitment."

"The stakes are high; in many ways, you might consider it a matter of survival."

"Do you mean a life-or-death situation?"

"*Tout à fait.*"

"I'm not in a position to grant carte blanche."

"In a manner of speaking, I'm asking you only to continue with something you're already doing."

"I'm afraid I must insist."

"The potential discovery would put someone at risk. You see, years ago when I arrived in England, I brought someone else with me."

Percival returned to his chair. "A member of your old household in France, you mean?"

"Yes. Since she's already in residence, I'd like her to remain until someone comes for her."

"You're speaking of one of our maids?"

"No, not at all. Please understand that her father spared no expense when it came to his daughter, and although she was a child when I brought her, she was already accomplished in a great many ways. However talented she may be, she also has the misfortune of sharing the same appearance as someone else in our acquaintance." He held on to Percival's unwavering study until realization dawned in the other's eyes.

The butler pursed his lips doubtfully. "You're not speaking of milady?"

Quenton allowed time for Winston to gather his thoughts but preempted his initial question before he could say more. "Now you understand the need for secrecy."

"To protect Lily?"

"This has nothing to do with her."

"But where is she?"

"If you are asking me about Lily Griffon, then I don't know."

"But when?"

"I'm unable to say more, except will you watch over her until her guardian can arrive to take her home? I notified him over the weekend, and I expect he'll soon be in contact with His Lordship."

"Who would this guardian be?"

"However he chooses to approach is his own affair. It's

not my place to reveal anything about why she is here, but you'll agree there'd be an enormous scandal if this were to become public knowledge. No one would like this to reach the newspapers, and the consequences could be devastating if she ran away."

"By Jove!"

"Not to mention the stain it would place on the respectability of the household. It might inflict a great deal of harm to Lord Griffon's reputation. Please just agree to look after her. As I've said, you've been doing so already without undue difficulty, haven't you?"

Percival harrumphed into his handkerchief. "Forgive me if I ask when you plan to share this information with milord. He has the right to know if he has a guest beneath his roof."

Quenton rose and collected his hat. "I'll consider how to tell him; however, whatever I reveal must not be discussed. Have I your word?"

"Of course, if you keep your end of the bargain," the butler finally conceded, climbing up to reach for the door.

"I will. *Merci.* In parting, I'm afraid I must admit that my charge was pampered as a child. She usually isn't too difficult to care for, but I can't remember a time when she wasn't particular. A word to the wise, should she become reluctant about eating: bacon, lean and well smoked. It's long been her favorite."

IT WAS FIVE STEPS from the table to the shelf. Quenton slipped his gold watch from his waistcoat to look at the time. It was not yet ten; he could still say what he needed to, but if Nicholas Griffon did not appear soon, his departure would leave a critical gap for Percival's conditional measure.

Annoyed, Quenton returned his timepiece to his pocket.

The singular gain from Lily's interference was a question of whether their estate had been confiscated illegally. The only way to find out was a return to France, but even if their rights were restored, what remained to be claimed of their fortune? He would not know until he arrived whether his house had a roof or the businesses were solvent. If he missed his ship to Calais, he would not get a refund. He turned and paced in the other direction.

He was thankful Alix was tucked in Lily's bed without knowing his plan to board the ship in the harbor. He would be on French soil by the time she woke in the morning. He could only hope the injuries she had sustained from the pile-up at the fence during the Oxley race would keep her out of trouble until Robbie arrived to take her back to the farm. Once Quenton found out whether it was safe for her to join him at home, he would seek her there.

When the stable door finally rattled, he found Nicholas Griffon drenched by raining drizzle and wearing a frown as he stood at the bottom of the steps. "Why the devil are you hiding in here?" Nicholas grunted, staggering after Quenton when he came to take Midnight to his stall.

He had precious little time to spare for the Englishman's intolerance. "You might wish to reconsider standing there," he advised, hefting Midnight's saddle onto the wall between them. "You'd hate it if your clothes got soiled."

Nicholas straightened away from the stall unsteadily. "I'll not take that tone from any man, no matter how long you've worked for me."

Quenton finished buckling Midnight's sheet and left the horse with his head deep in a manger of hay as he stepped out and closed the gate. "Apparently it's not a good time for a chat."

"Who in the devil do you think you're talking to?"

Quenton easily evaded the earl's clumsy swing at his chin and decided it was better to collect his belongings and leave. "Why not run along home and sleep it off?"

The earl staggered after him carelessly. "I don't take orders from servants."

"That's right . . . I forgot to mention that I've quit. Percival already knows, so you don't have to worry about remembering to tell him tomorrow."

Nicholas straightened indignantly and then caught himself on the handrail of the steps and lumbered after Quenton's ascent. "You can't just quit on me."

"It's already been done."

Behind him, Nicholas stumbled against the door frame. "What've you done with your things?"

"These are the quarters afforded with the stipend for your coachman. Since that is no longer me, I've packed to leave."

"But"—Nicholas pulled his soaking beaver-top hat from his head in clumsy confusion—"there's nothing in here."

Quenton retrieved his own hat and cloak from the antechamber. "Actually, there's a bit of furniture and a few utensils if you are intent on taking inventory. It'll all be here tomorrow," he concluded as he returned to the ring of waxy candlelight.

"This is Mackinlay's," the earl noted, helping himself to the bottle of scotch Quenton had put in his open valise.

Quenton retrieved his bottle from Nicholas's clumsy grasp. "You don't need to sound so astonished."

Nicholas fell into a chair heavily. Dissatisfaction had ravaged his polished appearance, and an intransigent scowl had etched haggard lines deep into his face. "What in blazes are you wearing?"

"These are my clothes," Quenton replied about his only

black suit, but then noted the earl's suspicion. "It's paid for, I assure you." He planted two cups on the table and poured scotch in each to appease Nicholas. "Here, we might as well have a drink. It'll be a nightcap for you and a final heave-ho for me. This is only twenty years old, so I hope you'll find it suitable."

"I never realized you were such a sarcastic bastard."

"Be careful whose parents you are insulting. Someone might take offense." He lifted his cup to touch the other on the table. "*Santé*," he finished, tasting his drink.

Nicholas blinked at his unusual effrontery. "You sound like a bloody Frenchman."

"Imagine."

Quenton sipped his scotch while Nicholas glared at him sullenly. His bargain with Percival weighed on him, but, judging the earl already inebriated beyond the point of reason, Quenton finally took his cup to the shelf where he had left the Bible from the family vestry at Mont Blanc. He studied the embossed cross on the cover absently, wondering how he was going to manage the cumbersome book on his journey to France.

"*Santé*," Nicholas finally agreed behind him. "If you can afford aged single malt, I must pay you too much."

Quenton laughed softly. "Some things defy compromise."

"What's that book?"

He tested the Bible's weight by hefting the binding. It was heavier than his valise was, and awkwardly bulky. "It's a Bible."

"It's rather large for someone of your position, isn't it?"

He refused to take offense. "They all tell the same stories of prophets and kings, don't they?"

"You're too well dressed to be running away to become a priest," Nicholas observed pointedly. "Did you shave, by the way?"

"When I cut my hair earlier."

"What do you want me to say next—that it looks good?"

Quenton laughed at his foolishness. "Only if it does."

"Blast you if you are fishing for compliments."

Quenton turned to splash whiskey into his empty cup and reseated the cork with a laugh. "I've lived without any for this long; I might manage a while longer."

"Good." The depth of his cup distorted Nicholas's reply. "Since you're not leaving to become a priest, why are you quitting? If you're going to work at the Royal Stud, I'll match whatever they've offered."

"It's business," Quenton responded vaguely, hefting his ebony cane from where it was hooked on the cupboard. Alix had gifted it at Christmas on the year North Star had won the Newmarket Cup. He could not help but smile at the gold image of North Star's head that shaped the handle, for it was a reflection of his brother's signet. He wore Henri's white chalcedony ring on the chain with his gold cross. It had an intaglio engraving of a knight chess piece with the profile of the great stallion Augustus Leopold II.

"Old business," he clarified for Henri's honor, and cupped the handle lovingly in his hand. "You know how it is: You think something's finished and find out it's not. I only hope it's not been neglected overlong."

"I don't suppose you'd understand about contractual obligations."

Quenton considered Nicholas with wry amusement, but now was not the time to delve into aesthetics of business. He was running short on time anyway, if he meant to keep his bargain with Percival, although he doubted that Nicholas would remember much in the morning. He turned to the Bible's delicate embossing, which matched the cross erected in the vestry at the old château. He had no idea if it stood any longer, but he was determined to find out.

"I knew a man once," he began his tale carefully. "He was a good businessman, or, should I say, he was splendid." He glanced at the other man circumspectly, but if Nicholas wondered why Quenton was beginning a story, he kept the question to himself as he stared into his cup. "I've never understood how he could've been used so easily. Give him a sale, and he'd nail down a contract so damned tight, it needed an act of God to change it, but all it took was an alluring glance across a room and a beautiful woman to inveigle him."

"Shut up, Quincy," Nicholas replied, surprising him. "I don't need you to tell me how my life has gone."

Quenton lifted his cup with recognition that it was only a bizarre twist if Lily had done the same to entrap Nicholas as her mother, Mary-Margaret, had done with his brother, Henri. "I guess, but I didn't mean you, and that's something to be damned glad about, because this man lost everything." Quenton closed his eyes against the regretful return of the past.

He cleared his throat in the stifling silence and wondered aloud, "Where was I? Oh, that's right, we were at the part about this beautiful woman—and, since the man was foolish enough to be a decent sort, he married her and took her home. You know about these things." He waved his cup vaguely. "After a while, she became heavy with child." He hefted his cane to study the eerie glitter in the jeweled eyes of North Star's image. "Have I mentioned the man's brother?"

Nicholas sprang to his feet, knocking over his chair. "Damn you, Quincy!"

"Sit down. This is not about you," Quenton advised bitterly. "Trust me, you'll soon notice the difference."

"I don't need you telling me about my life!"

"This brother was only nine years old at the time the child was born; does that make a difference?"

Nicholas planted his chair and fell into it. "Bleeding Phillip."

Quenton drew a deep breath and willed himself to patience. "Not surprisingly, the boy didn't care much for the woman who invaded his home. Not only did she take over the household, but she thought it her duty to replace his mother. He didn't like the idea, since his own mother had died bringing him into the world, and he grew up without one." Feeling her position even more secure, Mary-Margaret had ceased to worry about pleasing anyone but herself. He shook his head, remembering the frequent quarreling that had led Henri to stay away from the château. "Inevitably, the day came when the man returned to find someone else in his bed."

Nicholas bobbed his head in commiseration. "That figures."

"After that, he sent her away. She was making everyone's life a blasted hell anyway."

"Good for him. What'd he do about the man he caught with her?"

"What do you think? He took him out and shot him."

Nicholas lifted his cup in a gratified salute. "Wasn't a very tolerant sort, was he?"

Quenton laughed at his glib observation. "No."

"Good—I might get on with him."

He refrained from guessing what Henri's opinion would have been of the Englishman. "Anyway," he continued, "the boy was happy to see the last of her. His life returned to much the same as before, except he became inseparable from the child she left behind."

"Wait a minute." The earl stopped him. "What child?"

"She wasn't allowed to take everything, you know—only what her husband allowed. The child she left behind didn't remain small for long. When the boy was grown enough to make his way as a man, the father decided to take the child with him wherever he traveled, but whenever the family was together, there was always a celebration. Even apart, they never lost their connection."

"So everyone lived happily ever after."

"Happily ever after is for fairy tales." Quenton doused his enthusiasm sourly with the dregs of his scotch. "Incidentally, it was one such time, when they met at home for a few joyous weeks in the summer, that the brother left the château to take a ride up to the high country. Since he was gone, he never learned why they came to arrest the man for treason. The newspapers said the man was killed trying to escape, but the truth was, he was shot to death while sitting at his desk. The child ran for its life, fearful of being murdered. The brother barely returned home in time to save anyone, and although he grabbed the child and rode to safety, the child was shot during the escape."

"They were killed?"

"No, thank God, but not for lack of trying." He drank the dregs of his scotch with the acrid stench of that memory. "They rode away together, until the child fell off the horse behind him. The sight of blood drove him mad, I think. He headed for shelter in the nearby caves, where a friendly monk they knew managed to staunch the bleeding. After a long and bitter night, he ventured back to take care of what was left of his older brother, but when he returned to the cave, he found the child had fled. All that remained in the child's place was an unknown man who'd been shot to death with his own pistol."

The distant clock in the tower began to strike the bells of a half hour in an ominous toll, cutting his story short. Quenton checked his watch to find that if he did not leave right then, he would miss his ship. He reached for his cloak.

"Wait . . . where are you going?"

"I have to leave now, or I'll be late."

Nicholas looked around blankly. "But what about the child? Did it survive?"

"Yes," he replied, leaving off the admission that the punishment for her crime would be the guillotine, if she were ever caught.

Quenton buckled the valise as Nicholas doused the light. "What are you doing?"

"You said we're leaving."

"*I'm* leaving," Quenton corrected Nicholas, as he reached for his cane in the dark. "*You're* going to bed."

"Not here, am I?"

He fumbled for his hat. "It'd probably serve you right, but no."

"Here's your hat."

Quenton reached for it but ended up staggering under Nicholas's weight as the man slung his arm around his neck.

"You don't mind, do you?" Nicholas asked pleasantly, and then hiccuped as they wove a careless path to the door.

"You'd better wait for me," Quenton grunted, grabbing him as he nearly catapulted headlong down the stairs.

"Sorry. I don't know quite what happened."

Quenton braced himself against the handrail and began a stumbling descent. "Can you hang on long enough to reach the house?"

"Certainly," Nicholas replied, just before his legs gave out.

"Try harder," Quenton advised, leaving his valise by the door to carry his burden. "I'd hate to have to leave you for Percival to find on the lawn in the morning."

When he dragged Nicholas into the house, the butler spotted them in the entry and came running. "Milord!"

Quenton propped the master of the house against the door frame. "I'm sorry for his condition, but I'm going to be late."

"Think nothing of it. Allow me to help you, milord."

"Why, thank you, Percival," Nicholas replied, but toppled to the floor and lay unmoving.

Quenton clasped hands with the butler. "I'll never forget your kindness."

"What else are friends for? Hurry, now, or you'll miss your ship."

Quenton tipped his hat to the shadow of Mary Winston as he dashed into the night. The raining mist drowned the light from the windows, plunging him into darkness. Hoping he was not too late, he held on to his hat and began to run.

CHAPTER 10

LUNCH AT THE BOAR'S HEAD TAVERN

*ist caressed the earth with dewy tears. Stones wept, oblivious to the stoic leaf and twig where humbled birds flitted, too miserable to fly through the noonday twilight.

Jenny stopped in the doorway. "Come, now; if you don't take the weight off your leg, it'll never heal."

Alix replied without moving from the window. "Jenny, do you ever wonder why we are where we are and who we are, instead of someone, somewhere, else entirely?"

The metronomic clock ticked, and a black umbrella wearing trousers moved down the empty sidewalk. A brown spaniel on a red leash trotted alongside to lend it color. Alix glanced around, suspecting from the continued silence that she was alone, but the maid remained, with a frown puckering her forehead. Heartened Jenny was listening, Alix continued, "Do you think the Fates are only gaming with our lives, rolling dice or tossing cards to fill odd moments of whimsy?"

Jenny pursed her lips pensively. "I don't understand what you just said."

"I wonder if, as Shakespeare wrote, the world's a stage and

all the men and women merely players who have their exits and entrances. There can't be a more woeful pageant than the scene wherein we play, because as time slips by on sylvan wings, in a single blink of an eye, everything changes."

The maid came forward uncertainly. "You didn't tell me that you'd hit your head." She felt Alix's forehead suspiciously. "You don't have a fever—what's wrong? Why aren't you making sense?"

"How should I know? I'm merely a paltry player; I strut as directed, posing this way or moving that, spouting euphemisms with varying effect, but am at liberty to exit only when the time is ripe to clear the way for someone with a more meaningful presence."

"That's it—I think you've cracked."

Jenny's eyes were soft green pools of concern, smoothly lustrous, with a multifaceted resilience, reminding Alix of polished jade. She smudged their color on the palette in her mind, fascinated by their shading. "Has anyone told you that you have remarkable eyes, Jenny?"

The maid gaped, and her face flamed crimson. "Have you been at the sauce this morning?"

Realizing she had diverged too far from the role of Lily, Alix returned to her post at the window, where she waited for Quenton, for if he had tired of his role as Quincy the coachman, he must be planning to reenter as a new character. "If by 'at the sauce,' you mean have I been drinking, then no."

"Well, at least you finally said something I can understand. I've heard about women who go daft from time to time. You're not one of those, are you?"

"Not that I'm aware, but I'm certain you'll be kind enough to share it if I am."

Alix had planned to be home by now. She had trusted

Quenton to release her, but then Jenny had shared the news abuzz that Quincy the coachman had quit and disappeared. She had thought Robbie would come for her, but he had not even attempted a meeting.

"Perhaps you need a nice hot bath. While you breakfast, I'll prepare a manicure. I think those fingernails could use a different color of lacquer, don't you?"

Alix looked at her crimson nails dispassionately. "If you think so."

Jenny bustled to the couch to plump the gaudy assortment of pillows. "Why don't you relax on the couch until your breakfast tray gets here?"

The clock settled the swelling silence while Alix watched pipits bounce beneath the dripping shrubberies. Finches scuttled after sparrows fluttering to the privet, and a mournful pigeon dropped onto the lawn to dance solemnly in search of food.

Quenton had not even looked at her the day before. He had opened the coach door with aloof imperiousness. All the way back to Westminster, she had perched on the edge of the seat, longing to speak through the tiny shuttered window separating them, but had dared not, with Lily's husband riding alongside on Midnight. She thought her uncle must be more than angry with her for having attempted to race Dark Star. His temper was quick to flare, not because he lacked patience, but from his inherent drive for perfection. His abandonment left her feeling lost. If Robbie's detachment at Oxley Commons was puzzling, then Quenton's subsequent desertion was devastating. Were they distancing themselves from the inevitable fallout when Nicholas Griffon finally summoned the police to arrest her?

A gentle knock on the door signaled the arrival of the

breakfast tray, unless the butler was bringing the constable to question her. Realizing that Jenny had gone to prepare a bath, Alix ventured to the door, every step an agonizing reminder of why she should not have been walking.

A prodigious tray of silver domes filled the doorway. "Good morning, milady," Winston greeted her, with uncustomary effusiveness.

Only one pair of black-trousered legs supported his burden. Relieved there was not a second pair wearing the blue wool of the Metropolitan Police, Alix retreated to allow the butler to enter. "Oh, there you are, Winston," she replied, pretending to be Lily.

"I trust you're enjoying a splendid morning," he proposed cheerfully. He cast a bright glance at her in passing. "I don't know why Mrs. Winston had in mind to add bacon to your plate, but she thought you might find it a pleasant change," he explained while Alix followed listlessly. "Allow me to pour your tea, milady," he offered, busily setting her place.

"Thank you."

He glanced at her speculatively as he filled the teacup. "May I bring up a few books this afternoon?"

Alix hesitantly took her seat while he hovered expectantly. Perhaps the constable was lurking in the hallway, waiting to catch her stealing food.

"Of course. Thank you." She waited anxiously for him to leave and wondered if Jenny's disappearance signaled that the maid had already been arrested as an accomplice. But when the door closed without complication, Jenny bustled in belatedly.

"I don't know how everything got so behind suddenly, except Albert Frisk stopped by for the second time this morning. I still think he's up to something."

Alix sipped her tea glumly and picked over the food on her

plate. What she knew about prison could fill a thimble, but she was somehow certain that bacon was not on the menu.

IT WAS NOT THE FIRST MORNING that Nicholas had felt the aftereffects of the night before, but he could not recall ever having been late for an appointment. Not only was the oppressive weather against him, but his head pounded like a devil inside was having a go with a hammer when he met John for a hack across country. Midnight Star was not a horse to ride blindly, and he finally halted the questionable pursuit when his horse nearly unseated him.

"How now, Griffon? I never thought I'd see you swoon at the sight of a fence."

"Nor I, Johnny, but apparently I had too good a time last night."

John laughed, moving his gray hunter alongside. "I say, what were you doing? Celebrating your winnings from Oxley?"

"One might guess."

His friend laughed incredulously. "What? You don't remember?"

His troubling delusion about his wife was why he had been drinking heavily at the club, but he would rather lie than defend his lack of reason. "I'll deny it if I ever hear you tell anyone."

They reached the road at the five-mile marker and aimed for the Boar's Head Tavern. He realized the surrounding fields bore a semblance to the illustrations Frisk had found in Lily's desk, but subtle differences frustrated his desire to spot the exact location he hoped to recognize.

"We didn't come across you in Mayfair last night, or we might've joined you."

"I went to the club."

"Did you have another go-round with Lily?"

"All I know is, I awoke in my bed."

"Cheer up. All you need is a little hair of the dog to set you straight."

"I'm in no shape to argue."

"All right, come on; see if you can keep up, old man. We're not too far from the Boar's Head."

The words were no sooner out of John's mouth than Midnight Star nearly left him behind. As John's gray horse lunged into a gallop, only Nicholas's natural agility kept him in his own saddle for a spurious race to the tavern. By the time he collected his wits sufficiently to step down, John caught him around the shoulders and pulled him inside. "Barkeep, this unlikely blighter needs some help," he called cheerfully.

"Whatever happened to using a bit of bleeding discretion?" Nicholas complained. As embarrassing as his entrance was, it sparked a hazy memory of careening carelessly down steps in the dark and staggering toward his house. What sorry devil had helped him home in such bad condition?

John pulled off his top hat and tossed it into the next chair, before snatching Nicholas's to add with his own. "Now then, here we are," he laughed, as he grabbed the bartender's good-natured wife when she brought their ale.

"Go on, milord, keep those hands to yourself," she rebuffed him with a laugh.

After stealing a kiss, John released her and sat back with his beer. "Cheers, and drink deep for whatever ails you."

Nicholas lifted his tankard. "Cheers," he responded, but it took two beers and lunch before he regained a semblance of normalcy. He described the crux of his problem in a roundabout way as they worked their way through pan-fried fingerlings and a handful of chips. By the time the chicken and roast pork arrived, his friend was considering him doubtfully.

John washed down his mouthful of food. "I'm afraid you've lost me, chum."

Nicholas shrugged and stripped his chicken leg of meat with his teeth before tossing away the bone. He had come this far in explaining his dilemma; he might as well ask John's opinion directly. "You've not noticed anything, then?"

John shook his head, intent on sawing through his slab of roasted pork. "Lily is Lily."

"Yes, but then again, no," Nicholas countered, spearing a bite of potato and hoping he had not been remiss in asking the question. He had been friends with John for a long time, and John knew better than anyone else about Nicholas's mistake in marrying her. "I feel like I'm losing my mind."

"If you really want to know if she's Lily, take her to bed."

"How the blazes will that prove anything?"

"As her husband, you should know. If you have a good time deciding, who cares?"

"You're a bloody lot of help."

"Look, you've never really asked me anything about last summer, but it took me weeks to break it off with her. You of all people know how she doesn't take no for an answer—I mean, I'm sorry, old man, but I can't do it now; I'm still on my honeymoon."

"Don't get me wrong. I'm not asking you to roll her."

"Well, what exactly *are* you asking, then?"

"Simply if you've noticed anything different."

"I don't know," he protested and mulled it over with beer. "I make a practice of not paying too much attention; it gives her ideas."

Nicholas poked a roast carrot in frustration. "I don't know why I expected more from you."

"Give a fellow a little warning when you need an opinion.

You've obviously got the advantage, if you're suspicious. Just think it through logically: Who goes around impersonating someone?"

"That's my question."

"I thought your question was whether Lily is Lily."

"It's part of the same thing."

"All right—if so, then what makes you think she's not Lily?"

Nicholas finished his beer and signaled for more. "I don't know . . . because she's different. She's quieter, for one thing, and even likes Sarah."

John sat down his beer defensively. "What's not to like about Sarah?"

"Nothing, but that's my point. Lily wouldn't speak to Sarah last summer."

"Yes, but now they have me in common," John smirked.

"Be realistic." John grabbed the bartender's wife as she delivered another round, making her giggle and blush as Nicholas noted her husband's glare from behind the bar. "You'll not be fit to ride if you don't slow down."

John chuckled as the woman pushed him away. "You made it here, didn't you? I'll manage."

Nicholas let the subject go, ruminating on John's question while drinking the top off his ale. "She plays the piano."

"If that's what you want to call it."

"Yes, if we were speaking of Lily, but now . . . You'd have to hear her play to believe it."

"She plays better, do you mean? So, she took a few lessons."

"She's canceled all her upcoming engagements."

"I've heard; that's why everyone's saying you must have threatened her with something."

"I've nothing to do with it the fact she scarcely steps outside the house. She reads, she paints, and she plays piano as if she belongs in a concert hall."

John's brows knit together. "Have you spoken to her maid?"

"Don't you think she'd be in on it?"

John lifted his beer thoughtfully. "Now you're talking about collusion. Isn't that even more far-fetched?"

"Lily might be in a tight spot—there's speculation that she's pregnant."

John choked, spraying beer across the table. "Sorry," he said, mopping his mouth belatedly.

Nicholas pushed his plate aside. "I was finished anyway."

"Uh, congratulations," John ventured guiltily.

"It's not mine," Nicholas discounted disparagingly. "It'd have to be the next immaculate conception."

"I swear to God, I've nothing to do with it."

Nicholas had no wish to pursue the subject of the baby's father, and settled back in his chair.

"She's usually so careful. I mean, how could she—"

"With your wealth of experience, you really don't need me to explain it to you," Nicholas said, pointedly embarrassing John. With a sip of beer to settle the sour subject, he returned to his plate. "If it's true, then a bizarre plot might be conceivable, but even so, how does anyone find someone who's willing to step in and take over?"

John wagged his head. "It doesn't make any bloody sense. If Lily's . . . as you maintain she is, there's not only who and why, but how? How does anyone find a dead ringer? I don't know one bleeding devil I could tap to take over for me. Does Lily have a twin sister no one knows about? Cousins anywhere?"

"Lily Radcliffe is an only child; her father was lost at war."

"Aye, but stranger things have happened. That must be it: Lily found a relative who needs the money."

"But why would someone abandon her own life?" Nicholas insisted.

"I don't know." John shrugged and sat back. "Does it matter?" he asked eventually. "The important question is: What are you going to do about it?"

"So you believe me?"

"Whether I do or not doesn't count. It's what you do that makes a difference."

Nicholas shook his head doubtfully. "I'd look more than a fool if I accused Lily falsely. It'd be grounds to lock me up, don't you think? This might be a plot to have me declared insane. Especially if she's pregnant—how would it look to drag my wife into court and claim she's an impostor, when her friends would line up to testify differently? Even my own staff would prove witness against me. Having me put in Bedlam would work nicely for her, don't you think?"

"I say, old man, that's a bit harsh, isn't it?"

Nicholas shrugged. "She's pushed me too far, and I'll not stand for any more. A divorce is just as legal as a marriage is."

"A divorce! Why not just set her up in the country? Plenty of marriages end that way; don't you know the scandal will be enough to ruin your reputation?"

"As if it's of any worth now. Just because I've not said anything, I haven't reached any decisions irresponsibly." Nicholas did not add that he had had plenty of time to think about it while Lily flaunted the affair with Phillip under his nose. He was uncertain whether he would be able to return to the house where he had been born without burning every stick of it to the ground. If he could not undo his foolhardy marriage, he would be forced to relive it every time he tried to go home.

"All right, what do you want me to do?" John asked.

"*Do?*"

"Well, yes. You brought it up for a reason."

"I wondered only if you noticed anything, and I don't mind saying that you're absolutely no help at all."

"Well, damn it, what else do you expect? How was I to know I should've been watching her all weekend? Other than to concede that she looks like Lily, do you have something specific in mind for me, like taking the ladies dancing? I try to avoid it with her these days, but if there's one way for me to know for certain if she's Lily, a single dance ought to do it."

"I'd rather you didn't mention this to Sarah."

"You've my word on it, but you can't just give up the old ship. What've you got to lose, besides a lonely night at the club? If nothing else, you might have a bit of fun. After all, whether or not she's Lily, she's your wife, for all appearances, isn't she? You're a blasted fool if you don't realize there's nothing better than having an affair no one will notice."

"Your answer is to suggest a shameful exhibition of my own?"

"Well, you're not exactly unlikely-looking."

"Have you any idea what you're proposing?"

John laughed, crossing his arms as he leaned back to study Nicholas critically. "Of course I do—you'll clean up all right. Just remember to shave."

CHAPTER II

THE RETURN TO CHÊNES NOIR

The windswept clouds shifted with color as violet deepened the east. Twilight pooled in shadowy vales as the sun tipped the trees across the river. Cranes and storks posed in reeds, but ducks splashed noisily as Quenton rode by. Beneath an ancient oak, the poor livery horse stumbled where the road fell into a turn. Quenton gave his thin neck an encouraging pat. "Ce n'est pas trop loin maintenant; nous serons là bientôt." The meager animal snorted as it plodded along with a brighter eye.

Shifting to ease the discomfort of the hard rented saddle, Quenton was just as eager to reach their destination. His heart called him onward, yet he did not know what he would find. Upon his arrival at Nantes, he had purchased the ready-made riding clothes he wore and packed his British suit in the valise tied behind his saddle. Stagecoach and ferry had taken him farther, until he disembarked upriver from Limoges. The poor brown horse he rode was hardly adequate, but it had been the best available, and since he was too close to spend another night without seeing his house at Chênes Noir, Quenton had set out immediately. Now they traveled the opposite bank, looking at the trees marking the boundary of the black-oak forest that had once belonged to him.

When he had left on that fateful summer day years ago, he had ridden with his men, herding cattle for his brother's estate at Mont Blanc. The journey was to be only a routine delivery to his ancestral home in the Alps, and he had expected to return home with warhorses to fill the army contract.

Quenton had departed without an inkling of his future and now returned much the same. He had no clue of what he would find when he passed through the old ironbound gates. At one time, he had crossed over the arched bastions of the old Roman bridge without consideration of anything but its convenience. Now it marked his homecoming. On the opposite side, the darkening woods waited in dusky shadow. If his place survived, he would see the pointed rooftops of Chênes Noir before nightfall. As he put the thin horse into a shambling gallop, he experienced his return to the black-oak forest as far less auspicious than his leave-taking.

Bats flitted overhead between the trees, filled with twittering birds nesting for the evening. Frogs sang with crickets and toads, creating a peaceful harmony. Quenton could not remember if he had ever ridden a slower nag but was enjoying his remarkable voyage nevertheless. Here was the corner marker of the lower pasture, where red deer grazed by the pond with a sagging windmill. Over in the shallow cove, the old boat dock was afloat, but only as a barge for noisy geese and swans teeming toward the shuttered boathouse.

Before reaching the gates, Quenton slowed the tired horse. When the barrier of the imposing wall rose before him, he stepped down to walk. Silence echoed where a watchman should have hailed him, but his hand stopped shy of the lever hidden in the shelter of protective stone. Chênes Noir had been confiscated with everything else that his family once owned. While his heart denied it, by returning he had assumed undeniable risk. He pulled the lever, and the latch, in need of grease, released in rusty protest.

The companionable livery horse nudged his shoulder. Quenton gathered the reins and returned to the saddle. The horse puffed amiably and sauntered through the gloomy twilight, which lent the grounds an amorphous ambiguity. Bats escorted them past angled rooftops rising through the stark, billowing silhouettes of trees. Instead of following the curving driveway to the house, he went straight to the barn and found its stalls devoid of life.

Quenton cared for the shabby horse in the dark and left him free to wander for his food. When he emerged into the night, the house was a black shape without lights. He followed the lane along the overgrown rose of Sharon hedge under a sky of stars with a crescent moon and searched blindly for the courtyard gate. The sweet pungency of flowers filled the air with promise as he pushed through a scant opening. The melody of the fountain swelled with singing frogs, and the perfume of jasmine welcomed him up the steps beneath the broad portico. Feeling as if he were moving through a dream, he put his gloved fist through a square pane in the glass door and flipped the lock. Shattered glass scraped and hinges squeaked when he stepped inside to close the door.

His feeling of dreaming increased a thousandfold. The house was too dark for him to determine whether the furnishings were familiar. He finally struck his flint in the north salon, where denuded windows reflected closed shutters. Sheets covered everything not stripped, and the carpets had disappeared. Other than obvious neglect, the welcome home was suddenly worth celebrating.

"Damn me," Quenton murmured, lighting a few nearby candelabra. He rummaged swiftly through the sideboard, still complete with monogrammed glassware. As if the ensuing years stripped away, he searched his old liquor cabinet. Triumph filled him when he found a bottle of bourbon, and he gratefully kissed its embossed label. Polishing a dusty glass with his shirttail and pouring with a hand trembling with emotion, he dutifully lifted a salute to his eerie welcome home.

"*Santé.*" He quaffed his drink and threw his glass into the cold fireplace to bind his oath. Its crystal shattered the empty silence when it broke against the marble hearth.

AS THEY STOOD TOGETHER at the row of mirrors surrounded by other women ogling one another in the plush ladies' lounge at Brighton Hall, Sarah sighed with admiration, plucking at Alix's black tulle overskirt. "This is fantastic. Who would dare such creativity?"

Alix liked the enormity of the old building dating back at least a century. The ceilings were high and the hallways broad, designed when life had been a little richer than current fashion warranted. The ornate woodwork was heavily gilded, and old-fashioned tapestries still hung in places along the walls. Enormous murals of medieval hunts involving unicorns and lions made for a fascinating study that no one except Alix seemed to notice.

The invitation to join the Wesleys for an evening of dancing had been unexpected, and now, in response to Sarah's question, Alix could not share that she designed her own gowns or that experimenting with fashion had become almost an obsession during her long hours of seclusion. Lily's poor husband footed the bills, but Lily would pay the full price upon her return, because her sister would swiftly discover Alix's snug measurements would not fit her.

She turned from her reflection, uneasy, as always, about the close proximity of other women, and joined Sarah in the hall, where John Wesley waited to escort them to the ballroom. Alix scanned the crowd for the police she had expected ever since the near disaster at Oxley. As the hours eked into days, her initial presumption that their delayed appearance was to save Nicholas from public humiliation had transformed into a fearful puzzle of how and when she would be apprehended.

Now, as she passed a table, a barrel-chested man with a curled mustache noticed her. He looked as intelligent as a detective and sat with a man wearing a monocle who looked distinguished enough to be an official. Amplifying her suspicion, they leaned together to speak quietly. Alix's heart pounded when the man with the monocle pretended to polish it. He peered through it experimentally and looked directly at her.

Alix realized the time to escape was nigh. Desperately, she looked for the exit while following Sarah and John to their table. The monocle-wearing man commented to his mustached partner, surveyed the room, and then scrutinized Nicholas, who rose at their approach. The mustached man held his drink balled in his fist; was it a secret signal to seal the exits? Alix panicked. If she did not leave quickly, her flight would be useless, but when she jumped up, she sprang into John's waiting arms.

Sarah giggled commiseratively. "Of course Lily can't wait to dance with you, Johnny!"

John Wesley had steel-gray eyes and a pervasive smile too quick to be kind, but he assured her, "I'm delighted, of course."

"Sarah, shall we go, too?" Lily's husband suggested.

"Oh, yes, why not?"

"It's just a quick dance while they bring our drinks," John Wesley advised engagingly. He patted her hand encouragingly but then left his perched atop hers too warmly while leading her to the dance floor. "You don't have to worry; Sarah doesn't suspect a thing."

Alix propped Lily's smile on her lips and started dancing, but the monocle flashed in the light as it followed them.

His gaze probed her intently. "You don't mind, do you?"

Alix had forgotten to listen and had not a clue of what John meant. "No," she replied too quickly, using him as a shield against the monocle. Sarah's husband regarded her pensively, although he did not seem offended. He continued talking and finally began to chat about the weather. "Of course," she tittered in a mimicry of Lily, but the mustached man signaled someone. Was he calling a waiter or a troop of constables?

John Wesley had asked a question. His expression was pleasantly expectant while he awaited her answer, although Alix did not like his thin veneer of courtesy. "Oh, no, not really," she declined ambiguously.

He turned her around so that the men were behind her. Now they danced toward a corner. Were the people at the table police, too? Even though the woman wore feathers in her hair, she might be one of those secret agents working at Scotland Yard.

"I hope you don't mind."

"You know me," Alix responded vaguely.

"Really? You want to slip out together? Here, tonight?"

"Why not." Although she responded without under-standing exactly what he meant, she wondered if he was warning her of something, because the man with the monocle cut the corner of the dance floor, as if intent on intercepting them.

"We'll have to sneak away."

Was he offering to help her escape? The mustached man cast a glance at them while he passed behind the edges of the throng collected near the dance floor. "Are you certain?"

For a fleeting moment, his conscience seemed to trouble him, but he put on a brave show. "Of course."

"I couldn't ask it of you," Alix said, declining his offer. Perhaps he meant well, but he was clearly unreliable.

He blinked with surprise. "As long as Sarah doesn't learn of it."

Alix carefully watched Sarah dancing with Lily's husband, but they showed no signs of avoiding the public spectacle of her arrest.

"Are you scared?"

Alix giggled courageously as he danced her nearer to the exit. "Who, me?" The man with the monocle stopped to chat with the woman with feathers. The mustached man reached the orchestra to speak to the maestro, who finished the dance abruptly. Couples came to a standstill, and everyone applauded vaguely.

"Think about it, then, won't you?" John took her arm and led her through the crush toward his wife and Nicholas, before the music began again.

"I say, wasn't that the most fun!" Sarah laughed.

John stared solemnly at Lily's husband and then shrugged indifferently as Alix sank into her chair. The blue suits of London's finest were not here yet, but they were most certainly on their way.

A SHARP PROD in his back woke him. Quenton barely wondered what it was, before it rudely repeated. He opened his eyes to stare at his denuded room.

A rough voice came with another jab and the sudden realization that the cold steel he felt was the barrel of a gun.

"*Levez-vous! Qu'est-ce qu'au nom de Dieu faites-vous ici?*"

"*Ne me tuez pas,*" he mumbled into the mattress. "Don't shoot."

"Keep your hands where I can see them, monsieur!"

His slow wits failed to rally, although he lay sprawled ridiculously naked on a stripped bed. His clothes, strewn in the dressing room, included his only weapon: a foil concealed in the shaft of his walking stick. Even though a sword was no match for the carbine shoved in his back, it might have been worthy for a rudimentary surprise.

His hesitation earned another prod. "Get out, or you're a dead man!"

His dullard's mind shifted to seize on the voice. At one time, its owner had been as familiar as Quenton was to himself. Dare he guess? His situation left him vulnerable if he were wrong.

"May I have the decency of putting on pants before you throw me out?"

The response assured the man's identity. "*Cap de Dieu!* Maybe, monsieur, if you don't try anything foolish—I don't like my Estella seeing anyone naked, unless he's already dead."

He could only be Gaston, although why his old servant still worked here was a question. It was sufficient to suggest that Chênes Noir indeed still belonged to Quenton, but this was not a time for distraction, considering the fellow's nervous trigger finger. "Gaston?"

"Save your tricks for a simpleton, eh? Get up, and keep

your hands where I can see them."

He was in a senseless position to do otherwise. "Where else would I put them?"

"Oh, you're funny, monsieur. Where are you from, one of those traveling circuses?"

"On some days, I wouldn't be surprised." Gaston was a good enough marksman to bring instantaneous death, but if Quenton must die, he preferred to see who was killing him. He rolled over and recognized the man pushing the carbine under his nose. "Gaston, it's me."

Unwavering, Gaston groped for the nearby dustcover from the floor. "Wear this."

Quenton caught it reflexively. "I can't say you've grown kinder with age."

"Shut up, monsieur, before I forget I'm your host."

"You don't you recognize me?"

"I don't know anyone, monsieur, but if you insist I should shoot you, let's do it outside, where it's easier to bury you."

"All right, all right." Gaston was never one to overthink his situation. The same quality that allowed him to obey without question also made him balk at indecision.

Gaston retreated, but his carbine did not waver. "Where are your clothes?"

"In the dressing room. Where else?"

Gaston motioned with his rifle. "Let's go."

If asked, Quenton would think himself unchanged by the years in England. As he passed the mirror, the absurd fellow clutching a sheet with a rifle barrel aimed at his skull looked very little like the graceful noble once reflected there. It might be fitting if he died on the day of his return, but he would rather not make that statement. His old dressing room reflected a dream of familiarity; perhaps a connection to the past would jolt Gaston's memory. "Where's Bertrans?" he asked of his old manservant.

"Bertrans who?"

"Bertrans Havre. You remember—he used to work here."

"Bertrans Havre is dead. Where've you been, monsieur? If you want to trick me into thinking you know your way around, you'd better ask about someone who's alive."

"I've been in England awhile, but it's a shame about Bertrans."

Gaston inched toward the settee wearing the pair of trousers on its arm and, without moving his eyes from Quenton, felt through the pockets before tossing them over.

"I hope a priest gave him the last rites, at least," he concluded, and asked after his old majordomo. "What of Étienne?"

"Étienne moved up to Orléans. You must've been in England a long time."

Quenton stepped into his pants and buttoned them. "Longer than I'd like to think." Even if trousers were no protection from a bullet, he felt better wearing them. He reached cautiously for his shirt. "I know the man who used to own this place . . . and thought you'd remember him, too."

"The marquis and I were like brothers," Gaston vowed, crossing his fingers demonstratively.

Quenton hesitated as the rifle barrel lifted, and waited for it to wave permission to continue dressing. "I thought so, too."

Gaston decided to test him. "What was his name?"

"Quenton. He's about this tall." He slowly marked his height with his hand and then quickly pushed his loose shirttails into his trousers. "About my weight, give or take a few stone."

"Maybe he was taller; that shows what you know."

Quenton openly measured his reflection with Gaston's in the mirror but also slipped his foil free from his walking stick hidden in the folds of his riding coat, which hung over the chair. He continued in hopes that Gaston would recognize him before the servant put too much pressure on his trigger. "He has brown hair and eyes like mine. He even used to think he was good with a sword."

Gaston laughed. "He'd cut out your liver before you knew what happened."

"Really? I never thought he was that fast."

"Oh, sure, and it proves you didn't know him. You heard about him, maybe, or saw him ride on the parade ground."

"That's right—he trained destriers, didn't he?"

"Yes, and his family was famous for their horses. Keep talking, monsieur, but you're only proving you don't know anything about Quenton Saint-Descoteaux."

"You don't think I know him as well as you do, but there's something you've failed to recall."

"Take my advice, monsieur, and climb onto that nag of yours, and . . . eh!"

Quenton dropped onto his haunches, hooked his foot behind Gaston's leg, and swept the feet from beneath him. A deafening roar from the rifle split the room; an explosion of plaster rained from the ceiling. When Gaston banged his head on the wardrobe, Quenton grabbed his rifle and put his sword at the man's throat. "You're getting slow."

Gaston spread his hands in the air carefully and then froze. "Eh, don't kill me, monsieur; I have mouths to feed at home."

"After everything else, you still don't recognize me?"

Gaston blinked at him in a daze, until realization dawned. "Quenton? Marquis, is that you?"

Quenton relaxed his sword. "I thought it was, until you

came to tell me differently."

"Lord Marquis!" Gaston scrambled to his knees, grabbing Quenton's hand to kiss his ring, and squinted at his naked finger hesitantly before climbing up to hug him. "My God, I thought you were dead! I should've known. Forgive me!"

Quenton gratefully embraced him in turn and slapped his back congenially. "What're you doing these days, besides dragging men from their beds?"

"I'm the caretaker here—what else do you think? I would've recognized you at once if you had been wearing your ring."

"I sold the gold long ago, when I needed the money."

Gaston helped him with his coat. "By the cape of God, I almost killed you!"

Quenton laughed as he sat down to pull on his boots. "Tell me you have a cup of coffee and some food around here."

"Oh, sure, but you'll have to come up to the gatehouse, if you don't mind the accommodations." Gaston looked around for their hats. "It was in the newspapers that your family was killed; proclamations went up everywhere. The government seized this place for a while, but before anything could happen, the English captured Bonaparte. Now Chênes Noir is managed by an executor, but they say the King's been restoring titles ever since his election."

"That bodes well for me, I hope."

"God willing." Gaston crossed himself briefly. "Hey, I saw your poor horse in the field. Where'd you come by such a pitiful nag?"

"He was the only livery horse available. Do they pay you to live here?"

"Òc," Gaston answered, his old habit of mixing provincial language with French unchanged. "Moises Benoit handles it;

I'll tell you over breakfast. Just wait, by God," he laughed, trailing Quenton to the stairs. "I'm not the only one who's going to be surprised that you're alive and returned to Limousin."

CHAPTER 12

THE STRAY

❦

obert nursed his beer at an empty sidewalk table in the cluster between the street and the tavern. He sat in rolled-up shirtsleeves and a tan vest, feeling undressed. His jacket of faded green corduroy lay tossed on the adjacent seat. His supple boots were replaced by a stiff and unyielding pair overdue for polish. He had left his wool riding breeches with inset padding at the knees in England; instead he wore threadbare twill trousers stained in places. Customarily, he would not have worn such clothing, but ordinary habits had changed. He even shaved, leaving his face exposed.

Still, he welcomed the muslin shirtsleeves after years of wool sweaters. He was older and did not miss the bite of the English wind on his battle scars. With heat, those aches faded. Such was the difference a few hundred miles made in the temperature, and he enjoyed the warmth emanating from the nearby wall.

The rippling pigeons scouring the street were engaging. Near the crowded storefronts, a group of ragtag boys played soldier. Occasionally their captain drilled his troop in marching, when they were not sword fighting with sticks.

Robert had never had children. He had not been around enough to make any, he guessed. At least he wasn't stuck playing father to those not even his, like other men were. When faced with being alone, some women lacked Molly Gordon's dedication. Which ones ever knew if their husband would return from some foreign shore?

Robert might not have given Molly children to succor her old age, but at least they had Alix. She was a bright ray of sunshine in their lives, no matter how desperate her own situation had once been. How that blunder could have turned so fortuitous, he would never unravel; he could only be thankful for it. She was the something right he had done in his otherwise sorry existence, but even she would not be able to forgive him if this went wrong.

The pigeons surged away as a plow horse wearing a harness carried a farmer up the street, his muddy boots dangling without stirrups. He stopped at the nearby water trough and slipped off to let his questionable mount drink. First he lifted his patched hat to scratch his baldpate; then he dug into a pocket for his pipe. He found it with a lean pack of tobacco but not a light.

Obligingly, Robert left his beer and pushed up from the table to loan the man his tinderbox. "Bonjour, Monsieur le Fermier."

The farmer regarded him with mild surprise. "*Merci beaucoup*, Monsieur Genre." With a grin, he accepted the gift of the flint. "It's going to be a nice night, don't you agree?"

"Yes, I think it is."

"Have you ever been to Marseille?" the man wondered, puffing his smoke to life.

"Not for a long time."

He returned Robert's tinderbox with a bow. "You'll go again someday? I hear the best beer is at Hotel Argonaut."

"I'll have to try it if I go."

The farmer clamped his pipe in his teeth and handed back the flint with a folded scrap of paper before jumping onto the enormous horse with surprising agility. "Thanks again for the light."

"It's my pleasure," Robert replied, pocketing his tinderbox and the note as he returned to his table. He had just settled when his greyhen sandwich arrived with a fresh beer.

The boys had finished playing, and he ate in the silence of cooing pigeons and an occasional burst of conversation from inside the tavern. Somewhere, someone began to play an accordion. The sun shifted, leaving Robert's table in shadow, but the wall was still warm. After pushing away his plate, he leaned back to finish his beer and brought out his pipe with his pack of tobacco.

He retrieved his tinderbox to strike a flame and finally glanced at the farmer's note. He touched it to the flame and released it to the ashtray to watch it burn. After pulverizing the ashes with his spent matchstick, he blew a puff of smoke into the fading afternoon. He had a month to ensure that Quenton made it to Paris to petition the King for restoration.

QUENTON PLAYED HIS GUITAR and sang gently. *See that lonesome dove . . . sitting in an ivy tree.* The solid tick of a clock broke in, and awareness stole the sweet scent from the beeswax candles flickering. *She's weeping for her own true love, as I shall weep for thee.* Alix clung to her uncle's fading song, realizing it was only a dream, while the counter-syncopation from someone playing in another room stole Quenton's voice, until it dimmed into faint memory. *Ten thousand miles . . . rocks may melt and the seas may burn. . . .*

She lay alone in the darkness, listening to a different guitar playing in the night. With a displeased sigh, Alix rolled over and cuddled her pillow, willing the return of sleep. The upstart in the other room was singing Quenton's song, and while his rendition was pleasant, he could never match her uncle. Eventually, his music lulled her back into dreams.

Alix sat in a wooden chair. The floor where she scuffed her boot heel was gray slate. Pale light slanted through vaulted windows set in stone walls. The wood of the doors to the outside was bound with thick bands of iron. A floor clock ticked in droning silence. Alix drew a sharp breath of recognition of the rough-hewn room with armored suits guarding the corners. She was in the front hall outside her father's office. The tall-backed chair belonging to the doorman was empty. When the clock pendulum flashed and chimes rang out in a warning, an icy fear gripped her. She was locked in a dream and fixed in time, while the toll of the clock torched a terrible explosion.

Alix landed on the floor. With a disconnected awareness that it was too late to run, she fought the tangle of foreign sheets with a graceless displacement chasing her though a room of dislocated furniture. Stumbling and careening crazily, she toppled a chair that tripped her, banged into the rubbish can, and crashed against the door frame. The abrupt pain from a smashed toe brought her awake.

"Glory, what a mess." She fumbled for a light as her heart pounded away the residue of fear, and found that her split great toe was bleeding. "Oh, this is ridiculous," she muttered, as welling blood forced her to march on her heel to her dressing room in search of bandaging.

Purposely, she perched on the edge of a chair to tie a handkerchief around her toe. Her knee still hurt from the smashup at Oxley, and now this. Instead of staunching the bleeding, the thin linen blossomed brightly. Alix had seen blood before, but now it brought a strangely ominous oppression.

Resolutely, she closed her mind to the unresolved dregs of her nightmare and rummaged through cupboards for a rag. She ignored the weighty trap of blood by disguising it and hobbled to the couch. After lighting a reading lamp, she grabbed the nearest book and opened it randomly. *I am but mad north-north-west. When the wind is southerly* . . . She began where her eyes found the page, and let Prince Hamlet's predicament transcend her discomfort.

Jenny's exclamation woke her from a restless doze with a start. "Fie, what happened? It looks like a storm blew through here!"

The confused light of morning revealed the disastrous scene in the bedchamber. Haphazard bedclothes draped an upturned chair and a dented rubbish can. In the dressing room, where lamps burned low, the cupboards were ajar and the drawers swelled with tangled things Alix had tossed in her desperation to disguise her blood.

"A nightmare woke me. I fell out of bed and stubbed my toe," she explained weakly, surrendering to the maid's skillful ministrations.

Jenny busily reached for the footstool and unwound the hasty bandage to look at Alix's damaged toe. "If you miss this morning's fitting, it might be weeks before the dressmaker has another opening. Minnie says her cousin's shop has been crushed with new orders."

While the maid cared for her foot, Alix sketched a design for a necklace, a gift of gratitude for Jenny. In the alleyway near the dressmaker, there was a master craftsman's shop where Alix had once commissioned a gold-handled walking stick for Quenton. If anyone could create a jade collar lustrous enough to match Jenny's eyes, it was Cyril the stonecutter.

Jenny straightened at a rap on the door. "There's your tray."

Satisfied with her design, Alix folded the paper and slipped it into her beaded reticule. Later, while Jenny was busy with errands down in Piccadilly, Alix would nick over to Cyril's shop and put in the order, instead of lingering in the ladies' tearoom.

"Now then," the maid fussed purposely, while pouring a cup of tea and arranging the tray. "Here's your tea, milady. Don't worry about a thing; that sore toe of yours will soon be right as rain." She leaned closer and lowered her voice. "Take my advice and stay off it while you can. It's liable to be sore later on."

"Thank you," Alix replied, and took her time adding a drop of cream to her brew.

When Jenny opened the wardrobe, the mirror on the angled door reflected into the tilted mirror adjacent, creating a double reflection of Alix with her bundled foot propped on the footstool.

"I think you'd better wear slippers today, instead of shoes."

The combined reflection of the red dress hanging on the wardrobe in the mirror suddenly magnified disproportionately. It brought from veiled memory a sudden, suffocating image of the crimson-velvet riding outfit that Alix had been wearing in her dream.

Jenny regarded her with surprise when Alix rose from the couch unsteadily. "Is something wrong?"

A hasty attempt to flee the desperate vision met with a swift rise of darkness. Alix experienced a vague sensation of falling as it swallowed her, and nothing more.

❧

"MILORD, PERCY THINKS HE SHOULD send for the doctor," Frisk insisted, handing Nicholas a towel.

"What in the blazes for?" Nicholas retorted, blotting his dripping hair as he stepped from his interrupted bath.

"Milord, if milady is in the condition that we suspect—"

"Do you think I don't know?" Nicholas interrupted uneasily, tossing aside the towel in exchange for the white Turkish robe that Frisk produced. "No one needs a damned diagnosis."

"But if it's something else, it might be prudent—"

"What's the worst? She might die of complications. Good bloody riddance," he swore, tightening his belt.

"I find that I stand in agreement with Percival. There's a certain degree of civility—"

"Where the devil is the civility in having a child that will be calling his uncle Father and his father Uncle? You tell me," Nicholas bade angrily, and grabbed for underclothes.

"Even so, to deliberately neglect the well-being—"

"I've heard enough," Nicholas said, cutting off his objection. "No doctor. That maid of hers can handle whatever she needs; she's taken care of every other blasted thing thus far, hasn't she?"

"I apologize, but I find your decision unconscionable, milord!"

"Do not dare to suggest that I feel one jot of pity!" Nicholas dumped tea into his cup to settle his nerves. "As far as I'm concerned, she should've thought of this long ago, before she had fun rolling my brother and anyone else who came along. You'd do well to drop the matter entirely," he advised, rattling his cup and saucer. Roughly, he yanked his trousers from the wooden butler before Albert had the opportunity to reach for them. "The time has passed when I should be expected to feel anything for that woman. It's long been obvious she married me only for my money. Well, she's gotten what she wanted, hasn't she?" He buttoned his trousers and buckled his belt, incensed by Albert's silence. "Do you think I'd get any consideration in return? No! By God, all I got was a bleeding incestuous family. Don't expect me to swallow the gall of coddling a bastard as part of the bargain."

"If we don't send for the doctor, what are you going to do? You can't just ignore this!"

Nicholas bit back an angry retort of grudging truth. "I'll show you what I'm going to do," he decided instantly, buttoning his shirt on the way to the door.

Percival Winston was hovering in the hallway. "Good morning, milord—should I send for the doctor?"

"Good morning, Winston. I apologize for my delay; I was in the bath," Nicholas replied on his way into his wife's room. Closing his mind to his vow never to cross the damned threshold again, he steered a course straight to the bedchamber with the butler on his heels.

"Milord, no one understands quite what happened. Milady was in the dressing room with her maid and—"

"Yes, yes. Thank you, Winston. It's probably only an overly tightened corset."

"Milord, don't you feel it might be prudent to send—"

"I hardly think a doctor will be necessary." Annoyed by his insistence, Nicholas cut him off by closing the bed-chamber door abruptly. He continued blindly to his wife's dressing room, but momentum carried him only so far. Jenny was on her knees with Lily cradled in her lap as a chambermaid fanned her futilely, but they released her to scramble to their feet as he entered.

"You there," he addressed Jenny sharply. "What brought this on?"

"I don't know, milord. Milady was sipping her tea while we discussed her morning outfit."

"Nothing alarmed or frightened her?"

"No, milord. You can see her upended teacup there, on the floor."

Nicholas hunkered down to lift his wife's chilled hand in a show of concern. "It appears to be only vapors."

"Milady was awakened by a nightmare, and she fell out of bed," Jenny stammered, looking to the chambermaid for validation. "She stubbed her toe and decided to read awhile—"

"You don't say," he said, cutting into the flow of hogwash and putting a decisive end to the display by scooping his wife from the floor. He was fed up with her contrived manipulation and unending bid for control. What did she expect to gain now? Was he to find her latest plight pitiful? "It's a simple overreaction," he determined, but realized that she seemed more fragile than he had expected as he carried her to the mangled bed. While the maids scurried about to restore the tangled covers, he unwittingly became aware of her appealing vulnerability as her soft hair spilled across her pillow.

The maid abruptly usurped his place by tugging the blankets over Lily's thinly clad form. He turned aside from her tempting illusion, confused by an unexpected desire to join her, and nearly sprawled headlong over the upturned chair hidden in sagging bed curtains. "What's this?" he demanded, his damaged pride salvaged by the quick distraction.

"Part of milady's accident earlier," Jenny replied, busily tucking the covers under the mattress.

"I see," Nicholas replied cautiously. He hurried to the door, determined not to revisit the enticing image lying in his wife's bed. "Lily should feel better after a rest," he claimed officiously. "Winston, see to a new rubbish bin, and send someone up here to fix the bed curtains later."

"Of course, milord."

Nicholas stopped to look for the book that the maid professed his wife to have read. He cursorily flipped through the pages, but it showed no more evidence of her use than other books she purportedly enjoyed. Either her sudden penchant for reading was part of a superficial parody of reform or she had discovered their convenience for hiding secret correspondence. Noting that Winston was less concerned about why *Hamlet* was splayed on the floor than about questioning the maids, he tucked the book beneath his arm to review later, and escaped.

ON THE RIDE BACK to the Griffon house, Alix considered her afternoon outing a success. She had not only managed to complete her fitting at Mrs. Wimple's Dressmaking Shoppe, but had also slipped over to deliver the design for Jenny's necklace to Cyril the stonecutter, despite the throbbing reminders of why she should have stayed in bed. The maid filled the return trip with trivia about the Griffons' ancestral estate near Aberystwyth. The place was whimsically named Hollyrune, which Jenny explained came from the myriad of holly trees planted around the estate. While it suggested that at least one of Nicholas's forbearers had been imaginative, Alix knew little about Wales, save for its existence. As Jenny described the enormous stone house and the sea-swept beauty of the remote Welsh landscape, Alix watched the narrow streets roll by, longing for the green fields of Buckinghamshire surrounding Robbie's farm.

Alix shifted her position in the corner uneasily. "In ancient days, people thought holly was a charm against evil."

"I wouldn't know, but the house has a grand view of a lake."

A sharp snap from a whip startled Alix upright. A corresponding moan pulled her to the opposite window, where her nerves lit on fire at the outrageous sight of a junkman standing over a ragged horse as it collapsed in the traces of a rubbish cart.

"Stop!" she shouted, as he raised his whip again. Her command brought the Griffon carriage to a clattering halt as the coachman confused her order. She sprang through the door and landed poorly when she twisted her knee, but spared herself a fall by clinging to the door handle. Stumbling forward, she narrowly missed an oncoming coach with a shouting driver and hesitated long enough to dash around a startled man on a frightened horse. She finally reached the brute, wielding death with the lash of his whip. "You there! Stop!"

He snarled with surprise when she grabbed at his upraised forearm and spoiled his aim. "Leave me go, lady!" He shoved her aside, but she scrambled up from the ground, ignoring the painful protest of her injury, and resolutely braced herself against his intended blow.

"Stop it, I say!" she commanded, staggering under his strength. "What manner of foul beast are you?"

"Milady!" Georgie abandoned the driver's box and dodged the coaches careening to avoid him.

"God, move back." The junkman shook her off to recoil his whip. "Stay out of the way!"

Alix returned determinedly to shield the dying horse from another blow. "Leave off from this animal, you monster!"

"Are you out of your mind? Get away from me!"

"Give me this whip!" she insisted, grabbing for the slippery handle.

He cackled and spat around the smashed end of his cigar when he knocked her aside. "Someone oughta teach you to mind your own business!"

Georgie grabbed him from behind. "Here, mister!"

"This ain't your affair, kid—get back unless you want double!"

Alix scrambled to the ragged horse as it heaved a rattling breath. "Oh my God, my beauty, what's this brute done to you?" she mourned. It struggled to lift its head at her touch, rolling its sunken eyes pitiably. "Rest, my lovely," she begged, smoothing its rat-chewed mane with trembling hands.

Behind her, someone fell in the street, ending the sounds of a struggle as shouted confusion increased. Hunkering protectively over the horse while it wheezed its last, moaning breaths, Alix realized she heard the whining of a dog. She looked around to find a white terrier crouched in hiding by the front wheel of the reeking cart. "You poor thing," she told it. "You'd better run for your life." The starving dog was not much bigger than a barn cat; its bones poked through its sparse coat of filthy fur. It stood up to shiver convulsively and then cringed away when it noticed the looming return of the junkman.

"You're a churlish maggot," she bitterly accused the man behind her as his whip whistled overhead. "Back off and give this poor beast the benefit of a last breath without the taint of your stench."

"Those are brave words for a nosy biddy who thinks she's above a lashing!"

Ignoring his threat, she resumed her soft crooning as she stroked the dying horse's face. "Pass easily, my pretty," she whispered. The chilling whistle of the whip and the astonished outcry behind her carried no meaning, and an eerie silence settled as the poor beast shuddered and died.

A man behind her spoke up curtly in the hush, giving quick orders. "You'd do better to stay where you are. Someone find a constable. You there, help this lad back to his coach. Some of you see if you can't get the traffic moving before something else happens."

The blast of a bobby's whistle brought Alix to her senses. She was sitting in the street with a dead horse and a muttering crowd behind her. Guiltily, she staggered to her feet as police whistles began to sound stridently.

Her dress and white kidskin gloves were ruined. Peering over her shoulder fearfully, she saw a fashionable gentleman break the whip across his knee and toss it aside with disgust. He stood over the junkman on the ground, cupping his bleeding nose, while someone hurried forward with his top hat and the whistle-blowing constable pushed through the crowd. In shocked revulsion, Alix looked frantically for escape, but she was surrounded by gathering people caught in the stalled traffic. Horror tinged her vision with darkness as her rescuer turned to reveal his identity. Nicholas Griffon was busy explaining the circumstances to the constable, but he reached for her without hesitation when her knees buckled, and saved her from falling face-first into the street.

Summoning an approximate imitation of Lily, Alix gasped weakly, "This is naught but a grave misunderstanding."

Nicholas's rigid self-control kept the upper hand, and his response remained as bland as if he picked his wife up from the cobblestones every day. Coolly, he turned to the constable. "If you don't mind, I'll let you do your job here, Officer. If you need a statement, my secretary will be happy to make an appointment."

Alix moved forward numbly as he ushered her through the crowd. "I don't know quite what happened—"

"Don't say anything further." He cut her off abruptly and looked to Georgie as the coachman jumped to open the coach door. "Head home straightaway, lad—no stopping."

"Yes, milord."

Whistles began shrilling as Nicholas lifted Alix into the carriage, where she shrank unsteadily onto the red-leather seat. "I realize this is extremely odd—"

"Here, milord! That was my own horse!" The junkman shouted his protest over the group of constables crowding him.

Nicholas spared a backward glance as he secured the door. "Constable, add littering the streets to assault charges, and see that that mess is cleared immediately."

"How can I move my cart without me horse?" the junkman wailed, as Nicholas crossed to a white brougham waiting at the curb without a backward look. Police whistles began shrilling to move the traffic out of the street with shouts of "Move along! There's nothing more to see!" He boarded the coach sprouting men at the windows amid a collective ballyhoo, but his reply remained unruffled. "As I suspected, my coachman was attempting only to prevent an accident."

Alix stared numbly at her filthy gloves and avoided Jenny's scalding disapproval as the coach jerked into motion.

"Fie, what got into you?" the maid asked finally.

The sound of Jenny's voice drew a curious black nose from under the hem of her skirt, and the sight of the dog jolted Alix from her daze. She lifted her skirt with surprise as the maid gasped in disgust.

"What's *that?*"

"It's a poor little dog," Alix exclaimed, lifting the cringing animal.

"I can see it's a dog! What are you doing with it?"

"He was by the junk cart; he must've followed me."

"Psst," Jenny hissed, lowering her voice. "Tell Georgie to stop this coach immediately."

"I can't," Alix protested quietly. "He's supposed to go straight home—"

"You've got to put that thing off."

"Put him off?" Alix repeated in disbelief, brandishing the unhappy terrier with his tail tucked miserably. "How can I put him off? Where'll he go? The poor thing is hungry—look at his bones."

"Get rid of it. Milady doesn't abide dogs—and can't you see how dirty it is?"

"A bath would fix that, you know. Speaking of baths, I need one, too."

"You can't mean to keep him!"

"Why not? At least until he's clean and has something to eat—someone might take him if he looks better."

"That dog stinks!"

"Well, actually, now that you mention it, it might be the both of us."

Jenny sprang from the seat to open the windows. "Oh, phew!"

NICHOLAS SPOTTED JOHN AND SAM as he headed for the stairs, and abruptly turned into the adjacent hall to descend the old spiral staircase that led to the back hall exiting into the alley. After circumnavigating the abbey, he crossed Saint John's Square and continued down to the Archer for an overdue pint of ale.

He was not so much avoiding John Wesley as he was being cautious. After his friend's careless advice over lunch at the Boar's Head had led to an inconsequential evening of dancing in Brighton, Nicholas doubted that John grasped the delicacy of his situation. But, after all, how could he? To John, if the woman living in Nicholas's house was not Lily, it was the perfect lark to take full advantage of his unexpected position, but it was not Wesley's name that would ring with derision if Nicholas falsely called the constable; it was not John whose sanity would become questionable. Nor would John be the one standing in court, giving a bumbling explanation about why he wanted a divorce, when, for all practical purposes, his wife's lifestyle no longer bore the weight of his complaint. Even Nicholas's own household would bear witness against him, and while they described a homebody who might read or paint or play a bit of piano, he would emerge as the callous husband bent on ridding himself of an unwanted wife.

He sank into his beer thoughtfully. His aim was divorce, not a legal separation that would entitle Lily to a rich allowance to resume a flagrant lifestyle however she wished, but when he had found her swooning over a dead nag in the street, it had added another item to his growing perplexity about her new image. What was her aim? He could scarcely believe her display had been a completely innocent attempt to alleviate the animal's suffering. More than likely, she had intended to make a public showing of high moral standards, aimed at discrediting his charges against her.

However, at the end of that episode, she had collapsed into his arms, and therein laid the source of his conviction that she could not be Lily, despite appearances otherwise. Although she might reflect his wife's image and practice amused self-absorption well enough to fool even John, she did so with a quintessential difference, or so Nicholas had begun to hope, as the alternative was that he was inadvertently attracted to his wife's elusive appeal. He did not like to remember that he had once thought so enough to marry her, but even then, what he had felt was not comparable to what he experienced now.

How should he consider the mounting evidence that she was not Lily? John's question of what Nicholas was prepared to do about it might be better restated as: What did it say about Nicholas as a man that he had done nothing thus far? Who was she, and where was she from? Had she run away from somewhere? Was she a fugitive from justice? People did not just leave their everyday lives. If she was an impostor, the authorities would want to know why he had not immediately sounded the alarm to search for his wife.

Yet if she proved to be Lily, he would be an immediate laughingstock. What kind of man did not know his own wife? Now his intentional disregard of the woman he had married came home to roost. His blatant foolhardiness in his hasty decision to stand at the altar would be overshadowed by his neglect in managing his own life. His constant presence at the club would become suspect. His judgment in steering-committee action could be questioned and could even result in Lion Shipping Company's being put under investigation for mismanagement. Whatever remained of his tattered reputation was already at stake, and if his wife's affair with his brother became public, the scandal would deal it a death blow. Even moving Lion Shipping down the coast would be insufficient to salvage it. In the aftermath, their family fortune might be reduced to a fleet of tugboats.

Asking John's opinion had been worthless, but there had to be a way to know the truth without a direct confrontation, because if Nicholas merely demanded his own wife's identity,

Lily would be the first to trumpet his lunacy from the highest hill. He needed a subtler discovery. In that, perhaps Frisk's earlier advice to have a chat with her was not so unwarranted. If he did, it could not be at home, where the staff could later be called on as witnesses. It had to be somewhere without the distraction of a gathering crowd to lure her away. Somewhere quiet—even dinner, perhaps. Somewhere like Lexington's.

CHAPTER 13

DISCOVERY AT CABBIE'S PUB

*lix would have preferred to spend her evening with the terrier, instead of obeying the unanticipated summons from Lily's husband for dinner out. She had hoped for a quiet evening and wished only for a book by the fire, once she soaked in a warm bath to ease the swelling of her knee. Though that would not be possible, she had managed to give a good scrubbing to the stowaway that she had slipped into the house beneath her cloak. He had gorged on biscuits and cream at tea and then promptly curled up in a corner and gone to sleep. So far he seemed to be an engaging little fellow, but she did not know how long she could keep him hidden from the household. Although she had bathed him scrupulously, the chambermaid would notice any shedding hair, and the butler would wonder at her sudden penchant for walking at all times of the day.

Still, she could not simply put him out. Even with a clean and snowy white coat, he was so gaunt that every bone was apparent through his fur. He was lame in one hind leg and traveled on three, although she could find no obvious injury.

What she had at first suspected was a miserable tail tucked between his legs had turned out to be only a pitiable stub. He had not much to show for himself, except inquisitive ears shaped like a bat's, a pointed snout with an adorable black button nose, and a pair of chocolatey round eyes filled with curious hope.

The drive to the restaurant seemed to take forever. Alix endured the thick silence stoically. At least Nicholas seemed more interested in the passing scenery than in pursuing a conversation. Once, she thought the driver had gotten lost, because they seemed to go in a roundabout direction, but then she saw the river when he finally brought the carriage to a halt.

Even inside, at the table, Nicholas seemed more intent on his dinner than on her company. Her anxiety increased incrementally as the silence between them deepened. Was he waiting for her to spark conversation? Would Lily normally ignore him, since there was no apparent audience of a crowd to impress? She kept her hands beneath the table so he would not see her fingers tangle in the napkin while she strove to mimic her sister. Was his scrutiny whenever he chanced to look her direction as sharp as it seemed? His gaze settled on her briefly and then returned to his plate as he cut into his fish, but she saw that he had taken note of her covert observation.

"I thought it'd be nice to enjoy a quiet dinner for a change," he finally said in explanation of his unwarranted invitation.

Despite the mundane assertion, Alix was convinced that he had baited a trap. At the onset of their unprecedented engagement, she had expected the driver to swing the coach by Scotland Yard. When it brought them instead to the restaurant on Queensboro, she was uncertain if this place, with candlelit tables and music courtesy of a strolling violinist, was one that

Lily preferred. Carefully, Alix sipped her wine. Had Nicholas hidden a smile when he'd returned his attention to his dinner? Was he entertained by her puzzlement, or did he find the way she sipped her wine secretly amusing? Discomfited, she nervously plucked a morsel from her bread and then hesitated, because the act had regained his attention.

His austerity eased. "Your fish will get cold."

"It was a little too hot."

He blinked at her inane assertion and chose a drink of wine to consider it. "You like the chardonnay, at least," he noted, motioning the waiter forward to top off her glass. "It's a Moisson d'Épernay; I thought you'd enjoy it."

"Of course," she conceded easily, but propped up her assertion with a purposely astringent smile.

It seemed to unsettle him enough that he returned to his former critical regard. "Although I confess I've never noticed your preference before."

Alix nearly choked on the bite of fish she was swallowing. Who could believe that Lily had no preference for a good white wine? Did her sister not know that she was half-French, for God's sake? She struggled to keep the striped bass from sticking in her throat as she yearned to drink the suddenly suspect chardonnay. She swallowed again, desperate to find a quick resolution to her new dilemma.

"It's good to try something different occasionally," Lily's husband continued pleasantly. He waxed on his topic while finishing his fish. "Everyone has room to learn something. Take me, for example. Should anyone ask me about art, I'd have little to discuss, unless in consideration of maritime history. Of course, I had the standard courses in school, but faced with any of those old exams now, I'm afraid I'd give a lackluster performance." He waited expectantly. "You took art in school," he presumed with a wave of his fork. "Who would you consider, if I were to ask you, your favorite artist?"

The fish found a painful place to park in her attempt to squeeze it down her throat. Alix imagined fainting from lack of air, too afraid to wash down her bite. Nicholas studied her untouched glass and then lifted his own in an unspoken challenge.

"I . . . ," she managed to reply, swallowing a fearful gulp of air that drove the fish down far enough for her to swallow. "I don't know."

He did not believe her. His expression flattened in disappointment as he drank a liberal chaser of wine.

"I mean," Alix clarified, wondering if she was stifling his attempt at polite conversation with her reluctant reticence, "it would depend on the type of art, wouldn't it?"

His initial surprise turned thoughtful, and then he nodded in concession. "Yes, I suppose it would. Anything, I guess. Why don't we stick with painting?"

Was this a trap related to her request for a painting kit? She had not found anything bearing Lily's signature on his Westminster walls. Feeling a snare ready, she grasped at one of his books for an example. "Well, there's that Italian fellow, Michelangelo Caravaggio. I suppose he's famous."

Satisfied, Nicholas signaled for the next course. One waiter brought a fresh choice of wine, while others changed their plates. "Michelangelo . . . wasn't he also a sculptor?"

Alix was unable to decide if he was being facetious or whether he was honestly confusing the two different artists because of their common given name. He waited expectantly while sampling red wine for the next course.

"I don't think so," she ventured carefully. She had no idea how deeply Lily was dedicated to the arts. "At least, your book didn't address sculpting."

Her answer perturbed him. Setting down his empty wineglass, he motioned for their waiter. "Are you certain?" he insisted pointedly. "Isn't he the one who painted the ceiling of the chapel in Rome?"

He appeared to be genuine, but Alix did not see how anyone could confuse the two men, when their works were lifetimes apart. "Perhaps you're thinking of the infamous Master Simoni," she proposed gently.

"I distinctly recall his name as Michelangelo."

"Michelangelo was their common name. Merisi da Caravaggio was not even born during Lodovico Buonarroti Simoni's lifetime," she clarified glumly, hesitant to reveal more. "You see, his name was in the book."

"Ah," Nicholas replied, with a subtle air of discovery.

"It was *all* in the book," Alix quantified hurriedly, attempting to rescue her shattered facade. She pushed Lily's bored smile upon her face. "Of course, I wouldn't ordinarily remember such excruciating details, if I hadn't just read it recently." She finished by tittering her sister's dismissive giggle and hoped disaster had been avoided. At least, there did not seem to be any constables rushing forward.

The new wine with the entrée of roast beef and baked pastry posed a new dilemma. If Lily did not like white wine, dare she try the red? Did Lily find this pastry pleasing and care for sauce? Did she eat roast beef with horseradish or something else?

"What else did the book say?" Nicholas prompted, tasting his pastry.

"Book?" Alix surfaced from a sip of wine she had not meant to take. Guiltily, she relinquished the glass, but he noted her lapse. His eyes flashed to the waiter, who hovered nearby. Was he jotting notes on that towel he kept convenient?

"Yes, the book," Nicholas replied, with an impatient wave at her plate. "Yorkshire pudding isn't good cold."

Obediently, she retrieved her knife and fork. If she fled now, she could never make it to the door before she was caught. She concentrated on her roast beef and its delicious combination of garlic and thyme.

"What else was in the book?"

"Oh, you know." Alix smirked like Lily. "It was about his life, which was predictably boring."

He sawed at his meat vigorously, belying his forbearance. "It must have held some interest if you read it."

"No," she denied, suddenly realizing she was hungry. Just a hint of rosemary mingled in the wine sauce served with the meat, which was teased with a dollop of horseradish. She had not tasted a decent roast beef since she had left the farm.

"Yet you recall his complete name."

"Michelangelo Merisi da Caravaggio, yes."

"Are you certain he wasn't born in the fifteenth century?"

The freshly grated horseradish had just a touch of vinegar to ease it. "It was the sixteenth, actually."

"He was from Rome, wasn't he?"

Her reply that the artist had only escaped to Rome from Milan died on her lips when she glimpsed his overt interest. What was he planning? She washed down her guilty response with a gulp of wine. "It might have been Rome," she finished weakly.

Nicholas returned to his meal with flat dissatisfaction, but that allowed Alix to revisit her plate. She tested the pastry with the tine of her fork, dabbed it with sauce, and tried it carefully. Disappointed, she stabbed at a pea and, after a furtive glance at her suspicious host, rinsed her palate with a sip of wine.

The violinist stopped to play at their table. He bowed at

Alix for her notice, without a break in his well-rehearsed performance. In a sudden memory, she could almost hear a baton rapping against her instructor's music stand. Monsieur had been a perfectionist. *Encore une fois*—once again, from the beginning, he had ordered her. Now her customary repertoire on violin included jigs and flings, not the classical music she suddenly recalled as she listened to the troubadour's performance. "Bravo," she said at his finish, applauding gently.

Across from her, Lily's husband wore an uncharacteristic smile. "Good show," he agreed as the man bowed away. "Let's go somewhere," he proposed suddenly. His eyes glittered as he escorted her from the restaurant into the haloed mist and waiting coach. "It's a little early yet. What do you say to a nightcap?"

NICHOLAS GAVE IN TO HIS WHIM despite his crucial awareness that his impulse might be another blunder, but when it came to his wife, what else was there? He had walked a tightrope all night, and meant to end it. Her vacillation between careless disregard and cautious ambiguity made him edgy. When prompted by the violinist's charm, he had taken the plunge before the spell could fade. Was she Lily or was she not? For the moment, it did not matter, and when she shivered as he put her into the carriage, he cursed himself but sat on the seat beside her anyway. "Would you care to use my cloak?"

If she recoiled from him disdainfully, it was too dark to notice. The shadows hid most of her face; only the curve of her cheek and the movement of her responding lips were visible. "No, thank you," she declined gently. "I'm fine."

The odd disembodiment of her voice deepened the enchanting illusion. "Are you certain?" he pressed, just to hear her reply.

The coach jolted forward, and a passing street lamp illuminated her eyes as she glanced at him carefully. "It's a very nice offer, but I'm fine, really."

The magic strengthened. Was it because of her uncustomary courtesy that he felt she was a stranger? Angular patches of light slipped by with tantalizing predictability. She kept her face averted as she looked through her window at restaurants and storefronts, although Nicholas failed to notice anything different from what went on any other night in London.

Perhaps because of her closeness or his misguided attempt to confuse her about classical art in an attempt to define her familiarity, he felt on the verge of discovery. A greater question might have been if Lily would know the difference between art forms, but if his supposition proved valid, Nicholas would rather not ignore the implication of an impostor's education. Riding in this oddly companionable darkness, he found himself longing to break the silence. "It's damp tonight, isn't it?"

His observation was inane enough to invoke a simple response: "Yes, it is."

Did he detect a difference in enunciation without Lily's image to sustain her performance? When only the lower half of her face was lit, her uncertainty seemed obvious as she nibbled her lower lip. If she were Lily, she should recognize their destination, so why did she appear doubtful about the familiar streets of Mayfair? *Was* she Lily and now, in her attempt to redefine her image, reluctant to bump into her old crowd with him along as an escort, or was this neighborhood strange to her replacement?

Greater than a growing certainty that she was an impostor was his concern about why anyone who was fundamentally unknown would put herself in someone else's position.

Whether she had done it for a lark, for money, or as part of a desperate game, what was he prepared to do about it? He must be drunk to be dwelling on it. He pulled his eyes from the mesmerizing sight of her lips and stared through his window.

When their well-known destination, Cabbie's Pub, finally appeared, he nearly sprang for the door. Her careful dismount from the coach reminded him of the foot injury she had sustained before she had inexplicably fainted earlier in the day. But in the invasive light of the pub, his hopes took a pivotal turn. Why was he hooked on a delusion that someone would assume Lily's place, and how had he become desperate to believe in such a dangerous dream? In ushering his wife along as if she were a prize he had just discovered, was he not falling in with a plan for public reunification to legitimate the birth of her child?

If he was not mad or drunk, he determined he would soon be one or both as he checked her cloak with his own, giving the impression that they were here together. "A glass of brandy and a double scotch," he ordered stoically. Was her perusal of the room curious or speculative? Too little insight soured his questions, so he checked his watch in a search for clarity. "Cheers," he ventured when their drinks arrived. What would she say, if she could say anything?

Although Nicholas was intent on discovery, he was interrupted by "Ahoy there, Griffon, old boy." He looked around as his neighbors Reginald and Martha Burton wove their way through nearby tables. When Nicholas rose to greet them, he unvaryingly prompted the notice of the entire room. Soon, the flow of interruptions was oppressive. Excusing himself meant little to anyone, for when he shook free from one conversation, someone pulled him into another. Although his intent for the evening had been to confront his peculiar obsession about her identity without simply demanding an immediate explanation that might cast a doubtful light on his own sanity, he wound up glad-handing over drinks instead.

It should not have surprised him when he eventually looked around to find Lily's chair empty.

"Ahem—I beg your pardon," the club manager interjected. He bowed apologetically to the circle of men, looking between them inquiringly. "Lord Griffon?"

Nicholas knew instantly that the intrusion involved Lily. "Yes." Whatever spectacle she had contrived, it was too late to wonder about the cost of his embarrassment.

"I'm sorry," the manager explained, as he led Nicholas toward the back of the bar. "I'm afraid there's been an accident."

"Are you referring to my wife?" Nicholas supposed, knowing the man's answer. Anything including Lily customarily led to disaster, much like his marriage.

"I'm sorry, Lord Griffon. I'm afraid we don't quite know how it happened. Doctor Adamson is here tonight; he'd be happy to examine Lady Griffon."

Lily was determined to drag a doctor's opinion into the official announcement—what better way to prove her child's legitimacy? Nicholas felt as if he were heading to the gallows as he followed the manager down the dingy hall.

"I assure you that Lady Griffon is as comfortable as possible."

Nicholas was feeling foul enough to greet the very devil when he stepped into the manager's tiny office but was completely unprepared to see Lily sitting in a pool of lamplight. Surprised, she looked up from a magazine. Her demure satin toe was all that showed in a wealth of lace, cushioned on a satin pillow. The sight plunged Nicholas back into his redundant delusion about an impostor. "Lily?"

Her pitiable look of entreaty compelled him closer, to kneel at her side. "I'm sorry to have pulled you away! This is such a little thing!"

The anxious manager hovered nearby. "As I was saying, Lord Griffon, we've no idea how Lady Griffon may've fallen."

She cast a remorseful look at the manager. "It's my fault. I should've watched where I was going."

"Summon our coach," Nicholas requested, instantly regretting his decision not to return home after dinner.

"Oh, please," she begged, plucking at his sleeve imploringly. "I'm fine. Don't feel you must leave because of me. I'm capable of going home on my own!"

"You don't look fine," he said, cupping her shoulders reassuringly, but then the lacy cloud of her sleeve snagged on his cuff button. "I'm terribly sorry," he apologized quickly when she flamed with uneasy embarrassment. "Hold still; don't move—it's just a bit tangled." He looked for help, but the manager had stepped away to ring the service bell. "Here, I'll soon have it free," he insisted confidently, despite his fumbling and his uncomfortable memory of her panic at a similar occurrence with bonnet strings.

"It's my fault; I insisted on this lace." She offered her chary consolation distantly: "It's embarrassing enough to have tripped on it, and now . . . ," she protested faintly. Her face paled as she shrank even deeper into the chair to avoid his immediacy.

"Yes, well . . . ," he blustered, but quickly ran out of things to say, because he failed to find their predicament completely intolerable. If proximity to Lily always affected him as such, he could feast for a lifetime. More than his chest tightened as he tore his eyes from the soft swelling of her breathlessness beneath him.

"Ahem! Oh, I beg your pardon!"

Nicholas glanced up swiftly at the hesitant manager. "I say, you don't happen to have a pair of scissors handy, do you?"

"Please hurry," she gasped weakly.

If nothing else proved that she was not Lily, it was her singular entreaty, but Nicholas would have preferred to believe her excitement was from desire. "Here," he said, deciding to remedy their situation. "Simply because we're stuck together doesn't mean we can't stand up." He shifted his position to allow her to rise, hoping it would keep her from fainting. "Rescue is imminent—it's these blasted cuff buttons. Hold on for just another moment, sweetheart—" *Sweetheart?* He had never before used such an engaging term for anyone, but it suddenly seemed a suitable endearment as the manager returned, armed with enormous shears.

"Steady now, Lord Griffon. This should take only a moment."

"That's all right, man; do what you must." Lily clung to Nicholas apprehensively, her eyes widening with horror at the sight of the scissors. "This should do it," he proposed consolingly, but then caught her collapse as the shears closed on her lace and freed his sleeve.

The manager retreated fearfully. "Is Lady Griffon all right?"

"She's swooned, I'm afraid," Nicholas countered, as he cradled her in his arms. Even in a dead faint, Lily's mask never faltered, but beneath the cut-away portion of her dress, he found the evidence he had been craving. Where Lily had flawless shoulders, the missing lace revealed a terrible scar belonging to an impostor.

☙ ❧

CLOUDS STIPPLED THE SKY, and an afternoon zephyr sighed over golden fields where birds darted from the merlins skimming the meadows. Quenton disembarked from the ferry on the dock in Limoges with his pair of horses in tow, eager to reach home. He attracted avid looks as he mounted the gentle lead horse and led the impressive young Friesian along on a tether. He did not mind that everyone's attention was riveted on the eye-catching black colt instead of on him; in his opinion, it was better to pass unnoticed. The townspeople did not recognize him as the man claiming to be the marquis who had once owned the forest. Without official recognition by the Crown, he was innominate; without the chalcedony ring, Quenton could be anyone. When he had destroyed his own, he had done so for want of money to pay the fee for breeding Alix's mare with the Turkoman stallion that resulted in her champion, North Star. He had never considered that he might one day need it to prove his identity.

The archetype for the knight chess piece of the seal had been the founder of the herds of white horses that Quenton's family had once been renowned for. They were lost now, gone like so much chaff in the wind of the war after Henri had died. According to the attorney acting for the estate, they had been appropriated with everything else belonging to the family. After the emperor's collapse, the horses had simply disappeared.

The Friesian colt at the end of his tether was symbolic of a new beginning. Starting over, Quenton had chosen a versatile horse more relevant to modern times, rather than attempt to reconstruct the line of horses used for war. The stallion was too young to ride over distance, but he already regarded the world with imperial interest. Although he had journeyed overland and by ferry for two days, his glossy blue-black coat defied dusty stains. His furry fetlocks fell over the coronets of his hooves fancifully as he paced the homely horse escorting him through the outskirts of Limoges and to the bridge.

Upon an occasional whim, the Friesian cavorted with the breeze through the streets. Mostly, he traveled with a lively gait and played nuisance games with his companion. The saddle horse, in turn, swiveled his head away from a sudden nip or flattened his ears disdainfully. When the infractions became serious, Quenton tapped the errant youngster with the flat of the lead to remind him of his manners. Afterward, the colt would acquiesce pleasantly for a time, until his capricious humor returned.

They traveled the last leg of their journey through the aging afternoon, and Quenton was as relieved as his long-suffering horse was to see the oak forest ahead. The fanciful young stallion, as if aware of his destiny, became even more animated. He twisted his ears expectantly and looked for mares in the meadows but found only uninterested cattle. He squealed and pranced impressively but received a flattened look from his brown horse companion, and another tap of the lead.

"Baylor," Quenton admonished sharply.

The stallion knew his name and shook his head to tousle his mane, while the brown horse blew a rattling puff of resignation. Quenton gave its skinny neck an understanding pat, and, encouraged, the gelding lifted his head and picked up his step across the bridge to the pungent forest. The woodland was new to the young horse. He looked into the trees enthusiastically, but whether Baylor saw mares or unicorns, Quenton was in no mood for frivolity.

The tree canopy absorbed the sky as they passed into dappled shadow. The sound of their homecoming was swallowed by the forest, and cicadas filled the silence. Tall rock pillars braced the open ironbound gates. Beyond, the lane stretched to the arc of the stone bridge and the round gatehouse. A watchdog barked; the young stallion snorted warily in response as the brown horse whinnied a greeting. Quenton raised a hand when Gaston's wife, Estella, appeared in the gatehouse doorway with her fair-haired daughter perched on her hip.

Beyond the stone arch of the little bridge spanning the brook, Gaston drove a two-wheeled gig through the trees to meet him. "Bonjour, milord!" he called, reining in the spotted pony pulling his cart. "By the cape of God, will you look at him!"

"Bonjour!" Quenton stopped as Gaston clambered out of the driver's seat in a hurry to collect the colt's lead.

"How magnificent, eh?"

"It's too soon to know his worth as a sire, but he has the right qualities."

Gaston turned as a distant pair of riders emerged behind them. "Here come Jean and Michel—we'll take over from here, milord."

"I'll be down later to see how he settles in," Quenton agreed, as his brown horse continued toward the house without urging. "*Merci*. Take good care of him," he added, waving as he passed the approaching stablemen.

He would never tire of the welcome sight of pointed rooftops rising through billowy trees. Since his return, the ivy had been trimmed and the edging replaced with beds of lavender joining the pink and white roses of Sharon bordering the lawns. The new majordomo opened the enormous front doors and sent a houseboy out for his horse when Quenton stepped down from the saddle.

"Bonjour, seigneur." Marcel bowed with the lithe grace of a swordsman. Although he was not tall, the majordomo had the powerful build of a natural athlete. He waited in the vaulted foyer with an enigmatic smile half-hidden in his curling mustache.

"Good afternoon, Marcel—or is it now evening?—and why do you look like a cat with a bird?" Quenton asked, trading in his dusty fedora to tug at his riding gloves.

Marcel smirked mischievously. "I have what I hope is good news for you, milord. My cousin Simon has agreed to work in your kitchen."

Quenton chuckled as he dug the bill of sale for the colt from his inner pocket before turning over his coat. "First Jean for the stable, and now this; soon you'll have every hotel manager in Limoges up in arms."

"Is it my fault good men constantly seek new opportunity?" Marcel rejoined innocently. "He started work in the kitchen this morning. Whatever he's planning for dinner is a secret, but his assistant went out truffle hunting."

"There're plenty in the forest."

"Oh, but of course! We've pilfered them for years, haven't we?"

Quenton laughed as he continued to his office upstairs, where a stack of mail waited on his desk. Marcel had sorted the catalogs with the newspapers from Paris and London. More important were the copies of pending contracts sent over by Oliver Belfort, the general manager of Fontenot Porcelain, and a letter of response from the estate attorney, Moises Benoit.

Quenton dropped the bill of sale on top of the stack and took Benoit's letter along to open as he went to his chambers. It was a long way from Poitiers, and nothing was worth doing before he cleaned up and changed into comfortable clothes.

The house around him was in the process of restoration,

and the distant echoes of a hammer followed him through the halls. His rooms were far from finished, but they were clean, with new carpets spread on the floor. Unfortunately, Benoit's letter had failed to reassure Quenton that there would be money to pay for it. Until Quenton's audience with the King, Benoit's generosity would have to cover the invoices. How long would it be before Moises questioned his expenses? The attorney did not make any promises.

He sipped a glass of cognac while changing clothes. He wanted only what was his returned to him, but his uncertainty over Chênes Noir and Fontenot Porcelain were not his sole concerns, since the ownership of the lapidary business in Geneva, along with the rest of Alix's inheritance, also pended the King's recognition. If Louis Philippe chose to entertain his plea for restitution, his proclamation would indemnify the residual. In accepting Quenton's legitimacy, he would validate Alix's bequest and, inasmuch as Quenton's wealth was restored, the largess would extend to Alix's fortune.

In the meantime, Quenton did not dare to bring Alix home without protection from the Crown. Even as Moises Benoit systematically addressed the old claims against him, there was no guarantee of his complete reinstatement. Essentially, his return had raised him from the ranks of the dead, and while this was far from the pale existence he had left behind in England, it was not what it should be. The house was as far from completion as Quenton's affairs were from settled. There was no future to offer Alix until he met with the King. She would be terrified to return to France, and if Louis Philippe denied his petition, Quenton would not even have a roof to offer.

A cheery fire awaited his attendance in the north salon. A few of the vaulted windows were ajar, allowing in evening air to fan sparks up the chimney. Marcel waited, hovering between a pitcher of wine and a plate of stuffed mushrooms. He waited until Quenton sank into his favorite chair, and served both on a golden platter, while wearing an enigmatic smile. "For your pleasure; the wine was delivered yesterday. I tapped the barrel myself."

Quenton swirled it in his glass to study its ruby clarity before sniffing the fruity bouquet, and was pleased by its dry finish when he finally tasted it.

Marcel nodded appreciatively at his expression. "It's most definitely a Moisson Cabernet, no? Simon insists it's the perfect pairing for his mushrooms."

Suddenly, Quenton's return home was real. For years, a fine meal had entailed only holidays with Alix at the Gordons' farm. Now, as he sampled the mushrooms eagerly, he put his feet on his footstool, deciding that his future might be indeterminate but the quality of his dinner was certain.

CHAPTER 14

JENNY'S NECKLACE

lix plucked hopelessly at what was left of the collar on the dress she had worn to dinner with Nicholas, but the cutaway in the lace revealed the ugly scar on her shoulder vividly. "I don't dare try this style again," she decided anxiously. "The bodice on the amethyst velvet is going to have to be altered if I'm to wear it." The delicate overlay was attractive, but after the mishap the night before, she felt it best not to push whatever luck she had left, in what was becoming a limited store.

Jenny came around front and tried to rearrange it better while Alix watched in the mirror. "I still say that if milord had noticed your scar, he would've demanded an accounting straight away."

Alix whispered, "He'll summon the constable when least expected. He must be waiting until even the officials are positive there's no mistake." Abandoning her reflection with a sigh, she dropped onto the settee by the terrier. "I can't make sense of it," she confessed, stroking the dome of his head carefully. Not only was the poor dog sorely flea-bitten, but his neck was raw from the frayed rope that she'd had to cut away when bathing him.

"You've got to be mistaken. If milord had noticed that scar on your shoulder last night, we'd be having a different sort of chat."

"Glory, if only my knee hadn't given way!"

"Why were you trying to hide in a broom closet anyway?"

"Lily doesn't stay underfoot all the time, does she?" Agitated by Jenny's critical look, Alix rose and went to the dressing table to rearrange her curls.

"You'd do well to keep the weight off that leg of yours."

They fell into sudden silence when a knock at the door interrupted them. Automatically, Jenny straightened her cap and smoothed her apron as she headed to answer it, but the terrier surprised them with a bark and jumped down to scamper past her.

Alix gasped, "Oh, glory!" She lunged after him, despite the pain wrenching her knee.

"Fie, I knew this would happen!"

"Stop, you!" Alix scrambled to catch the dog before he could reach the door, but he was too fast. She grabbed him just in time, but her overtaxed knee gave out and she crashed against the door. Frightened, the terrier let out a yelp and squirmed away behind the couch. Outside, the butler rapped urgently as Alix staggered to the chair.

When Jenny rushed to open the door, Winston looked between them, his straight brows incredulous. "Ahem," he acknowledged them hesitantly. "I say, is everything all right in here?"

"Fine," Alix answered faintly.

"Are you hurt, milady?" he asked, with a piercing look askance at Jenny, as he hurried inside to put down the package he had brought.

"No, I'm fine," she replied smoothly, struggling for composure. "I was a bit unbalanced, that's all. I wasn't expecting a knock on the door at this time of day, and I'm afraid it startled me."

If Winston did not believe her, he withheld his argument as he entered assiduously. "A package has arrived for you, milady."

"Oh." Alix looked blankly at the unassuming brown paper–wrapped parcel on his polished silver tray.

"I'm afraid it didn't arrive with any salutation," he continued, eyeing the maid as he reached into his breast pocket. "I've some scissors to cut the string."

"No!" Alix gasped, suddenly remembering the enormous shears the nightclub manager had wielded. In memory, all she could see was their pointed approach as the earl's suffocating closeness squeezed her. "It's quite all right! I mean . . . thank you, Winston—that'll be all," she finished faintly.

Jenny drew herself up stiffly. "I have scissors, should milady find them necessary."

"Of course," he conceded without conviction, and reluctantly bowed through the door.

"By Jove," Alix breathed when he was gone.

Jenny hurried forward with a furious whisper. "I'll be summoned to the office now for sure. I told you that keeping the dog was a bad idea."

"He didn't mean any harm," Alix responded, sparing a glance for the cowering terrier while retrieving the package to slip off the knotted string. "He was only trying to protect us."

Jenny was distracted by a knock on the serving door in the dressing room. "That's probably young Percy now, summoning me down to speak with his father."

Alix peeled the brown-paper wrapping from the white pasteboard box after the maid hurried away, and realized it was the jade necklace she had ordered for Jenny.

"Oh, hello, Albert." Jenny greeted Nicholas's personal servant distantly through the dressing-room doorway. "What might I do for you?"

Alix opened the lid to dig out the velvet pouch inside while the maid queried, *"Dinner?"* As the coiled necklace for Jenny slithered into her palm, she reckoned its arrival could not have come at a more opportune time. Now the perfect occasion to wear the new jade collar at a meal with a gentleman presented itself, and when Albert Frisk saw how it brought out the luster in Jenny's eyes, he would never forget them. Alix smoothed the strand of polished stones, delighted by their opalescence. "Oh, Cyril, you've clearly outdone yourself!" she exclaimed happily.

FRISK PULLED OUT A STACK OF TOWELS, left one at hand on the rack by the washstand, and took the rest to the shave tray. "According to Percival, he was in the hallway and heard every word plainly."

"Cyril?" Nicholas echoed dubiously and plunged into the water in the washbasin while groping for the bar of soap. "Who the devil is Cyril?"

"I've no idea, milord. I've never heard the name mentioned before, except in connection with the courier who stopped in during lunch. 'Cyril, you've clearly outdone yourself.'"

Nicholas rinsed his face clean and reached for the towel blindly. "I was unaware Winston has developed a penchant for eavesdropping."

"I dare not speculate, but I understand the courier insisted that Lady Griffon was expecting the package forthwith."

Albert clattered the steamer lid as he retrieved hot towels for the evening shave. "Also that he was not from the lot that we usually see around the neighborhood and refused to say who sent him. I found the outer wrapping in the rubbish bin this afternoon, but it was unmarked."

Nicholas balled the towel and tossed it aside as he went to join Frisk at the chair for his shave. "A courier wouldn't need to remember, if it was his only delivery."

"Just as odd as the package was the way Percival approached me to share what he'd heard."

Nicholas was afraid to speculate after the revelation that he had not tripped beyond the edge of reason by imagining a beautiful changeling in his wife's place. "How so?" he inquired carefully.

Albert clattered the lid onto the steamer again after wrapping a hot towel over Nicholas's face, and with a shave brush beat soap to a lather as he responded. "When Percy holds himself to the highest standard, I find his air of confidence peculiar. He found me in the library when I went to shelve a few books. If I didn't know any better, I'd think he was already privy to what you've just learned."

Nicholas cleared his throat. "Do you mean that you think he knows who she is?"

Frisk's guarded testimony mingled with rhythmic sharpening of the straightedge. "Not precisely, but I'd venture to say that he is aware of the stranger in our midst."

"The devil you say—I was not so drunk to lose my recall of events last night, and you're the only one I've taken into my confidence, unless he's been listening at every keyhole."

Frisk removed the warm towel from Nicholas's face and tossed it aside to lather his beard. "After all his years of service to this family, it's inconceivable to think so."

"When I get to the bottom of what's happening around here, if Winston has to go, I'd rather face it now. As for Lily's maid, I always knew she was not to be trusted."

"I find it hard to believe that Jenny would confide in Percival, unless he questioned her about something amiss."

"That's still a mark against him, if he didn't report it immediately."

Albert tested the sharpness of his straightedge before beginning the shave. "I don't know, milord, but I understood Percival to be of the impression that the package was from you."

"Me?" Nicholas echoed doubtfully. "Why would I send something, when she's already making free with everything I own?"

Frisk paused to clean his razor. "It was too small for the routine bonnet or pair of shoes. He guessed it was a trinket of jewelry."

"Have I made a habit of sending my wife gifts?"

"Not that I've noticed."

"Bite your tongue, lad," Nicholas advised acerbically. "You're suggesting Winston knows, and he thinks I'm sending gifts because of it? Is he mad? Does he think I know who she is? And where the devil is Lily? If he knows so much, then why hasn't he shared any of it?"

Albert coughed uncomfortably. "I'm afraid our conversation didn't go so far, milord. It's not exactly my place to demand a full reckoning."

"No, by God, but it won't stop me."

"On the other hand, there's the alternative of Jenny Smith. If anyone knows the details, it is she. The trick is getting her to reveal them."

"Good luck," Nicholas scoffed.

"I've already made arrangements for dinner. I'll see how far it goes."

"Before I interview Winston, I'd like to be certain whether he has any part of this conspiracy."

"Aye, milord."

WHAT TO DO WITH THE IMPOSTOR posed a new problem. Nicholas's discovery at the pub had been frighteningly simple to accept on the drive home, when she was secure in his arms. If he had been a different man, he might have taken advantage of his unexpected position, but whether it had been from finding herself in his embrace or from knowing he could end her charade with a single word, her terrified reaction upon awakening had been impossible to hide. It was difficult to forget her vulnerability, and the way she had nestled comfortably, with a smile curling her lips, as he carried her to the coach. He had been sorely tempted to taste the shape of those lips while cradling her on his lap. But the illusion had lasted only until an inopportune pothole jolted the coach and sent her fleeing to the furthest corner to ride in silence the rest of the way to the house.

Of the myriad questions surrounding this impostor's involvement, Lily's connection was not the least. Nicholas was already the butt of jokes about marital indiscretion and could ill afford worse innuendo. Nothing would end his career in Parliament faster than an illicit scandal, and this sudden change of circumstance threatened to plunge him in over his head.

Had anyone warned him of this escapade the preceding summer, he would have laughed heartily. If someone had suggested the contemptible affair between Nicholas's wife and brother, he might have called the man out. Now he was too aware of the precipice beneath him to ignore its consequences.

In some ways, he might be damned without a trial, but others were too promising to ignore. Despite what he did not know about the stranger taking his wife's place, he could not deny a fascination with her allure.

INSTEAD OF HAULING ALIX around to Scotland Yard, Nicholas treated her to the ballet. The graceful choreography of the dance was more extravagant than she had expected. At length, she decided if ballet had been this exciting when she had taken classes, she might not have dreaded her lessons.

Nicholas Griffon's private balcony offered a commanding view of both the stage and the packed audience near the orchestra pit. The strains of music made Alix long for her violin. When the leading lady rose from her grave to dance with her lost lover across the stage, Alix realized her host's attention was riveted on her, not the performance. She snapped open Lily's hand-painted fan defensively and hid while rearranging her expression into one of boredom to reflect her sister's.

While a bevy of ghosts followed the lovers down the stage, Nicholas leaned close to comment quietly, "It's easy to see why this show has won such acclaim."

Heretofore, their exchange had been perfunctory, so his observation was unsettling. "Yes, it is," she conceded uneasily.

He seemed pleased with her response but studied her critically. "Do you like it?"

"Of course," she replied, but then hesitated as his gaze fixed on the fan with annoyance. Lowering it, she showed her teeth in Lily's tired grimace of appreciation. "It's lovely."

Unconvinced, he glanced at the stage as the scene ended with an embrace. "They say it's a smash hit in Paris. Critics rave that Gautier has revolutionized dance." A swell of applause drowned their spurious conversation as the curtain lowered for intermission. "Let's see if we can find a glass of champagne," he proposed, while ushering her out to the mezzanine.

"Griffon, old man," someone hailed from the crowd. Progress halted as the tide of black suits flooded the room and carried Nicholas away, and Alix found herself alone to suffer a withering inspection through the diamond-studded lorgnette worn by someone's plump wife.

"Lily." Her sister's name came as an unfortunate surprise.

Alix maintained Lily's tired facade. "Good evening."

"Oh, Lily!" Millicent Fabersham hurried to rescue her through the thickening crowd, and her approach drew the lorgnette's attention.

"Oh," the woman noted drearily.

"Hello, hello," Millicent sang expansively. "How are you, Lily dear? Good evening, Martha. Isn't this show amazing?"

"Millicent Fabersham," Martha remarked disdainfully. "It appears as if everyone is here."

"Doesn't it?" Millicent agreed brightly. "Even your unfortunate niece," she noted with a glance at the shy woman shrinking against the nearby wall. "Hasn't it been a brilliant performance?" she continued with a laugh, as she took Alix's arm presumptively to usher her away, and then lowered her voice conspiratorially. "Lily, for God's sake, why are you talking to Martha Burton? You must be bored to tears. I just came across William. He said he saw you the other night at the pub, but when he tried to catch you alone, you disappeared. "

Nicholas suddenly stepped into their path. "There you are, Lily. Why, hello, Millicent."

While Millicent Fabersham tittered with displeased surprise and stammered out a reply, Alix reluctantly acknowledged that it was too late to try to slip away and hide. Wistfully, she looked across the crowd to Martha Burton's unassuming niece, wondering why Lily's friend had called the woman unfortunate and her aunt had not disagreed.

"I must dash," Millicent decided, squeezing Alix's hand. "I see Cynthia—*yoo-hoo!* Cindy!"

Nicholas watched Millicent walk away and then turned to Alix to hand her one of his two glasses of champagne. "I'm sorry if I interrupted something."

"She was looking for Cynthia anyway."

"I'm afraid old Reginald gets a little carried away. You'd never know we were the occasional neighbor. I suppose he feels cheated, living in town; as luck would have it, of all places he'd like to see, wouldn't you know, it's Wales. Who'd have guessed he'd be wild about hunting?"

"Oh," Alix responded, stunned by his sudden garrulousness.

"I suppose there's nothing like the chase, is there?"

"No," she agreed, stifling her unbidden litany of indignity against hunting for sport, rather than necessity, and looked for a clock, wondering how soon intermission would end.

"Do you miss it?" He looked away abruptly when she turned to him questioningly. "The country," he clarified vaguely.

Alix sipped her champagne before responding carefully. "Somewhat."

The act made him gauge her glass critically. "You'd better hurry; it'll have to hold you through the end of the show," he advised, signaling a wandering waiter for more. "I know how you hate to go dry, and we've only five minutes."

Alix suddenly found she had a flute in each hand, scarcely able to finish one before he exchanged it quickly. He glanced around as the room began to empty.

"We'd better hurry, or we'll miss the final act."

Annoyed, Alix finished the glass and took along the other, for it promised to be a very long night.

NICHOLAS HAD RESOLVED to make a decision during the ballet, but the evening would have been a triumph had she fallen into his arms to confess. Although she remained a complete stranger to him, he deemed her well enough acquainted with Lily to adopt his wife's most infuriating habits. In gauging her afresh, he recognized the penchant for delicate hesitation was only an impostor's uncertainty. Each subtle pause was a precursor of a response from a memorized store of Lily's affectations.

He was unaware of when he had distanced himself from his emotions, but as the evening progressed, he realized that he was at liberty to experience the moment as enjoyable, although the woman accompanying him gave no hint of desire to succumb to his dubious charm. In fact, the impostor rarely seemed to consider him as more than a stage prop for her act as Lily. If she guarded her conversation with others, she was vigilant in his presence. If she was careful with everyone, she was wary of him, but how could he defeat her foreboding when he distrusted his own intentions?

Before he had brought her out to the ballet, he had decided it was safer to proceed as if unaware that the woman on his arm was not his wife, but a desire for self-preservation was not his only reason. He knew nothing about the impostor or her motivation to undertake this dangerous subterfuge. Without any evidence of Lily's whereabouts, a judge might send this woman to the gallows for her crime.

Regardless, gossipmongers had sufficient fodder for speculation about Nicholas's sudden appearance at an unofficial function with his wife. Once begun, rumors were impossible to defray, so he went along with her ruse as both a willing accomplice and a covert observer. As the victim, he reserved his right to establish the degree of culpability involved, and once he found where Lily was hiding, he would decide his next course of action.

The uncertain lighting as they drove to dinner on the wharf was an unexpected co-conspirator. Sensing unease by the way she stared wide-eyed into the mist swirling outside whenever a street lamp rolled by, Nicholas retained a discreet distance, unwilling to chance scaring her back to the corner to which she had withdrawn when he'd touched her. What was she looking for in that shapeless obscurity? What was she thinking? Moreover, what did she think of him to find him so terrifying?

"It was an astounding production, wasn't it?" When he broke their tenuous silence, her gaze flickered to him briefly. "I guess the ending was no surprise, considering she had already died."

Tenebrous melancholy swam through the depths of her eyes. "Not really."

Was she that sensitive, or was her reaction only another part of her act? "It's been a while since we've frequented the ballet together," he lied blatantly. He never went to a show with Lily. "It's the finest premiere I've seen in some time."

Unspoken words hung in the gloomy coach, the silence broken only by the steady sound of the horses, until the street brightened and Georgie slowed through the roundabout. "Ah, here we are." Nicholas did not wait for the driver but reached for the door as they stopped. "I thought we'd try someplace new tonight. The Triton has a fine reputation." Nicholas reached for her hand, feeling on the verge of a new beginning.

He steadied her ginger descent carefully, determined to support her act as Lily as long as possible in an attempt to gain her trust.

ALIX DREAMED THAT SHE WATCHED herself racing through nondescript halls darkened by obscurity. She ran blindly, careening around corners and crashing into walls. The only direction in which the girl in her dream looked consistently was behind her. She fell over a table and got caught up in chair legs. Chessmen rained onto the floor and foiled her struggle to rise. The pithy recognition of her ruined game with Quenton pulled Alix inside that frantic child. Horror overwhelmed her, raising her hair by the roots. Her heart pounded faster and filled her hearing. One thought propelled her forward toward the stairs: *escape*. Monsters were everywhere. She could hear them behind her. They were coming.

Papa! Her mind froze. She challenged his murderers to the stairs, where even Quenton could not catch her. She flew to the safety of her father's room and wedged the door with his chair. Gold was stacked on his table, and with it his seal, which he wore as a ring. She scooped it together with frantic hands. She would not leave it for the invaders.

His safe stood open. Had they been here? No. The purses and jewelry bags were still secure. She stuffed everything she could inside her shirt. A litany of "just in case" scenarios flooded her mind. *Just in case I escape. Just in case I survive. Just in case I ever wish to wear them. Just in case.*

There were too many papers everywhere. There were stacks and packets of things. Why did Papa need so much paper? How could he need it, if he was . . . Her heart denied everything. She grabbed all that she could, knowing it had to go somewhere. The safe was not secure. The killers would look there. Who knew what they wanted, besides Papa? Her mind stopped thinking.

She was in the dressing room in front of the wardrobe. No one would look through Papa's clothes. She bundled papers and pushed them into the sleeves of his coats. "Don't play in the wardrobe," Nana would scold if she could see her. Where was Nana? Alix's thoughts teetered wildly.

There was noise in the hall. They were outside the door. *Escape.* Alix dove for the laundry chute. The shutter was tiny. They could never follow her there. *Escape.* She had done it before. She dove in headfirst.

When Alix landed on the floor, the blow to her head was stunning. She awoke with the terrier whining and licking her face. "Glory," she muttered and pushed him away. "I'm awake."

She gathered herself and draped the bedcovers around her like an Arabian thief. She stole through the room in the darkness to find a tinderbox and light the lamp. Taking up a book as she nested on the couch, she opened *Macbeth*, making room for the dog by her feet. The terrier climbed up her length to perch on her side, licking his nose sympathetically.

Hang out our banners on the outer walls; the cry is still "they come." Our castle's strength will laugh a siege to scorn. . . . Macbeth's concerns conquered all.

IT WAS A STANDARD AFTERNOON in the House of Lords until John caught Nicholas on the stairs. His appearance was as aggravating as Fitzgerald's request for the dossier that Nicholas was obliged to deliver. It was past the hour of three, but, determined to enjoy an evening without reeking of scotch, Nicholas had chosen to relinquish the file instead of indulging in the ceremony of hammering details over drinks. Had he been paying attention, rather than thinking about the stranger sleeping in his wife's bed, he would have noticed Wesley sooner. He knew from John's determined expression that he was in for a confrontation. When Nicholas had agreed with John's previous suggestion to take the ladies dancing, his friend had displayed undue interest in a woman whom he had professed he wished to avoid. Nicholas knew why, now that he had seen the proof for himself, but John had never once confessed if he realized the truth, or his intentions toward the impostor. Now it was too late for Nicholas to turn the opposite direction, and so he feigned interest in the committee findings.

"Blast you, Griffon. Don't try that old trick," John hailed, as he purposely blocked Nicholas's path.

Nicholas looked up hesitantly. "Ah, good afternoon, John; I'm afraid I didn't see you."

"More than likely."

"Well then, allow me to apologize for my haste, but Fitzgerald—"

"Blast you for a liar," John said, blocking Nicholas with a forearm before he could pass.

"Do you dare insult me?"

Wesley frowned, incensed enough to grab him by the arm and usher him on a return trip upstairs. "You know damned well I've been looking for you. Why in the blazes are you hiding?"

Nicholas balked. "*Hiding?* Why, that's the most preposterous thing I've ever heard."

"Don't protest too much, old fellow; it doesn't become you. Look, what in the devil is wrong?"

"I don't know what you're talking about."

"I'm talking about Lily!" John snapped in exasperation. His declaration rang along the stairs, stilling conversation as everyone in the hall turned in their direction.

Nicholas reclaimed his arm indignantly. "A little quieter, why don't you?"

John followed him doggedly. "You know what I mean!"

"If you are asking after Lily's health," Nicholas rejoined stiffly, "as far as I know, she's fine."

"That's not what I'm asking, and you know it!"

Nicholas made a beeline toward his office. "Do you mean that you don't care?"

"Of course I care about Lily!" John spouted, once more drawing awkward notice along the corridor. John returned their surprised stares helplessly. "I'm a married man!" he protested indignantly, and ran to catch Nicholas before he could disappear into his office. "What're you trying to do, ruin my reputation?"

"I understand they can be slippery devils," Nicholas discounted briefly, as he pushed his door closed. "Now, if you'll excuse me—"

"Not so fast." John slipped in behind him and perched on a chair expectantly while Nicholas exchanged his file for the bottle of whiskey he kept in the desk drawer. "Stop playing games, Griffon. Tell me who she is."

Nicholas dumped liquor into identical glasses and passed one over his desktop blotter. "I've no idea what you mean."

"Who's taken Lily's place?"

"Ah, so you finally concede that you believe me. It's too bad you didn't care to discuss it when I first asked your opinion at lunch the other day."

John surfaced from a hasty gulp of his drink. "I didn't know then!"

Nicholas lifted his glass in a silent salute. "But you do now."

"I told you I needed only an evening, and since then, you've been seen together all over town. My nod at least put you in the right direction!" He looked at his drink, blustering without conviction. "Blast you—you haven't had to listen to Sarah rave about Lily. I thought I was going to have to live in my office when she heard you went to the ballet premiere without us."

"Cheer up, chum. There's always the club."

John looked desperate. "You've got to help me out. Now I hear you've tickets to the opera."

Nicholas sipped his drink distrustfully. "You hate the opera."

"And you don't?"

"I've never hated it; I just prefer other things. Tonight is a comedy."

John swizzled his whiskey dismissively. "Their singing is comedic enough . . . but look, tickets to the premiere are sold out! If Sarah finds out you're going—"

"Damn me, Wesley, but you sound henpecked."

"I like to keep my wife happy."

Nicholas laughed at his disconcerted expression. "Right."

"Think what you want," John rebuffed grudgingly. "I'm asking for a favor; you've got to take us with you."

Nicholas expected as much when John brought up the subject. "Take you? Come, now, Lord Wesley, you know I don't have to do anything of the sort."

"I've admitted it's a favor. Remember, you owe me a favor."

"You're trying that fickle old line?"

"It's for not laughing in your face when you told me about your . . . obsession."

Nicholas smiled coolly over his drink. John never did like it when Nicholas came out on top, and with women, John was usually the spoiler. "It's sounding as if the subject of my wife is an obsession of yours." He waited for his friend to absorb his barbed response, and then attempted to be reasonable. "Look, John, if you wish to see the opera, you can use my balcony anytime, whenever I'm not in it."

"Just be a decent sort and invite us along. Please."

"If you're having a problem affording your own seats . . ."

Angrily, John reached for the whiskey to refresh his glass. "Damn you, I never knew you to be so condescending. Look, Sarah is dying to see Lily."

"Are you certain it's Sarah?"

"I knew you were bloody well avoiding the subject!"

"Everything has a limit, John."

"What? You're jealous already?"

Nicholas finished his drink in annoyance. "*Jealous?*" he repeated skeptically. "For what reason? It doesn't make sense to involve you any further; don't you see how the press will have a field day if this gets out?"

John splashed more whiskey into Nicholas's glass. "Don't you think having witnesses might prove beneficial? I'm willing to substantiate your claim of not knowing this woman before she turned up in your house—or your bed, or wherever else you choose to discover her."

"How do you expect to do that?"

"If you already knew her, you wouldn't have ridden all the way to the Boar's Head with such a ripe hangover to ask for my help. You're as innocent a devil as the day you were born; I'd be happy to swear to it."

"You know this is ridiculous. You don't really want your name called out in court. Better yet, what about Sarah? Don't be naive."

"But that's my point! Who wouldn't believe Sarah?"

"You can't seriously be considering putting your wife in such a position."

"We're already involved up to our necks, aren't we? Everyone knows we were together for the weekend at Oxley."

"We were together in hundreds of people," Nicholas corrected. "There's a difference."

"You're only fooling yourself; everyone knows we were shipmates, and classmates before that. How long would anyone believe you wouldn't confide in me? You'll be risking perjury, along with your reputation, if this thing blows up."

"John, it's none of your business."

"What do you mean, it's not my business? She and Sarah are friends, aren't they?"

"Perhaps, but friends usually know who one another are."

"So? Why don't I just ask Sarah to find out?"

"Are you out of your mind?"

"Why? Women always talk about everything. Ten to one, she's already told Sarah something of herself."

"I find that hard to believe; she's very . . . careful."

"Well, careful with *you,* perhaps; after all, you're supposed to be her husband. You know, you can be a rather frightening fellow at times. I'm not saying it hasn't had its uses—don't forget, I've seen you in battle. Still, when it comes to women . . . And besides, Sarah's another matter entirely. What do you say? A few drinks, and then a night at the opera. I'll even take care of the tab."

"Damn you, John, if you breathe one word of this to anyone—"

"Who, me, old man? You forget to whom you're speaking. Now, what time shall we swing by to pick you up?" he asked, spinning out of the chair. "Seven o'clock too early?"

"I'll have Winston add your names to the reservations."

"Good. I'll see you later; I've got to dash off a note so Sarah'll know to be ready. Thanks a lot, old chum. She'll be ecstatic."

"I'm certain. Just remember to go white tie tonight," Nicholas added, before John could breach the door.

He laughed in response. "That's impressive."

As John closed the door on his exit, Nicholas drained his scotch. "God knows I'm trying."

CHAPTER 15

A WALK ON ROTTEN ROW

❦

*M*oths danced in the candlelight or died in the flame. Strolling troubadours played tired music on badly strung mandolins, cheap guitars, and a leaky accordion. Couples strolled through light spilling from hotel windows. Empty curricles and cabriolets for hire parked beneath glowing street lamps. A crowd of sailors gathered at the end of the boulevard.

The distant quay was ablaze with torches as men unloaded barrels from the frigate for the line of waiting drays. Reflecting ship lanterns made spindly shadows of its spars against the sky. The moon hung with stars might spark Robert's memory some other time.

He ate alone at a sidewalk table. His beefsteak was grilled with mushrooms sautéed in burgundy wine. The earlier course of swordfish might have been enough to eat, but he never could resist a decent steak, and it was too late now to reconsider the blancmange he had ordered for dessert.

He had a weakness for a good blancmange, even though he knew it could never compare to Molly's. The girl had a gift when it came to finding her way around in a kitchen. He was a lucky man to have a seat at her table; not many men could say the same about their wife. Her talents exceeded a capability to fill the lonely night, and even fewer would maintain that sentiment, especially as years slipped by. He counted himself among but a handful of men who agreed they would never regret the day they found their bride.

The ship's captain ventured down to the quay. Robert could not see him, but the men working around the gangplank stopped to pay attention. That he was an important man was apparent in the way they held their obeisance until after he passed. Robert was down to his last morsel before the man's outline emerged briefly in the streetlight at the end of the wharf. The captain climbed into a barouche hitched to white horses, remarkable for their spectral appearance in the dark.

The waiter appeared to exchange his plate for custard piled high with berry compote. Robert had no idea what he planned to do with it; the cup of coffee that the man poured looked more appealing.

"*C'est tout, monsieur?*"

"*Oui, merci.*"

The waiter took his tray away. Robert realized belatedly that he scrubbed his upper lip with the napkin. It was an unnecessary habit for a man without a mustache. He dumped cream into his coffee and stirred it deliberately while tasting one of the berries. The barouche wheeled onto the boulevard as the ghostly horses assumed earthly form and filled the night with the clatter of their hooves. The coffee was brewed strong in Marseille, and its flavor was not disappointing. There was nothing like a good cup of coffee on the Mediterranean coast. It blended well with the blancmange, although the compote was too sweet.

The doorman spotted the barouche before it stopped. The entrance splintered into a maze of activity. Glass doors split as the manager emerged. Lackeys spilled past with lamps to light the street before the carriage opened. The ship's captain sent everyone away with a word.

Darkness returned, but the manager hovered at the entrance. The captain stepped onto the shadowed curb. His silhouette was tall and lean, but instead of carrying himself with the rigidity associated the discipline of his station, he moved with fluid ease. The lining of his cape flowed crimson in the lamplight when he touched his cane to the walkway. He wore a low-crowned topper, instead of the bicorn of his rank. A lackey had a light ready when he paused with a cigar.

Robert did not remember finishing his blancmange. He pushed the plate aside with the back of his hand in exchange for his coffee. Did the ship's captain expect him to rise with his approach? If so, he was disappointed. Robert did not meet his eyes until the man sat down opposite him.

He was younger than Robert had expected, and not bad-looking. Intelligent eyes considered Robert from beneath expressive brows. If Robert did not know better, he might mistake this man for his father, the notorious Count of Mandelieu, but that would have been years earlier, when Robert was a younger man himself. The fleet of ships belonging to the count's Cyclops Freight Line had increased over the years, but Robert doubted the man sitting opposite did little more than ride his father's coattails.

"*Vous devez être* Robert Peltier."

"And you are Claude Rouget."

He directed a puff of cigar smoke between them, but laughed gently. "*Vicomté* Rouget."

Robert accepted the correction impassively; the title of

viscount meant little these days. "Pardon."

"You've eaten, yes? The food here is good, no?"

His father would beget an idiot. Robert sipped his coffee and returned the cup to its plate. "Yes."

"Oh, how nice."

He had expected something more substantial. Apparently, the weather changed with the times. The other's cigar, combined with Robert's satiated appetite, made him long for a pipe, but he was in no position to relax yet. His waiter scurried close to refill his coffee when he approached with a tulip glass of cognac for the guest.

"*Santé,* eh?"

"*À vôtre.*" Robert's reply drew a narrowed focus when the viscount tasted his drink.

"You're a carefree man," Claude Rouget decided. The crowd of sailors had moved to the shadows across the street. The younger version of the Count of Mandelieu was perhaps not so different after all. "You may have guessed I've been sent with an apology. You see, my father is out of the country at the moment . . . You understand."

If the younger man had intended for Robert to find his insincerity engaging, it missed its mark. "Yes, of course."

"Otherwise, he would have been delighted to see you. Imagine his surprise to learn that after all this time, you'd returned to France."

"One can imagine." Robert had not expected a fanfare of welcome. The viscount's gaze failed to weigh as heavily as the younger man might have liked, but it was enough to achieve its purpose.

Viscount Rouget made up his mind not to vacillate. "I understand you are not the only one making an unprecedented return to France."

"Even pilgrims come home whenever they may."

Claude's smile was cold. "There's a reason Frenchmen emigrate to foreign lands."

"Times change."

"And history remains."

"It depends on who's writing it."

The viscount laughed appreciatively. "Touché, Monsieur Peltier." He enjoyed a generous swallow of his drink and a satisfied drag on his cigar. Its smoke ran out with his sympathy. "Ah, but what is done is done, is it not? At least, that is what they say . . . and in the case of our friend, it is already too late."

The enjoyable dinner he had just finished turned, regrettably, to stone upon the viscount's insinuation. "How so?"

Rouget chuckled amiably. "At last I have your attention." He sipped from the tulip glass and waved his cigar vaguely. "You may relax—it's just a reminder of what's at stake."

Only dead men lost their tempers, but Robert came close, goaded by the viscount's youthful insolence. He hid his defiance in his coffee cup. The apple sitting opposite had not fallen far from his father's tree. The sailors on the dark side of the boulevard held counsel silently.

"Don't worry—it's too early to tell. In fact, it's not yet been received, but the wheels are in motion. So as they say, *quello che sarà, sarà*—what will be, will be—and we'll see what comes of it, eh?"

Robert would not give him the satisfaction of asking questions to inflate his self-infatuation. He finished his coffee and boldly signaled for his check, but did not miss the quick shift in the younger Claude's attention, which gave the waiter permission to approach.

"It's a pity you are leaving, when you've only so recently arrived."

Robert dropped a coin on the waiter's tray. "Don't let it bother you. I've never cared much for Marseille."

The younger Claude laughed, and one glance at the door pulled out a handful of help to clean up the place. Finishing his cognac deliberately, he rose as Robert prepared to leave. "It's a pity, but not everyone realizes they're someplace unsuitable until they experience a little discomfort."

"With the right persuasion?" Robert presumed, donning his trilby as he collected his walking stick from the hatcheck hurrying to deliver it. At least the viscount's presence elicited impressive service.

Claude touched the brim of his own hat in an odd show of respect, considering their circumstances. "Perhaps. Thank you for meeting with me, when I've heard so many things about you."

Robert had plenty of insight into the younger Claude's reputation without having to ask anyone about his character. "Please tell your father that I'm sorry to have missed him. Another time, perhaps. Good night."

The viscount seemed to have a penchant for Italian. "*Addio*," he responded evenly, as Robert walked into the darkness.

IT WAS NOT UNTIL ALIX lay in Lily's bed, with music from the opera playing in her mind, that she wondered at Nicholas's sudden desire to attend premieres. The shows were wonderful, but the events were completely different from making official appearances at formal affairs. She turned over to bend her tender knee more comfortably as she curled with the warmth of the dog. The terrier snuggled into the crook of her arm and licked his nose contentedly.

She played violin for their visitors, and as Bach's partita

filled the room, people stopped to listen. Brightly liveried servants moved through the gathering with laden trays. The round room was decorated with mosaic frescoes of fantastic sea creatures and aquamarine stone. A statue of Poseidon rose from frothy waves on a pedestal beside her and then disappeared when darkness absorbed her, leaving her cold and alone. Terror swallowed her in a tomb of stone. She clung to its walls and crawled through the narrow opening as the suffocating stone squeezed the breath from her lungs.

Alix woke when she landed on the floor. The terrier emerged from beneath the blankets, whining encouragingly. "Shush!" she warned, struggling free while he licked the tip of her nose. The round beacon of his eyes in the shadowy darkness moored her confusion. "God," Alix gasped as she struggled to her feet. "You know, this is completely ridiculous." Wearing her blanket like Caesar, she marched to the sitting room.

The dog sank to his haunches while she built up the fire and struck a flint to light the lamp. "What are we going to do with you? We can't keep you a secret forever." She reached for the book on the end table and arranged herself on the couch. "Come up if you want," she said, making room by her feet. The terrier hopped up and curled in the crook of her legs. Plumping the occasional pillow beneath her elbow, she opened *The Song of Roland* at random and began to read, while somewhere she heard a distant guitar begin to play. Finally, the elusive melody became so peaceful that she closed her eyes and listened, until she fell asleep.

NICHOLAS HAD INTENDED TO PLAY "Jump at the Sun." He broke his rhythmic strumming to pick out a tantalizing melody. It was delicately complicated but simple, when he considered the combination of notes. He played it through another time, and then his guitar rang silent. He sipped his scotch and began "Jump at the Sun" again.

The intrusive notes flummoxed his timing. He stopped playing the fling to repeat the pervasive melody, but it faded away unfinished. Usually he did not hear new melodies; they merely manifested while he was playing. The taunting refrain was unique in this but ended before it was complete. It was a peculiar puzzle, intriguing in its sudden inclusion and then disappearing, as if his obscure muse had been suddenly sidetracked.

Finally, he set aside his guitar with an idea that the tune might return if he did not consider it. Retrieving his cold pipe from the ashtray, he knocked out the ash and filled it with Virginia tobacco. The spark of flint flared in his darkened room, and he settled back to prop his slippers on the footstool. When he blew out his tinder in a billow of smoke, his eyes touched on the stacked illustrations that Albert had pilfered from across the hall.

Paging through the drawings had become a habit. The impostor had a fondness for rich color and bold shadow, as well as a critical eye with a whimsical twist of fancy. Why, he wondered, did birds flit around the windows of the old fairy-tale castle and the horses smile for their portraits? Who was to care if the bunch of mares in the edelweiss meadow shared the pond with a turtle, or if the clouds stacked high on the cliffs resembled elephants? Then there was still the question of why she included Quincy Hill in the guise of a nobleman astride his fine horse, gazing out at the castle in the valley below.

Nicholas considered the penned painting while blowing smoke rings and watching them dissolve. What was her fixation with Quincy? Was he someone familiar, or an instant fascination?

If only he could remember what he and Quincy had discussed on the night the stableman disappeared. A salute of *santé* over drinks was his most remarkable recollection of the incident, besides the surprising transformation in the man's appearance, and yet Nicholas had a feeling they had exchanged words. It was impossible to know if his dim memory of having taken a swing at Quincy was real or illusory, but whatever had happened, the stableman had vanished without consideration.

Quincy had appeared in much the same manner one summer day, simply walking in unannounced from the street to inquire about the advertisement Winston had placed for a stable master following Old Rory's death. As it happened, Nicholas had been ashore to assume control of Lion Shipping, after the same hunting accident that killed the old stable master had ultimately claimed Nicholas's father's life. Quincy and Nicholas were near the same age, and something about Quincy Hill had struck him with an immediate liking. It had not mattered that Quincy had not come without references. In retrospect, it was a decision he had never regretted.

Now the man was gone, and here was a painting implicating him in connection with Lily's disappearance. It came with so many questions that Nicholas felt if he could but grasp the right one, the web of deceit surrounding him would unravel with answers. In that, it was similar to the refrain haunting him. He reached for his guitar and played it again, adding to it as another fragment of the mystery began to make sense.

The idea of Lily's being involved with Quincy Hill was not as ludicrous as it had first seemed. She must have skimmed sufficient funds to set up temporary housekeeping, with intent to pass off her unwanted child and return to resume her position as his wife, but she had an enormous surprise awaiting when she found her bags packed and a taxi waiting to take her anywhere but here. In the meantime, Nicholas had the problem of the woman across the hall. Should she remain, Lily would imagine her plot secure. Nicholas would be in prime position to use the charade if Lily balked at his terms for divorce.

MUTE SWANS SAILED LIKE BARGES with gangly cygnets in tow. Graylag geese herded noisy goslings down the grassy slope to splash into the water rambunctiously. In the center of the lake, a single rowboat carrying a fair-haired family splashed a course. The sky reflected blue on a sun-sparkled surface but rippled green near the grassy shore.

Alix walked with the terrier without concern if he wandered, for he invariably returned. He might stray a few feet to investigate, but a leash would have betrayed their connection. Men tipped their hats and ladies bade good day as they passed, yet no one said, "Hello, how are you?" or "Nice to see you," or offered any other invitation to stop for a conversational exchange. Alix did not mind. Public ostracism did not offend her; in her position, she was even happy for it, because it allowed her relief from juggling Lily's show.

A couple strolled by, each holding a hand of the young girl splayed between them. She had tawny pigtails and a red shepherd's hat tied with an enormous white bow so appealing, Alix wished to paint it. The man touched his bowler politely, but his fashionable wife sniffed under the rigors of speaking. The wandering terrier had returned from an investigation of shrubberies and skipped ahead on three legs, when the girl's voice rose above the distant noise of rancorous ducks. "Oh, Mummy! Look at that pretty horse!"

Alix turned automatically, but it was only Midnight Star, prancing as if on parade. As swiftly as her heart leaped in joy at the sight of her beloved pet, she cringed from Lily's husband in the saddle. Who would guess that such an inexorable person would be riding through the park on a lovely day?

"Oh no," she sighed, caught in a quick dilemma. Helplessly, she looked for a hiding place, knowing she and the dog could not pass without Midnight's spotting her. She hurried for the safety of a divergent path, but the gap in trees near the water exposed her. Walking briskly, she kept her face turned to the lake in a slender hope that neither man nor horse would notice her, or the dog that dashed at her heels.

Midnight's excited whinny froze her in place. She knew from experience that if she ignored him, he would only think she was playing. Determinedly, she mustered Lily's practiced smile and turned, trying to ignore the earl's perplexity as Midnight paced forward, fighting the tightness of the reins.

"Good afternoon," she began with absurd delight, as if they met in the park every day. She held her gloved hand out for Midnight to nuzzle as her pet pushed closer. "It's a lovely day, isn't it?"

Obviously annoyed with his horse, Nicholas Griffon pulled himself together sufficiently to reply. "Hello . . . Lily." Abruptly, he kicked his feet from the stirrups and bounded to the ground to take control of Midnight's head. "Watch him, there. Sometimes he's unpredictable."

Alix backed away a pace, leaving him to suffer the worst of it when Midnight abruptly crowded Nicholas away from Alix.

"What the devil? Midnight, old son, mind your manners," he admonished his horse, but found himself in a scuffle. "I'm sorry, he doesn't usually act like this," he protested, promptly losing his top hat when Midnight knocked it askew.

Alix struggled not to laugh as she came to his assistance. "He probably wants a treat," she suggested, reaching into her pocket for a lemon drop. It disappeared from her palm immediately, leaving Midnight with a surprised look that she had given him a candy. She stroked her pet's nose while Nicholas scooped his hat from the path.

"He's not usually so misbehaved," he explained, but then spotted the dog coming close to sniff around hopefully. "Scat!" he ordered, making the terrier cringe away.

"Oh, don't!" Alix pled instantly, but he misunderstood her entreaty and caught her arm as she reached for the terrier.

"Be careful!"

"No, it's all right! I-I know this dog," she stammered, hurrying to lift him protectively. Now she not only had a horse pushing against her back companionably but also was cuddling a stray dog. Fortunately, Nicholas was so stunned, he did not realize it when she slipped Midnight another lemon drop and shifted the terrier more securely. "He's a surprising little gentleman that's been following me for a few days. He's a little thin but should fill out admirably, don't you think?"

"Well, I . . . ," he replied hesitantly, and then Midnight suddenly lifted his head and tried to steal his hat. "Stop that!"

"He's mischievous, isn't he?"

"More so than usual, I daresay."

"It must be the weather," she suggested inanely, moving along to distract the horse. "He's quite the character."

Nicholas caught his balance as Midnight pushed him after her. The normally unflappable man was disgruntled and cast a confused look at his horse as Midnight fell in line at Alix's back. Despite the critical barbs in his eyes, whatever he was about to say was interrupted when Midnight helped himself to a snack of her bonnet ribbons.

"Here." Nicholas jerked on the reins. "What the devil has gotten into you?" They reached the street, lined with waiting cabbies outside the tall iron gates. A line of hooded prams packed the sidewalk near benches where nannies chatted in the shade. "Would you care for a taxi?" Nicholas offered considerately.

"Oh, no, thank you," Alix declined, releasing the dog to the ground. With any luck, he might wander away a bit to investigate and Nicholas would ride on. "I like to walk."

"Wait," he cautioned, and then guided her through the passing traffic to the opposite side of the street. "At least let me offer you a ride on Midnight Star. He's really very docile," he added quickly, misreading her doubtful look at the saddle.

Nicholas had no idea what he had just offered, but she was not reckless enough to add stealing his horse to her lengthy list of transgressions. Since he intended only that she sit on his saddle while he led his horse along, Alix politely declined. Midnight would not understand why she was acting so strangely. "Thank you, you're very kind, but I really do like to walk."

Midnight abruptly towed him after her when she started down the street, still attempting to reach her ribbons. "I say, Midnight Star's developed a quite a fondness for your bonnet."

She resisted the urge to swat Midnight for being a nuisance and collected the fluttering strings beneath her collar. "It's probably because they're green," she said, fabricating a reason for his fixation. It was fortunate that it did not have silk flowers as decoration, because he really fancied those. She stepped off the curb, just as a foursome of white horses careened around the corner, pulling a white carriage.

"Wait!" Nicholas abruptly pushed her back as the terrier dashed, barking furiously, at the oncoming horses. The driver shouted and stood in his box to haul on the reins, pulling the coach to a precipitous halt in the middle of the street.

"Hoy there, Lord Griffon! Is milady all right?" the driver called. Sarah's red hair appeared when she lowered the coach window.

Nicholas stepped out to meet him angrily. "You should bleeding well watch where you're going! Don't you know there're speed limits in the city?"

Sarah laughed as she poked her head through the window. "Yoo-hoo! Lily, is that you? What're you doing in the street? Hello, Nicholas!"

"Good afternoon, Sarah." He paused to lift his top hat stiffly, but no sooner had he replaced it than Midnight playfully pushed it askew.

Alix stared at the coach assiduously, struggling to control a laugh. "Hello, Sarah . . . I suppose I should watch where I'm going."

"I understand it's particularly helpful when stepping into the street! Since we nearly killed you, it would be the polite thing to offer you a ride, at least!"

Recognizing it as the simplest solution, Alix conceded. "If you insist," she replied, as the driver opened the door with a contrite bow.

"What about you, Nicholas? Won't you join us?"

He declined as he helped Alix into the carriage. "Midnight Star needs a bit of exercise."

"Oh, why don't the two of you join us when we go up to Stragglethorpe this weekend? Sam and John want to do a little fishing. Oh, Lily! We could have such a grand time! What do you say, Nicholas? You and Johnny have been appointed to almost the same committees. Please, please come! It's only for a week!"

"I'll check my calendar," Nicholas pledged hesitantly, as he stepped back for the driver to close the door.

"Would you like to come and visit my childhood home, Lily?" Sarah asked, reaching for Alix's hand.

Alix automatically collected the terrier when he jumped into her lap. He was already becoming a fixture, but she had no idea if he would be accepted. Sarah did not even seem to notice him, but Nicholas's gaze landed on the dog as he settled in his saddle. "I'm sure it's beautiful," she replied ambiguously.

"I'll see you in a while," Nicholas tipped his hat in farewell, and without another word, Midnight carried him away.

"Don't worry," Sarah insisted, reaching for Alix's hand as the coach jolted into motion. "Johnny'll make sure Nicholas agrees to come along. You can bring your dog, too . . . My goodness, Lily, don't you ever feed him? What's his name?"

"He's a stray," she admitted hesitantly. "He doesn't have a name."

"He seems to like you. What does Nicholas say?"

"I don't know."

"Well, my goodness, you'd better think of a name straightaway if you plan to keep him!"

"Don't worry, I will."

CHAPTER 16

WINSTON'S CONFESSION

⊙❧≈⧾≈❧⊙

*T*he gentle trilling of evening replaced the shimmering of cicadas. Quenton blew a puff of smoke at mosquitoes hovering in the balmy twilight and sipped his bourbon. Crimson clouds stretched in the azure distance as the evening awoke without promise of stars and the feeble moon hid from a change of weather.

If his ride home had been lackluster, it was not due to his Friesian saddle horse, for Chiron had pranced along the road with typical savoir faire. Quenton had returned across the bridge wearing the same suit of clothes that he had donned in the morning, when his life still bore some normalcy. The garments were not as crisp as they had been, but neither was Quenton's thinking. His usual preoccupation with his life's resurrection had dissolved in his recognition that the process had renewed something sinister.

The letter did not appear threatening; in fact, it was so innocuous looking that he had not even realized what it was until he had opened it to read it, without an inkling of its meaning. That was when he had realized the letter was meant not for him but for his brother. Stunned, he had examined the envelope, but there was no mistake. The address read: *L'Honorable Marquis Henri Saint-Descoteaux, aux bons soins de Fontenot Porcelaine, Limoges Haute-Vienne, Limousin.* There was no confusion except on the part of the sender, although why someone would think to find Henri alive at *Fontenot Porcelaine* was as great a mystery as the letter, which was not even signed. One might expect it to carry cryptic or crucial information, but it was no more than a mundane message from someone who thought signing his name was superfluous.

Quenton had mulled over its contents during lunch at Georges, and when Moises Benoit had come into the restaurant, Quenton had put the opportunity to use by inviting his attorney to join him. Although Benoit's legal practice was far from Paris, it did not mean that the fellow was a third-rate poseur. So far, Quenton trusted the man's keen grasp of his precarious situation. Weeks had passed without a visit from the authorities who Quenton had anticipated would throw him out of his house.

"You shouldn't do anything," Moises had counseled over peach tart and coffee. "There's no reason to react. You go about your business, just like everyone else."

"You're suggesting I ignore this, but how? Who'd think my brother is still alive?"

"So what if anyone does," Moises shrugged. "It's just an old colleague who's mistakenly assumed the rumors of your brother's death are as exaggerated as yours were." He waved the subject away. "What matters more is that you're not dead, and as a French citizen, you're protected by a constitution that guarantees you not only civil liberties but the same inalienable rights as everybody else."

"The reason for my concern—"

"Of course, it's for your niece, is it not? This is one of the reasons you didn't bring her along with you; am I wrong? Now, take my advice and let it go. Whatever you do, you don't want this to end up in the newspapers. There's no sense in resurrecting those old charges, especially when your niece arrives. You see why it's better just to burn this letter. Get rid of it now, before someone wonders why you're keeping it."

"You're right, of course," Quenton had agreed then, but later, alone in his office at Fontenot, he had been unable to dispose of it. He had finally replaced it in his pocket, determined to discard it later.

Now, as he had come outside to enjoy his cigar, he could not quite touch a flame to the paper. Ordinarily, he did not consider himself a superstitious man, nor did he harbor a desire to cling to the past. Yet he was undeniably gratified to see his brother's name written on a letter, as if the horrible deeds of that day had vanished, leaving Henri alive and the future whole. Soon Alix would be where she belonged, and considering respectable suitors for her hand. The approving of a husband should have been Henri's job, but it was somehow as if the letter were a missive passing that torch. After she was settled, Quenton could focus on a family of his own. The idea of children's voices echoing through the silences of Chênes Noir filled him with anticipation.

His laughter surprised him and hushed the evening serenade, leaving the musical fountain to fill the silence. What would he do about Henri's letter? Its unwarranted appearance was a trick without meaning. Whatever its sender imagined by its conception, Quenton would not rush back to England to live in fear. He knew he should destroy it but kept it instead, as a talisman for the future.

WHEN FRISK'S QUESTIONING of Jenny Smith predictably fell flat, Nicholas summoned Percival, determined to learn the truth about the woman impersonating Lily. He strode through the library doors to find the butler shelving books at the far end of the room. "I say, Winston, am I late?"

Percival placed the volume in his hand and turned with a bow. "Good afternoon, milord. I was a bit early, so I decided to put away a few books," he explained as he came to join Nicholas.

"I take no more offense at keeping things organized than the next man," Nicholas replied. He positioned the wing chair opposite his desk and then walked around to his own. "Please sit down."

"Thank you." The butler waited until Nicholas was settled before taking a seat. "Am I to presume this is about the dog milady brought home today?"

Nicholas immediately found Winston's ignorance promising. If he were to sack Percival, it would involve getting rid of the man's entire family, and their tenure with the household exceeded two generations. "You didn't know about the dog?"

"I beg your pardon for asking, milord, but how could I, if she only just brought it home?"

"Apparently, it's been following her for days."

Winston hesitated thoughtfully. "Ah, I thought I heard a dog when I knocked on her door . . . I beg your pardon, milord."

Nicholas clasped his hands together on the desktop blotter. "I would've thought she'd confide in you."

Winston's surprise was evident. "Me?"

Nicholas pushed away from his desk and rose to pace. "Yes, why not?"

"Forgive me, milord—but why would she?"

"Perhaps the pithier question is, why would she not?"

Percival blinked at him blankly and then looked around the room with a stupefied frown that was hard to mistake. Either he was a good enough actor to be onstage, or Nicholas might be assured that his butler was not part of Lily's conspiracy. Still, he had to be certain. He went to stare into the fireplace, to allow the butler a moment of reflection. If Winston were going to confess to his part, now would be the time to do so.

"Milord, I'm afraid I don't quite know what to say."

"Say anything you'd like, but it'd be better if you started with the details surrounding how she came here."

"You mean, when did she arrive?"

Nicholas turned from the fire to see that the butler's incredulity was fixed in place. "Yes, you *do* know whom I'm referencing, don't you?" He noticed that the library doors were still open, and went to close them for privacy's sake. "The impostor," he clarified, when Percival remained silent.

"How would I know? Didn't you ask Quincy?"

"Quincy!" It was Nicholas's turn to reflect over the connection that he had previously suspected. He waited as Winston went to the liquor cabinet and began his confession.

"Yes . . . Quincy promised he would speak with you before he left. Well, of course . . . when he brought you home in such a state . . . Naturally, you were in no condition to ask, but I'd assumed that he'd explained everything."

Nicholas could not remember if Quincy had or not, but he took the butler's word for the moment, since he had no other choice.

"He said it was important to keep mum—please don't say it was all poppycock!"

Nicholas accepted the scotch the butler delivered and

tasted it with a wave at the liquor cabinet. "Don't stand on ceremony; feel free. I daresay you look as if you could use one."

"Thank you, milord."

Nicholas returned to his chair and reassessed the situation while the butler poured himself a drink. "You might as well bring the decanter over," he advised. "Did Quincy tell you who she is?"

"No." Winston returned to the desk fully equipped and topped off Nicholas's drink, before putting the bottle aside. "If you still don't mind," he said of the chair, and arranged his coattails silently. "He said only that she was someone from his old family where he worked in France. Or maybe it wasn't France, but he speaks French . . . No, blast it! He didn't even say he was French—he just said he was *many things*."

"I can vouch for that, the bloody beggar," Nicholas returned sourly.

"He did state plainly that he'd been in touch with her guardian and that he expected him to contact you shortly. When you began to take milady out for dinner and to a few shows, I assumed you were only trying to keep her entertained."

"Oh, come now, Mr. Winston!" Nicholas pushed himself away from the desk. "I wasn't entertaining anyone, least of all myself," he said, emphatically denying the insinuation. Though he had an inkling that he might be protesting too much, that sort of nonsense was the last thing he needed circulating. "And, to date, I haven't been contacted by anyone."

"You haven't?"

"No. As a matter of fact, I'd barely discovered that Lily was missing, when it became obvious that you were already privy to it. Frankly, Percival, it puts you in a suspicious light."

"Me?" the butler echoed, mystified again. "What did I do? Do you think I'm an accomplice?"

Nicholas turned away from his innocent pose and went to the window, where he gazed down at an empty curb. All of a sudden, he recalled when Quincy had brought the impostor into their midst. It had been the afternoon after Lily's disappearance, when she had supposedly spent the night with her friend Beth D'Arcy, after the D'Arcys had already sailed for Europe. That was why she had panicked and nearly throttled herself when his cuff buttons had snagged on her bonnet strings and tangled around her throat. Lily had probably filled her with stories about how Lily came and went as she pleased.

"Aren't you?" Nicholas pressed the butler.

"No—I . . . I only found out when Quincy asked me to care for her! He said he had been called away and gave his resignation."

"Well, then why don't you tell me what he said?"

He saw the realization of what was at stake finally occur to the butler. Winston looked around the room uncertainly and ran his fingers through his thinning hair as he dropped his eyes to the floor. "I don't know . . . I was polishing silver, actually. Young Percy came to fetch me, explaining that Mr. Hill was waiting in my office. He said he didn't recognize Quincy at first, until Quincy revealed himself. I didn't quite believe it until I walked into my office and saw him myself. A more astonishing change, I've never—"

"Yes, yes," Nicholas interrupted. He recalled that transformation, because he had seen it as well. The man's haircut and shave had revealed a cleft in his chin and dimples the same as those in the painting of Quincy upstairs. With his hair combed back, his distinguished brow and widow's peak were apparent. Nicholas turned from his post abruptly and rejoined the butler. "What did he say?"

"Well, firstly, he said he resigned. When I asked if it was due to his obvious change in fortune, he said that he had received a summons to return home."

"A summons."

"Yes, that is the exact phrase he used: 'a summons from home.'"

"Where is this home?"

"He didn't say."

Nicholas recalled something of the sort from when he and Quincy had been drinking in the stableman's room. He pushed aside the awkward disparity of drinking in a servant's quarters and pursued the butler's explanation: "He told me that it was business."

"Yes, I suppose. And when I asked why he was not more forthcoming, he claimed that years ago, when he came to England, he brought with him a child from his old family. He said her father spared no expense with her education, and cautioned that if the secret got out, the scandal alone could ruin your reputation."

"Yes, well, he was right about something, at least." Winston's abrupt finish left Nicholas facing the gaping hole in his shoddy memory. "He didn't say anything more?"

"Only that she likes bacon, but for me to attest either way—"

"Bah," Nicholas cut him off. "Never mind—what the devil difference does that make? These people could be gypsies, for all we know."

"Gypsies!"

"Aye, why not? The continent is overrun with them, especially after the wars—always looking for a dupe to make a penny on."

"Milord, I hardly think—"

"Did Quincy Hill admit to any established facts, such as anyone's name or where they're from?"

"No, milord—but nothing about Quincy Hill has ever suggested such a history!"

"If they're gypsies and I approach the impostor for the truth, she'd reveal nothing but the same kind of nonsense that Quincy gave to you."

"I can't agree, milord. Quincy spoke of her with affection."

"He would, wouldn't he? Haven't you looked at her?"

"I didn't get the impression that Quincy was lying—only that he spoke a limited truth."

"Then that's the extent of it?"

"Yes, milord; he asked me to care for her until her guardian came. He said that he notified him over the weekend of the races at Oxley Commons and thought he'd be contacting you any day. Other than leading me to believe she was a member of the family he'd once worked for, he promised to explain the situation to you before he left. He accompanied you up to the house and then went to catch his ship. That's really all I know, but I must say, it explains a great deal about a few delightful differences I can't have failed to notice."

Nicholas did not need those delightful differences catalogued; he had enough in his own store. "Very well," he granted. "If that's all of it, then you may go—but with a word of caution to keep this under wraps for the time being."

"Don't worry about my keeping mum—but do you mind if I ask your plan?"

"Simply to carry on as we've done before, Winston, until I'm able to get to the bottom of this, before the press gets wind of anything. Should I go to Scotland Yard prematurely, the cost might be everything for the woman upstairs, unless I can learn what's happened to Lily. From what you tell me, if Quincy Hill is a gypsy, then this impostor may've been stolen from her family as a child. Send a note to Terrence Poole, will you? Have him meet me at the office tomorrow morning."

"Terrence Poole, of Poole Investigations?"

"Yes. Make it at nine—no, wait, better yet, eight thirty. That will leave him plenty of time to make arrangements. Once I know which ship Quincy sailed on, then I'll know his destination. That will be all, unless you have any further questions for me."

Winston paused as he rose to leave. "Just one, milord: What are we going to do about the dog?"

"Nothing for now—it'll distract her from questions that might arise during the investigation. We've been invited out of town for a few days, so we'll be leaving to Stragglethorpe this weekend. In the meanwhile, just make sure to feed it. The blasted thing's a disgrace."

"I SAY, I'VE NO IDEA WHAT YOU MEAN!" Albert Frisk's exasperation rang through the dressing room, but Jenny's curt response cut it off.

"You know exactly what I mean, you bounder!"

"Ouch, Miss Jenny!" he yelped at a resounding slap. "I must say, that violence is uncalled for!"

"Albert Frisk, you're fortunate that I'm the type of woman who keeps my thoughts to meself!" Jenny's angry retort ended with a slamming of the door that rattled perfume vials and sent talc canisters careening across the floor. "The cheek!"

Alix cautiously peered around the edge of the wardrobe. "I suppose this means you'll not be joining him for tea."

"Tea!" Jenny fumed, feeling for pins holding her flowered

hat. "Why, I'll never share another cuppa with that rake!"

"Oh. I'm sorry." Alix returned to the wardrobe to look for a cooler blouse.

"You're sorry? Why, when you don't have anything to do with it? Here, what're you doing in there?"

The depths of the clothes muffled Alix's response. "I'm looking for a blouse."

"Come out and let me do it."

"This is your afternoon off. You shouldn't be here."

"I'm back to work, milady," Jenny insisted emphatically.

Alix paused to meet her imposing look and retreated meekly. "Why are you upset with Albert?"

"Upset—who, me?" Jenny's voice got lost as she vanished inside the wardrobe, but then she poked out her head and peered at Alix. "What am I looking for?"

"Only something a little cooler, you know."

"It's warmed up nicely, now that the fog has burned off. Here we are," Jenny concluded, reappearing with an ecru lace blouse. "This'll work nicely, don't you think?"

"Yes, that's fine," Alix consented, unbuttoning her starched pintuck. "If Albert didn't do anything to upset you, then why are you angry with him?"

"I'm not angry; I just caught him at lunch with Martha."

"Martha the chambermaid?"

"She's the one."

"Weren't you dropping by the abbey?"

"I finished earlier than expected, didn't I? I thought I'd surprise him."

"Well, it sounds as if you did," Alix murmured, stripping off the stifling blouse.

"I'm sorry?"

"Exactly," Alix amended. "I am, too."

The maid held the lacy top for her to slip into and took the other to the laundry chute. Alix turned to avoid the harmless door, troubled by an earlier dream of climbing inside a laundry chute as a child and tumbling out onto Quenton's dressing-room floor. He was so surprised that he cut his chin while shaving. "Everyone could use a little fresh air now and then," she added weakly, haunted by her dream of squeezing through the chilling depths of the château. "A walk sometimes helps."

"You're taking the dog out again?"

Alix arranged the lace collar in the mirror and watched Jenny sweep up spilled powder, thankful for the diversion. "No, but perhaps you should invite Albert for a walk instead of working—you know, just to sort things through."

"Albert's trying to outwit me. That's a man for you, always thinking the grass is greener next door."

"Well, it's a fact, you know: The grass does looks greener from a distance. It's the perspective . . ." Alix trailed off under the weight of Jenny's glare.

"I was not talking about grass. Oh, fie." Jenny paused, retrieving one of the fallen perfume vials from where it had rolled, by the washstand. "The lid's come off."

Alix turned when she saw in reflection that it was her rose perfume, the only possession she had brought from the farm. It was more than just her favorite perfume; it was the only scent she liked to wear. She'd had the vial for so long that she did not know when she had acquired it, but until now she had taken it for granted.

"Thank goodness it didn't spill everywhere, but it's nearly empty, don't you think?"

"I've never noticed before."

"Well, there're plenty of other perfumes to wear," Jenny said, fitting the crystal stopper.

"But I like this one."

Confidently, Jenny peered underneath the bottle. "We'll order some more—but wait, this doesn't have a label."

"Does it need it?"

"Every perfume I've ever seen comes with one," the maid explained, glancing at Alix knowledgeably. "It says who makes it, so when it's empty, you can get more of the same."

"It's never had a label."

"Well, then where'd you get it?"

"It has its own box," Alix replied, turning to look through the dressing-table drawers in search of the velvet container, instead of answering the question.

Jenny went to the highboy and opened the middle drawer. "I put it with the jewelry chest to keep it safe. It's distinctive enough that someone might notice it. It's purple, isn't it?"

"Yes, that's right."

"It's not going to do much good," the maid decided as she retrieved it and gave it a cursory inspection. "There's not a label on the box anywhere."

"There must be something," Alix refuted, dismissing the maid's overt speculation as she took it to examine for herself. The pentagonal box, covered with tucked velvet, was the same as ever, and the tiny edelweiss emblazoned on the inside of the lid did not mean anything.

"What's this?" Jenny asked helpfully, pinching a bit of the folded fabric.

"It's only where the velvet is tucked—"

"No, look!" the maid insisted, pulling it loose. The entire bottom lifted away, revealing a folded card beneath. "Fie, what a place to put something! It's like one of those magic boxes!"

"Is it a label?" Alix asked, trying to see it.

"You'd better read it." The maid handed it over generously.

"It looks like nonsense to me."

"Glory, it's an order form—just what we need!" Alix hesitated. "You can't read?"

"I read enough," the maid sniffed dismissively, and busied herself restoring the lining to the box, before putting it away. "The money for school was better spent on my brothers' futures. Now, I'd better get this mess cleared away. Once you have your order ready, I'll run it to the post office myself."

Alix looked at the perfumery address, in Grasse, France. "I wonder how long it will take to arrive." She had the one order card, and only a blank address to complete for a return shipment. Heading for the desk in the sitting room, she determined to copy it faithfully. "I'll have this ready in a minute."

"I'll take it straight away."

Alix retrieved a note card and uncorked the inkwell, pulling up the chair to jot notes about the perfumery and the order number. The series, beginning *2-5-1-21,* was as much gibberish to her as the rest was to Jenny. "You'll go alone?" she asked, when the maid came into the sitting room, pinning on her hat.

"Of course."

Alix ran the blotter across the Westminster address she had finished inscribing, feeling awkward about using such a transitory destination for its delivery. She wished to put her own London post drop for Sterling Wood Stable, but without Quenton's help, there was no way to retrieve it. Finally, she handed it over to the maid. "Albert might wish to walk with you."

"That'll be the day."

"I'm sure as you walk along, you'll think of the right things to say."

Jenny hesitated. "What do you mean by 'the right things'?"

"You know . . . how you felt when you found him sitting with Martha. From the way he sounded at the door, I think it safe to assume he hasn't a clue about how you've come to admire him."

"*Admire him!* Why, he's a scoundrel!"

"If you think about it from his viewpoint . . . Well, you know how men are. Quite possibly he was going to lunch, and he saw Martha going to lunch, and they just ended up going to lunch at the same time. After all, men have to eat, don't they? I can't pretend to know about your brothers, but every man I've ever seen likes to eat, especially when they're working. Do your brothers get hungry?"

Jenny tucked the card into her coat pocket. "Fie, they'd eat the larder bare if Mum let them."

"You can't let Albert Frisk go around ravenous, can you? Why don't you invite him to tea? That way, he can eat a biscuit or two while you chat about what happened."

"Haven't you listened to a word I've said?"

"Do your brothers like biscuits with their tea?"

Jenny buttoned her coat. "Those four louts could eat an elephant if someone cooked it first."

"Exactly. I don't know a man who doesn't eat well, except for one of those peckish sorts. Albert Frisk doesn't strike me as one of those; does he strike you as one?"

"Albert?" Jenny wondered, pausing on her way to the door. "Why, no, not at all. He's not one of those overstuffed sorts, either. He keeps himself fit, doesn't he?"

"Yes, and he doesn't strike me as a weakling. After all, he's been carting coal and collecting your parcels lately, hasn't he? He must have strong arms, at least."

Jenny nodded. "Of course. In fact, when he rolls up his sleeves, it's easy to see how strong he is."

"In that case, I think eating would be necessary, don't you?"

"No one could expect a man like that to live on air."

"Even if he had to share his table with someone, he'd still be eager to sit down to a meal after working all morning, wouldn't he?"

"Yes, I suppose he would."

"Good. I'll see you after your tea with Albert."

Jenny turned to her. *"My* tea? Who said *I'm* having tea with Albert?"

Heading for the other door before the maid gainsaid her proposal, Alix replied, *"You* did, remember? And see he eats a few biscuits," she added, as she stepped into the front hall and the terrier dashed past. "He'll need plenty to keep his big, strong muscles."

ALIX HAD BEGUN WITH A BALLAD, but it had transformed into Beethoven's *Moonlight Sonata* when her fingers strayed along with her thoughts. For a magic moment, the bright English parlor faded in the shadowed recesses of a deep conservatory with colorful frescoes and a piano surrounded by potted palms. A white frieze of horses galloped from the marble above the enormous fireplace. The vision faded, but not the memory. It remained behind, another piece of her past reclaimed.

Somehow, the junkman's dog had climbed up to lie in her lap. He pricked his pointed ears pleasantly at the changing tunes but jumped down to charge the door with a barrage of barking at their unwitting host's unprecedented intrusion.

"Oh no!" Alix gasped, almost tripping on her skirts in her haste to stifle the dog. To his credit, Lily's husband spared a cool glance for the unseemly attack and continued on his way to the hearth while Alix scrambled to contain the clamor.

"I'm sorry," she said when silence settled.

A fleeting smile quirked his lips after his boisterous welcome. "Hello," he responded with a swift survey of the room. "I didn't mean to interrupt."

"Oh, but you didn't!" Alix rushed to assure him, and belatedly bit her tongue on her too-quick response. Collecting her sister's disdainful reserve, she released the recalcitrant dog without a scolding and clasped her hands together as the terrier slunk beneath the nearest chair.

"Please, play if you wish."

"I was finished, thank you."

He seemed unconvinced as he watched the butler's silent entrance to arrange the tea tray—or maybe he was distracted by the terrier crawling on his stomach toward the plate of biscuits in an overdue display of discretion. "I thought you might wish to know the arrangements, since we're leaving this weekend to Stragglethorpe to accompany the Wesleys. Sarah's brother Sam has gone on ahead, of course. We'll be escorting Sarah's cousin Mary." He noted her hesitation and moved toward the couch. "We might as well sit and enjoy a cup of tea; there's no reason to remain standing, is there?"

Alix looked at the door wistfully but went along when he took her arm to guide her to a seat.

"Since Stragglethorpe is near Nottingham, we'll take a schooner up to Skegness and travel overland from there. The voyage shouldn't take too long if we catch the tide."

"Of course," Alix answered uncomfortably, while pouring his tea. She was supposed to know his preferences, but she had not a clue about how he liked his cup. As she fussed with the pot, she could not summon an image of him drinking tea.

The sight of the creamer in her nervous grip softened his austerity. "Just a drop, if you don't mind. I'll forgo the sugar for a twist of lemon . . . That is perfect, thank you."

When Alix passed him his cup, his hand embraced her fingertips—whether by foul or by accident, she did not know, but she felt her face flame. Grateful for Lily's makeup to shield her embarrassment, she fumbled with her own tea while he filled the silence with details of their agenda.

"It'll still necessitate a night on the road, but it's faster than driving from London. I didn't think you'd mind, considering how you love to sail."

Alix absorbed this informative tidbit silently, unable to define his intent. Was he instructing her about how to carry on as Lily? She wondered, since he had yet to summon the Metropolitan Police. For herself, she did not remember ever having sailed on a ship, although she must have at least once, or she would not be in England. The idea of an ocean voyage excited her; she imagined a map of the rugged coast, though she failed to summon the location of Skegness. Nottingham, she knew about from reading old tales of Robin of Loxley, and that gave her a hint of where they were heading. To think she might ride beneath trees where Robin Hood had once lived was thrilling.

Nicholas watched her critically, but the sharp barbs in his eyes had softened to a gentler inspection. To her surprise, he reached out to snag a biscuit from the tray to toss to the terrier. "Have you named it yet?"

"No," she admitted.

"What about Limey?"

"Oh," Alix sighed, repressing a sardonic response. Who would name a dog something so disagreeable? "I don't think so."

"Spot?"

She struggled not to roll her eyes, watching the dog lick crumbs from his chops. "No."

"Whitey?"

Alix promptly hid her reply in her teacup. When she surfaced, she managed a smile. "I'll think of something."

"Ah, well." He finished his own cup and spoke with confidence as he put it aside. "I'm sure you will. If you'll excuse me, I must be off. Don't worry about anything; I'll make sure Frisk shares the schedule with your maid."

Alix found another bright spot in the upcoming adventure. Nothing could speed love's wings faster than a romantic change in surroundings. "Thank you." She realized that she was smiling when he stopped to look at her as he neared the door, but instead of speaking his mind, he left quietly.

CHAPTER 17

VOYAGE TO SKEGNESS

❦

𝓣he bitter wind promised snow. Robert adjusted his great cloak and buckled the toggles beneath his fur mantle. Julius shifted uneasily beneath him, swiveling his tail to the cutting gusts. After digging into fur-lined gauntlets, Robert picked up the reins and moved his sturdy horse onto the open road. Julius reluctantly lowered his head and trudged uphill in the stiff downdraft from the cliffs.

Robert would not be long, and when this was finished, he did not plan to come this way again. He had been here only once before and wondered at his decision now, but if he waited longer, the weather could be worse.

Julius puffed with exertion up the lonely grade. For a highway, there was not much traffic besides the locals, unless a stage from Geneva or a merchant caravan passed, but with the change of seasons, none would dare this road much longer. Winter came early in the high country, and Robert had not passed more than a few shepherds and a monk since he had left Moûtiers. No matter—he found the solitude agreeable.

When the castle appeared through the trees, he did not

slow his horse but changed direction. The forest swallowed the pointed rooftops and thickened when the track angled from the open road. Julius appreciated the shelter it offered from the wind but twisted his ears as the gales' fury rattled the copse. Robert followed the unkempt track deeper into the forest, through the dark trees.

The great gates closed on the road sooner than he had expected and were higher than he remembered. The rustle of the wind in the forest was his only greeting. Robert turned Julius beside the wall and stood on the saddle. It took him an instant to scale to the top. On the opposite side, he opened the gate and beckoned his horse through with a short whistle. After he mounted again, he urged Julius faster.

Robert had expected the place to be abandoned, but caretakers would secure the grounds. On a day like today, they might be anywhere, and he had not come to answer questions. Wary of activity, he rode through the wilderness around the fringes of old gardens.

Reaching the lonely graveyard in this roundabout fashion, he spurred Julius through its rusted gates. The moaning wind swept away the sound of his horse on the gravel road as Robert rode in search of the tomb he knew he would find, slowing Julius only when he reached the white granite crypt.

He recognized it at once. A single cross sealed its black doors, which did not bear the name of its occupant. He felt riveted to his saddle. It was worthless to have ridden all this way to stare at the engraving of a cross. He stepped down and crunched his boots on the gravel. A gust of wind tried to take his hat, so he moved to the lee of the mausoleum.

What did he expect to find? Men died every day. Sometimes they went in sleep, and other times when they least expected. They died in flood, famine, sickness, by happenstance or in war, and the lucky ones went with a family weeping for their loss. What could any man say about the prospect of dying, when it was the inevitable conclusion to life?

He found the need to clear his throat as the wind whipped into a whistle around charnel houses and forgotten tombstones.

"Henri."

The lonely wind howled in answer, and scattered with it whatever he had come to say. The place did not dissolve as smoke in a magician's mirror, and the stone doors did not split open. Robert lifted his eyes away from the sepulchre and scanned the bleakness around him for witnesses, but he was alone in the graveyard. Determinedly, he touched the frigid cross marking the doors to the crypt.

"There wasn't time to say good-bye."

The wind moaned. Had he anticipated absolution? Resolutely, he clamped his hat back onto his head and retreated to his horse. Julius did not shift when he climbed into the saddle. Robert took a final look at the unmarked grave, then spurred the horse toward the gate as a flake of snow found him.

THE ADVENTURE BEGAN with the morning tide on a Lion Shipping topsail schooner. Whether from Alix's excitement or because the owner was aboard, it seemed that the sails snapped crisply even in the lackluster fog. She would have preferred to remain topside but went belowdecks to the cabin with Sarah, while poor Cousin Mary retired early to the captain's cabin, seasick before they even left the river.

It was to be a quick trip up the coast, and Sarah promised that when the fog lifted, they would be able to see the distant shore. Alix hoped by then her friend would like to venture out onto the deck, because there was too much to see to be closeted. In their tiny cabin, Alix sat opposite Sarah at a small table, sipping tea with cream and nibbling on crumpets with honey, as unseen bridges over the Thames sailed by. While Sarah made herself comfortable with her magazine, Alix strained her eyes to catch a glimpse of something beyond the splash of water and the mist through the portholes. Finally, she resignedly retrieved her borrowed copy of *The Odyssey* and fed her crumpet to the dog.

She was unaware when the fog broke apart. She was determined to keep the terrier from being a nuisance, and lifted her eyes from the page when he slipped off her lap. He cocked his head to the side and pricked his ears, looking at her expectantly. "Oh, don't tell me . . ."

Her comment drew Sarah's attention. "Is something the matter?"

"He wants out, of course. I've lost track of time reading," Alix explained, reaching for the door.

"The wind is going to ruin your hair."

Alix laughed gently, stepping into the narrow corridor to follow the scampering dog. "That's what bonnets are for."

"Milady." The first mate bowed when she emerged. "Lords Griffon and Wesley are astern. Please, allow me to escort you."

"Thank you," Alix replied. She did not wish to find the pair as much as she was afraid of getting lost. Not only would a wandering Lady Griffon be an embarrassing gaffe, but the ship was full of rough sailors whose job it was to sail it. They were on their best behavior with their employer onboard, but who knew how accountable any one of them might be if she chanced upon them unescorted?

Apprehensively, she followed the jaunty dog trotting ahead. He traveled on four legs until reaching the narrow steps to the upper deck. Alix took it as a hopeful sign that his injuries were healing. Already the rope-worn rawness on his neck was fading, and he had an air of buoyancy that promised he was feeling better. With daily baths, his white fur had become snowy, and what she had initially thought was ingrained filth had transformed into a sable-and-tan mask on his head and face. Anyone who looked at the terrier would think him gaunt to the point of emaciation, but Alix believed his bony appearance was lessening, even if his former neglect was still apparent.

The wind tore at her skirt. As the first mate strode into the open across the quarterdeck, Alix hesitated to secure her fluttering ribbons and gather her dress to keep it from ballooning in the shifting wind. Cries from the pirouetting seagulls above the mizzenmast punctuated the splashing of the ship and the slapping of the rigging. Shouts relayed orders to sailors scaling rope and crawling along spars in towering masts where billowing sails were brilliant against the blue marble sky. To the east, Alix saw the dark coastline marked their scudding progress north, but she had hesitated overlong, and the mate hurried toward the poop deck without noticing that she had failed to follow.

The terrier sat on his haunches and regarded her quizzically, as if awaiting her decision. Instead of venturing across the quarterdeck, where an unwarranted wind gust might lift her skirts in an unseemly display, she decided to edge away from unwitting disaster and turned toward the protection of the forecastle at the bow.

Despite her earlier trepidation, the sailors were too busy to notice her or do more than cast a cursory glance at the dog trotting past. Alix slipped around the foremast and, buffeted by the wind, came to a stop where she could watch the bowsprit challenge the waves. A herd of gray seal cut across their path in the distance, swimming for a faraway beach past rowboats with fishermen tending the nets dragged by larger trolleys.

The viewpoint was the same as the painted design on Nicholas's porcelain dishes, but instead of sailing into a nameless harbor, the schooner skirted the shore. The fishing boats were different, but they created a connection that formed a memory of the familiar cathedral by the seawall scene on the household teacups. Alix had seen it thus, sailing into the Bay of Lyon in the Mediterranean, during her long-ago and forgotten lifetime.

"Hello."

A sharp bark from the dog helped to disguise her startled reaction to Nicholas's unexpected advance from the quarter-deck. "Quiet," she admonished the terrier, scraping together the sensibility to smile. "Hello," she replied, scooping up the dog while trying not to appear as disoriented as she felt.

Nicholas smiled in return, but his eyes held secretive amusement. He joined her, and removed his hat before losing it in the wind. "That's the Norfolk Klif." He pointed out the brown smear of land to the left. "The Wash looks deceptive, but it's too shallow for ships. That little town on the edge of the beach is Hunstanton."

Alix did not recognize the names but suddenly remembered the famous white cliffs that had been her first sight of England. The memory returned with throbbing pain through her old scar, and an overwhelming sense of numbing oppression.

Fortunately, Nicholas was too distracted to notice her confusion, as he called up an order to the sailor clinging to the foremast. "Six degrees starboard, and drop the mainsail!" Behind them, someone echoed the order as the ship's captain approached.

"I'm sorry, milord! The navigator—"

"This is a devil of a place to take a nap, Perry. Get more men up the mizzen and trim those sails."

"Yes, sir!" He saluted before hurrying away to call out orders.

Nicholas glanced at Alix apologetically while his command echoed in relay and men jumped in answer. "I'm sorry, but this crew isn't accustomed to having me onboard," he continued, clasping his hands behind his back. "I haven't traveled up the coast in a while."

Jenny had cautioned that Nicholas was a master who ran a tight ship, but Alix had never considered the man beyond his obvious connection to Lily. "Oh," she replied, as the ship slowed. Men clambered like monkeys on the rope netting above, and Nicholas rode the deck so easily that he even steadied her as the bow shifted slightly north.

"The shoreline along here is sandy, and the shallows can wreak havoc even when the tide is high. More than one ship has gone aground in this area."

How he was able to determine so much by looking at the blank expanse of water was mystifying. "That would be unfortunate."

"Quite," he admitted with a brief laugh, and glanced at her speculatively. "I've just been below, checking the horses before we put ashore. I daresay they're ready to get off this ship, although John's hunter, Donny, doesn't seem to mind being down in the hold as much as Midnight Star does."

Alix nibbled on her lower lip to stifle a response that Donny Boy had more experience on a ship than Midnight did, since the colt had been brought over the Irish Sea from Wexford as part of an agreement between stables. It had been a surprise to see the young horse that she had culled from the racers and trained for the hunt over the winter. It had not been hard to deduce that John Wesley had purchased him shortly after her arrival in London, but observing the old stablemates together this far from Robbie's farm had been an oddly comforting coincidence.

"It won't be long before we dock," Nicholas continued. "It takes a bit of doing to put in at the pier. I daresay you'll be more comfortable below."

There was nothing Alix would have liked more than to stand at the bow and watch the approach of land, but she knew she would be in the way of the sailors hurrying to secure the enormous ropes and heavy chain spooled neatly near the bowsprit. "Of course," she conceded obligingly when he reached for her. Overhead, men scurried along the spars, working to furl the sails as the activity on deck increased and shouted orders changed as the ship straightened.

"Have you thought of a name for him yet?"

Alix looked blankly at the dog she carried. "No."

"There's always Laddie."

"I'll think of something."

Was he laughing? Nicholas averted his face to the sea but glanced at her circumspectly when he replaced his hat as they stepped into the relative shelter of the forecastle. "Ah, well— I'm certain a name will come in time." He guided her to the steps leading down to the cabin where Sarah waited. The ruddy-cheeked first mate waiting near the door snapped to attention and hastily opened it with a bow.

"Here we are," Nicholas stated needlessly. "Hello, Sarah."

"Hello, Nicholas! I see you've found Lily." Sarah laughed as Alix released the terrier and came in to join her.

He lounged against the door frame briefly, bracing himself against the uneven rise and fall of the ship. "As you might imagine, we've made good time up the coast and will be docking soon."

"Wonderful. Poor Mary is beyond ready, I'm sure. We'll let her know."

"Good. I daresay she'll be grateful for a little dry land. If you'll excuse me, I'm due topside," he replied with a nod at Alix, and pulled the door closed.

"Oh, Lily, I'm so jealous," Sarah laughed. "Only you could go out in the wind and look better than ever."

"Don't let my maid hear you say so," Alix replied, swiftly fixing her hair to restore her sister's image.

UNFORGIVING RAIN FELL from the leaden sky and washed the horizon. It drowned the river and swallowed boats in a showery veil. Smoke wreathed chugging chimneys and clung to eves around houses where occasional dogs barked half-heartedly from the comfort of shelter along the Paris highway. Chiron paced through the sodden landscape placidly, with nostrils narrowed and ears flattened by the rain. Quenton patted his black horse encouragingly. They could have taken the ferry all the way into Paris, but he had decided it was better to avoid any crowds.

Had it been left to him, Quenton would have entered the city unannounced, but someone, somewhere, had deemed his arrival worthy of a newspaper article. It was short and hidden near the editorials, but it cited Henri's name in connection with his own, stirring old scandal for eye-catching appeal. Quenton might have been the only one who noticed it, but he preferred not to tempt the Fates. He disembarked with his horse before entering the city gates and opted to ride to his hotel.

He followed a river of swollen sky after buildings claimed the horizon. Pigeons crowded in rain-washed alcoves above the empty Sunday sidewalks. In a passing tavern, a lone viola challenged a reluctant oboe, and Chiron's hoofbeats echoed the rhythm until it drowned. Quenton chose to ride a labyrinth of streets, despite the doubtful day, and turned from the north onto the avenue where his hotel was, to approach from an unanticipated direction. Years of looking over his shoulder in England had not dissipated easily. On the sidewalk, a man stood beneath an umbrella near the over-flowing fountain, a hackney waited under the awning, and a red-liveried doorman stood inside the lobby, watching the sheltered driveway.

A flock of pigeons surged aside when Quenton rode through their midst, and Chiron snorted the rain from his nostrils. Quenton collected his saddlebags as the doorman hurried out and a hostler ran to collect his horse.

"Come with me, milord." The liveried attendant bowed and signaled for the concierge as Quenton entered the lobby.

He shook the rain from his fedora and shrugged out of his sodden great cloak as the bellhop came to take his saddlebags. Bellhops and concierges were busy everywhere; Quenton snapped his fingers at a hatcheck to come along and collect his wet things.

"Right this way, milord," the man beckoned, leading him to a nearby office.

Quenton followed, wondering if Moises Benoit had anything to do with the impressive service, but realized belatedly he had walked into a trap set by the notorious secret police. He froze and lifted his hands away from his body as the uniformed officer in charge rose from his prominent chair, motioning for his men to seal the room.

"Quenton Riche-Ives Acelin Saint-Descoteaux?"

He had forgotten he had so many names. "Yes."

"I have a warrant for your arrest, on the charge of subversion."

For a stunned moment, he felt a ridiculous sense of relief. They had trumped up the old allegations against his brother, instead of charging him with the murder of the man he had found dead in the cave. "Would it help to maintain my innocence?" Why would he return with a plot to overthrow a cousin who was in the perfect position to help him? Quenton stood stoically when they relieved him of his sword and looted his pockets.

"As you may realize, tonight's lodging will not be what you expected," the gendarme captain warned primly, slapping a fine pair of white leather gloves against his palm to stress the importance of his position. "Tomorrow you'll have an opportunity to enter your plea with the King's magistrate. Until the court makes a decision, your belongings will be kept by the bailiff and reclaimed if you're released." He poked through Quenton's possessions with ill-concealed interest. "Take him away."

Quenton tempered his frustration with resignation that the arrest had been prearranged to demonstrate the efficiency of the secret police. Why else would a room have been reserved for staging the rank of soldiers who would march him out on display? It was of more interest than apprehending him alone in the rain, and proved that reestablished order reigned in the streets of Paris. Now he might warrant a headline in the *Gazette*. Especially since the captain's thumb paused when paging through the papers that his men seized from Quenton's pocket.

He cursed himself a thousandfold for playing the unwitting dupe, for he had become so accustomed to carrying Henri's letter that he had forgotten to leave it at Chênes Noir when he came to Paris.

෨෧

NICHOLAS COULD NOT REMEMBER the last time he had been in Skegness, but it was a regular stop for John, whose home was in the neighboring county. It was the first night of their journey, and the ladies wished to dine in and retire early. John dismissed the hotel bar as stuffy and took Nicholas on a tour of taverns along the waterfront. Nicholas had been in enough ports that they were all the same, except for the language. John had not been to sea since their days of chasing pirates for the King and still reveled in the old excitement of the Gold Coast. To Nicholas, those days were better forgotten. He found little glory in bloody memories of men dying by the sword or of cannonballs hitting below the waterline to sink entire ships to watery graves.

"Unless my investigator finds a quick answer to the impostor's identity and her connection to Quincy Hill's whereabouts, I think it's time to leave London."

John gave Nicholas a second look as they went for another round, and tugged him to a stop before they reached the crowded bar. "What do you mean? You're thinking of going home early?"

"A few weeks isn't early," Nicholas rationalized evenly. He had expected Wesley's reaction and pushed him forward. "Come on, if we don't get our drinks now, it might be a while. This place is packed."

"It's the weekend," John complained dismissively. "You can't just leave London at the drop of a hat—where's your sense of responsibility?"

"All the tariff reform I've submitted is effectively tabled by committee until next year. Everything else scheduled to come onto the floor is routine, and you're a capable proxy."

"Proxy? Who, me? Why?"

"Because I've asked and you've accepted."

"When did I accept?"

"Right now, and since you insist, the first round is on me. A couple of Mackinlays here," Nicholas ordered, palming a farthing onto the bar as John propped himself on his elbows to survey the crowded room.

"You're joking, old chum; I wasn't consenting."

"It sounded like it to me, and I accept. Thanks, Johnny. I can't tell you what it means."

"Wait a minute, Griffon!" John protested suspiciously. "This isn't about an investigation! It has to do with *her*, doesn't it?"

Nicholas swept up his drink from the bar. "I don't know what you're talking about."

"That's it, isn't it? You're intent on staying away from London. You're afraid someone is going to find out about her, before you've seduced her!"

"Even if I were, you should be more careful about casting such unfounded accusations."

"Oh, come on—admit it! This is Johnny you're trying to fool. Do you think I'd blame you? God knows I would've taken her away somewhere already!"

"Wesley, pull yourself together; it's nothing like that at all." Nicholas took his scotch to a nearby empty table and claimed a chair.

"Damn me, but I'm beginning to think you're stuck on your little bluestocking—not that I can say I'd blame you."

"Just because she plays a bit of music and might paint now and again—"

"Listen and learn, lad. Sarah said your friend was reading *The Odyssey* on the ship; buck up, old man. Any woman who reads Homer is a bluestocking."

"It's an act," Nicholas revealed, half-convinced. "I've found books in her proximity but not in her hands."

"I don't know where an impostor would come up with the impression that Lily's a bookworm, but the only real way to find out is to put it to the test. Time will tell—and we've a week together."

"Not that it matters," Nicholas said, dismissing his intimation.

"You can't tell me that you don't find it odd. She's a rather ripe-looking plum to be at loose ends. By now you must have some kind of clue about who she is and where she's from."

"I've naught, Johnny," Nicholas denied. "At least Sarah saw her with her nose stuck in *The Odyssey*. It's more than I'm privy to, except that she gave Roddy the slip, and I found her up on the bow, watching the spray."

"I've told you, mate: Let Sarah ferret out the details, and you decide what they're worth. Women can't keep secrets from one another."

"And I've told *you* before, Johnny: I'd rather keep Sarah out of it."

"Sarah's bound to realize something's amiss before very long."

"You know Lily better than any one of us, and yet she had you fooled until I started asking you questions, didn't she?"

"Yes, but as I've explained, I wasn't exactly paying attention. And speaking of Lily, what *are* you planning to do about finding her? When all this goes before the magistrate—"

"Don't worry; Even Scotland Yard won't discredit Terrence Poole and his investigation."

"Of Poole et al.? Of course not, when he's lured away some of the finest detectives ever trained by the Metropolitan Police."

"That's one of the reasons why I've brought the impostor along—I thought it best to give them a little room to work. Once they start making connections, it'll become apparent where Lily's hiding. Until then, it's better to stay out of the way."

"It sounds smart but doesn't explain why you're taking her home—any man can understand, but that won't satisfy the masses."

"The public will make of it what they will, but it's another reason why I've a thin line of propriety to walk."

John laughed with rueful recognition. "As long as it doesn't make a priest of you."

Nicholas paused, prickled by a sudden memory of drinking with Quincy Hill on the night the stableman had disappeared from London. The man had been standing at the shelves in his tiny room, looking at something. Was it a book? Nicholas had asked him, *Since you're not leaving to become a priest, why are you quitting?*

It's business, Quincy had said, and then had lifted a black walking stick with a beautifully executed golden horse-head handle. It must have had jewels for eyes, for they had glittered in the yellow light. *Old business . . . You know how it is: You think something's finished and find out it's not.*

I don't suppose you'd understand about contractual obligations, Nicholas had responded.

Quincy had then turned to consider Nicholas with both a perceptive and mordant amusement that transcended his former role. Nicholas did not know who Quincy Hill was, but the dimly recalled conversation convinced him that the man was a master who had taken up the role of a servant. It was a clever disguise, and in the painting by the impostor, Quincy had not merely pretended to be a wealthy noble; she had traced his image faithfully.

Abruptly, Nicholas finished his drink and stood up, barely hearing Wesley's surprised reaction.

"Where are you going?" John quaffed his drink in a hurry and grabbed his hat to chase Nicholas out to the street. "What in the blazes has come over you? Why are we going back to the hotel so early?"

Nicholas was eager to write a letter to Poole that would go out in the morning post to London. Given all the ships passing through the busy harbor, the detective would never find Quincy Hill's name among those of other servants on the third-class passage lists. Quincy's transformation suggested that he was restoring his life. Even Winston had been misled by the ambiguous claim of the stable master as a faithful retainer returning to his old family. "I've just remembered something unmistakably important, but I've a feeling I've recalled it too late."

CHAPTER 18

THE GYPSY AND HIS MONKEY

❦

Quenton considered buying a coat. He sat with his back to the wall and his knees drawn to his chest to conserve his warmth while waiting for the afternoon sun to crest the rooftops and light his floor. His riding coat of merino wool was no match for the reluctant stone of his cell, but he was not anxious to purchase one of the lice-infested rags that the guard bargained as such.

Although his recent self-image still reeled from the lunacy of having forgotten about Henri's letter, he did not consider himself stupid, and deliberated about a coat for something to do. Even though La Prison Sainte-Pélagie might never be as bad as the notorious Bastille, the prison was still a prison, by anyone's consideration. His cell was ten paces by twelve, if he moved the metal cot serving as a bed. Otherwise, he could deem it only ten paces square. He preferred the twelve paces, even if he was not going anywhere.

He should have burned Henri's letter when Moises had suggested it. Now he found himself with an uncertain future. While waiting for someone else to decide it for him, he might count flies on the windowsill or roaches in the slop served for his daily meal, or listen to lice sizzle in the hot embers from his meager supply of cigars.

When would Moises arrive from Limoges? How could he know? There were no special couriers running in and out at the prisoner's behest. Quenton would feel lucky if the guard whom he had bribed actually mailed his letter to Benoit. He could hope only that the promise of reward provided sufficient motivation, and the soonest Moises could appear might be in days or weeks or even months, depending upon the night guard outside his door.

He found himself scratching the back of his neck and determined it best not to consider the vermin crawling there. Restlessly, he pushed up from the flea-ridden bed and pumped his arms as he made the long walk from one wall to the next. Another unlucky soul had once measured the days of interment by etching marks in the rock in standard groups of five. Quenton counted fourscore and ten for the ninety-eighth time. If he were to start a tally, would there be a need to add more to them before his own release?

Dismally, he regarded the straggled lines scratched in stone. He dared not ponder what his thoughts would be like after that many days. Now he recognized what Alix had gone through when kept in her mother's cellar. She had been just a girl, and had survived things that no one could have believed would happen. How had she managed all those years ago?

He found himself rubbing an itch on the small of his back. As annoying as it was to be unable to scratch between his shoulder blades, he knew he needed a challenge to absorb his attention; otherwise, his next cell might be in an asylum. All he had was his determination to endure, until Moises Benoit's round face appeared in the square grate of the ironbound door. It was roughly ninety leagues from Paris to Limoges. He might spend a few minutes calculating how many steps needed to travel those miles, and then he would know how long it would take to walk home.

Inspired by something different than waiting for the sun, Quenton retrieved his pilfered pencil stub from beneath the scraggly straw mat serving as a mattress. Sinking down cross-legged, he ciphered on stones worn smooth by thousands of footsteps. With luck, Moises would appear before Quenton walked the leagues to Limoges, one step at a time, between the walls of his prison cell.

THE MORNING HAD DAWNED dreary for travel through the notorious marshland surrounding the shallow bay known as the Wash. The baggage carts and servants went ahead, and although Alix rode with the other ladies bundled beneath blankets and heated by foot warmers in the carriage, it was a miserably damp ride. While the road was boggy in places, they journeyed with cheerful certainty that soon they would leave behind even the dankest of fens. By the time they stopped for lunch at a wayside tavern, the marsh was behind them, and their journey continued through fertile cropland.

The planned stop for the night was at the inn in a tiny village, and the last thing Alix expected after the wearing day of sitting in a closed coach was to experience excitement at the idea of a local fair, but as soon as she heard music, she forgot her hours of confinement.

She was not alone. Sarah caught her husband's arm while tugging Mary along. "Johnny, can you believe it? We're here in time for a fair!"

The owner of the inn was a cheerful man with arms like a blacksmith's, evidenced by his rolled-up sleeves. He wore the half apron of his dual role as bartender, and his family worked in the place of employees. "They say today's the day that Little John freed Robin of Locksley from jail in Nottingham," he shared jovially. "Whether 'tis or not, 'tis a grand night for all."

Mary laughed, hugging Sarah's arm. "How exciting! I wish Sam were here!"

"Did I hear my name?" Samuel Newton answered, surprising everyone with a theatrical appearance from the adjacent tavern.

"Sam!" Sarah exclaimed, throwing her arms around her brother.

"Sarah, my sweet," Sam laughed, and began a round of greetings while explaining his unexpected appearance. "Well met," he vowed in conclusion. "I knew you'd be here for the fair, and thought I'd best come keep John and Nicholas out of trouble."

Sarah giggled as she hugged his neck. "Oh, Sam! You're incorrigible!"

"Since you're here, we'll have to make a night of it," John conceded readily, and began to steer them to the stairs. "If we're going to enjoy the evening, we'd better give you ladies a few minutes to change."

"Bully," Sam agreed, helping himself to Mary's arm to escort her. "There's dancing in the square tonight, and I hear they're crowning the winner of today's archery tournament."

"Oh, Sam! Will it be you?"

He laughed heartily about his skill as a bowman as they climbed the stairs. "No, blast it! I was outmatched by a few others—all this rot about rushing off to London for the season has played the devil with my aim."

The gay rumpus of the music from the street followed them as they found their rooms. "They're a little small," Sarah noted apologetically about the rustic lodgings, "but it's only for a night."

"We won't be spending much time in them anyway," her husband added cheerfully. "And tomorrow's ride down to Stragglethorpe won't be too taxing."

"Don't be late, Lily!" Sarah bade, as their group splintered off to their respective rooms. "Sam says there's a calliope in town!"

"Of course not," Alix promised, scarcely able to contain the sudden thrill coursing through her. She could not remember the last time she had heard a calliope play, but the prospect added an air of enchantment to the evening.

Nicholas Griffon stepped closer, but he was only reaching for the door handle behind her. "I'll be right across the hall. Is an hour enough time?"

Her swift response sounded strangely breathless to her. "Certainly," she managed to reply, and then he was gone, leaving her staring numbly at the closed door.

"Psst," Jenny whispered from the antechamber. "You'd better hurry if we're going to get you ready."

Alix scraped together her oddly scattered thoughts as she obeyed. "Jenny, did you hear about the calliope?"

"Yes, we passed it on the way into town. It was with a caravan of gypsy wagons, all painted with bright colors."

"How exciting! You have another date with Albert, to go out dancing tonight, don't you?" Alix tugged on the fingertips of her gloves as she settled on the dressing-room chair for Jenny to unlace her shoes.

"I might."

Alix could scarcely believe the maid's indifference. "Do you mean that Albert hasn't asked you yet?"

Jenny laughed as she put Alix's shoes away. "I haven't said yes."

"Oh," Alix chuckled with relief, and then noticed the mauve brocade gown hanging on the rack for tonight. "What's that?" she asked, dreading the thought of putting it on.

"It's your gown, of course."

"Oh no, I can't wear that," she insisted. "It's so formal! This is a country fair."

"It's the same as what the other maids have put out for your friends."

"Oh, well, then I certainly can't." Alix laughed, determined to strike independence from Lily's dictum for just a few hours. Once the sun set, everyone would be too busy having fun to pay attention to whether or not she acted like Lady Griffon, and she was in a place where no one had any idea about her sister. She would not have to worry about hiding behind curtains or stumbling through broom closets; she could simply slip away from the fringes and dance in the shadows. "Didn't we pack something simple?"

"Well, yes, of course, but . . ."

In the town square outside the hotel, a hurdy-gurdy wound to life. "I'm not in the mood for anything pretentious," Alix said. "We're on holiday, so why not have a little fun?"

IF WHILE IN THE CANDY SHOP to find peppermints at Sam's request, Nicholas should choose to buy lemon drops for the impostor, no one should consider him odd. Just because his indecision over licorice and saltwater taffy prompted him to buy both did not mean he was pampering her. When he returned to learn that the woman had disappeared, his immediate concern was for her safety. After all, they were in a strange place surrounded by people from everywhere, but then he realized that she might have simply returned to her family.

She could be a gypsy; how would he know? Her father might be the stocky fellow playing the calliope. Her brothers might be the jugglers, her sisters shaking tambourines. Nicholas pushed the paper sack of lemon drops into his pocket, determined to investigate. Even if gypsies were notoriously well versed, the impostor's talent belied formal training. Quincy's tale that he had brought her to England as a child, coupled with Nicholas's slow realization that his servant had been a man of former worth, could mean that the pair were fugitives. If so, the impostor might be valuable if she were recognized from a missing-person's poster that the local gypsies might have come across in their wanderings.

Nicholas did not expect to find the woman beneath a nearby strawberry tree. While the calliope continued to draw a gay crowd to the lighted square, the impostor stood wrapped in thought and hidden in shadowed darkness. She did not realize his approach, even when he stopped beside her.

"Hello," he said to break her spellbound silence, and immediately reached to steady her when she startled fearfully. "I'm sorry; I didn't mean to frighten you."

She turned with a shaky laugh. "I'm sorry—you didn't frighten me; I was listening to the music."

Nicholas withdrew the candy from his pocket. "I thought of you at the candy shop."

Her surprise was absurdly gratifying, considering his small concession. "Why, thank you." Darkness stripped her of Lily's mask, and while he listened carefully for clues to her history, she sounded as British as ever. "Would you care for a piece?"

How could Nicholas decline, even if he did not want it? He could not remember the last time he had tasted a lemon drop, and savored its bittersweet tartness now, if for no other reason than to have this common bond with her.

"I say," he proposed, prompted by the ridiculous idea that they might stop their maddening game for the moment, "have you seen the dancing monkey?"

"No."

Nicholas grabbed her hand to tow her into the crowd before she could gainsay him. "Good, let's go! It's over by the candy store," he exclaimed, and found himself laughing for no reason.

He might have guessed that John would spot them across the square and pull Sarah along with him. "Wait up there, Griffon," John hailed from a distance. "Where're you headed?"

Frustrated, Nicholas stopped to wait for them at the edge of the crowd. "We're going to watch the monkey."

Sarah laughed, reaching for the impostor curiously. "Hello, Lily! Isn't this fun? What did you find?"

"Nicholas bought lemon drops; would you care for one?"

"Candy! What a nice surprise! Oh, Johnny!"

Nicholas stoically met John's weighty measure, but Sarah's engaging entreaty inevitably led them to the little sweetshop at the edge of the square. Nicholas waited outside with the strolling jugglers and dancing jesters while the hurdy-gurdy played, listening to the distant rumpus absently.

"How now, Griffon—look lively, mate," John called cheerfully as they emerged from the shop. "Here," he added, pushing a sack of taffy at Nicholas as they fell in line behind the ladies moving toward the clock tower. "Have you gotten anywhere with your little friend yet?"

Noting that John's choice of candy did not seem of interest to the impostor, Nicholas replied, as he tucked the bag into his pocket, "Dare I remind you that it's none of your business?"

"Tell me to butt out if you'd prefer, but don't think I won't warn you that you're making a mistake. Who'd care if you stole a kiss, when everyone thinks she's your wife?"

"This is a ridiculous conversation."

"Why? Admit that you owe it to yourself to have a little fun. What in the devil's happened to you? I've never known you to be cavalier."

"I've explained my reasons heretofore," Nicholas reminded him, and then resolutely guided the women to the front of the merry audience while digging through his change pocket for a few farthings. Although the impostor's grateful reply was lost in the noise, there was no mistake about her generosity. She immediately tossed a farthing for the monkey and shared the rest with Sarah.

It was absurd to feel that she was the picture of innocence when Nicholas knew the depth of her deception by posing as his wife, yet he found himself helplessly entangled in her artless illusion. Applause rose as the tune ended and the monkey scampered avidly for a rain of coins. While it scooped up its bounty, the gypsy began to play "My Love Is Like a Red, Red Rose."

Perhaps Sarah's chortle of delight distracted the capuchin, because it suddenly waddled forward with upraised arms, looking like a spindly child. "Oh! Isn't he adorable? Come on, I've got another coin!" But Sarah's laughter turned to a dismayed cry when the monkey jumped up to use her as a springboard and plunged deep into the tree branches overhead. John's automatic grab for the wayward animal was clumsy and missed, igniting screams and shouting as it bounded away through the trees.

Nicholas was familiar with the spindly capuchins that sailors sometimes kept as pets and, knowing they were smart, expected it to double back to its owner, who was whistling frantically for it. While John charged to the dais and called for order, Nicholas gauged the animal's progress through the treetops by the wildly swaying lanterns tied to branches across the square. He shifted into position, ready to intercept its flight before its precipitous escape turned to disaster. The monkey was only a shadow when he jumped to catch it, and came down with a handful of fur amid a shower of leaves and earsplitting screams of calamity. The struggle he anticipated was suddenly a warm surprise, because in his arms was not just the capuchin but also the irrepressible impostor, with the monkey clinging to her desperately.

"Blast," he swore, and began a fumbling attempt to strip it away from her, until he realized her gentle laughter was mingling with its cries.

"There now, me boy-o," she sang to it gently, spinning a mesmerizing charm over the terrified animal and Nicholas alike. "You're safe now, aren't you?" Her eyes flickered with silver fairy fire in the shifting light when she cast an inclusive and grateful glance up at him. "He's only a little scared, Nick. It's all right; he's not hurting me."

Her melodic prosody stunned him into releasing her, even as he wondered why he did so. He would much rather have clung to her as tightly as the monkey did, but only watched while she straightened its sultan's cap with a laugh. "See, what did I tell you?" she continued to comfort it as she turned to Sarah. "Look, he didn't mean to frighten you; he only wanted a piece of your candy."

"My-my candy?" Sarah answered with a shaky laugh.

A constable's whistle was blowing when the impostor reached down for one of the spilled pieces of Sarah's taffy littering the cobblestones. The monkey grabbed it with excited chatter and sprang to the gypsy, who was emerging from the confusion. The owner collapsed to his knees as he reached for the impostor's hand. "Milady, by the sainted Virgin, I swear—"

"Here now, that's enough out of you," Sam ordered, as he arrived to take control. He crowded the stage with the bewildered and breathless Mary, demanding tersely, "Why isn't that animal on some kind of restraint?"

Sarah rallied to its defense and sided with the impostor. "Sam, it only wanted a candy!"

The constable finally arrived. "Let's have some order here! Quiet everyone, please. Lord Newton first, if you don't mind!"

John stepped forward to interrupt furiously. "This man's monkey . . ." His accusation was quickly drowned in the gabbled rise of protests.

"Milords and ladies, please!"

"Really, Officer," Lily's impostor entreated gently. Her voice beckoned with a surprising strength that stilled the crowd. While the constable grinned at her foolishly, she granted him the concession of a smile. "The poor thing wished only for a piece of candy."

"Candy? And who are you, miss?"

A moment of weighty silence rang in the wake of his inquiry, but Sarah laughed and reached for the stranger's hand. "This is Lady Griffon, Constable. She's going to be our houseguest for a few days."

Immediately, the policeman straightened and clicked his heels into a smart bow. "I beg your pardon, milady."

"Oh, my lords and ladies." The gypsy collapsed in an anxious plea for clemency. "I swear to God, by the sainted Virgin—"

"Constable," Nicholas finally interrupted, moving to adjourn the session with a sense of reason. "Capuchins are intelligent animals," he began, and tried to ignore the impostor's surprised admiration for his statement. Silence fell, granting his speech importance as it resonated above the confusion. "Seamen often keep them as pets. Typically, they're well behaved, but they've an innate curiosity that occasionally leads to mischief. I'd suggest by the way this one's eating candy that we allow this man to take his animal and feed it."

"See how docile he is?" the impostor chimed in, giving the monkey another confection. "He's only hungry."

"Right," Sam agreed, harrumphing officiously. "You there, give this animal something to eat."

"Lady, how can I thank you?" the gypsy implored as he bowed gratefully.

Nicholas produced the sack of candy that John had bought earlier. "Here's this, and buy yourself some dinner, too," he proposed, adding a shilling for the gypsy's benefit, as much as his own. If he could but foster the impostor's elusive regard, it might make the trip to Stragglethorpe worth something after all.

ALIX DREAMED OF RIDING a carousel, spellbound by the dizzying lights showering her. Her painted pony was a unicorn adorned with roses and ribbons, and she clung to its gilded pole, thrilled by the thumping calliope. A faceless crowd spun past in the outer fringe of darkness; when she glimpsed her father, she called to him, but her voice brought her awake. She whispered his name again, hoping to restore her bittersweet dream. Turning onto her side, she cuddled the warmth of the sleeping terrier and drifted back to sleep.

She scuffed her boot on the gray slate floor, watching the pale light slant through the vaulted windows. She stared at the smoky pillows of clouds stacked in the brilliant sky beyond diamond-shaped panes, while the clock ticked in lonely measure. Her horse, Snowball, suddenly lifted her head, patiently waiting where she was tied to the post. Alix had been about to go riding; she wore her favorite red velvet dress with colorful braiding. Outside the window, the day was fine. She knew from experience it would not remain so for long; it was the time of year when weather moved down swiftly from the mountaintops to chill the rocky slopes.

The tall-backed chair was empty where she usually found the doorman sitting with his dog, Tigre, at his feet. The hall was quiet save for the heavy toll of the clock. When was the house ever so still? Where was everyone?

The impatient pendulum flashed in the sun. Alix scanned the hall uncertainly. The familiar empty suits of armor, and shields hung with helms or swords, were her only company. A faint murmur of voices finally lifted above the ponderous clock, and Alix froze fearfully. The regulator clicked, freeing the whirr of chimes. Her scream shattered the stillness and was obliterated by a booming discharge from a gun.

Alix landed on the floor, awakened by the surprised yelp of the terrified dog. He struggled for his freedom and sprang away beneath the nearby table as she clumsily floundered in the sheets. "Glory," she avowed breathlessly, as the terrier watched with fearful eyes. "Poor thing! You're all right, aren't you?"

She shuddered convulsively and found her feet. Pulling one of the bedcovers around her shoulders, she began a march like an Egyptian queen to the tiny hotel sitting room. "God, whatever happened to a good night's sleep?" She barked her shin on an ill-placed footstool that reignited the throbbing of her great toe, but the blanket protected her from the worst of it. "Where is a tinderbox around here?" she wondered, rummaging through empty hotel drawers until she found one in the dark. "There," she sighed, grateful for the light as she replaced the chimney and hung the shade.

"Now"—she reached for *Hamlet* as she dropped onto the settee and made room for the dog—"let's see what the old prince is doing tonight, shall we?" Opening the book at random, she began reading as Hamlet commanded his friends, *"Come hither, gentlemen, and lay your hands again upon my sword. Swear by my sword never to speak of this that you have heard."*

ROBERT COULD NOT DENY his habit of picking up newspapers. Depending upon the town, it might prove entertaining. Contingent to the population, it could be informative. How contemporary the news was was subject to distance, but if the story was printed from outside the locality, it was usually riveting.

He came across such an article when least expecting it, while riding the ferry south to Avignon. The newspaper was not the latest edition, but Robert propped his chair against the wheelhouse in the shade to peruse it nonetheless while enjoying a pipe.

The weather had warmed after he had left Lyon. The farther the Rhone River carried the ferry south, the more intense the heat. Even his good horse, Julius, appreciated the difference after the trek into the mountains. The animal waited belowdecks in the hold, along with other livestock.

Robert read about politics. He read a fragment of a serial story he had never seen before. He perused the advertisements for anything interesting. He stopped when he reached the editorials and a scathing column about an upstart claiming to be one discredited Marquis Quenton Riche-Ives Acelin Saint-Descoteaux.

Who else would wish to claim an infamous name? Not just

anyone would seek such notoriety, despite the fortune involved. The article dredged up old rumors of espionage, conspiracies, and subversion, despite the change in regime. It cited crimes no one cared about, if only to cast further dispersion on the allegation that the miscreant deserved a prison sentence unless he were marched to the guillotine.

Automatically, Robert checked the date of the newspaper and calculated the timing from his meeting with the viscount in Marseille: *It's too early to tell. In fact, it's not yet been received, but the wheels are in motion. So as they say,* quello che sarà, sarà—*what will be, will be—and we'll see what comes of it, eh?*

Robert had no reason to doubt that the Rougets were behind the article and the arrest in Paris, before Quenton had the opportunity to involve the King. The newspaper claimed that, conveniently, the spy carried proof of his guilt in a recent letter to his brother, whom the authorities had also thought deceased. Further inquiry by the secret police was pending, but the article concluded that either the notorious Saint-Descoteaux brothers had faked their deaths to avoid prosecution and now tired of exile, or the man claiming to be the Marquis of Limoges was a charlatan and a fraud. Either way, the man arrested in Paris was sitting in a prison cell, where he deserved to remain.

CHAPTER 19

HORSE RACE AT STRAGGLETHORPE

⟡

erhaps the triumphant capture of the escaped monkey
had prompted the rise in Nicholas Griffon's humor, but
Alix determined to tread lightly. One never knew when another
change would transform his newfound buoyancy, and a lapse in
her vigilance could quickly end in disaster. Still, she was
grateful for his improved outlook as the merry company
wended along the road to Stragglethorpe. Seeing him relaxed
with his group of friends gave Alix hope that he might not be
as terrifying as she had originally thought.

She took the opportunity to consider him as an individual
separate from Lily, instead of frantically trying to outwit him
with her tenuous act as his wife. It would not be long before
they would be blood-related through Lily and Phillip's child.
She had always thought that wavy hair on both sides of the
family boded well for a baby's curls. Nicholas's high forehead
denoted intelligence, his honed nose a solid character, but his
stern eyebrows made a crease where they met that eased only
when he laughed.

Otherwise, Alix could not detect any problems when he

was eating and concluded that his teeth were sound. He was definitely tall and well built, free from physical abnormality, as his agile capture of the monkey had evidenced. The act marked an adequate capacity for planning and execution and exhibited fine reflexes, and from all indications, his family was decent stock. If Phillip shared the same traits, she supposed Lily's child would be healthy.

Alix poked thoughtfully at a carrot on her plate. Perhaps his brother was not as intelligent—after all, he had recklessly impregnated Lily—but then, Lily was her sister, so how could Alix hold that against him? The child should still have a chance to become its own person. She dared another covert look at Nicholas and wondered if he would help to give it one.

She ducked her eyes when his friend John noticed her looking at Nicholas, but it was too late. From his pensive pause, she knew he was about to address her. Defensively, she put the bite of carrot into her mouth.

"Don't you think so, Lily?"

Why did he stress the first syllable of her sister's name, so that it smacked of incredulity? Did John suspect something, or did Lily's husband tell all, as unwitting people sometimes did? Perhaps she should revise her estimation of Nicholas's innate capability, since he did evidence a lack of prudence by having married Lily. That alone was worthy a mark against his capacity for foresight; if it were the same as his brother's, then it might suggest a mental instability. In that case, the poor child could be doomed to an asylum, because Alix's complete loss of memory marked her own unfortunate tendency toward lunacy, which notoriously ran in families.

Without a clue about the topic of conversation, Alix chose a careful answer: "It remains to be seen."

Her response surprised the men, and the trio exchanged

glances amid robust laughter. Alix looked to the other women for salvation, but Sarah was busy picking through the peas on her plate and Mary had eyes only for Sam. She hoped her equivocation was sufficiently artful to avoid notice, because Lily would never have shrunk from an opportunity to monopolize the conversation of a group of men.

John Wesley was not the type to ignore an opening, so he pressed on: "Really? How so?"

Alix had pulled a piece from her bread, but his question forced a response. Nicholas watched her expectantly, his cobalt eyes containing a curious light that was of no avail. Sarah and Mary continued to be oblivious, but how could Alix find an opinion without knowing the subject?

Again, she tried to be vague. "Why, on the outcome, of course."

For an extraordinary reason, Nicholas took an inordinate amount of pleasure in her answer. He chuckled as he sat back to drink from his beer cheerfully. "There you have it, Counselor."

The laughter finally pulled Sarah's attention away from her food. "Have what?"

John lifted his glass merrily. "We were discussing the worth of our horses, and Lily thinks we should put it to a test."

Alix felt her mouth drop open but quickly popped her bread into it. There was no need for a race to know that Midnight Star was a better horse than Wexford's Donny Boy.

"A race!" Sarah exclaimed with predictable excitement. "When?"

"Now, Sarah," John concluded, "it wouldn't be fair to race our horses while we're on the road."

In Alix's estimation, to make any race fair would require added weight on the saddle to handicap Midnight, but she hid her opinion in a slow drink of wine, awaiting their deliberation while Sarah clapped her hands, bouncing with anticipation. "Oh, what fun! We've something brilliant planned before we're even home!"

"Isn't that wonderful!" Mary added happily, blushing when Sam reached for her hand beneath the table.

"Lily, you've good luck picking horses! Who do you think'll win?" Sarah asked, reaching for Alix's hand.

John laughed. "Lily suggested a race for a reason, didn't she?"

Alix bit her tongue to keep from joining the ensuing debate, for whatever she added was certain to reveal too much. By the time they returned to the road, she found herself reconsidering her appraisal of Donny Boy. Not every horse made a good racer just because it had speed. Without a doubt, as long as Nicholas Griffon could manage to stay in his saddle, Midnight should win. It would not take long to find out: As they approached the Newton estate called South Hill, the contestants decided to let Sam choose the course and race on the morrow.

MAURICE THOUGHT QUENTON was bluffing and called his hand. The night guard smirked triumphantly as he pushed his tower of pennies into the middle of the pot between them. "All right, monsieur. Show me your cards."

"Be careful, Maury—you've mouths to feed at home," Quenton cautioned, unwilling to take the man's slender earnings with his royal flush, and then hesitated when Moises Benoit appeared in the open doorway. "*Mon Dieu!*" he exclaimed in disbelief. "Moises," he laughed, springing to his feet.

"My lord marquis, I've brought someone to meet you."

Maurice scrambled to retrieve the carbine he had put aside at the beginning of their poker game. "You can't just come in here," he protested. "Who the hell are you? Where's the bailiff?" he added, rushing to the door suspiciously.

"This is my attorney, Maury," Quenton supplied gladly. "Moises Benoit, from Limoges."

"And this is Josef L'Argan, my colleague from Paris. Josef, this is the Marquis Saint-Descoteaux, as I promised."

"It's a pleasure, Marquis," the other responded, appearing thin and mousy beside the hearty Benoit as he shook Quenton's hand. After a brief inspection through his lorgnette, he looked to the guard. "The bailiff knows me. He'll be along shortly with paperwork to move the marquis to a more appropriate cell. He'll be released in the morning."

"What do you mean, he'll be along shortly? He's not allowed to let anyone in without a guard!"

"I assure you that he is on his way. In the meantime, Marquis, please allow us to collect your things."

"I've nothing but what you see—"

"Hey, you still haven't shown me your cards."

"I fold." Quenton quit easily, turning to grab up the strewn cards to hide the ones he still held in his hand.

"I warned you," Maurice chuckled cheerfully, eager to claim the meager pile of pennies.

Moises Benoit pulled Quenton aside. "Please forgive my seeming delay, milord. Your letter only just arrived, and . . ."

Quenton was so happy to see him that he could have shouted with relief. "The mail service in and out of this place is as fine as the rest of its accommodations."

Moises nodded knowingly. "Of course, but don't worry," he replied, lowering his voice further. "I thought I advised you to burn that letter. My friend Josef is at his finest with these types of political affairs. We've already filed a petition for immediate release, and they'll take you to a preferable cell until you're free."

"I readily concede that I was extremely foolhardy, Moises, but at this point, isn't retrospection rather futile?"

"Our problem is now the unfortunate result of unprecedented collaboration by an affidavit that was filed in Alpes-Maritimes."

Quenton's short-lived elation at seeing his attorney dissolved in disbelief. "A sworn statement?"

"Yes, a sighting of your brother in Naples. Assuming it false—"

Outraged, Quenton forgot about speaking quietly. "What do you mean, *assuming?*"

Moises stepped back cautiously. "Please keep calm, milord," his attorney advised, exchanging a quick look with his companion. "Due to the distance involved, we've not yet seen this affidavit for ourselves."

"For God's sake, Moises, what difference does it make if you've seen it firsthand!"

Josef L'Argan intervened hastily. "The affidavit claims that Henri Saint-Descoteaux was having coffee in Naples, but the origin of such a document must be verified. The signature and seal are most important—"

"Henri Saint-Descoteaux? Henri, my brother? How can that be, when I buried him with my own hands? I carried him into the crypt and wrapped a rosary around his fingers!"

Moises stopped him. "Ahem, Quenton, my friend"—he patted Quenton's filthy shoulder but then looked at his hand uncertainly—"we don't doubt you." He banished his soiled hand behind his back. "But these things take time, and if the witness is credible—"

"Witness! What witness?" Quenton did not care that his voice echoed throughout the hallway, or whether anyone was privy to his reaction to such an insane suggestion. "Henri Saint-Descoteaux is dead! How dare anyone claim differently?"

"Marquis," Josef stepped closer to put a placating hand on his chest to separate him from Moises. "We believe you, of course."

"*Of course.* What's not to believe, when you're looking at someone who's dead? Everyone knows a man is dead when he's dead, especially if he's your brother!"

"Marquis, this is not the time," L'Argan warned sternly, but Quenton pushed past in pursuit of Benoit.

"Damn it, Moises! What do you mean by enlisting this idiot? Does everyone think that I've only imagined the years since?"

"Quenton, please calm yourself!"

"You bargain with restraint and plead forbearance? How dare you or any man claim that my brother's alive!"

"Mar-Marquis!" Benoit choked, as Quenton grabbed him by the collar. "It's a sworn statement and nothing more!"

Suddenly realizing he was dangerously close to losing all control, Quenton released Benoit and pushed him back, although sorely tempted to add his fist on the man's chin for good measure. "This is ludicrous," he said, turning away. He went to stare at the gray stone wall opposite his narrow window, with bars so closely spaced that not even a cat could slip through. His ridiculous position rendered him completely helpless without the men behind him, whom, a second ago, he had been willing to alienate.

As Quenton struggled to control his livid reaction to his circumstances, L'Argan raised the stakes. "We beg your pardon, Marquis. Your friend Moises was only attempting to caution that your case is not a simple matter. With the filing of the affidavit, no matter how inconceivable," he hastened to add when Quenton turned to look at him, "you must understand the court's obligation to entertain it. Unfortunate or not, the scales of justice are blind, and since the statement was given under oath—"

"Not everyone is intimidated by eternal damnation, Monsieur L'Argan."

"Even so, it's the right of due process. We take civil liberty seriously in France."

"And in the meantime, I'm to wait patiently? Who is this soulless devil who claims to have seen my brother?"

"It's one of his friends, which makes his claim sound sincere, does it not? Certainly you must know him; it's the Count of Mandelieu, the Honorable Monsieur Claudius Rouget."

"From Côte d'Azur?" Quenton asked skeptically. "Since when did he become so significant?"

"Count Rouget is an important merchant tycoon—"

"Bah, he has a handful of broken-down ships. So what? Henri may've invited him over whenever he was down in Aix-en-Provence, but a business acquaintance hardly makes him a bosom friend."

"You would call Cyclops Freight a handful of ships? The count's business prevails throughout the Mediterranean and up the coast of Spain," Moises replied incredulously.

"Be that as it may," Quenton conceded dismissively, although he had not realized that Rouget had waxed so fat after Henri's demise, "being rich doesn't make him right. Henri might have met him on occasion, but that hardly counts as closeness."

"If this is so, and I have no doubt of it," L'Argan

countered, "it'll be determined in our discovery. Monsieur Marquis, as you realize by now, we're hampered by the distance, but the courier from the Alpes-Maritimes court should be here tomorrow. Your accommodations tonight might still be cheerless but will be . . . shall we say, better than here."

"Fantastic," Quenton replied in defeat.

"We've arranged for a bath and new clothes from your luggage. With a decent dinner and a window looking onto the courtyard—"

"The one with the guillotine, no doubt."

Josef found a reason to smile as Quenton shuffled to the door. "Don't worry, Marquis—we're permitted our own investigation. In fact, we've already started."

ALIX ADJUSTED THE FIRE before she returned to her nest on the couch. The little dog lifted his chin and blinked at her sleepily. She settled beside him carefully and returned to a fresh page in *The Song of Roland*, but it failed to lure her mind away from the dream that had awakened her. Quenton had never asked any questions about those frantic hours in the terrible aftermath of her father's death, but if he had, Alix could not have answered with any certainty until she began having nightmares of those old memories after she arrived in London.

The murderers had never imagined that she would worm her way through the walls of the house. Had she never played in the laundry chute when she was small, the idea might not have occurred to her. Had it not, she would not have been able to dream of it in retrospect. She had no clue about the kind of woman she might have become had that day never happened. Now she sat in place of Lily—a sister she never would have known existed.

She had awoken one day with the realization that she was

cold, and had found that she was locked in a windowless room in a cellar. The air was dank, and her hair needed washing. Dirt had crusted beneath her broken fingernails; she wondered at them in the uncertain light from the shuttered lantern allowed her in that small space. A spindly chair and table, and a thin mattress for a bed, were her comfort. *It's for your own safety,* the housekeeper charged ominously when she answered Alix's tenuous pounding on the door. *Where would you be, if not for madame?* she whispered. *You should be thankful for her benevolence.*

A-lex, Lily had sung, after her sister had found Alix. Neither one knew of their relationship yet, but Lily had fun spinning her diamond bracelet before Alix's eyes. *A-lex . . . A-lex . . . why were you named for a boy? Mother says I may play with you, but we must pretend you're a ghost, and you can't go outside. She says no one can ever, ever see you, so I'm casting a spell to make you invisible. If you're good, I'll bring a lump of sugar for your tea.*

Alix shivered as she set aside the book and left the couch to look out the window, waiting for the gloaming light of dawn. The Lily of those days had not been kind. Her sister had poked and prodded her to make her cry, but the cruelty had helped, for the aggravation had kept Alix from slipping back into a stupor. When Alix had finally been bathed to make her a suitable playmate, her sister had been delighted to discover they were as alike as mirror images, save for the differences in expression. That was when their mother, Mary-Margaret, had revealed the secret that they were twins, and Lily had contrived to convince Alix to copy her in all things.

When Lily had suddenly visited the farm to reveal her grand scheme to switch places, Alix had been as woefully unprepared to deal with her sister as ever. Now she wished herself back in Lily's apartment, plucking the plum of Robbie's farm title from the nearest vase. With it in hand, she would be free from this idiotic escapade. Without it, the future of Sterling Wood Stable teetered precariously.

The approach of Apollo's chariot of the sun finally glimmered in the east. Above, the star-strewn heavens glittered, promising a fair dawn, at least. Beyond the planned race between Midnight and Donny, the day's events were uncertain. Alix pulled the draperies open and settled on the kissing chair, determined to enjoy the sky without the city crowding the horizon.

THE AFTERNOON WAS WARM. Halcyon clouds floated in a sea of blue, mimicking ships on the ocean. Sarah rode her white mare, Sugar, and Alix followed on a black-and-white piebald called Domino. Mary's horse was a sweet, ginger-colored mare named Goldilocks who liked to trot with her head held high to look around.

Alix's initial trepidation about mimicking Lily on sidesaddle eased when no one seemed to notice a difference. She merely copied the same casual riding style as her companions and let Domino carry her in their wake. Perhaps the men were too absorbed with their upcoming race as they trotted their horses in the opposite direction. Sarah was charged with showing the way to the Millpond, where the race would end at the three-mile post.

While Sarah and Mary chatted back and forth, Alix trailed behind silently. She had not perched on the sidesaddle for long before her knee, still aggravated from the smashup at Oxley, began to protest its position wrapped around the pommel. She did not have much time to dwell on the vexation, though, because the ladies riding ahead suddenly remembered her.

"Lily, where did you learn to play the piano so well?" Mary wondered pleasantly. "I heard somebody saying that you've been taking lessons. I didn't even know you played until last night—I must say, your performance was beautiful."

"That's kind of you to think so." Alix snickered Lily's snide laugh smugly.

"Where've you been taking lessons? I've been dying to find a good instructor."

"I haven't, really. I've just practiced, practiced, practiced. You know what they say."

"No, what?" Sarah asked, slowing Sugar alongside Goldilocks.

"Practice makes perfect, silly," Mary laughed. "Actually, I'm sad to learn of it, Lily. I thought for certain that you'd know a good tutor. I hate to ask, but will you share some of your techniques?"

"At least something, while you're here," Sarah suggested eagerly. "Once we're back in London, you'll be too busy with preparations to leave for Wales, but we'll make time this week, won't we, Mary?"

"If *you* don't mind, she means," Mary finished, while Alix tried to sort through the surprising announcement. She had thought to find the title and finish the charade before the London season ended. She made a quick calculation. Lily's baby was not due to be born for weeks. A new kind of panic seized Alix upon the realization that she had not heard anything new from Lily. Her sister had promised that their arrangement would be over once the baby was provided for, but Alix had no idea how Lily intended to switch places again.

"I can't imagine living in Wales. It seems so far away!" Sarah said.

Mary squeezed Sarah's arm in gentle agreement. "Don't you wish we could live in London all year?"

"Look, is that the millpond?" Alix redirected their

attention as the enormous wheel spilling water from its paddles became apparent through distant trees.

"This is going to be exciting!" Sarah exclaimed, returning to the topic of the race. "Lily, Nicholas is so fortunate to have a beautiful horse like Midnight Star! I can't believe he's from the same place as that horse we bet on at Oxley Commons. Do you think he was ever a racehorse?"

"Possibly," Alix demurred.

"Sam said that they met the owner at the sales when John bought Donny a few weeks ago. Oh, how I wish I could have joined you at the races!"

"I forget the name of the black horse that we bet on in the Hunt Cup, but you would've loved him, Mary; he looked just like Midnight Star."

Alix would never have sold Midnight had it not been for Quenton's persuasive argument to separate the colt from North Star. Even though Dobbins was Midnight's father, it did not stop the challenge between the two. When Midnight nearly battered down his stall as Finghin brought North Star into the barn one winter afternoon, Alix knew it was only a matter of time before the rivals battled for dominance. Then Quenton had worked in the Griffon stables, and selling Midnight to Nicholas had been an easy choice. But now her uncle was gone.

Alix turned Domino in line with the other horses as they reached their spot in the shade to watch the racers finish. They had not waited long before Sam galloped past on his lanky chestnut to wait at the three-mile post.

He doffed his hat as he bowed in his saddle. "They should be coming in a few minutes, ladies!"

"This is so exciting!" Sarah chortled.

"Isn't that the master gardener coming along in the cart?"

Mary asked of the red two-wheeled gig careening around the pond.

"It looks as if he's bringing the butler and half the staff." Sarah laughed as they watched the little wagon crowded with servants coming to watch the end of the race.

Mary gasped suddenly, directing them to the gray horse that appeared in the distance. "My God, do you see? It's Donny!"

The drumming of hooves marked the advance of the riders, and there was no mistaking the dappled-gray Donny in the lead, outrunning Midnight Star by an incredible three lengths. John lay flat along his horse's neck, while Nicholas Griffon galloped Midnight in his wake.

Sarah laughed in excitement, turning to her brother, Sam. "I knew he'd win!"

Alix longed to swing her sore leg free from the pommel, clamp her knees to the unwilling piebald, and set him into a flat gallop straight up the road to interrupt the race. She had worked too hard to build a reputation for Sterling Wood Stable to see it sullied because she had unwittingly sold one of her best horses to a worthless fop.

"I thought I heard Nicholas boasting that his horse has never been beaten!" Mary said to Sam.

"Just take a look now, Mary!" Sam directed, pointing up the road with his riding whip. "Midnight Star is a prime bit of blood if I've ever seen any."

Sarah laughed. "Oh, he's a gorgeous horse, but Donny's the one winning!"

"Not for long, little sister," Sam cautioned merrily, as the black horse suddenly flattened out his stride.

Alix nibbled her lower lip anxiously. Nicholas was finally riding as if he had decided to join the race, but Donny had increased his lead by another full length.

"John'll be so pleased! You've no idea how he measures everything by Nicholas. They've been friends forever; they might as well be brothers." Sarah's squeal of excitement was so loud that even Domino lifted his head to look around.

Alix forgot her role as Lily in dumbfounded disbelief. Midnight closed the gap incrementally, but his rider did not seem to realize that John and his horse had run away with the win right in front of him. "What a bleeding idiot," Alix proclaimed in stunned dismay. Belatedly, she realized her own good fortune that everyone was too busy cheering to hear her. She did not know what was more shocking: the idea of Midnight losing a race, or that she had completely misjudged Donny Boy's ability when she had culled the Wexford progeny from her racers. Wexford horses had an impressive history on the track, and valiant Donny was living up to his erstwhile reputation. She could only wonder how many other horses she had erroneously dismissed by discounting a couple of shoddy performances.

Impossibly, Sarah's and Mary's screams lifted higher, but no amount of cheering could rally poor Donny when he faltered short of the final mark. The gray fell to sudden defeat as Midnight charged past to victory. The exultant finish, accompanied by tossed hats and collective cheers, left Alix seething with frustration and incredulity. She stared purposefully into the trees, struggling with a sharp desire to share her opinion with Nicholas Griffon about his utter stupidity. Meanwhile, the unfortunate Donny was heaving for air with his head down because John Wesley was an oversize braggart with insufficient intelligence to keep from killing his favorite horse in a wager.

"I don't know quite what happened at the end; he was

giving it all his worth," John happily explained as he patted Donny. "Too bad, old boy. We'll get him next time."

"It's all right, Johnny—he ran beautifully," Sarah said.

Whatever vindication Alix might have felt that her estimation of Donny Boy had not been completely in error was tempered by Midnight's reaction when he noticed her and lunged against the stablemen's attempt to lead him away.

"Go easy there," Nicholas advised sharply, turning back to assist with his horse.

"Here, milord," Georgie called confidently, towing forward a fresh saddle horse from the stable.

In the confusion, Alix moved Domino behind the cart while Nicholas helped to contain Midnight. "Good lad," he said, before exchanging reins with Georgie. "John, you set quite the pace," he offered as he mounted.

"Damn me if someone didn't move the three-mile post," John laughed, climbing up on his own fresh horse to ride home.

As the party splintered into groups, Alix consigned Domino to lag behind the others on the road. When Nicholas twisted in the saddle to look for her, his dubious attention drove her eyes to the clouds as she willed a pair of wings to materialize. As swiftly as she could fly, she would speed away to forget this madness and leave these poor fools behind.

CHAPTER 20

LOST IN THE WOODS

Robert chose the table in the corner of the empty restaurant, from which he could watch the door as the maître d' snapped for a waiter to pull out the chair.

"White wine or red tonight, monsieur?"

"A blond ale will do."

"Certainly." The man bowed and sent his staff scurrying.

Robert unbuttoned his jacket and adjusted his cuffs in his sleeves as a server came to set his place. "May I suggest the special stuffed snail?"

"The squid persillade, I think."

"Ah, yes—very well, monsieur," he bowed, and tucked his tray beneath his arm as he went away.

Robert pulled his watch from his pocket and noted it was not like a seaman to be late. As he snapped it closed, the wind blew a man through the door. He was tall enough without the black fedora he swept from his head, and still thin, despite his cloaked illusion. His hair might have faded, but there was no mistaking the newcomer's fierce gaze when it stopped on his table.

"Robert." The Count of Mandelieu stretched out a hand in greeting and gripped Robert's shoulders to kiss each cheek as if they were compatriots.

"Claudius."

"*Asseyez-vous;* sit down, sit down," Rouget insisted, his habit of mixing French and English unchanged. It was the other man's meeting, and sufficient for the count to play the host, so Robert reclaimed his chair dutifully.

Claudius looked around for the waiter while tugging at his gloves. "Cabernet," he ordered, circumventing the man's hasty course. "*Actuellement,*" he grunted, taking the opposite chair, "I'm sorry to be late. It's not so far, but some idiot dropped a wagonload of melon a few streets over. *Mon Dieu, quel gâchis.* It makes one wonder if it is worth it to even come away from the harbor." He paused to taste his wine. "*Bon,*" he deemed with satisfaction, and ordered a carafe, along with a plate of stuffed mushrooms. After the waiter had gone, the count considered Robert over his wine. "*Comment avez-vous été;* how have you been? How's your magnificent wife, Maureen?"

"She is well, thank you."

Claudius smiled and tipped his head to the side. "Well? Just well?" He chuckled amiably. "What has happened to your joie de vivre, *mon ami?* Or perhaps things have not gone so well as you had planned up in England?"

The door opened to admit a trio of burly men. Robert kept his focus on the count while the maître d' showed the men to a nearby table. They scarcely had time to scrape into chairs before the bell on the door jingled, signaling the beginning of a crowd.

Now Robert only went through the motions of drinking the thin foam from his beer, while the count's men found places between his table and the door. He wore his saber on his belt and packed twin pistols beneath his coat, but the two-bullet limit of each taxed him as much as it ever had. None of the newcomers evidenced any weapons, but the rough-looking gathering was not here for a show.

The Frenchman continued his cordial banter as the waiter brought wine and the hors d'oeuvres, split onto a pair of plates. "Bon appétit." The Count of Mandelieu was not above speaking around the food in his mouth. "Not bad, eh? *Le secret est dans l'ail.*"

"If you like garlic."

"Who doesn't like garlic?" the count chortled, tossing another mushroom after the first. "Maybe only someone who's been in England too long."

Robert withstood his barb impassively. "I was surprised to read about Quenton Saint-Descoteaux's arrest in the newspaper."

"Ah," the count said, grinning appreciatively. "*Mon ami,* you're as blunt as ever."

"I have a ferry to catch."

"Oh, there's always the next one," Rouget reasoned enthusiastically. "How often is it that we see each other—how many years has it been? *Ici,* eat a few of your mushrooms and tell me of Maureen. How many children she has given you? *Vous savez,* Robert, there are more important things than miscreants rotting in prison."

"Descoteaux is far from a troublemaker. That letter was a fake, and you know it."

"*Eh bien, oui, bien sûr*—but who was foolish enough to carry it?"

"Henri was his brother," Robert reminded him pointedly. "You're intent on perpetuating this hoax?"

"*Moi?* I'm not the one holding him."

"Perhaps not, but you can arrange for his freedom."

"*Peut-être*—that remains to be seen—but since when does Henri's brother mean so much to you?"

Robert sat back carefully when his plate of fried squid arrived. No longer able to stomach the thought of eating, he reached into his pocket and palmed a silver coin onto the table for payment. His fare did not slip past the count's notice, but the nobleman shrugged forgivingly.

"Come now, Robert; you know what they say about silence speaking for you."

"He reminds me of Henri," Robert revealed reluctantly. "Why shouldn't he? And it's not odd that we'd become acquainted in England."

"No," Rouget replied, and drained his wineglass, before reaching across without invitation and helping himself to a ring of squid. "I suppose not." He tossed it into his mouth and savored it briefly. "You are close."

"No," Robert refuted, appraising their silent audience. "He's a business acquaintance."

"You don't mind if I observe that you've gone through a good deal of trouble, for an acquaintance."

"I'll admit to using his expertise from time to time."

The count laughed. "Expertise, eh? Of what kind, Robert? Or is that a question I might better ask of Maureen?"

Robert found his feet and sword simultaneously. The blade sang to life with deadly swiftness that froze the scrambling reaction of the count's men. He kept the tip of his rapier beneath Rouget's aquiline nose and, making his meaning evident, freed a pistol from beneath his coat with his left hand. He wagged it with the barrel pointed at the ceiling. "Mind that I don't take offense."

"*Mon ami.*" The count grinned, testing the sword tip with a cautious finger. "*Je suis désolé; s'il vous plaît, pardonnez-moi.* I meant no disrespect. All Frenchmen have a certain . . . *charme,* a *savoir faire, un goût pour la vie,* don't you think?"

"Don't bother to apologize; just get Descoteaux out of prison and forget about him."

"Oh, now, Robert—"

"I'm leaving," he finished, pinning the frozen group with a sweeping gaze to leave no doubt about his seriousness. "Thank you for clearing up the unfortunate misunderstanding about le Marquis de Limoges. I'll look forward to reading about his release in the newspaper."

"But you don't know what you ask. Paris is a long way from Marseille, and I keep telling you, it's not up to me."

"Then I suggest that you find someone to convince," Robert countered. Keeping his sword en garde and his pistol aloft, he edged toward the door.

"Be careful, Robert. Have you considered that you might be mistaken?"

"It wouldn't be the first time I've regretted a decision," Robert revealed, as he maneuvered to the door. "With that, I bid you adieu."

He did not stop moving once outside, but stashed his sword as he crossed the avenue in spotty streetlight. Feeling the weight of the conversation when he reached the opposite side, he holstered his pistol and buttoned his evening jacket. Before the restaurant door opened, he turned away from the ferry waiting at the dock and sought the cloaking darkness.

THE MEN WERE AFIELD, bow hunting, so, after an early lunch, Sarah took Alix and Mary on a tour of the Deer Park. Alix did not mind that she was again riding the black-and-white gelding, even if he preferred to walk with his eyes half-closed, complacently trailing the other horses. She ignored the protest of her knee around the sidesaddle pommel, while Domino followed so readily that she might have been a pasha riding in a caravan, for all the skill required of her.

Although the afternoon was fine, it had rained earlier. Patient sheepdogs tended unshorn sheep and fawn-colored cattle dotting forest-green meadows. When they stopped on a knoll before entering the forest, Sarah regarded Alix and Mary solemnly. "You're not afraid of getting lost in the woods, are you?"

Alix typically frequented the King's old Salcey Forest almost daily at home when training horses cross-country. The woods were darkly deep bordering Robbie's fields, but she could not admit to her adventures riding through there. "Have you ever been lost in the Deer Park?" she asked instead.

"Once or twice," Sarah admitted. "When I was small, I was never allowed to ride out here alone, so stay close. If we venture in the wrong direction, we might end up with spiderwebs in our hair."

Alix hid her amusement about what the others might think if they came across her galloping through the countryside around the farm. Domino shifted into a shambling trot after the other horses while Sarah explained the forestland's history.

"They call it the Deer Park now, but in medieval times, these woods were part of Sherwood Forest. I suppose that's why the men in our family have always been so keen to pursue archery. Mother once told me that we're descendants of William Scadlock, who, according to ancient texts, was Will Scarlet."

"Will Scarlet of Robin Hood's band?" Mary asked eagerly.

"The very same, but I'm not certain that it's wise to claim an outlaw as one's most illustrious ancestor," Sarah cheerfully conceded.

"He was supposed to be related to Robin of Locksley, so that would mean the same for you," Alix proposed.

"How exciting," Mary giggled. "Can't you imagine Robin's men hiding in these trees? Look there—is that Little John?"

Sarah caught herself looking when Mary pointed her riding stick into the trees, and laughed. "We might've picked a better day to venture through the park. I didn't realize it'd be so wet this afternoon. There's a meadow up here where I've found deer before."

"I love deer. Don't you?" Mary asked eagerly.

"Yes, one might suspect they know they're protected, because they're scarcely afraid of anything."

Mary sighed. "It's so beautiful here! This reminds me of those old tapestries where armored knights are riding on white horses and all manner of animals are hidden in the trees as they pass."

"I suppose so." But Sarah's laughter dissolved when they reached the clearing.

Alix stopped Domino before he bumped into the white horse. "Is something amiss?"

"This isn't the meadow I thought was here."

"It's certain to be ahead, isn't it?"

"I guess so," she decided, starting her horse again. "That's one thing about trees: They all look alike."

Goldilocks was not the type of horse to watch her feet, and the mare stumbled over a root in the path, nearly unseating Mary. The sudden mishap frightened Sarah and Sugar, which caused Domino to balk suddenly and shy from their abruptly rattled company.

"Perhaps we should turn around here," Mary urged, recovering to survey their surroundings.

Sarah laughed unsteadily as she regained her composure by

fussing with her bonnet. "We might turn around now, but where are we?"

"Oh, don't tell us we're lost!"

"It shouldn't be difficult to backtrack," Alix proposed, turning Domino to survey the muddy tracks their horses had left.

"Sam!" Mary called out into the forest hopefully. "Sam!"

"Careful," Alix cautioned, as their unnerved mounts shifted uncertainly, frightened by the shouting.

"Sam could never hear you anyway; the woods are too close," Sarah agreed anxiously as she took the lead. "Lily's right —it's easy enough to see our trail. This is most embarrassing."

"One doesn't lose oneself on purpose," Alix replied.

"I should know these woods after growing up here."

"Don't worry—we'll find our way now," Mary said.

"Here's a road, but I don't remember it before."

"It's bound to lead somewhere," Alix reasoned, but then was surprised to see a gray horse moving through the distance. She slowed Domino while her companions went ahead. He shifted uneasily, eager to join his stablemates, but Alix held him back as Midnight Star emerged from the woods with a stranger riding him and then vanished on the far side of the road. "Glory!"

"Glory is right!" Mary repeated with merry relief, turning Goldilocks in place as they waited for her to join them. "What're you doing, Lily?"

Alix had no time for tomfoolery or the furthering of Lily's games. She steered Domino to the others with unforgiving urgency. "Sarah, was anyone from your stable instructed to exercise our horses this afternoon?"

"Which horses?"

"Wexford's Donny Boy and Midnight," Alix clarified,

drawing up Domino sharply. She realized she may have revealed too much, judging from the stunned surprise on the others' faces at her inexplicable emergence from Lily's amused self-absorption.

"No," Sarah replied, exchanging mystified looks with Mary.

"Do your grooms routinely wear their livery?"

"Yes, of course!"

"Then you'll have to hurry home," Alix replied firmly, using her riding stick to push Domino in a hasty circle to follow the distancing men. "Find your stable master and get help, Sarah—I think I just saw some men stealing Donny and Midnight in the woods!"

"But, Lily! What are you going to do?"

"Someone has to follow to see which way they go . . . Mary, make certain that Sarah stays true to the road!" Determinedly, she set Domino after the men. When she slowed at a stream, the gentle horse was puffing heartily.

"Don't worry, me boy-o." Alix crooned her standard disclaimer. If her mount had been a mare, she would have called her a sweet bonnie-o. There was something soothing about the cadence that animals seemed to respond to. Safely out of sight of the others, she forgot about the sidesaddle stirrups and secured her seat by clamping her legs around his barrel. "I'm not sure where the road leads, but I'd guess it comes down on the west side of the hill, so we'll follow the wash, where the going is easier."

Alix guided the black-and-white horse along the gurgling stream, and while the piebald picked his way gingerly, she wondered at the cost of her presumption. The men taking Donny and Midnight had not been riding as if fearful of pursuit, but they could have thought their plot secure so far from the stables. She hoped she was wrong, but horses were stolen every day and sold on the enormously profitable black market, especially on the Continent and in the United States. Who looked at registration papers, when so many animals were imported? Midnight might end up pulling cabs in New York City, and Donny a fish-wain piled high with shrimp on the docks in Louisiana.

She finally turned Domino toward the empty road and stopped him beneath a spreading oak. She had hoped to see the thieves clearly enough to sketch accurate images for the authorities, but, as unconcerned squirrels scuffled in the forest duff and chased one another, Alix realized that the men might have already passed or gone in another direction.

Domino's ears swiveled as he plodded forward upslope grudgingly. A man's laughter drifted through the trees and faded while Alix immediately steered the horse from the road. If the approaching riders were leading a search with Sarah, then she would feel foolish, but if they were the horse thieves, Alix would wish only to disappear.

On one side of her, the land banked steeply; to the other, it rose sharply. Alix turned the piebald back the way they had come. Poor Domino was not nimble-footed and slipped on the muddy track, protesting with a wary snort when she urged him into the trees.

Her heart began to hammer wildly when the riders on Donny and Midnight emerged uphill, traveling at a leisurely pace. Domino shifted anxiously, reminding Alix that he was not accustomed to being alone. Hastily, she slipped from his back, but he crowded forward when she scrambled to keep him from revealing their hiding place. A sharp pain knifed through her knee when she slipped, and she grabbed his neck for support. Frightened, Domino plunged aside frantically and tore the reins from her hands. Above the crashing of the piebald through the undergrowth, she heard a surprised shout.

"Look out down there!" The horse thieves did not guess that she was a woman alone. Alix ducked behind the nearest tree to avoid being spotted as her horse charged for the road while the riders flashed past. It would not take long for the men to realize that they were running away from a riderless horse, and it was an impossible hope that they would not notice the ladies' sidesaddle.

"By Jove!" Alix gasped, as she shrank behind a tree and peered after them, horrified when Domino broke onto the road before they were out of sight. The piebald kicked up his heels at his flailing stirrups as he doggedly chased the fleeing horses. Donny and Midnight were matched in a heated contest until the man stealing Donny dared to look behind them. Alix could almost see his puzzlement as he straightened in the saddle.

She could wait no more. Hefting her bedraggled skirts, she stumbled deeper into the forest. Never had she wished more for the woolen breeches and tall boots she wore at the farm. She had no time to worry about the price of her folly when her overtaxed knee gave out at the stream; even a drenching in icy water was subsumed in her overwhelming rise of terror.

"Who have we here?" one of the thieves asked, as she stumbled into the stone wall of his chest. Hard hands clamped off her scream. Only colorless eyes showed through his hood, and when he laughed harshly, Alix saw that he was missing a yellowed upper tooth. Oddly, a swiftly humming arrow pierced his hat and pinned it to the adjacent tree while darkness rushed over her.

OF ALL THE MOMENTS to miss his mark—but the shaft was enough to convince the outlaw. Nicholas had scarce time to nock a new arrow when the brigand dropped the impostor and lunged for the stallion tied to a scraggly rowan. Midnight Star reacted with a wild sideways kick and shied violently, tearing the reins from the tree.

"Stewart, are ya stone daft?" the other thief shouted, as he yanked Donny to a precipitous stop at the edge of the road.

Nicholas responded by unleashing his arrow at the easy mark of the second outlaw. It flew high, attesting to an ill-fitted fletch, but struck the robber in the shoulder. Echoing the man's surprised scream of pain, Newton's hunting horn blew a long summons. Nicholas responded with his own, while John's sounded distantly.

The outlaw who had been trying to regain control of Midnight Star changed his mind and ran to the gray horse instead. He clambered up behind his wounded cohort on Donny and took over the reins. Nicholas raced pell-mell downhill through the trees while they galloped away on John's horse, leaving Midnight Star behind.

The rebellious stallion's hooves danced dangerously close to the impostor lying motionless on the ground. Nicholas caught a branch to stop his careless advance short and spoke to his horse soothingly. "Whoa, old son. Be careful there. Easy now, Midnight."

The animal's nervous whinny ended with a wary snort. The whites of his eyes rolled watching Nicholas, but he dropped his nose to nuzzle the unmoving woman beneath him. "Whoa, Midnight." Nicholas edged in low, ready to snatch the impostor from harm, but his horse backed away, only to whicker plaintively when Nicholas scooped her from the forest floor and cradled her in his arms.

Sam shouted with surprise when he saw them from on high, but lost no time in trumpeting a final summons on his horn. He was breathless from running by the time he reached Nicholas. "What's happened?" he asked, panting for air. "Did Lily take a tumble from her horse? What's Midnight Star doing here?"

"Donny's been stolen; the rest I don't know. I didn't take the time to ask any questions."

"Nick!" John called, as he paused on the hill and looked around. "Over here!" he shouted to the huntsmen converging from the forest with their horses.

"Help me out here, if you don't mind," Nicholas requested, exchanging his burden with Sam to mount Midnight Star.

"Hurry it up, men," Sam called over his shoulder, and then eased the impostor up onto the saddle in front of Nicholas.

"My God, what's all this?" John gasped in wonder when he reached them.

"Donny's been stolen," Sam advised tersely, glancing up at the search party from his stable. "Mick," he instructed the nearest man, "ride up and fetch the stable master. They've come looking for the horses; if we hurry, we might still catch them."

"Yes, milord!"

Sam briefly watched his servant ride off to do his bidding and then turned to John. "They nearly got away with Midnight Star, too, and no one wants to think what may have happened to Lily," he finished, as he grabbed his horse and landed in the saddle. "Davy, ride home to alert the house that Lady Griffon's been hurt. Richard, guide Lord Griffon home; the rest of you men will come with us."

Nicholas took his cloak from one of the servants and tugged it around the bedraggled woman in his arms. "They can't have gone far; I clipped one of them."

"There'll be more than clipping when this is done," John vowed, as he spurred his horse forward to lead the search.

Midnight Star stepped out readily, snorting with displeasure as the others rode off in the other direction. Nicholas held the senseless woman against him as his horse carried them back to South Hill. As the silent aftermath of the near tragedy settled, so did recognition that in one fell blow, he might have lost her. Should the thieves have kidnapped her, he might have thought she had simply run away with them. She might even have been branded a horse thief and been left to suffer the same fate as the outlaws, for how could she have explained herself while pleading for mercy?

She stirred against him, murmuring something. Nicholas lifted the edge of his cloak to check on her curiously, but her eyes were closed. With a sigh, she slipped her arms around him and nestled childishly. *"Nous allons maintenant à la maison?"*

"Yes," he promised hesitantly, "we'll go home," but he was uncertain how to keep his end of the bargain.

ALIX FELT CAUGHT in a peculiar stasis, for which she was grateful. If nothing else came from the tumultuous aftermath of the attempted theft of Midnight and the subsequent capture of the horse thieves who had made off with Donny Boy, she had at least gotten an abrupt reprieve from the constant suffering her knee was causing her. The assumption that she had been hurt in the woods granted her the liberty of coddling herself for a change, and then Nicholas chose to return to London, rather than to remain at South Hill through the week. He cited concern for his wife's comfort at home and made arrangements to leave for Skegness in the morning.

They made good time. The roads were fast, and the weather held until they were nearly to the coast. Rain started midway through the marshes around the Wash while the water was high. Nicholas joined Alix in the carriage when he tired of riding through the pervading wetness. It struck her as odd that what should have been a discomfiting journey had instead evoked deep appreciation. Had it not been for Nicholas Griffon, who knew what might have happened to her? Alix repressed a shudder at the thought and held the terrier closer.

Nicholas looked at her over his drooping newspaper. "Have you named him yet?"

"No."

With a slight smile, he shook his paper into shape and resumed his reading. "Have you perhaps considered Barkley?"

"I'll think of something."

"Fang?"

"It'll come to me."

Nicholas harrumphed gently, dropped one corner of the news to peer at the dog, and then straightened it. "I'm sure it will," he relented, and returned to his story.

Alix released the terrier to the plaid blanket she had placed on the seat and blindly reached for a book from the basket. After she sat back to read *Hamlet,* she felt the weight of Nicholas's eyes without looking up from her book. Finally, she dared to peek at him covertly, but he appeared absorbed in the newspaper. Alix was about to lower her eyes again but stopped when she noted a familiar name in an upside-down article on the front page.

She looked again at the topsy-turvy type. Someone named Quenton was on the crease of the folded page. Earlier in the column was a reference to Limoges and Fontenot Porcelain. It summoned an image of the factory's trademark golden oak tree printed on the bottom of the blue-and-white dishes at Nicholas's house. Why did she suddenly remember a black-oak forest? Chênes Noir—the name came to her, and although her uncle's name was not readily apparent, she was afraid that the article was about him. She reread what she could see of the text but came to no conclusion. It left her with the fear that her uncle had returned to France without telling her.

CHAPTER 21

SNAP FINDS A HOME

After Quenton's release and fulfillment of his delayed appointment with the King, he put his horse on the first southbound ferry leaving Paris, despite his attorneys' pleas to remain. His initial dislike for the city had deepened to outright aversion, and he cherished his liberty better than he did his fleeting popularity. In his opinion, the public approval garnered by the King's favor was only artificial; the newspapers would make of his restoration what they could. They had stirred old scandal about Henri's downfall, but now they were making Quenton's reinstatement the latest sensation.

Quenton passed by people gathering to meet him, blinded to their accolades by his singular intent to return to England for Alix, but Benoit and L'Argan immediately argued against his plan, fearful that he would never get beyond Calais without recrimination. "How would it look," L'Argan had bargained convincingly, "if you take your renewed status to London before the ink is dry on the King's decree? Are you French or English?"

"You'll be followed," Benoit agreed. "If the secret police

don't like what they find, you might not be allowed to return."

When Quenton had argued, L'Argan had trumped him. "How easily you forget about prison. Whatever enemies you've invoked might have abated for the moment, but until our investigation of its source is complete, how can anyone be certain?"

"You should wait," Benoit added. "If you return to Limoges to redouble your worth, the King will look upon his concession favorably. Don't forget that paying taxes fills his coffers, and in the meantime, opportunity is everything."

QUENTON HAD CHANGED HIS FERRY for a barge on the outskirts of the city and made better time traveling south. He parted ways with the river at Orléans but was too eager to reach home to remain. After dinner and a few hours in a hotel, he was on the road to Limousin before the sun had time to crest the horizon. It was a wearying ride, but Chiron's enthusiasm made up for Quenton's fatigue with sufficient verve to clatter into the yard.

"*Monseigneur, bienvenue chez vous!*" Marcel burst through the door with a laugh.

Quenton ignored his obeisance and clasped forearms to embrace the majordomo. "Marcel, my God, it's a relief to be home!" He laughed then, with the dizzying realization that his restoration was complete.

With a grin, Marcel clapped his hands and rubbed them together, returning to business. "Helis, lights in the north salon! Tatienne, get to the kitchen! Milord, Chef Simon hopes that a filet and Dauphiné baked potatoes might be acceptable for a light dinner."

"If he suggested slop, it'd be far better than what I've been eating."

His rejoinder lifted the majordomo's eyebrows in surprise. "Should I relay your response?"

"No!" Quenton laughed. "Filet will be a most welcome change."

"Of course, Lord Marquis," Marcel replied, as he headed to the bell rope. "But first I have arranged a bath."

NICHOLAS CLIMBED THE STAIRS to his room, relieved to be home. For the first night in recent memory, his only plan for the evening was to spend it quietly. It was too much to hope that the impostor would deign to share it without holding fast to her jaded act as Lily. He could only wonder what it would be like if she would just be herself. He looked at her closed door across the hall as he entered his own. How easy it would be to knock on it, even if only to say hello.

Albert looked up as Nicholas entered the dressing room, and gave a final tug to the paisley bow tie he had fixed around the terrier's neck. "Good eve, milord; I've been expecting you."

Nicholas unhooked his timepiece and unbuttoned his waistcoat. "Since when do dogs sit on tables?"

"I bathed him when we first arrived home," Frisk replied, reaching for the towel to swab the lowboy after the dog jumped down. As if understanding their conversation, the terrier approached Nicholas and sat at his feet, cocking his head quizzically.

"He's a hardy lad," Nicholas admitted, pulling the stickpins from his tie, "but doesn't he belong somewhere besides my dressing room?"

Albert clattered the steamer heating towels for the evening shave. "I daresay he's only here because I gave him a few biscuits."

"At least he needn't worry about starving, but he may yet

prove to be a nuisance," Nicholas said as he unbuttoned his shirt.

Albert hastily beckoned to the dog and put him out. "Did you learn anything new from Sir Poole this afternoon?"

"Hardly," Nicholas answered, peeling out of his shirt while Frisk came to help. "It's always the same mumbo jumbo about who said what, but at least Terrence had a credible lead from Burton's butler."

"You mean Daniel Clive?"

"The very same; do you know him?"

"We chat now and then, but it's not as if we meet for tea. My experience with Mr. Clive is limited to his rounds when he's out walking Lady Burton's spaniel, or mayhap the odd run-in downtown."

"More's the pity; apparently, Clive bumped into Quincy at the bank about the same time that he disappeared."

"At the bank? Why would a coachman have business at the bank?"

"Precisely," Nicholas responded, loath to share his uncertain impression of Quincy's being more than an ordinary servant until he had collaboration from a reputable source.

"Mr. Clive may've been mistaken."

"Except that Quincy's in this up to his bloody neck." Nicholas stepped out of his trousers and headed for his waiting bath. "So far, the interview's inconclusive. He couldn't be certain the man was Quincy Hill. Clive had finished Reggie's business, and a man resembling Quincy held the door. He didn't seem to notice Clive, and upon further questioning, the butler admitted his acquaintance was limited to seeing Quincy in the neighborhood. He remarked more on the quality of his suit and ebony cane than on anything else."

Rain smeared the bathroom window. Nicholas stepped into the tub of heated water with relief. After holding his breath and sinking to the bottom for a count of 120, he surfaced for a breath of air, suddenly remembering that Quincy's cane had matched the description. "I don't suppose you might learn when milady's next outing will be."

"Funny you should mention it, milord. Jenny was quite pleased this evening when the errand boy brought a message confirming a fitting tomorrow at one thirty."

"Good. It's high time to get to the bottom of this. There is bound to be some concrete evidence somewhere, and the best place to begin is with the impostor's drawings that she keeps in the desk."

ALIX RECOGNIZED THE TERRIER'S WARMTH when he licked her nose, breaking the darkness of her dream. She fled the suffocating nightmare of the laundry chute and opened her eyes to the shadowed room. "*Qu'est-ce que tu fais?*" Then she amended the question, realizing the dog did not understand French: "What are you doing?" He wiggled his stubby tail in response. "Did I wake you? *Merci* for returning the favor." Unrolling from her cramped, creeping-through-the-laundry-chute position, she stretched in the satin sheets. The mantel clock in the sitting room chimed a lonely hour of two. "When we're at home, we'll be getting up soon." She stifled a reluctant yawn and rolled over to push her pillow into shape, hoping for sleep.

Alix counted the seconds in her mind to match the minute hand. "This is impossible." Throwing aside the bedcovers in defeat, she shivered and fumbled for her dressing gown. After floating into the sitting room like Cleopatra, she lit the desk lamp and held it aloft to consider the highest shelves. Since the accident at Oxley, she had not been able to climb in search of the title. Now she kicked off her slippers and wedged the desk chair into the corner, determined to use it as a ladder.

Soon she was perusing knickknacks and found a mirrored carousel with painted porcelain horses. Posed unsteadily, Alix wound its brass key, and the ballad "Fair Margaret and Sweet William" began to play while the turning carousel illuminated the walls and ceiling. *"The rose is red, the grass is green, the days are past that I have seen,"* she sang softly, as she climbed down clumsily. The terrier dropped from the couch and bounded to her. "You really like music, don't you?"

She wound the music box again and put it aside on the table. While the mirrors danced delightful reflections around the room, she scooped up the terrier to rumple his pointed ears. "You're quite the character." While the music box played, she studied the bookcase. If the title were there, she would find it tonight. In a handful of hours, she might be on her way home. Ozzie's racing clothes bundled in the back of the wardrobe would make a suitable disguise. No one would think to look for a missing woman wearing a man's clothing.

For the first time, the idea of leaving without saying good-bye troubled her. Alix had not considered it before but did not know when she might see anyone again. She released the dog to the floor and shook her thoughts free of the question. What difference would it make if she did? She had a business to run and a future to pursue. Worrying about what happened to Lily's life was Lily's problem to manage.

As soon as tomorrow, Alix might return to her old routine. She would be up at three to start the morning feeding, and by the time Ozzie came to work at four, she would be in the storage room, rationing grain. Smooth execution of the schedule was imperative to training horses. She had no time for idle reflection. She reminded herself that she was here only because Sterling Wood Stable was in jeopardy.

The terrier dashed to the desk chair and eyed the shelves

speculatively ahead of her advance. "Oh, no you don't," she scolded, as she returned him firmly to the floor. "You're not a cat." Resolutely, she climbed to the shelf where she had found the carousel, and reached for the Oriental vase. To her surprise, there was some paper inside. Just as she found it, the vase wobbled precariously, toppling from her grasp as her perilous purchase slipped. She dropped amid a hail of knickknacks and landed in a muddled heap of curios crashing to the floor. The terrier yelped and sprang to her rescue.

"No, stay down! Quiet, for God's sake," Alix groaned. Helpfully, he whined and licked her face while she struggled to her feet, trying to ignore the reignited sharp stab of pain in her knee.

She froze fearfully at the sound of a door and rapid footsteps in the hall, and the realization that Nicholas was coming sent her scrambling. She fell in a frightened tangle, tripping on her nightdress. "By Jove!" she gasped when the dog pounced playfully onto her back. A fearful pounding on the door brought her bolt upright. The terrier, delighted to join the hubbub, dashed in a circle, barking hysterically. Alix struggled to her feet and frantically grabbed the knitted blanket from the couch.

"Quiet," she hissed, as the handle rattled insistently before the banging resumed. "Just a moment," she begged, but her plea drowned in a thunder that shook the door in its frame. Praying for the lock to hold, she threw her shoulder against it to prevent his bursting in on her undressed condition.

"Stop," she begged, as the dog dug furiously at her bare foot, which she was bracing against the panel. Her voice sounded surprisingly sharp in the sudden silence. "Stay," she maintained, hoping it was clear that she intended the reprimand for the terrier. She flipped the lever of the lock and cracked the door slightly. "Yes?"

"Hello," Nicholas replied with surprising restraint.

Her terrified reply sallied forth as a whisper. "Hello. What might I do for you?"

His eye drifted down the length of the crack in vague disbelief. Uneasily, Alix tucked aside the telltale ruffles of her nightgown. The terrier's eager snuffling at the base of the door grabbed his attention, and he looked at the dog as she shoved him back with her foot. Did his eye widen at the sight of her naked toes? She leaned on the door more heavily.

"Is everything all right in here?"

"Fine," Alix replied glibly.

"I thought I heard something fall."

Alix's knee wrenched with painful prickles. "My apology; it was only me."

His eye narrowed skeptically. "You fell?"

Was Nicholas trying to push inside? The door seemed resistant. "No. I . . . was playing with the dog."

His hand appeared as he grasped the panel, and she watched his hand, adorned with a diamond ring, slip dangerously near her thinly clad shoulder. "You're playing games at this time of night?"

"Yes," she lied desperately, and readjusted her foot firmly as the terrier dug at the narrowed opening. "Stop that, you. We've caused enough trouble."

Nicholas brought his face so close, she felt the heat of his breath. "You haven't named him yet?"

"Who?"

His eye sharpened. "The dog."

"Oh," she responded, collecting her thoughts desperately. "Of-of course," she stammered. "I was teaching him his name."

Nicholas's eyebrow lifted in disbelief. "What is it?"

Alix wished her hands were not slippery with anxiety. If she lost her grip, he would think it an invitation to come in, and not only was she undressed, but he would spot the wreckage on the floor. She dared not loosen her hold on the blanket, but pushed her shoulder against the panel as her foot slipped, and opened the door incrementally. Incredibly, the terrier scrabbled excitedly at the toe of Nicholas's slipper in the opening. "Whose name?"

"The dog's name."

"Snap!" It was the first word that came to mind. She smiled brightly when he blinked at her in perplexity, and took advantage of his inattention to narrow the gap in the door.

"Snap," Nicholas repeated doubtfully.

"Yes, Snap," she confirmed, dismissing her own misgivings about the oddity of the dog's name by looking at the terrier with his muzzle parked in the fissure of the door. "Snap, stop it; there's a good boy." Luckily, Snap looked at her solely from the tone of her voice. Alix smiled until she found Nicholas studying her. "See, he likes it. We're very sorry for disturbing you."

"Snap is a name for a dog?"

"Yes, and now that you realize nothing is amiss, I really should be going."

Nicholas's eyebrow wrinkled into a frown. "Going?"

"Yes, you know, back to bed or something."

"That might be a good place for you."

"Thank you. Perhaps you should consider it as well. We apologize for disturbing you." Unable to withstand his withering inspection, Alix looked at the terrier trying to squeeze past the slipper incredibly wedged in her door. "I'd hate to remember the time."

The pressure abated on the door so abruptly that she scarcely saved it from slamming closed. "Oh, I'm sorry!"

"Yes, so I understand. Go to sleep," he added, before turning to disappear into the darkness.

Alix closed the door and locked it, turning to test the terrier's name. "Snap." The dog cocked his head and lolled out his tongue in an absurd dog smile. "All right, Snap it is," she decided, and turned to look at the wreckage of broken bric-a-brac scattered by the shelves. The papers inside the broken vase were not the missing title but a hidden diary. She hurried to remove the mess, keenly aware that, despite her apparent chumminess with Jenny Smith, Jenny worked for Lily, for a reason.

QUENTON SUSPECTED HE WAS difficult to please, but he pushed the unremarkable collection of Louis figurines aside. "These are unacceptable."

"But, Marquis," Oliver protested, "they're reasonable!"

Quenton snatched one up demonstratively. "Bah! It's cheaper to look at your own wife than at this. Destroy the molds."

"But, Charles . . ."

Quenton rose from his desk to retrieve his hat and overcoat. "If Charles Lesage wants to work here, he'll make another lot. Otherwise, give him a week's pay and turn him out."

"Marquis, I don't think—"

"No, obviously not. I'm leaving; I have a lunch appointment with Moises Benoit."

"God help him," Oliver retorted on his way out

"Don't forget to send someone to clean up this mess."

Whatever Oliver had to say was lost in the slamming of

the door. The paradox of French temperament struck Quenton while shrugging into his coat. He might not have noticed the difference if he had never lived in England. Businessmen there seemed more equitable.

The sky was leaden with swollen clouds, and Michel was waiting at the curb in the hooded curricle. The cathedral bells marked the hour as they wheeled through traffic on the roundabout, but even the passing showers could not keep patrons from lining the walkway outside Georges Café.

"Lord Marquis," Petrie bowed at the door as he dropped the gold cord to allow him through. "Bonjour, bonjour."

"Bonjour," Quenton replied, shrugging out of his coat while scanning the crowded tables. "Has Moises Benoit arrived?"

"*Mais oui, naturellement.*" The maître d' snapped his fingers for the hatcheck and unhooked the gold braid to the dining room. "Right this way."

Moises rose at his approach. "Thank you for agreeing to meet on such short notice."

"Everyone has to eat," Quenton reasoned, as he took the opposite chair. "Bring a bottle of merlot—Moisson."

"Oh, but of course," Petrie replied with a cheerful snap of his fingers. "Bon appétit."

"It's pouring outside, eh?" Moises ventured amiably.

"Yes, but it'll bring up new green in the pasture, so, all in all, the day is fine. I hope you didn't ask me here to discuss the weather. I've a stack of contracts waiting on my desk."

"Business is good, eh?"

"Good enough," Quenton allowed, tasting the splash of wine the steward poured for him to sample. "This is fine."

"I know you're busy, so I hope you don't mind that I took the liberty of ordering for us," Moises replied.

"As long as you don't ask me to dance next."

His attorney laughed. "I hadn't considered it, but I suppose I should get straight to the subject."

Quenton sipped his wine judiciously. "I'd appreciate it."

"I returned last night from Poitiers."

"Welcome home."

"I can't say that traveling in the rain is my favorite way to tour the countryside—"

"You're not going to dwell on the weather again, are you?" Quenton interjected.

"No. I'm trying to tell you of my meeting with Josef."

"L'Argan? What was he doing in Poitiers?"

"He was returning to Paris from La Rochelle. Poitiers was . . . convenient."

His meaningful hesitation caught Quenton's attention. "Conveniently away from Paris?"

"Yes, something of the sort," Moises maintained, as a plate of *gougères* arrived.

Quenton helped himself. "Am I to guess this has something to do with the Count of Mandelieu?" The more he learned about Claudius Rouget and his business, the less he liked it. If Henri's old friend had summoned L'Argan, it could not bode well for anyone.

"The count is making you an offer."

"Whatever it is, no."

"You don't want to hear about the schooner he has placed at your disposal? I understand it's a wonderful vessel."

"His ships are for the damned. What does he want in return for such a generous present?"

"Nothing." Benoit shrugged as the soup arrived. When the waiter left, he broke the crust with fanatical zeal. "He thought you might use it when you bring your niece home from England."

"It's none of his business," Quenton answered, but then he sipped his wine thoughtfully. If the count had been as close to Henri as the man claimed, he probably knew Alix, and the idea that the Count of Mandelieu took interest in her well-being was disturbing.

ROBERT NEVER SHOULD HAVE trusted fate by walking to the café from his hotel in Avignon. He was passing a stack of crates in an adjacent alleyway when he was suddenly dealt a numbing blow. He awoke on the floor of a fast-moving coach with a hood pulled over his eyes. He knew better than to react, but he must have given an indication of increasing awareness, because he received a kick in his gut that drove the air from him.

Soft laughter mocked his discomfort. An *"Arrêtez-vous!"* abruptly stopped the rollicking ride. With another command —*"Le délogez!"*—Robert was hefted and dumped roughly into the road. "Monsieur Peltier," his scornful tormentor continued, "I presume that I have sufficiently garnered your attention."

Robert was uncertain whether a response was expected, but the expression was familiar. He dimly recalled Viscount Rouget's having made the same sort of assertion when they met in Marseille, but the voice of his unseen tormentor did not belong to Claude. Apparently the Count of Mandelieu and his son were reluctant to dirty their hands and so had sent a henchman with their message.

"I understand that your friend the marquis is home in Limousin."

"Wouldn't it have been easier to send a copy of the Limoges newspaper?" Robert should have kept his mouth shut; the second kick to his gut hurt worse than the first.

The mocking laughter continued appreciatively. "Perhaps,

but the article would have been incomplete, you understand. There are people asking too many questions. Someone will inquire of the wrong person and won't like it when he finds himself dead. Don't you agree it would be inconvenient? Your friend's attorney, Josef L'Argan, is one. Another is that slipshod detective from London—what is his name? Stanley, I believe."

Robert might have taken solace that he did not know either man, had he had time to consider who they were, but the one-sided tête-à-tête was interrupted by the abrupt arrival of a swift rider on horseback. "Marquis du Périer!" a man called, pulling his mount to a precipitous halt. "I bring an urgent message from the viscount!"

"*Idiot!*"

The finality of a surprised cry and marked silence ended the conversation. Robert might not have connected the man's identity with the prestigious Harlequin Stables if they had not just crossed paths at Oxley Commons earlier in the summer. A blow to the base of Robert's skull stunned him as someone shouted dimly, "Carl! Take care of that horse," and then he heard nothing more.

ALBERT SLIPPED into the sitting room and closed the door silently. "They're gone, milord."

"In a moment," Nicholas cautioned, peering around the edge of the drapery to watch Georgie secure the carriage door. After the driver clambered up and gathered his reins, Nicholas let the curtain fall and turned to Albert. "Wait for me in the hall."

"It'd be more prudent to allow me to handle this risky business, wouldn't it?"

"There's only one way I'll be satisfied. Have you the art

that I'm to replace?"

"Here, milord," Albert said, as he retrieved the stack of illustrations from the drawer.

"Sound a warning the instant you suspect anyone coming," Nicholas instructed, as they slipped out together. Silently, Albert walked to the head of the stairs while Nicholas waited with his hand on the latch to his wife's chambers. When Albert waved the all clear, Nicholas stepped inside and closed the door.

He never had been able to stomach the apartment once Lily had had it remodeled, but he ignored his distaste by crossing immediately to the window and peering at the quiet slice of street. Releasing the lace, he turned to the desk, intent on a systematic search, and did not disturb the careful arrangement of paint pots and crayons. The middle drawer contained little more than a stacked variety of paper, paintbrushes, and extra pen nibs. The lower drawer was where Albert had found the other paintings, but Nicholas hesitated at its atypical mess before rummaging beneath the correspondence with Lily's name and finding neat stacks of the impostor's hidden art.

Calling cards and notes fell from the sheaf of pages as he put them on the desk. Settling into the chair, he compared them. There were fewer illustrations of the English countryside than the prevalent images of Quincy. In these portraits, Quincy played chess, pall-mall, or tennis, and fenced without protection, but he was customarily depicted with horses of prized heritage.

If they were to be believed, then Quincy might have been younger. Perhaps it was the difference of a beardless chin and slighter build, but they seemed to evidence a lapse of time. If that much were true, then where was the castle in the background? The high mountain cliffs and jagged peaks evidenced Europe, but it was impossible to imagine where inside the enormous length of the Alps or Pyrenees. Nicholas dimly recalled a new piece of their final conversation when Quincy had told him about a man who had everything. He had the feeling that he was looking at pieces of that story, but how did that translate to the other drawings of the English countryside?

Who the devil are you, Quincy? he wondered. He stacked the artwork in preparation to return it to the drawer but then stopped to study the scenes of the English farm. It had a pair of barns and a mew nestled among stone outbuildings. Apple trees lined the lane, and a windmill rose in the background of the comfortable house, where meadows were populated by a multitude of horses.

He was tempted to keep more than one to share with Terrence Poole's investigators but put aside only the house with the windmill and returned the rest. He was littering the top of the stack with Lily's letters, when he stopped, noticing a card written in bold, upright pen. It bore the address of a perfumery in France, and perhaps an order number.

The card was blank on the reverse, without solicitation or advertisement. When he retrieved a piece of notepaper, he found that the stationery matched. Realizing that he had discovered something written by the impostor, he jotted down the information, before replacing it along with everything else. Then he tucked his evidence away in his coat's breast pocket and turned to survey the room. His wife's shelves contained the regular clutter of meaningless trinkets that included the mirrored carousel Lily had received for her birthday from an admirer.

The sight of it brought his mind to a halt. Lily's birthday

was in a handful of days. Her friends would wonder about a celebration. The impostor was probably unaware of its advent, but the party down in Haymarket had cost Nicholas nearly a small fortune the year before. At the time, he and Lily had not been married; he should have recognized her wanton extravagance as a formidable sign, but in those days, he had been foolish enough to indulge her slightest whim. No wonder she had been so keen to marry him.

He tore his mind from reflection and discovered that he was holding the carousel. What should he do about the impostor? As far as anyone knew, she was Lily, and forgetting her birthday would not bode well in court when he posed his position as the maligned husband.

He replaced the music box and postponed the problem. After making a cursory inspection of his books stacked on the shelf, he determined nothing was different than he had noted before; the volumes were as unadulterated, as if used for display. Shakespeare, Scott, the collection of Raleigh's poetry, and *The Song of Roland,* the singular book misplaced on the end table—none bore dog-eared tags or markers on a special page.

Nicholas continued to the bedchamber and promptly found Lily's diary tucked in the nightstand drawer, resolving any mystery about how the impostor knew of his wife's habits. He moved on to the dressing room and blundered to a stop on his way to the dressing table, startled by his multiple reflections in her collection of mirrors. Wondering about her vanity, he rummaged through the bottles until he found the vial of rose-scented perfume that the impostor habitually wore. Its crystal vial was ornate, but its lack of a maker's mark obscured its origin. Satisfied when there was nothing else, he turned to the wardrobe, determined to find a monogram on something, even if it was the least likely handkerchief.

The very first drawer was daunting. His eyes fastened on the cubed sections fitted for rolled stockings. The next billowed with silky garments of various hues and trimmed in lace that were better left unconsidered. He finally plunged into the racks of gowns in the wardrobe and pushed to the end, wondering if he might find a gypsy costume. Without any other choice, he climbed onto his knees and rummaged blindly along the bottom. Racks of shoes and boots stacked in boxes filled the floor, but in the back corner, he found an awkward sack. Triumphant, he pulled it into the light, but the coarse bag was tied with a frayed cord that refused to yield. At last, he dug for his knife to pry it open.

"I say," Albert spoke up cheerfully in the back hall. "Martha, fancy meeting you here. I didn't know you intended to clean milady's room so early."

"Blast," Nicholas breathed, staring blindly at his half-realized discovery. He scarcely had time to dig into a roll of cobalt silk before he was required to relinquish the bundle quickly.

"I was just on my way downstairs," Frisk maintained further.

Next, a pleased laugh mocked him in reply. "That's a likely story!"

Nicholas resurfaced from the wardrobe depths and, after closing the mirrored doors, paused to smooth his disheveled hair.

"How could I pass by without begging a word with you?"

There was no time to consider the recriminatory evidence of his presence should the maid push through the servants' door as he hurried to the sitting room. With only a cursory glance up and down the front hall for witnesses, Nicholas escaped silently.

He straightened his clothing as he went to the library,
where he had left his morning paper. He opened it on the desk,
but his eyes blurred with wonder about what he had found
hidden in the wardrobe. Heavy and ungainly shoes and cobalt
silk might not be evidence, and a bottle of perfume without a
label might mean only that the label had been lost. Coupled
with the images of Quincy and the castle, Nicholas had
discovered only more mismatched pieces for a misfit puzzle.
He had gone in search of answers but found more questions.

CHAPTER 22

A BIRTHDAY SURPRISE

❦

*N*icholas had thought that he might come upon the impostor walking the dog through Hyde Park, but after meeting Terrence Poole at the detective's office, he rode Midnight Star blindly down Rotten Row on the way home. While the detective had been reviewing the evidence that Nicholas had produced from Lily's desk, Terrence had paused at the jotted bit of information from the impostor's note.

Leaning leaned forward in his chair, he had spun the copy around on his desktop for Nicholas to read. "It appears relatively straightforward, milord. It might be a standard formula really. If we assume they're corresponding letters, the two is a *B*, and the five is an *E*, and so on." He reclaimed it to note on his jotter. "Just give me a minute, and I'll have it for you . . . Yes, it appears to say *Beau Trésor*, milord."

"Beautiful Treasure."

"Quite."

"But what does it mean?"

"I'd say it's a perfume, considering the combination of the address of Laval Perfumery."

Without knowing why, Nicholas felt it was more important. When he was a child, his father had claimed their family's capacity for second sight was an inherited trait from their ancestry of soothsayers and sorcerers, and Nicholas had learned early not to discuss it, since it was impossible to explain. When he was a lad, it had teased him with a feeling of familiarity in new situations, but later, when battling pirates on the high seas, he had gained a fighting edge. Since then, it had failed him. It had been missing for so long that had forgotten of its existence, until his premonition when Terrence Poole uttered the words *Beau Trésor*. "Is it a place somewhere?"

"It might be." The detective shrugged. "One of our best men is in Paris; I'll have him inquire."

"Was there anything further on that fellow who supposedly returned from the dead to claim a fortune?"

"The Marquis Saint-Descoteaux? No, his attorneys have declined all interviews, and he left Paris upon his release. Everything about the man and the charge of treason is veiled by innuendo. He might have returned to his home in Limoges, but French newspapers are notoriously indeterminate. Shall I put Stanley on it? It might be nothing but a red herring."

Nicholas reached for his hat, prepared to leave. "No, it makes no difference to me why the devil tucked his tail when he was freed."

HAD HE BEEN ASTRIDE another horse besides Midnight Star, Nicholas might have passed the impostor, but her bonnet had already caught the animal's eye. They were nearly upon her when Nicholas realized that the barking dog charging up from the lakeside was the stray terrier with the peculiar name of Snap. Midnight Star was not typically rattled by dogs, and only curled his neck to snort at the tiny assailant, but the impostor was aghast when she noticed their approach.

"Snap!" She hurried to scoop up the beast and clamp a hand on his muzzle. "Quiet, you!"

"Hello," Nicholas replied, doffing his hat. He hopped to the ground, ready to stave off his horse with a well-placed elbow in the chest to halt Midnight's blithe over-exuberance. "I'm happy to see you're well enough to come out walking."

"Thank you," she replied, clearly unsettled by their unexpected meeting. She stroked the dog's ears with a trembling hand and released him to the ground.

"You know," Nicholas continued, as a way to ease her concern and broach the uncertain subject of Lily's birthday while escorting her toward the gates, "it won't be long, and the season will be over." The idea was unsettling; he could feel her trepidation as they walked, although her gaze was fixed on the jaunty terrier leading the way. "Last year you told me how you love to go out with a bash . . ." His blatant prevarication forced him to keep his eyes on the pair of black swans sailing overhead, lest she see the truth in his expression. "But this year, I thought a party might be a little difficult to manage dancing all night, after the incident in the forest up at Stragglethorpe."

"Oh." Her soft reply sounded like the coo of a dove.

"Since you love sailing," Nicholas ventured, and was happily rewarded by her delightful quickening of interest, "I thought we might take a trip downriver to Southend-on-the-Sea." If he had any doubt about her desire to visit the popular resort, her response quickly reassured him.

"Oh!"

It was ridiculous how she managed to express so much in one simple word. Pleased with her willingness to join him, all he needed now was to decide on a gift. "We could spend the day at the beach, if you'd like, or we might take a drive through Westcliff, toward the island. It depends on what you feel like doing; after all, it's your birthday."

"Oh."

As Nicholas had suspected, she did not have the slightest clue that Lily's birthday was in a few days. Had the circumstances been different, he would have put his arm around her shoulders to offer her consolation, but he loathed the prospect of the chance return to the lost wariness of her prior regard. Behind her, Midnight Star had taken to walking with his eyes half-closed contentedly. At least the horse was not trying to devour her bonnet strings.

"I had hoped you'd like the idea," he vowed truthfully, meeting her cautious glance with a reassuring smile. "Now, please allow me to find a cab to take you home. There's no sense in overtaxing yourself," he insisted, steering her toward the likeliest hansom parked in a line of cabbies at the curb when they passed the gates. "I'll be home later."

"Thank you," she responded, as he secured the door.

"It's my pleasure always, sweetheart."

Sweetheart? he thought when the unwarranted endearment slipped out again. A flash of her blue-gray eyes was all he received in response as the cabbie popped his whip overhead, startling the cob into a trot. The terrier's head appeared in the window as the carriage pulled off, lending the impression that Snap watched him expectantly.

Midnight Star was anxious to be under way; Nicholas barely had time to find a seat in the saddle before his horse started out after the taxi. He had a mind to swing down the Piccadilly for a pint but, for some reason, had a devil of a time convincing his horse. Finally, he turned around and rode along Knightsbridge in the other direction.

❧ ❧

"I STILL FIND IT SURPRISING," Alix protested, as Jenny shaped her hair into ringlets for the evening. She could not admit that it was contrarily unwarranted, since she and Lily shared the same birthday, November twenty-fifth. Only Lily would fabricate a birthday during the haute season—the London high summer, when Parliament was in session—simply to enjoy a party in her honor.

Jenny glanced at her speculatively in the mirror. "I understand that last year milord footed a huge party down in Haymarket. I wasn't hired on yet; another maid worked in my place, but everyone belowstairs has been wondering what milord had planned this year."

"It would have been nice to know," Alix replied glumly, and then realized her slip. It was kind of Nicholas to commemorate Lily's supposed birthday, but the idea brought the uncomfortable reminder that Alix deeply desired to be home for her own, as well as for Christmas. "When is Nicholas's birthday? I wouldn't like to miss it."

"Milord's birthday is January fifth."

"Oh," Alix replied, toying with the hairpins in the canister on the dressing tray. Certainly she would be gone by Epiphany and the New Year. She wished that she had been astute enough to inquire of Lily how she planned to enact the endgame of her unprecedented ploy.

"That will be Albert," Jenny said knowingly of the gentle rap at the door. "Snap!" she called the terrier from his woolen blanket in the corner. "Time to go out."

"It's kind of Albert Frisk to walk Snap in the evening."

"He likes dogs, doesn't he?" Jenny replied as she opened the door.

Alix could hear Albert's calming baritone voice in the

hallway as he chatted with Jenny. Since the jaunt to Stragglethorpe, Nicholas's man had taken on the responsibility of caring for the dog, although Alix wondered if it was mostly for the opportunity to visit her maid.

"Now then," Jenny said as she returned, "let's finish your hair."

"Has Albert asked you out for an evening again?"

"Fie, no. He hasn't mentioned a thing since we've been home."

"Perhaps at dinner."

"Pishposh—I don't count my eggs before they hatch."

"Oh." Alix watched Jenny move in the mirror. She was tired of looking at her own reflection and seeing Lily there.

ALIX INCHED FORWARD IN DARKNESS, too terrified to make a sound. Her raw fingers slipped on the reluctant stone of the laundry chute inside the château. New horror overwhelmed her when the rumble shaking her imprisoning walls indicated that the murderers were searching for her with the dumbwaiter. She squeezed her eyes closed, wishing the invaders away.

"Don't panic; you have to think in a tight situation," Quenton had counseled often when she was small. It was easy enough when sitting by the fireside. Alix squeezed forward, wishing for her forgotten riding gloves in her mad scramble from the terror in the front hall. Her escape from her father's murder had been instinctive, but despite the horrible evidence in his office, she had not truly realized that he was dead until she found herself trapped inside the laundry chute and incredibly alone, with no one to save her.

Her grandmother's coronet was gouging her side, and if Alix died, too, her bones would not hold the treasure trove of jewelry she had grabbed from her father's safe. As her body decayed within the laundry chute, pieces would drop out one at a time and land in the vat below.

Remembering the laundry lent an idea of a way out. Sliding through the walls would evade the murders ransacking the upper floors. By the time they realized she was not hiding, she could be safely past the gardens in the wilderness. She would find Quenton before he could ride into the deathtrap waiting for him! Alix took a deep breath as she pushed forward and let go.

She did not know when she met the carpet, but the terrier dug frantically to free her from the muddle of bedcovers. She heard whimpering, but confusing images overwhelmed her, until Snap somehow squirmed in to rescue her with a lick of his tongue.

"God," Alix gasped. She collapsed on her back while the fear drained from, leaving her vaguely empty. "*In nomine Patris, et Filii, et Spiritus Sancti,*" she whispered as she crossed herself weakly. Her forgotten habit had a strangely calming effect. Just because she had lost it for a while did not make her peculiar. As a child, she had been taught to attend Mass diligently. No one would think her strange just because of Lily's difference as an Anglican, rather than a Catholic.

Lily. The dregs of her past were drenched by complications of the present as she pushed the dog aside and climbed to her feet. Quenton might be right that the terrible deeds of the past no longer held sway, since she was safe in England, and that if the criminals remembered their crime, her father's death would be only an unsettled memory left over from the war. It was sage advice in daylight, but in the darkness of the witching hour, she shivered at the horrible recollection. The nightmare of what had happened on that terrifying day had returned too much. She willed it to go away.

She shrugged into a blanket and stalked though the darkness like an ancient priestess. A low-burning lamp guided her to the sitting room, where she reached for *The Song of Roland* as the terrier curled by her feet. *"'Come, swear me here to Roland's fall.' 'Your will,' said Gan, 'be mine in all.'"*

Across the lonely hall, Nicholas gently started a tune on his guitar that created a fragile melody to echo her thoughts.

NICHOLAS FOUND AN ANSWER in a dream where he wore the raiment of a king and danced with the impostor as his queen. The circlet of hammered gold and the necklace that she wore in it worked as talismans. He awoke with the desire to give the impostor a gift so rare that she could not fail to keep it. Such a generous trinket would work in two ways, for wherever he found her after the finish of the charade, he would recognize her by it immediately.

Despite the contrary evidence, Nicholas was not a fool. He knew Lily would return just as suddenly as she had vanished. As summer had waned, Nicholas had realized he had become more concerned about the impostor than about his wife's reemergence. Lily's pending displacement was a foregone conclusion, but how his wife had coerced the impostor to take her place would be the stranger's cost to pay at the end of it.

The realization that he was thinking instead of sleeping made him toss about in his sheets restlessly. He had no reason to lie awake when he wished for sleep, if only to dream about holding her and her willingness beneath him. He groaned and tossed his arm wide in frustration as he rolled to stare at the darkness. What was she doing now, but sleeping? How easy it would be to steal across the hall to glimpse her, but he knew not to give in to that temptation, because he would not be able to restrain himself.

He reached for his dressing gown and stuffed his feet into slippers. He went to build up the fire burning low, but as he finished, he imagined her lying in his rumpled bed, watching him sleepily. Whether she was a by-product of wishful thinking or second sight did not matter. She was gone when he blinked but did not change his surge of emotion or his feeling of being left cheated.

Tightening the belt on his dressing gown, he went to check the fire in the sitting room and reached for his guitar when he had finished, wishing that he had kept some of the impostor's illustrations. He had already given the one he had pilfered of the farmhouse as evidence to Terrence Poole.

He picked out a melody gently. It was her song, or it would one day be her song, because when it was complete, he would play it for her. Now it did not have words and was largely unfinished, but his fingers always seemed to return to it whenever he dwelled on her. What was her name? Was she Elizabeth, or Samantha, or something prosaic, like Jane? One of his greatest fears was what she would say if he asked. The guardian Quincy had promised had never materialized, and the idea that the impostor had been abandoned was disgraceful. If Nicholas revealed his knowledge of the charade and the news caused her to run away, where would she go without protection? It was reason enough for him to keep his silence, even without the circus that the exposé would create. He had ceased to care if his name became synonymous with the reputation of a cuckolded dolt, except for what it would mean to her. People bowed to him now in deference, but would she look on him the same if they mocked him?

He tinkered with the distraction of an addition to the song's refrain. His idea for a distinctive gift by which to recognize her later could be genius, but where could he find such a delectable something on the day before the promised trip downriver? It was impossibly short notice to order anything, and it would take time to comb the shops of Mayfair and the Piccadilly.

The longer he thought about the opal set in a diamonds from his dream, the more familiar it became. Finally, he put aside his guitar and went to open the coronet on the hearth, which concealed a secret vault. The last time he had been inside had been to add the documents from his mother-in-law's estate. Now he dug into the depths, where silk pouches and velvet boxes were placed. His mother had often remarked on how old-fashioned some of the jewelry was, but now her diamonds and pearls mingled with the rest.

When at last he was about to deem the safe empty, he came across a velvet purse crammed in the corner. Knowing instantly that he had found it, he hurried to the lamp to empty the glittering opal into his palm.

THE MEETING WITH MOISES BENOIT had given Quenton plenty to consider on his ride home as the day turned to evening. An afternoon storm had left behind a muddy road, and the clouds blanketing the horizon swallowed the setting sun. Stars pierced the violet darkening overhead as bats flitted through the gloaming. Trilling frogs drowned the sounds of cicadas before they reached the bridge as the stagecoach to Compreignac careened past.

Quenton moved Chiron to the shoulder, but a wheelhorse slipped and the coach lurched amid the collective surprise of its packed occupants. His horse plunged aside instinctively, but they were showered with mud. The stagecoach thundered away with Quenton's epithets in its wake. "Damned country! They let anyone drive here!" Chiron agreed with a disgusted snort.

Quenton gratefully entered the forest and turned toward home, unable to refrain from dwelling on his meeting with Benoit. Moises had practically jumped from his chair when Quenton had entered his office, and had hurried to pummel Quenton's hand anxiously. "Marquis, thank you for stopping by!"

Quenton should have known immediately that the meeting was about more than his trip to England. "I apologize for my delay, Counselor; as you might imagine, I've been busy with a few things before my ship leaves at the end of the week."

"I'm afraid I've unsettling news," Moises replied, reaching for the file on his desk. "Regrettably, it's something that couldn't wait. Marquis, Josef L'Argan is dead."

In the silent aftermath of the unexpected declaration, the wall clock was suddenly deafening. "Dead?"

Benoit passed over the file as he mopped his brow with a handkerchief. "Murdered, I'm afraid." He blotted his upper lip. "His body was fished out of the canal on the Rue Basse." He crossed himself swiftly. "May he rest in peace." With a nervous cough, he put away his handkerchief. "Before he died, he hid this file in the mail. It's evidence of what Josef discovered, and, to be frank, I'm nervous about keeping it."

Quenton opened the folder to find bank records in different languages, with only one name common to them all. "Claudius Rouget?"

"Josef has—*had*," Moises corrected hastily, "an astute perception of inconsistency, and he was curious about your account of the count's mediocre circumstances at the time of your brother's death. You see, there are many ways to make money—and not all are legal."

Quenton looked up from the documents, which listed enormous sums of wealth. "Do you mean that all this is undeclared?"

"Cyclops Freight manages quays in many countries; ships come and go. Cargo is delivered, gold changes hands, but sometimes the ledger is neglected."

"Or someone keeps an alternate set of books."

"Precisely, and who inspects the tariffs if the port commissioner is on someone's payroll?"

"It makes a lucrative pastime for everyone involved."

Quenton returned the file with not only new appreciation but also the question of why it would have led to L'Argan's death without the murderer's having attempted to leverage the attorney's connections first. "While Josef was following his nose, did it lead him to the departmental auditor's office?"

"Not only in Côte d'Azur, but in the Bouches-du-Rhône as well—and you're aware of the zealousness of local tax assessors. It might come down to percentages on paper, but when cargo completely bypasses levy in port and enters overland—"

"Now you're speaking of smuggling?"

Moises had gone to stare through his window to the street below. "One dare not speculate, Marquis. The implication earned my friend a sudden end."

"May I assume that you're concerned about your own future?"

The attorney clasped his hands at his back but did not turn around. "I'm sorry to admit it."

"I should go," Quenton decided then. "I suggest you that enjoy a long holiday with your family."

Moises turned in surprise. "A vacation? Now?"

"After all, your work here is done, so why not enjoy the lucrative bonus you've earned for your services? In the meantime, I'm off to London."

Obviously relieved, Moises trailed him to the door. "You

won't forget your appointment with the King in June next year. The finalization of your family's case tops his calendar."

"Don't worry—my niece and I will meet you in Paris. Expect to see Marcel tomorrow with your bank draft. It'll be sufficient to keep you awhile. If you're nervous with L'Argan's dossier, he'll keep it safe until it's needed."

"*Merci beaucoup*, Quenton, my friend. Until Paris, then—adieu."

Quenton had gone his way, unable to shake the growing suspicion that the bank records had raised. If L'Argan was correct about the Count of Mandelieu and smuggling, it put Henri's death in a harsh new light. Had his brother learned enough about his erstwhile friend Claudius Rouget to have warranted his own murder?

ROBERT SHOULD HAVE KNOWN to avoid the alley. The day had been too quiet, Aix-en-Provence too peaceful, and too late he realized the silence, when it was shattered by the slamming of a door. He stopped. The crisscrossed lines of laundry overhead were all that stirred in the lazy afternoon. As he eased a step backward, sun flashed on metal in the corner of his vision.

He dove for cover behind a nearby crate, grabbing his pistol as gunshots blazed. In the deafening aftermath, Robert scarcely felt a bullet impact his shoulder, but he managed to squeeze off a return shot before landing. His weight shattered the crate that broke his fall. As he collapsed in a pillow of sawdust, a telltale yelp meant that his bullet had found a mark. Across the street, another pistol snapped. A woman's scream eclipsed the breaking of glass and echoed a baby's cry.

Robert realized that he was caught in crossfire. "Damn it!" he cursed, rolling free of splintered wood. He had blundered blindly into an ambush, and the wound to his shoulder would render his left arm useless. Pain shot down his back, but his arm was mercifully numb. It threw off his balance as he reeled into the shelter of the doorway, but he could not remain in the open.

The woman and the baby were still sobbing miserably, and somewhere a man shouted. He scanned the vacant doorways and blank windows of the adjacent buildings until a man toppled out of the shadows and lay unmoving. Robert moved impulsively to flush out his adversary as a ready target. His aim with his right hand was never bad, and, while scrambling to the shelter of the neighbor's door, he returned fire with his last bullet. He lost his balance again and fell with a grunt.

Sprawled on his back, he tossed away his spent weapon and fumbled for his auxiliary pistol beneath his coat. It was slippery with blood from his shoulder, but he could not afford to be clumsy. Deafening silence followed the echo of gunfire. It was the same every time. One day he would not live to hear it, but it appeared today was not that day. Then a shadow blotted the sun.

"Robert." The Count of Mandelieu greeted him as if they had agreed to meet for coffee. "I thought you'd be home by now, safe in Maureen's arms."

"And I'd have thought you'd be getting tired of arranging meetings like these." Robert could not read the expression on the count's silhouetted face, but imagined it to be gloating. He quickly learned that he was right.

Rouget lifted the tip of his cane and placed it against Robert's gaping wound to waffle excruciatingly, patiently waiting for evidence of torture. "A man of your age should know better than to play this game. I'd have thought you'd take Du Perier's warning seriously. How have you forgotten the cost of putting your nose where it doesn't belong?"

Robert gritted his teeth, unable to reply even if he could think of something to say.

The count laughed gently. "Oh, Robert," he sighed, as he removed the torment of his cane and pushed back his fedora. He watched his men cart the injured away and then shook his head. "Why did you come up to Aix? There's nothing to see out at Beau Trésor. You should have been content with the hot springs, instead of trying to visit Henri's old estate."

"Imagine my surprise to hear that your sister's living up there," Robert revealed cautiously.

"You know, sometimes this business makes it difficult to keep friends." He returned his attention to Robert. "It's too bad that it carries such impressive rewards, eh?"

"It depends on who's getting rich," Robert grunted, struggling not to evidence his weakness, but his gouged wound tainted the street with the hot blood soaking through the back of his coat. How long before it leaked his life away? He had known men who had died from less.

In the meantime, Rouget barked a dry laugh. "I should have expected you to be cynical, even facing death."

Death would be appropriate—Robert had expected it since the day Henri had died. Despite the inevitable, his instinct to survive was undaunted. His thumb slipped when he pushed on the hammer of his pistol, but it seated soundlessly.

Claudius cackled when he released the switchblade concealed in the tip of his cane. Robert squeezed the trigger just as the knife slashed at his throat. His pistol roared, searing shirt to flesh and tearing his coat, but his bullet centered on Rouget's forehead and unbalanced the man as it lifted his hat away.

"That's for Henri," Robert grunted, rolling from the carnage as the notorious Count of Mandelieu toppled onto the street. He gathered the strength to climb to his feet and waved his pistol meaningfully at the stunned men staring at him in silence. They held uncertain ground until police whistles began. The gendarme was finally coming, too late to save anybody. Robert spared not a glance at what was left and staggered woodenly away.

ALTHOUGH THE MORNING WAS CRISP, Quenton breakfasted with his newspaper in the dappled sunlight on his balcony. The glass doors to his sitting room stood open, and the fire blazed uselessly. The chill sucked the steam from his coffee, along with most of its heat. Marcel wore his overcoat just inside the room, with Quenton's meal in chafing dishes to keep it from growing cold.

Draped in his fur coat, instead of a dressing gown, over silk pajamas and wearing snow boots on his bare feet, Quenton was aware of his picture of eccentric frivolity, but he was determined to enjoy his last morning in the forest. It was cold now, but when the sun was high enough to warm the shade, the afternoon would be comfortable. As of today, his schedule was free to ride around or take the sloop for a run upriver while André packed their things, because tomorrow would find them on the way to Paris.

"Would you care for a warm-up?" Marcel asked, coming forward with the coffee urn.

"A little, perhaps. After I finish this section, I'll eat," Quenton promised. Marcel would undoubtedly be happy to take off his coat and enjoy his own breakfast.

"*Très bien, monseigneur.*"

There was little doubt that Quenton's return to England with his personal servant would be far different than the long-ago journey with Alix had been. The years between were little more than a marker for his guilt for not having been at the château on that fateful day. As it was, he had barely been in time to save Alix. He might never know if she had purposely run into the open courtyard when he appeared at the gates. Had he hesitated, his horse, Titus, might not have been fast enough to carry him through the barrage of gunfire in time to scoop her up behind him before clearing the wall into the forest. When she slipped from his horse unconscious and bleeding, it had been too late to ask any questions or hope for a solution while their lives crumbled to ruin. He never knew how much she had seen; he knew only that what had been left of Henri was enough to sicken Quenton when he buried his brother the next day. Poor Henri had not needed a face for Quenton to identify him, and so when the unfounded claim that his brother was in Naples had emerged, Quenton had scarcely contained his outrage.

His journey had not yet begun, and he was already anxious to return home with Alix. Her stable of horses would be welcome at Chênes Noir for as long as she wished to keep them here, but he knew that after they had toured their landholdings, her preference would be to settle at Beau Trésor near Aix-en-Provence. The pastures near the Mediterranean were lush, and the old black castle would not evoke the horrible memories that the Alpine estate at Mont Blanc would.

Quenton could not expect Alix to ever live there. One day, perhaps, when their affairs were settled, she might agree to visit, but when they went to Geneva to tour her lapidary business, they would take another highway. They would stay awhile at Chênes Noir, while Alix arranged for a wardrobe and a maid, and since Geneva would be postponed until the mountain passes opened, they would visit the wineries first and split their time between Troyes and Épernay. From there, they would journey south to Aix-en-Provence. Once Alix was at Beau Trésor, he might have to pry her away. Quenton had not been down there in years, but the last he had seen the place, Henri had been intent on expanding the riding halls. Alix would not rest once she saw them again.

Unable to keep a smile from his face, he shook out his newspaper and was in the process of folding it when Marcel ventured forward with his warmed plate. He paused at an article about the murder of the Count of Mandelieu. Quenton scanned the limited disclaimer; the column was more of an elaborate obituary that included a list of surviving family. To think that Alix had once been included in their company was disturbing. Quenton had had the dubious honor of meeting the younger Rouget only once, and in his estimation, Viscount Claude Rouget was no match for his father. Cyclops Freight was too big to fail, but his son was too weak-kneed to manage a smuggling operation, and any criminal activity would quickly crumble.

Quenton reached for his cup thoughtfully. He could not be sorry about the news of the Count of Mandelieu; the only unfortunate part was that it had not happened sooner. He set aside the newspaper. *Good riddance*, he decided as he finished his coffee.

CHAPTER 23

THE RUINS OF HADLEIGH CASTLE

It was a subdued morning. If not for the outgoing tide, the fog was so thick that progress would have been futile without Nicholas at the helm to guide the slender cutter through the flotilla of frigates and past fishing boats bobbling in the waves. The sky brightened as the mist burned away, making it easier for Alix to see her book in the tiny cabin. Only moments ago, Albert Frisk had stopped by to invite Jenny down to the galley for breakfast, and Nicholas had soon followed.

"Hello," he said, poking his head through the door, waiting patiently for Alix to calm Snap's noisy response. "You're alone? I thought your maid would be with you."

Alix tucked away the borrowed book of sonnets she had been reading. "Come in, won't you? The pot is still warm, if you'd care for tea," she added, automatically opening the cozy to pour. "Albert Frisk dropped in a minute ago," she continued, as Nicholas took the opposite chair, completely at ease in their cramped surroundings. "They should return soon."

"It's not like Frisk to take liberty."

"Not at all—I've been reading," Alix demurred, unwilling to cause trouble after insisting Jenny should accompany her once she learned that Albert was to care for Snap on their adventure. Ever since Stragglethorpe, his only regular visit had been at Snap's evening walk, and Alix had determined that a day at the beach was the impetus their budding relationship needed.

Nicholas lifted his gaze to the row of windows. "We're just passing the Essex marshes and will put in soon. I thought you might like to walk around the shops in Southend before lunch."

"I might," Alix replied, clinging to Lily's haughty reserve as she gazed out at the tattered fog hiding the famous Hadleigh estate.

"We can take a drive out to see the castle later, if you wish." He smiled at her surprise, as she wondered how he had acquired the talent to read her mind. "Most of Hadleigh has crumbled now. My father gave me a tour of the old keep when I was a lad, and shared more about the Hundred Years' War than I could ever remember. Is this afternoon soon enough, or—"

"Oh, after lunch is smashing!" Alix bit off her excitement belatedly but could not regret her undue enthusiasm when he grinned appreciatively.

"All right. I'll be sure Frisk has a coach ready." As if he was aware of her discomfiture over the awkward slip, he finished his tea and reached for his hat as he rose to leave. "Don't worry—today belongs to you alone. I'd better get back to the helm. Thank you for the tea," he added, and then was gone.

Alix watched Snap snuffle at the closed crack of the door while wiggling the stub of his tail expectantly, and then Nicholas's voice returned distantly as he hailed his man from the hallway. "Might I have a word, Frisk?"

The door slid open, and Jenny entered, her cheeks pleasantly flushed. She waited for the terrier to scamper through before closing the door, and then turned to fix her hat busily. "I promised not to be long."

"Yes, but was it long enough?" Alix hid her interest by assuming a new place in her book while the maid's forehead wrinkled with perplexity.

"Long enough for what?"

"Please, sit down. Nicholas said we'll be docking soon."

"Milord was here?" Jenny said suspiciously, putting aside the evidence of his empty teacup when she took his place.

"Yes, he came by looking for your Albert."

"He found him right enough, but he's not my Albert."

"Did you see what you went to see?"

"We just went down to the galley. Why?"

"No reason."

"Fie, I know that innocent look by now; you can't pull the wool over my eyes, milady," Jenny protested brusquely. "There is absolutely nothing going on between Albert Frisk and meself. If you listened to anything, you'd know he is nothing but a rake and a rounder."

"Yes, I recall you saying something of the sort before."

"I've four brothers, haven't I? I should know."

"Yes, I recall your family as well."

"Then why are you sitting there looking like the kitten caught with cream on her whiskers?"

"Who, me? You're exaggerating," Alix replied, blindly paging through the book. "I was just wondering if you enjoyed breakfast."

"Breakfast? Who said anything about eating?"

"Precisely."

❧ ❧

NICHOLAS ESCORTED THE IMPOSTOR through the storefronts along High Street, aware that he had lied when promising the day belonged to her, because he was thoroughly enjoying it himself. In the candy shop, he realized that she was not beyond her own artifice by insisting her maid should sample the chocolates, rather than tasting them herself, all the while covertly watching Frisk's reaction.

Nicholas thought that Albert appeared to be more stoic than interested as he stood aside with the terrier. Frisk's initial intent to pursue Jenny Smith had been an effort to find information about the impostor, but since Nicholas's search of the chambers and the enlistment of Poole Investigations, Albert had retreated—whether because of frustration or disinclination, Nicholas had no particular desire to know. But he was on the cusp of meddling in his servants' affairs to discover if the impostor was one who had stacked the cards to watch them fall, or if she was merely an incurable romantic.

They finally left the shop with more sweets than anyone could eat, and the impostor offered Nicholas a peppermint stick when he settled beside her in the brightly painted shay. As Frisk shook the reins at the rented horses and drove their fanciful carriage past the cutter waiting at the pier, Nicholas struggled with a desire to stretch his arm behind her. Oblivious to his proximity, she watched the windswept dunes sprouting marram grass, holding the dog, which eyed him with quick intent. Undeterred, Nicholas rolled the peppermint stick in his mouth and commented, "It's turned into a fine day."

"Yes, it has," she agreed with what he now recognized as her singularly melodious prosody. When she turned to him, her crystalline eyes reflected the sky, and her wind-tousled curls tugged loose from the careful coiffure of her hair.

Nicholas could not help but grin, although it drove her eyes away. "We're passing Two Tree Island," he said to appear informative, even if they had sailed this way earlier. "It shouldn't take long to get up to the castle. There's a splendid view, but despite repeated attempts at renovation, it's long been an impossible loss."

"Did you by chance have the opportunity to see the exhibition of John Constable's paintings of Hadleigh?"

Nicholas should have anticipated her interest in the famous studies of the ruins. Her innocent question raised a thousand in turn, including how ridiculous she thought his clumsy investigation into how much she knew about Caravaggio, when he had suspected only that she was not Lily. "Unfortunately, I was at sea that summer."

"Oh." The impostor's gentle response taxed him greatly. As if anticipating that Nicholas longed to touch her, the terrier cast him a cautious look while sitting up to sniff the breeze.

"I enlisted with the navy before finishing the university and shipped out soon after," Nicholas shared affably, looking over the distant estuary, instead of at her. "Because of my experience at Lion Shipping, I was given the rank of second lieutenant. I suspect it was only natural that John and I became shipmates. We were assigned to a frigate patrolling the waters between the Mediterranean and the Gold Coast. We served two years together, before the end of duty."

"Oh."

Was he boring her with unwanted trivia, or would it eventually lead to an enlightened exchange? Nicholas felt a keen edge of anticipation as they stopped at the top of the hill overlooking the marshes.

"Isn't this beautiful!" she exclaimed. The crumbling ruins of the medieval Hadleigh Castle lay scattered across the landscape, but round drum towers guarded a section of barbican and roofless walls stood bare, with ceilings of sky.

"I daresay it was more impressive a few hundred years ago," Nicholas cautioned while hopping out to help her down.

She laughed as she released the terrier and clasped her hat to her head when the breeze sent its ribbons fluttering. "What a smashing view!"

Faraway music from a lone bagpiper drew them toward the castle ruins in the wake of the scampering dog across the greensward. When Alix spared a backward glance to see that Frisk helped the maid from the rear of the wagon, her step faltered, and Nicholas caught her shoulders to steady her. Once his arm was so well-placed, he refused to relinquish her until they reached the barbican, where she pulled away to take in the scenery.

Her unaffected smile was the only sight that Nicholas wished to see, but the flaxen curls streaming with the ribbons of her hat made him long to release the tawny length of her hair. As he turned away from his unbidden memory of its softness, the bagpiper began to play "Highland Laddie." When Nicholas looked around, she had vanished.

Wind whispered in gusts across the marshes. Music followed Nicholas's search for the impostor across the old bailey through the ruin, without success. He wondered if she was amused by such games or if her penchant for vanishing was intrinsic to her character, but even if she had the opal he planned to give her for Lily's birthday, Nicholas would have to find her first, before he could look for the talisman of the necklace.

How Nicholas would present the opal so that the impostor would keep it close was another issue. His own St. Christopher medal was the only thing that he wore consistently, and women changed jewelry as they did their shoes. The jewel would need a sentiment to bind it, and beyond the adventure of sailing to Southend, his plan was flimsy.

He would have overlooked her entirely had it not been for the terrier roaming nose to ground near the barbican at the base of the tower. If he had not specifically searched inside, he might not even have noticed her perched high overhead, clinging to what remained of the crumbled staircase and looking through the narrow window designed to conceal medieval archers. His initial surprise was quickly overcome by a fear of her falling from such a height, and he scarcely had time to muse over her daredevil spirit as he found his own precarious way up to join her. She noticed his clumsy arrival and hastily motioned him to silence.

"What are you doing?" he wondered, as she grabbed his sleeve and pulled him down next to her.

"Shush, they'll hear you."

"Who'll hear us?" Nicholas whispered. He used the excuse of steadying himself on the narrow ledge to gather her closer, but she was too intent to notice. "Dare I look?"

"Oh! Be careful, but now do you see?"

Nicholas was not surprised to find the object of such clandestine scrutiny was Frisk, walking with Jenny Smith on the hillside, but he was uncertain if it was the sight of his man plucking wildflowers or the sudden inclusiveness in her regard that was overwhelming. "Yes," he answered as she pulled him away from the window. When she gazed up at him earnestly, he became captivated by the clarity of her eyes. For the moment, there were no secrets between them, only a riveting connection.

"Good," she responded, as she pulled her restless gaze away to survey the rubble of the tower. "Oh, I forgot about Snap! He's going to give us away!" She reached for the window ledge and peered outside carefully. "Glory, there he is, too!"

"Where?" Nicholas asked, grasping at any attempt to be closer. He could feel her warmth as he pressed behind her at the narrow opening. He could not see anything, but it was not his intent. Her breathing beneath him quickened and stopped with a gasp, igniting a fire within him.

"Oh!"

"What?" he wondered, half-fearful that her answer might pertain to his unwarranted closeness.

"Albert's given his wildflowers to her!" she sang in quiet triumph, and then spun around beneath him. "Oh!" she repeated in sharp surprise, and shrank against the wall.

"Sorry," Nicholas lied about his indecent proximity, and shifted his position carefully, reaching for his handkerchief to blot his prickling brow. "There's not much room up here, is there?"

From the way she was judging him warily, he doubted that he fooled her. "No," she conceded breathlessly.

"Right . . . Well, I think Snap's decided to follow them." Nicholas opted to change the subject when he saw the terrier bound along the hillside.

She craned her neck to peer after the dog without shifting her careful position against the wall. "That's a relief."

"Getting caught like this might be a little embarrassing," he suggested, and bravely weathered her withering eye.

"Yes," she agreed heavily.

She gave no sign of falling into his arms to benefit him with a kiss, so he felt pressed to end the maddening moment. "Come on," he said, and grabbed her hand without waiting for concession. "We'd better get down from here before something happens," he added, leaving the rest to her imagination as he clambered down to help her navigate the broken staircase.

"Now then," he said, breathing more easily outside the tower, pulling her along the trail with him. "That's that, isn't it, then?" he asked nonsensically. "A marvelous view from up there."

The impostor recovered her sensibility quickly and turned to the view where the land sank to the sea, the Thames reflecting silver in the distance. Nicholas could not help but remain beside her, drawn as a moth to her flame. The bagpipe wheezed into the tune of "The True Lover's Farewell." The sound of music startled her, and before she realized his closeness again, Nicholas clasped her hand and pulled her into a dance. At first he sang the lyrics because she regarded him doubtfully. As her surprise turned to delight, he continued only to amuse her, but when her eyes became compelling, the lyrics of his song swelled with emotion. He felt as if he could sing to her forever, and when she joined in, he wondered why he had never guessed that she knew the words.

EVENING FOG FLOWED IN WITH THE TIDE. The sails slapped limply, but Nicholas guided the cutter through the slower frigates and brigantines upriver toward harbor. The difference in the afternoon was that Alix remained at the helm, rather than going below, into the cabin. The lackluster breeze tugging on her ribbons was scarcely sufficient to do more than jostle rigging tied with stout rope.

Nicholas glanced at her expectantly. "Come here. Would you care to try it?"

Alix paused. "Try what?"

"Take the helm. Come here; I'll show you," he promised, reaching for her when she hesitated, loath to leave the support of the railing, despite the gentler river as they sailed away from the sea.

"Roddy," he ordered, summoning his First Mate to hold

the wheel while he helped her to the helm. "The rudder is the easy part," he assured her.

Alix felt that he was lying but came forward obligingly. For whatever reason he had decided to indulge her with the excuse of Lily's birthday, she could not deny that the trip to Southend and Hadleigh Castle had been wonderful.

"Now, place your hands thus; just imagine the wheel as a clock, and hold it thus. Feel the rudder? Good . . . If you turn this way, you're steering starboard; the other is port; and here in the middle is straight ahead . . . It's simple. See?"

"Yes," she laughed with relief.

"Good," he replied, appearing pleased. "Now, hold her steady as she goes, and you can sail her all the way to London."

"London!"

"Of course, and why not, when the best way to celebrate a birthday is by doing something new, isn't it?"

"Mayhap, if one is so fortunate, but . . ."

"Well, then, why not?"

"Why not?" Alix laughed incredulously as he steadied the helm expertly, so that the cutter glided past a listing frigate.

"Mr. Jackson, signal that ship to learn if they've summoned assistance. Darkness is a devil of a time to block the traffic lane."

"Aye, milord."

"Now, where were we?" he wondered, as Jackson shouted his orders to a flagman. He kept his hand on the wheel while he glanced down at her. "Ah, that's right—we were on the subject of birthdays, and since this one is yours, I'd be remiss if I didn't offer a token of my regard."

"Oh," Alix replied, at a loss. "Please, don't worry. Today was gift enough."

"Do you think so?" Nicholas smiled down at her for a

moment, then lifted his eyes to the river and adjusted their course slightly. "You're supposed to be steering," he reminded her gently.

"Oh, sorry," Alix replied, pulling her eyes away from him to watch where the bow of the ship was aimed. At the moment, there was nothing in front of them, more than likely because he had been guiding the ship while she had gaped at him. Resolutely, she put her mind on business and caught the sway of the rudder quickly when he released the wheel to her care.

"Do you have her?"

"Yes, of course."

"Good . . . Can you hold her steady for a moment? There's a good girl . . . Roddy!"

"Yes, milord!"

"It's time to drop the mainsail."

"Yes, milord!"

"Can you still manage?"

"Yes," Alix answered, holding on to the wheel firmly.

"Good. Not just anyone can sail a ship, but I'd say you have a knack for this."

"Do you think so? I'm not certain—"

"Of course, which is all the more reason to give you this," he said, dropping a diamond-encrusted black opal from his hand to dangle in front of her.

"Oh!" Alix gasped.

"Roddy, if you don't mind," he interjected, summoning the First Mate to take control. "Now, let me see if I might manage this," he added, as he fastened the chain around her neck. "So saying, happy birthday. Now, turn around and give us a look at it, won't you?"

Alix was so stunned that she was scarcely able to find voice to protest. "You shouldn't; it's too much." She could not believe that he still imagined that she was actually his wife! Had she been completely mistaken about him?

"Not in the least." He laughed at her concern. "I'll admit that it's an old piece with sentimental value . . . but now methinks it's so well placed, it should never come off. Promise me."

"No," she replied, thoroughly confounded.

Incredibly, he continued to laugh, although he placed his hand over his heart as he bowed. "Then I accept your word as a pledge, and I'm humbled by your guarantee to wear it always."

"But I can't!"

"It's too late for a retraction, because I've already accepted. Now then, you must learn if you're going to sail a ship, to keep your mind on your destination. Thank you, Roddy," he added, reaching for the wheel. "Back to business. You're supposed to be guiding the helm, remember?"

"Yes," Alix replied meekly, numbly regaining her position at the wheel.

"You'll note as we get closer to London, the traffic on the river gets heavier . . ."

Nicholas remained close, with his arms around her to steady the wheel, and she felt almost caught in his embrace. It must have been a combination of the day and her surprise at the beautiful necklace that made her feel as if she were in one of those fairy-tale stories. The billowing fog that smeared the lights of the harbor added to the mystery. The only thing missing was a kiss from the prince.

ROBERT STOPPED HIS HORSE in the empty breezeway and surveyed the quiet stable from the saddle. After a pause, he retrieved his watch to check the time. Although Julius had stepped lively on the road from London, it was unusual to find the yard empty.

"Tim," he called, and stepped down stiffly. His shout brought the dogs barking from the paddocks. Penny came first, as usual, and old Chief limped behind. Alix's scatterbrained Cinders scrambled to catch up and bounded past to greet Robert first, but he staved off her over-exuberance with a well-placed knee. "Quiet, you mongrels; it's only me." He cuffed their ears in turn and ruffled old Chief's thick mane of fur, grateful to see each of them.

"Robbie!" Tim's surprised head appeared in the overhead loft.

"What in the blazes are you doing up there?" Robert demanded, pulling Julius into the grooming room.

"I'll be right down, Robbie!"

"See that you do it in a damned hurry. Did someone start paying you to sleep all day?"

"No, Robbie, I swear to God, I wasn't sleeping!"

The throaty giggle and slender arm catching the stableman's neck to hold him back provided sufficient evidence for Robert to turn away in disgust. His right hand was not of much use, and he wore a jacket thick enough to conceal the dressing over his wound. He had been lucky that the bullet had missed anything vital, but he would have been better off without Rouget leaning on his cane tip to make it worse. "Damn it, man," he snapped, as fatigue began to tax him. It had been the same since Aix-en-Provence, but a wound needed time and rest to heal. "You look like a man who needs to be fired."

"No, Robbie, I was just moving hay for tonight's feeding!" Tim blustered, as he came around to unsaddle the horse.

Unimpressed, Robert hefted his saddlebags from Julius's

back with his left hand and ignored the sight of the blond head up in the loft as the woman reached for her clothes. "Where's Finghin?"

"He's down at the track with Ozzie."

"Don't they quit soon, or has there been a blasted schedule change?"

"No . . . no, they'll be here any minute!"

"Then who's doing your work for you, since you're not doing it yourself?"

"I'm doing it all, Robbie, I swear!"

"It's damned obvious how much your word is worth. I don't suppose your wife knows how far you've slipped from your vows. You'd better be quick, or I'll ride down to the Crossroads to see if Mickey Harrison is still interested in working for me."

"Mickey can't work half as hard as I can!"

"When I left here, you started at dawn, didn't you?"

"Aye, Robbie!"

"Not today. Don't be surprised when your wages reflect the same. Tell Finghin I want to see him when he's done."

Robert headed for the house. Somehow he had managed to make it full circle, and all that was left was to finish what Lily had fecklessly started. If she was up to playing lovers' games in the loft, she was ready to pack her bags and take the shortest road to London. He crossed his threshold, scarcely able to believe that he was home.

THE SWIRLING CLOUDS BLUSHED with the setting sun as the sky turned violet indigo. It had been a long time since Quenton had wielded a paintbrush, but he thought about mixing colors while walking to the ferry. At last, he was on his way to bring Alix home. She was the artist, although he had had his own share of lessons as a youth. Now that their rightful places in life were restored, she would have time to pursue her passions.

Quenton was uncertain why painting had occurred to him. In his youth, Henri had engaged a tutor from the university in Marseille, but Honaire Montfort had remained at the château beyond Quenton's lessons to assume Alix's instruction. Quenton's interest had always been in horses, and under the guidance of Master Robichon, he had spent more time in the stables than on Montfort's instruction.

A few geese clamored to a noisy stop on the canal. On the sidewalk above the dock, a pair of lovely ladies strolled behind their fancifully clipped poodles walking on leads. Had Quenton not been absorbed by the appealing sway of their hips, he might have noticed the man approaching. His blood chilled with distaste when Claude Rouget stopped in front of him.

"Eh bien, eh bien, qui est-ce que je vois?"

Although the viscount was from Côte d'Azur, only someone as supercilious as Rouget would have assumed a Parisian accent that was thicker than the locals'. Quenton's response was cool. "Your enthusiasm suggests you've forgotten our last meeting, Claude." Alix had gone to Aix-en-Provence with her father after Quenton had moved to Chênes Noir to join the cavalry, and, for whatever reason, the Rouget family had become involved enough for Henri to bring the young viscount and his sister up to Mont Blanc in the summer. Quenton had not stopped to consider the source of Claude's audacity in touching Alix. Without forethought, Quenton had dangled the arrogant fool over the edge of the precipice, while Claude's eyes bulged as he clung frantically, fearful of his last breath.

Rouget smirked bravely, but at least Quenton's bluntness flattened the amused light in his mud-colored eyes. "I can't say that living in England has done anything for your manners, if you've returned to France an even bigger boor than before you left."

"I'm sorry I can't say it's been lovely to see you, but since I'm on my way somewhere, I'd prefer to keep going."

"Oh, you're catching the ferry. It shouldn't surprise me that you've developed a preference for public transportation, but don't worry—I understand there's been a mix-up at the last stop and your ferry's delayed."

"I suppose it was designed to give us time for this little meeting?" Quenton was not fooled by the viscount's foppish imitation and shouldered his walking stick deliberately, prepared to use the razor-edged rapier concealed inside, if necessary.

Claude cocked his head in a parody of concern. "I'm sorry that you didn't wish to use our schooner that Father put at your disposal. It would have been a more appropriate method of bringing the countess to France, wouldn't it? Or have your niece's standards fallen as far as yours?"

"As I recall, it's none of your business."

"Our services were offered, at least."

"Of course, and one may consider that they were proposed through someone who is now dead. So, then, if you'll excuse me," Quenton insisted, and lifted his hat in farewell.

"Are you certain that you'll refuse the ship? It would be so much more convenient; a private schooner isn't tied to shipping schedules."

"While I must admit it's a generous proposal," Quenton replied, looking purposefully down his nose at Claude, "I prefer the freedom to do as I please . . . You understand."

"As you wish, then," Claude conceded with a bow, as he stepped aside to let Robert pass. "Although not many would turn down such a lucrative suggestion, including your niece."

"Kindly remember how our conversation nearly ended so unfortunately for you on Mont Blanc. Nothing has changed, and your concerns about my niece are ill-founded. Good evening, Viscount."

"That is 'Count' now . . . after my father's untimely murder."

"I beg your pardon, then," Quenton responded, as the booming whistle from the approaching ferry echoed along the canal. "There is my boat."

Rouget tipped his hat in farewell. "Of course. Bon voyage."

Quenton headed for the ferry dock with marked relief, but if he had not known what he did about Rouget and his family, he might have accepted the use of their schooner. As he waited for his manservant to push through the crowd, it occurred to Quenton that perhaps his brother had not been so fortunate. Henri had been too trusting of those close to him; otherwise, he never would have married a woman as greedy as Mary-Margaret. It was not surprising that his brother would not have realized the Count of Mandelieu was a criminal when he accepted Rouget's assistance, and Quenton could not deny his satisfaction at the memory of dangling Rouget over the edge of the cliff. That fleeting gratification might continue to be worthwhile, as long as Claude Rouget kept his distance.

When the ferry to Calais pushed away from the dock, he was on board. This time when he crossed the channel, the sight of the famous white cliffs of Britain would be worth celebrating. In a handful of days, he would return with Alix, and while they could never recapture the years they had lost, they could finally pursue their future.

CHAPTER 24

The Final Masquerade

❧

Puzzled, Alix looked up from painting roses with red ink and stared at the gown of gold arrasene draped over Jenny's arm. "I'm going to a masquerade?"

Jenny lowered her voice to a whisper. "Fie, don't tell me that you've nary heard about the Clarence Masquerade in St. Albans at the end of the season—it won't be long, and we'll be leaving for milord's estate in Wales." As she moved to return to the dressing room, she added in a normal tone, "It's ready for a fitting whenever it pleases you."

Alix cringed inwardly at the idea of traveling anywhere but home to Buckinghamshire, as she jumped to follow the maid. "When's the gala?"

"It's Friday. That doesn't give us much time, and Albert thought this gown might be perfect for your costume," Jenny said as she hung it on the rack.

"*This* Friday?"

"Yes." She spread the silky skirt experimentally. "He said that milord hadn't decided to go until the last minute, and had found this dress while shopping in Piccadilly Square. It's not bad for something ready-made, is it?"

"The fabric has a lovely sheen, but what are our characters supposed to be?"

"Milord thought to go as a medieval king and queen."

"Oh," Alix replied, too astounded by the idea to make sense of it.

"First things first, though. After a proper fitting, we'll decide what to do with it."

Alix sank onto the dressing couch as Jenny responded to the soft rap on the door. When the maid lingered in the opening to exchange a few words, Albert pulled her into the hall. Alix could see no more than a shadowed outline of their shapes when they kissed, and then Jenny stepped back hastily, straightening her cap as he pulled the door closed with a grin.

Snap scrambled narrowly through, trailing his leash, and dashed for a place on her lap. Alix ventured, "It certainly was kind of your Albert to pick up this dress."

Blushing pleasantly, Jenny hung out a dressing gown. "It saved a step or two."

The maid's lack of denial about her newfound connection with Albert Frisk lifted Alix's spirits. Triumphantly, she affected innocence as Jenny came to help her undress. "Especially with the ball in a few days. Has he asked you out on Friday night yet?"

"Not yet. Why?"

"We'd better decide what you're wearing, too. After all, it's only a matter of time."

"ONE MOMENT MORE, MILORD," Albert insisted, as he tightened the lacing on the brocade doublet of Nicholas's costume.

Despite Poole's having called an end to his investigation in Paris because of the recent murder of his detective, Nicholas was pressing forward with a new plan, to attend the masquerade ball. He hoped that the false security of a costume might foil the impostor's practiced role as Lily and was still determined to get to the bottom of the bizarre affair. Besides, there was always the hope that if he assumed the role of her protector and king, she might fall straight into his arms. Then, when he pursued his passion until she surrendered, there would be no secrets left between them.

"Now then, is your doublet too snug?"

Nicholas flexed. "No, it's good. Was Jenny certain the queen will be on time?"

Albert gave the doublet a final tug and reached for his clothes brush. "So I hope; my own arrangements for tonight depend on it."

"Good show. I assume that you have something special planned?" Nicholas's reflection in the mirror might have stepped from an illustrated page. He fitted the black velvet flat cap atop his unbound hair to make his image complete.

Albert fussed briefly with the hat's white ostrich plume. "Jenny's fond of a show; there's a comedy playing out in Paddington. I thought we'd catch dinner up there and then take the long way home."

"Good luck to you, then. It sounds as if you're thinking of getting serious, old man."

"A man could do worse than to look for a wife in someone as astute as Jenny Smith. Now, may I say that you look splendid?"

Nicholas preened briefly in the mirror while Frisk straightened the ruffle of the collar. "If so, it's your doing. Since you've a date with your maid, don't worry about waiting up for me. I've no idea when we'll be home, so consider yourself at liberty."

"Knowing Jenny, I'm sure it'll hardly be necessary, but thank you, milord."

Winston bowed when he noticed Nicholas on the stairs. "Good eve, milord. I say, you look superb!"

Whatever else came of the masquerade, Nicholas had no fear of a mundane evening. "Good evening, Winston," he responded, as young Percy hurried in with the fur cape he would wear instead of a cloak. "Has the coach been brought around?"

"Georgie's already at the curb, milord."

The impostor appeared on the stairs as if the striking clock had summoned her, clad in a satin dress true to medieval fashion. Ivory brocade inset beneath crisscrossed lacing accentuated her scandalously slender shape, and the old-fashioned collar parted only to reveal the opal necklace he had given her as they had returned from Southend the other day.

She had eclipsed the image of even the queen in his dreams and descended with the terrier dressed in his own costume, of black velvet, and a gold collar trimmed with miniature sleigh bells. As she approached, Nicholas scraped together sufficient sensibility to doff his cap. "Well met, milady."

Her high color deepened as a tenuous smile revealed her uncertainty. "I hope you don't mind," she responded, allowing Nicholas to lead her toward the door. "Snap's promised to be on his best behavior, rather than to be left alone."

Nicholas took the black velvet robe from Winston to place on her shoulders while the dog waited with an absurd parody of a smile on his canine face. "I think it's safe to say that he'll be the most distinguished terrier in the room."

"You're very kind," she said as he guided her to the coach.

At least that much in her consideration of him had changed during the weeks since the discovery that she was an impostor. How much more of a transformation could he manage, given the right opportunity? The long winter stretched ahead with promise as the carriage took them through the crowded streets. Nicholas felt on the cusp of an ending and a beginning; tomorrow began the uproar of packing for home. Would the rambling relic of his estate at Hollyrune enthrall the woman as had the castle at Hadleigh? He had become so accustomed to loathing the idea of the place that it surprised him to feel excited about going home.

ALIX WISHED TO DANCE ALL NIGHT. There was something mystical about a gathering where even the familiar seemed strange. Who would have thought Sarah would dare to be Cleopatra with red hair? Mary was fetching as Maid Marian, opposite Sam's predictable Robin of Locksley, and John Wesley was vain enough to wear a Caesar's robe with knobby knees. They moved through a procession of kings and queens, knaves and priests, whimsical shepherdesses and curious beasts, all swirling together around the dance floor.

Nicholas lowered his eyes from the crowd to watch her while she lingered in his arms, dancing. Ever since the day at Southend, his erstwhile elusive regard had turned pensively tender. The music finished, and they stopped to applaud briefly, then began to dance again when the orchestra struck up Beethoven's Symphony No. 6, Op. 68. The first movement was one of Alix's favorites. She followed Nicholas blindly as a vivid memory of playing her violin in the old conservatory overwhelmed her.

"Are you enjoying yourself?"

"Yes," she replied as she returned to the moment. Their round table was littered with glasses of champagne in various states, and Snap waited on a nearby chair, watching them intently.

"Snap's something of a character," Nicholas said, noting her attention to the dog. "Who would have guessed from his unlikely start? You have quite an influence over a certain questionable few; would you take offense if I suggested that they include me?" He attempted to ease her alarm by removing her from the dance floor with a sympathetic smile. "So saying," he continued, as if they were involved in nothing untoward, even as he steered her through an adjacent corridor, "since we're on the verge of spending the winter together, I feel it's time to speak. I've said nothing about your company heretofore and pledge my silence hereafter. By now, you must realize that I'm trustworthy."

Alix's racing heart plummeted. His honor would never bear the weight of the deceptive Alex Sterling, Esq., the proprietor of Sterling Wood Stable. Now, she not only gambled her own future but threatened to discredit the victim of her unintentional hoax. "I know not how to tell you who I am," she prevaricated faintly.

He smiled, obviously recognizing her rendition of Shakespeare. "Think you that your name could ever be an enemy to me?" he paraphrased Romeo in response. "I take thee at thy word."

"That which we call a rose by any other name would smell as sweet," she replied desperately, because if he realized her relationship to Lily, any bargain with her sister would certainly be finished, and in the aftermath of his outrage, they might both be in prison.

"I'm not interested in reenacting *Romeo and Juliet*," he said, as he guided her through the thinning crowd, with Snap's merry bells jingling at their heels, "inasmuch as I wish you'd trust me."

When they reached an unoccupied antechamber, Nicholas pulled her inside and closed the door silently. Alix sank numbly into the chair he offered and clasped the terrier close when the dog joined her. Here was the reckoning she had dreaded, but at the most unlooked-for moment. The shock left her woefully unprepared to answer.

"Look," Nicholas began, as he drew up a chair to sit opposite. He clasped her chilled hands reassuringly and adopted a confidential tone. "I can see I've surprised you, but you didn't really think we could go on like this forever, did you? If so, then I beg your pardon, but give me a name, at least, unless I'm to assume it's Rose."

Her heart hammered so loudly in her ears, she scarcely heard her own reply. "As you wish."

He rose with displeased frustration and cast a calculating look at her, before returning to peer out through the door at the hallway. After closing it again, he leaned against it, his arms crossed. "After everything, you still don't trust me."

Why did he sound so disappointed? She was a charlatan, a perpetrator of fraud, an insubstantial vision, a poor look-alike. "I've no answer in my own defense."

His silence delivered judgment in a weighty pause. "No answer," he repeated finally. "Well, then mayhap I should share what I already know." He paced, guarding the door. "You're French. You came to Britain with Quincy several years ago . . ."

Alix's protest died before it found a voice. *He said Quincy, not Quenton.* Her uncle's identity was yet secret, and he was safe. Should anyone learn of their history, it could mean the ultimate price of death. Now, she realized her uncle's disappearance was a result of Nicholas's investigation. She listened for further clues as Nicholas ticked off his list of evidence. He did not mention Sterling Wood Stable or Robbie. He said nothing about her relationship with Lily. He knew about Mont Blanc and its horses, but he thought her a victim held in a plot, without consideration that she might be the criminal.

He was gently deliberating and pledged his assistance, but little did he know how he forged the probability of his own downfall with his allegiance. To give him a name that would not reveal her sham would be a small concession, especially if it bought time to find a solution without endangering the teetering foundation of the stable.

"Allie," she offered anxiously. "My . . . my friends call me Allie."

She could not blame him for regarding her doubtfully. "Allie."

"Yes."

He came forward to clasp her hand. "How is Lily involved with Quincy? How did they coerce you into this?"

"I cannot say," Alix pledged hurriedly, to stave off further questioning. "I dare not," she added, clinging to his hand in return, although she could not afford the reassuring connection. She wormed her fingers free and folded them around the dog. "It's not my story to tell."

Nicholas sat back on his heels and rocked to his feet in defiance. "Not your story—faced with this degree of knavery, you'd quibble about what's honorable?"

"You have every right to demand a full reckoning," Alix replied carefully. She was in no position to equivocate with a parliamentarian like Nicholas Griffon, who feasted on daily debate. "But I cannot provide the answers you seek; they are questions for another."

He turned away in disgust. "By 'another,' you mean Lily."

"Yes," she replied, helplessly drawn to his distress. The bells stitched on Snap's collar rang as she released the terrier to follow Nicholas. Her fingers itched to feel the velvet brocade of his doublet, but she folded them together instead.

"I don't give a fig about Lily or her lies—" He broke off at the sound of laughter ringing in the corridor. Nicholas turned away as the door opened to allow a redheaded Cleopatra and a raven-haired Maid Marian to stumble through, bringing extra glasses of champagne.

"We've come to the rescue," Sarah pronounced deliberately, and giggled as she delivered a glass to Alix.

"We thought you might be getting thirsty down here," Mary added, benefiting Nicholas with her extra flute, while John and Sam filled the doorway.

"A man can't turn his back on these two for a minute," John explained apologetically, as he reached for his wife.

"I think we were finished," Nicholas replied, giving his glass to John as he abruptly strode away.

"I say," Mary laughed, "we didn't interrupt a quarrel or anything?"

"These two lovebirds?" Sarah chortled. "I'd guess kissing is more likely!"

Sam took charge of the gathering as John followed Nicholas. "Allow us to escort you, Lily," he suggested, and captured his sister's elbow. "Come along, Sarah. I think you've done enough."

Alix followed mutely, but when the ladies decided to visit the lounge, she slipped down the hall, carrying the dog, and put him down once they reached the back hall, where the telltale bells on his collar would pass unnoticed. When he led her into a darkened corridor, Snap stopped with a throaty growl.

"Snap," Alix cautioned, and scooped him to safety.

A mocking laugh revealed a cloaked figure as it emerged from the shadows. "My, but you never cease to amaze me."

"Lily!"

Her sister dropped the hood of her cloak. "Of course it's me . . . I'm not interrupting anything, am I?"

"I—what are you doing here?" Alix stammered in surprise.

"Even *you* cannot possibly be so naive," Lily jeered as she turned down the hall. "I've come to change places. Follow me."

"But what happened to your baby?" Alix insisted, suddenly suspecting the entire game had been a trick.

"I lost it, thank God, but I'd rather not talk about it." Lily glanced meaningfully at the staircase. "It's up here. Tell me, what've I missed this summer? Have you been enjoying the high life in my place?"

"Not especially," Alix replied with quickening annoyance. "Even *you* can't think this has been a holiday."

Lily sniggered while leading Alix to a barren maids' lounge. "I can't wait to try on that dress. It's more than I can say for the rest of your wardrobe."

Alix released Snap to the tiny settee in the corner. "I hope you set aside what you used so I can put a torch to it."

Lily tittered appreciatively. "My, my, the kitten's discovered her claws."

"What am I supposed to change into? I can't walk out of here dressed like a maid," Alix protested, upon seeing the uniform Lily wore beneath her cloak. "I'd be spotted in a minute."

"Mabel packed riding clothes. I placed them behind the couch, in case anyone stopped by while I looked for you."

"How long have you been here?"

"Long enough to be certain that we won't be discovered if we hurry. Robbie sent a horse for you to ride; it's waiting at the edge of the hotel mews."

Alix's annoyance dissolved while she stripped off her clothes. At long last, she had the freedom of release, but now leave-taking felt unexpectedly bittersweet. Pushing aside these emotions, she was heartened by the welcome sight of her bundled clothes. "I hope you had the decency to thank Robbie for letting you stay."

"Why, when he was away?" Lily answered, as she unbuttoned her blouse.

The revelation that Robbie had not been home explained why he had not come to Alix's assistance, but she did not know of any trips he'd had planned when Lily had interrupted her life. "He went somewhere?"

Lily was short in response. "To Ireland, to visit his wife," she said dismissively. "Now, hurry up and hand over that coronet you're wearing so I can fix my hair. And don't forget that's my necklace, too."

Alix touched the opal briefly, daunted by her promise to Nicholas. Hurriedly, she finished dressing with rueful acceptance of its loss. "You'll have to remove it for me, because I can't take it off," she told her sister finally.

"Oh, don't worry; it's my pleasure," Lily sneered. "I'm not a bit shy when it comes to taking what I like."

"So I've noticed."

Her sister taunted her when she came to claim the necklace. "Do you know that this is quite a trinket! Where'd you find it?" she asked avidly, as she hurried to examine it under the nearby lamp.

"It was a birthday gift from your husband."

"*Ooh!* Dear Nicholas cut loose his purse strings? It's a little understated, but pretty, isn't it? What did you do to inspire such generosity?" she continued with a knowing look. "Dare I ask if you kept our secret?"

"Don't worry overlong," Alix replied cryptically, as she climbed inside her black riding sweater. A wild swing of emotion threatened to bring on tears when she saw Lily preening in the mirror, admiring the black opal. Resolutely, Alix dropped onto the settee beside the terrier and reached for the riding boots that Quenton had given her the preceding Christmas. The reminder of her uncle was sufficiently steadying to anchor her uneven reaction.

"You should've warned me to tighten my corset before I put this dress on! Come here and loosen the laces so it'll fit!"

"Don't you think I've done more than enough for you?" Alix asked, as she twisted her unbound hair into a knot.

"I can't go anywhere like this!"

Glancing around, Alix had to laugh at Lily's helpless flailing in the dress. "It'll come at a cost . . . Where's the title to Robbie's farm you promised as payment for this little stunt?"

"I gave it to Robbie before I left!"

"You've had it with you this entire time?"

"You don't think I'm stupid enough to leave it where you'd find it, do you?"

Alix should have known that she had spent the better part of the summer trying to outwit a fox. She untied the nearest ribbon on the dress. "Consider this the sum of my kindness. Jenny still has a few things of mine. Will you allow them returned to me?"

"As if I'd care for anything of yours!"

Alix would not be the one to point out that even with the ribbons untied, the dress was still too snug. "There, sister dear. Please don't bother to darken my door in the future, for you'll find a much different kind of reception."

"Don't worry," Lily retorted, busily gauging her warped reflection in the narrow mirror. "Oh, God, this dress can't possibly make me look this awful!"

"No, of course it doesn't," Alix lied, and realized from her own reflection that she still wore Lily's makeup. "Which way is the fastest out of this place?" she asked, as she hurried to the washbasin.

"To the left," her sister replied, while trying to adjust her lacing. "The hall leads to the lading area, where you'll find the alley with your horse."

"*Merci*," Alix said into the towel, and reached for her coat as she followed the terrier through the door.

Lily's derisive laughter followed her. "Are you pretending you're French again?"

Alix let the door close on the question. Lily refused to believe that anyone but Richard Radcliffe was their father, since Mary-Margaret had raised her on the premise that he had been lost at war. It had worked conveniently for Lily, who had inherited everything upon their mother's death, and Alix had no wish to change anything.

Snap darted past to take up their new direction as Alix pulled the sweater hood over her hair. Away from the noisy crowd and the orchestra's music, his harness-bell collar jangled noisily as they made their way to the exit.

"You'd better come here," Alix decided, scooping him up to button him inside her riding coat before opening the door. "It might be a little snug, but you'll never keep up with a horse."

Movement on the nearby stairs caught her attention, and as a pair of familiar-looking laced boots descended, fear pushed her out into the night. What could she say to Nicholas Griffon now, if he caught her in this ridiculous situation?

Fog dimmed the street lamps and wet the cobblestones in the alley crowded with waiting coaches. Through the mist, Alix saw the saddled horse where Lily had promised it. As she neared, she recognized North Star before the stallion turned his head to look at her.

"Dobbins!" Alix gasped with relief. North Star's mixed Turkoman and Arabian breeding gave him unparalleled speed over long distances. Mounted on her champion, she could be home in time for breakfast. Cradling Snap against her, she jumped into the saddle and caught up the reins while the horse wheeled away from the parked coaches.

Nicholas Griffon suddenly appeared directly in front of them through the fog and stopped with astonishment as North Star reared onto his hind legs to avoid him. "Oh, God!" Alix gasped, as the animal squealed with surprise. He came to earth while she clung to his neck, and bounded forward into the mist.

Did Nicholas shout something about learning to ride in their wake? If so, Alix could not blame him. The quick tattoo of North Star's hooves clattering through the streets of St. Albans did not fade until the highway.

NICHOLAS REALIZED WHY he'd lost the sound of Snap's bells in the hallway as soon as he saw Lily stuffed into Alix's dress. His wife was hard not to miss; if its strained seams held together for the rest of the evening, it would be a miracle. Even Lily's bosom chums looked embarrassed for her, and John came forward to offer her his red velvet Caesar's robe.

Nicholas avoided the scene as if it were rife with the plague and called for his coach immediately. He did not have to guess if the change had been well planned; as with everything else in this frustrating charade, its timing had been perfect. Searching for the impostor now would be futile. She would not linger in St. Albans, but she might return to London for the forgotten bundle in Lily's wardrobe. If not, it would still provide him with vital clues about how to find her.

Once home, Nicholas climbed the stairs two at a time past Winston's surprise, and he towed the butler upstairs in his wake. "Lily's returned," Nicholas explained briefly as he pushed through Lily's door. "Our impostor has fled, and I'm sure you would've noticed if she had returned for her things." He plunged headfirst into Lily's wardrobe and dug on the bottom to find the bundle wrapped in bagging. He pulled it forth and slit the knotted cord with his knife while Winston hovered over his shoulder.

"Is that a shirt of sorts?"

"Apparently." Nicholas relinquished it to the butler and tugged out black woolen breeches. Finally, he upended the sack to dump stiff and mud-caked boots onto the floor with a black jockey's cap and filthy riding gloves.

Winston peered at the silk shirt near the lamp. "By Jove, the name on this label is Ozzie Gladstone, Sterling Wood Stable."

"Why the devil would Allie hide racing silks in Lily's wardrobe?"

"I'd say they've been carelessly cared for," the butler continued, returning the shirt to Nicholas. "They were put away hastily, at least."

"Aye," he agreed with puzzlement. The jockey Ozzie Gladstone had been hurt and unable to ride in the race. The Sterling Wood entry Dark Star had run only because Alex Sterling had suddenly appeared to race his horse. "*My friends call me Allie.*" A conjured image of the rider in the dark who had nearly run him down suggested the impossible, and the connection with Quincy, Sterling Wood Stable, and Midnight Star's unconcealed attraction to the impostor suddenly made improbable sense.

"What should I do with these things, milord?" the butler asked, as Nicholas headed for the door.

"Return them as they were," Nicholas replied. If his

suspicion were correct, then he had been an incredible fool. He broke into a run once he was out in the night and did not stop until he reached the stable.

The horses lifted their heads when he came through the door, and their nervous sounds of surprise followed him up wooden steps to what had once been Quincy's quarters. He stopped to fumble for a light, but the thick candle was scarcely bright enough. A bottle of Mackinlay's single-malt scotch and a pair of battered cups remained on the table, and the Bible Quincy had been standing by was still on the rough-hewn shelf. As Nicholas lifted the light to survey the barren room, a hazy memory returned.

He carted the Bible to the table. In the uncertain flicker of a single flame, the ornate cross embossed on the cover glowed darkly. On a fragile page, in hand-illustrated letters, ornate script declared it the property of the family Saint-Descoteaux.

"The bleeding devil!" Nicholas exclaimed in surprised recognition of the mysteriously missing marquis who had been imprisoned in Paris. "You know how it is," Quincy had told him. "You think something's finished, and you find out it's not."

The Bible was full of illustrations, commissioned works hand-painted by priests. Nicholas pulled the cork from the bottle to drink a long draft as he settled in the chair. Thus prepared, he turned to the center, where the family chronicle detailed generations. The script changed through the years, but Nicholas's immediate concern was for the most recent entries. His mind stopped working when he reached them, stunned by the names inscribed at the end. Alix Rose Juliette and Lily Marie-Margot were the last entries—twin girls born on a November day.

"Sisters." His lips moved without sound.

Alix was Alex Sterling; he knew instantly it was she whom he had recognized as a jockey at Oxley. He pulled his mind together to look for the nearest family. "Her uncle Quenton must be Quincy; her father was Henri, Quenton's older brother," he murmured, recalling the story that Quincy had told him, and when he turned to the list of family deaths, the unfortunate Henri was the last entry, dated just before Quincy began working as a stableman.

The puzzle that had troubled Nicholas for so long slipped together. The scar Allie bore was from having been shot during her escape. Quenton had brought her to England to save her from the guillotine. *"I know not how to tell you who I am."*

He finally had the answer. "Alix Rose Juliette Saint-Descoteaux." His whisper kissed her name.

Acknowledgments

⟨❧⟩

Anyone who has ever attempted to write even the simplest letter knows that words don't always just appear. This book would not have been possible without the understanding support of my family and friends, but most of all, my mother, who encouraged me to pursue my dreams. Mom was eighty-five when she passed last year, and even though she suffered from macular degeneration and could not read even the largest print on my computer screen, she listened faithfully to my clumsy readings until falling asleep.

I'd like to think it was from the sound of my voice, and not from my story, but I can still see her sitting at the kitchen table pretending to do a word search puzzle she could not see, pen in hand. "Have you finished your book yet?" she would ask me. "No, not yet," was my only answer at the time. "Am I in the book?" she would never fail to continue. My mom ever loved to see her name in print. "No, it's a work of fiction," I would remind her gently. "The characters aren't real." Mom would get her indignant look and tap the table with the end of her pen. "I want to know why my name is not in the book," she would ask emphatically. "Don't worry, Mom, your name will be in the dedication," I promised every time we had this discussion. Now I wish I could have it just one last time, so I could tell her "yes."

I'd also like to thank my daughter, Elizabeth Smith, and one of my best friends, Donna Christiansen, for having the patience and strength to read through the back drafts of *After Midnight* and still have the grace to encourage my endeavor.

Finally, I would never have been able to pull it all together without the hard work of my enormously talented writing coach and editor Annie Tucker, along with the hardworking professionals at She Writes Press. They have managed to take my manuscript and make it into a book. Without them, *After Midnight* would still be a shapeless Word document in a computer file.

ABOUT THE AUTHOR

Growing up in the Salinas Valley in the shadow of creative giants like John Steinbeck and Alfred Hitchcock, Diane's father inspired her to write before she could even read. She still lives in Central California and has written *After Midnight* for her children and grandchildren, hoping to inspire a future generation of literary art.

SELECTED TITLES FROM SHE WRITES PRESS

She Writes Press is an independent publishing company founded to serve women writers everywhere. Visit us at www.shewritespress.com.

Trinity Stones: The Angelorum Twelve Chronicles by LG O'Connor. $16.95, 978-1-938314-84-1. On her 27th birthday, New York investment banker Cara Collins learns that she is one of twelve chosen ones prophesied to lead a final battle between the forces of good and evil.

In the Shadow of Lies: A Mystery Novel by M. A. Adler. $16.95, 978-1-938314-82-7. As World War II comes to a close, homicide detective Oliver Wright returns home—only to find himself caught up in the investigation of a complicated murder case rife with racial tensions.

Fire & Water by Betsy Graziani Fasbinder. $16.95, 978-1-938314-14-8. Kate Murphy has always played by the rules—but when she meets charismatic artist Jake Bloom, she's forced to navigate the treacherous territory of passionate love, friendship, and family devotion.

Portrait of a Woman in White by Susan Winkler. $16.95, 978-1-938314-83-4. When the Nazis steal a Matisse portrait from the eccentric, art-loving Rosenswigs, the Parisian family is thrust into the tumult of war and separation, their fates intertwined with that of their beloved portrait.

Water on the Moon by Jean P. Moore. $16.95, 978-1-938314-61-2. When her home is destroyed in a freak accident, Lidia Raven, a divorced mother of two, is plunged into a mystery that involves her entire family.

Watchdogs by Patricia Watts. $16.95, 978-1-938314-34-6. When journalist Julia Wilkes returns to the town where her career got its start, she is forced to face some old ghosts—and some new enemies.

CPSIA information can be obtained
at www.ICGtesting.com
Printed in the USA
BVHW07s1346290618
520404BV00001B/5/P